GLOUCESTER

The Serpent of Venice

ALSO BY CHRISTOPHER MOORE

Sacré Bleu

Bite Me

Fool

You Suck

A Dirty Job

The Stupidest Angel

Fluke: Or, I Know Why the Winged Whale Sings

Lamb: The Gospel According to Biff,
Christ's Childhood Pal

The Lust Lizard of Melancholy Cove

Island of the Sequined Love Nun

Bloodsucking Fiends

Coyote Blue

Practical Demonkeeping

The Serpent of Venice

Christopher Moore

An Imprint of HarperCollins*Publishers*

THE SERPENT OF VENICE. Copyright © 2014 by Christopher Moore. All rights reserved. Printed in the United States of America. No part of this book may be used or reproduced in any manner whatsoever without written permission except in the case of brief quotations embodied in critical articles and reviews. For information address HarperCollins Publishers, 10 East 53rd Street, New York, NY 10022.

HarperCollins books may be purchased for educational, business, or sales promotional use. For information, please e-mail the Special Markets Department at SPsales@harpercollins.com.

FIRST HARPERLUXE EDITION

HarperLuxe™ is a trademark of HarperCollins Publishers

Library of Congress Cataloging-in-Publication Data is available upon request.

ISBN: 978-0-06-229865-2

14 ID/RRD 10 9 8 7 6 5 4 3 2 1

LARGE TYPE F Moo

The Cast

Chorus—a narrator

Antonio—a Venetian merchant

Brabantio—a senator of Rome, father of Desdemona and Portia

Iago—a soldier

Rodrigo—a gentleman soldier, friend of Iago

Pocket—a fool

Portia—a lady, younger daughter of Brabantio, sister to Desdemona

Nerissa—maid to Portia

Desdemona—a lady, elder daughter of Brabantio, sister to Portia

Emilia—wife of Iago, maid to Desdemona

Othello—a Moor, commanding general of the Venetian military

Shylock—a Jew, Venetian moneylender, father of Jessica

Jessica—Shylock's daughter

Bassanio—friend of Antonio, suitor to Portia

Lorenzo—friend of Antonio, suitor to Jessica

Gratiano—young friend of Antonio, a merchant

Salanio—young friend of Antonio, a merchant

Salarino—also a young friend of Antonio, interchangeable with Salanio, may have been born of a typo

Drool—a fool's apprentice

Jeff—a monkey

Cordelia—a ghost. There's always a bloody ghost.

The Stage

The stage is a mythical late-thirteenth-century Italy, where independent city-states trade and war with one another. Venice has been at war with Genoa, off and on, for fifty years, over control of the shipping routes to the Orient and the Holy Land.

Venice has been an independent republic for five hundred years, governed by an elected senate of 480 men, who in turn elect a doge, who, advised by a high council of six senators, oversees the senate, the military, and civil appointments. Senators come mostly from Venice's powerful merchant class, and until recently could be elected, by neighborhood, from any walk of life. But the system that has made Venice the richest and most powerful maritime nation in the world has changed. Recently, privileged senators, interested in passing the legacy of power and wealth to their families, voted to make their elected positions inheritable.

Strangely, although most of the characters are Venetian, everybody speaks English, and with an English accent.

Unless otherwise described, assume conditions to be humid.

The Serpent of Venice

ACT I

Fortunato's Fate

Hell and Night must bring this monstrous birth to light.

—Iago, *Othello*, Act I, Scene 3

CHORUS:

INVOCATION

Rise, Muse!
Darkwater sprite,
Bring stirring play
To vision's light.

Rise, Muse!
On fin and tail
With fang and claw
Rend invention's veil.

Come, Muse!
'Neath harbored ship,
Under night fisher's torch,
And sleeping sailors slip.

To Venice, Muse!
Radiant venom convey,
Charge scribe's driven quill
To story assay.

Of betrayal, grief and war,
Provoke, Muse, your howl
Of love's laughter lost and
Heinous Fuckery, most foul . . .

One
The Trap

They waited at the dock, the three Venetians, for the fool to arrive.

"An hour after sunset, I told him," said the senator, a bent-backed graybeard in a rich brocade robe befitting his office. "I sent a gondola myself to fetch him."

"Aye, he'll be here," said the soldier, a broad-shouldered, fit brute of forty, in leather and rough linen, full sword and fighting dagger at his belt, black bearded with a scar through his right brow that made him look ever questioning or suspicious. "He thinks himself a connoisseur, and can't resist the temptation of your wine cellar. And when it is done, we shall have more than Carnival to celebrate."

"And yet, I feel sad," said the merchant. A soft-handed, fair-skinned gent who wore a fine, floppy velvet hat, and a gold signet ring the size of a small mouse, with which he sealed agreements. "I know not why."

They could hear the distant sounds of pipes, drums, and horns from across the lagoon in Venice. Torches bounced on the shoreline near Piazza San Marco. Behind them, the senator's estate, Villa Belmont, stood dark but for a storm lantern in an upper window, a light by which a gondolier might steer to the private island. Out on the water, fishermen had lit torches, which bobbed like dim, drunken stars against the inky water. Even during Carnival, the city must eat.

The senator put his hand on the merchant's shoulder. "We perform service to God and state, a relief to conscience and heart, a cleansing that opens a pathway to our designs. Think of the bounteous fortune that will find you, once the rat is removed from the granary."

"But I quite like his monkey," said the merchant.

The soldier grinned and scratched his beard to conceal his amusement. "You've seen to it that he comes alone?"

"It was a condition of his invitation," said the senator. "I told him out of good Christian charity all his servants were to be dismissed to attend Carnival, as I assured him I had done with my own."

"Shrewdly figured," said the soldier, looking back to the vast, unlit villa. "He'll think nothing out of order then when he sees no attendants."

"But monkeys can be terribly hard to catch," said the merchant.

"Would you forget about the monkey," growled the soldier.

"I told him that my daughter is terrified of monkeys, could not be in the same room with one."

"But she isn't here," said the merchant.

"The fool doesn't know that," said the soldier. "Our brave Montressor will cast his younger daughter as bait, even after having the eldest stolen from the hook by a blackfish."

"The senator's loss cuts deep enough without your barbs," said the merchant. "Do we not pursue the same purpose? Your wit is too mean to be clever, merely crude and cruel."

"But, sweet Antonio," said the soldier. "I am at once clever, crude, and cruel—all assets to your endeavor. Or would you rather partner with the kindly edge of a more courtly sword?" He laid his hand on the hilt of his sword.

The merchant looked out over the water.

"I thought not," said the soldier.

"Put on friendly faces, you two." The senator stepped between them and squinted into the night. "The fool's boat approaches. There!"

Amid the fishing boats a bright lantern drifted, and slowly broke rank as the gondola moved toward them. In a moment it was gliding into the dock, the gondolier so precise in his handling of the oar that the black boat stopped with its rails only a handsbreadth from the dock. A louvered hatch clacked open and out of the cabin stepped a wiry little man dressed in the black-and-silver motley and mask of a harlequin. By his size, one might have thought him a boy, but the oversize codpiece and the shadow of a beard on his cheek betrayed his years.

"One lantern?" said the harlequin, hopping up onto the dock. "You couldn't have spared an extra torch or two, Brabantio? It's dark as night's own nutsack out here." He breezed by the soldier and the merchant. "Toadies," he said, nodding to them. Then he was on his way up the path to the villa, pumping a puppet-headed jester's scepter as he went. The senator tottered along behind him, holding the lantern high to light their way.

"It's an auspicious night, Fortunato," said the senator. "And I sent the servants away before nightfall so—"

"Call me Pocket," said the fool. "Only the doge calls me Fortunato. Wonder that's not his nickname for everyone, bloody bung-fingered as he is at cards."

At the dock, the soldier again laid hand on sword hilt, saying, "By the saints, I would run my blade up through his liver right now, and lift him on it just to watch that arrogant grin wither as he twitched. Oh how I do hate the fool."

The merchant smiled and talked through his teeth as he pressed the soldier's sword hand down, throwing a nod toward the gondolier, who was standing on his boat, waiting. "As do I, in this pantomime we perform for Carnival, he is our jibing clown. Ha! The Punchinello in our little puppet show, all in good fun, am I right?"

The soldier looked to the boatman and forced a grin. "Quite right. All in good cheer. I play my part too well. One moment, signor. I will have your instructions." He turned and called up the path. "Montressor! The gondolier?"

"Pay him and tell him to go, be merry, and return at midnight."

"You heard him," said the soldier. "Go celebrate, but not so much that you cannot steer. I would sleep in my own bed this night. Pay him, Antonio." The soldier turned and headed up the path.

"Me? Why is it always me?" He dug into his purse. "Very well, then." The merchant tossed a coin to the gondolier, who snatched it out of the air and bowed his head in thanks. "Midnight then."

"Midnight, signor," said the gondolier, who twisted his oar, sending the gondola sliding away from the dock silent and smooth as a knife through the night.

Outside the grand entrance of the palazzo the fool paused. "What's that above your door, Montressor?" There was a coat of arms inlaid in the marble, ensconced in shadow. The senator held up his lantern, illuminating the crest, showing the relief of a man's foot in gold, trampling a jade serpent, even as its fangs pierced the heel.

"My family crest," said the senator.

"Reckon they were all out of proper dragons and lions down at the crest shop so you had to settle for this toss, eh?"

"Think they'd have thrown in a *fleur-de-lis*," said the fool's puppet stick, in a voice just a note above the fool's own. "*Montressor*'s fucking French, innit?"

The senator whirled around to face the puppet. "*Montressor* is a title bestowed upon me by the doge. It means 'my treasure' and notes that he holds me highest in regard of the six senators of the high council. This is the crest of the family Brabantio, one our family has worn with pride for four hundred years. Do note the motto, fool, '*Nemo me impune lacessit.*' " He bounced the lantern with each syllable as he read through gritted teeth. "It means, 'No one attacks me with impunity.'"

"Well, that's not fucking French," said the puppet, turning to look at the fool.

"No," said the fool. "The puppet Jones is quite fluent in fucking French," he explained to the senator.

"But *Montressor* is French, right?"

"Froggy as a summer day on the Seine," said the fool.

"Thought so," said the puppet.

"Stop talking to that puppet!" barked the senator.

"Well, you were just shouting at him," said the fool.

"And now I'm shouting at you! *You* are working the puppet's mouth and giving it voice."

"No!" said the puppet, his wooden jaw agape, looking to the fool, then to the senator, then back to the fool. "This bloody toss-bobbin is running things?"

The fool nodded; the bells on his hat jingled earnestly.

The puppet turned to the senator. "Well, if you're going to be a bastard about it, your bloody motto is nicked."

"What?" said the senator.

"Plagiarized," said the fool, still nodding solemnly, the bringer of sad news.

The merchant and the soldier had caught up to them and could see that their host was incensed, so they stood at the bottom of the steps, watching. The soldier's hand fell to the hilt of his sword.

"It's the Scottish motto, innit?" said the puppet. "Bloody Order of the Fistle."

"It's true," said the fool. "Although it's *Thistle*, not *Fistle*, Jones, you Cockney berk."

"What I said," said the puppet Jones. "Piss off."

The fool glared at the puppet, then turned back to the senator. "Same motto is inscribed over the entrance to Edinburgh Castle."

"You must be remembering it wrong. It *is* in Latin."

"Indeed," said the fool. "And I am raised by nuns in the bosom of the church. Could speak and write Latin and Greek before I could see over the table. No, Montressor, your motto couldn't be more Scottish if it was painted blue and smelled of burning peat and your ginger sister."

"Stolen," said the puppet. "Pilfered. Swiped. Filched, as it fucking were. A motto most used, defiled, and besmirched."

"Besmirched?" said the fool. "Really?"

The puppet nodded furiously on the end of his stick. The fool shrugged to the senator. "A right shite crest and a motto most besmirched, Montressor. Let's hope this amontillado you've promised can comfort us in our disappointment."

The merchant stepped up then and put his hand on the fool's shoulder. "Then let's waste no more time out here in the mist. To the senator's cellar and his cask of exquisite amontillado."

"Yes," said the senator. He stepped through the doorway into a grand foyer, took tapers from a credenza, lit them from his lantern, and handed one to each of his guests. "Mind your step," said the senator. "We'll be going down ancient stairs to the very lowest levels of the palazzo. Some ceilings will be quite low, so, Antonio, Iago, watch your heads."

"Did he just besmirch our height?" asked the puppet.

"Can't say," said the fool. "I'm not entirely sure I know what *besmirched* means. I've just been going along with you because I thought you knew what you were talking about."

"Quiet, flea," growled the soldier.

"That there's a besmirchin', " said the puppet.

"Oh, well, yes then," said the fool. He raised his taper high, illuminating a thick coat of mold on the low ceiling. "So, Montressor, is the lovely Portia waiting down here in the dark?"

"I'm afraid my youngest daughter will not be joining us. She's gone to Florence to buy shoes."

They entered a much wider vault now, with casks set into the walls on one side, racks of dusty bottles on the other; a long oak table and high-backed chairs ran down the middle. The senator lit lanterns around the chamber until the entire room was bathed in a warm glow that belied the dampness that permeated the cellar.

"Just as well," said the fool. "She'd just be whinge-ing about the dark and the damp and how Iago reeks of squid and we'd never get any proper drinking done."

"What?" said the soldier.

The fool leaned into Antonio and bounced his eye-brows so they showed above his black mask. "Don't get me wrong, Portia's a luscious little fuck-bubble to be sure, but prickly as a gilded hedgehog when she doesn't get her way."

The senator looked up with murderous fire in his eyes, then quickly looked down and shuddered, almost, it seemed, with pleasure.

"I do not reek of squid," said the soldier, as if over-come by a rare moment of self-consciousness. He sniffed at the shoulder of his cape, and finding no squidish aroma, returned his attention to the senator.

"If you'd be so kind as to decant the amontillado, Iago," said the senator, "we can be about getting the opinion of this distinguished connoisseur."

"I never said I was a connoisseur, Montressor. I just said I'd had it before and it was the mutt's nuts."

"The dog's bollocks," said the puppet, clarifying.

"When you were king of Spain, correct?" said the merchant, with a grin and a sarcastic roll of the eyes toward the senator.

"I've had various titles," said Fortunato. "Only *fool* seems constant."

The soldier cradled the heavy cask under his arm as if he was strangling a bullnecked enemy and filled a delicate Murano glass pitcher with the amber liquid.

The senator said: "The wine dealer has five more casks coming from Spain. If you pronounce it genuine, I'll buy the others and have one sent round to you in thanks."

"Let's have a taste, then," said the fool. "Although, without it's poured by a properly wanton, olive-skinned serving wench, you can't really call it authentic, but I suppose Iago will have to suffice."

"Won't be the first time he's filled that role, I'll wager," said the puppet Jones. "Lonely nights in the field, and whatnot."

The soldier grinned, set the cask on the table, and with a nod from the senator poured the sherry into four heavy glass tumblers with pewter bases cast in the shape of winged lions.

"To the republic," said the senator, raising his glass.

"To the Assumption," said the merchant. "To Carnival!"

"To Venice," said the soldier.

"To the delicious Desdemona," said the fool.

And the merchant nearly choked as he looked to the senator, who calmly drank, then lowered his glass to the table, never looking from the fool.

"Well?"

The fool swished the liquid in his cheeks, rolled his eyes at the ceiling in consideration, then swallowed as if enduring an especially noxious medicine. He shuddered and looked over the rim of his glass at the senator. "I'm not sure," he said.

"Well, sit, try a bit more," said the merchant. "Sometimes the first drink only clears the dust of the day off a man's palate."

The fool sat, as did the others. They all drank again. The glasses clunked down. The three looked to the fool.

"Well?" asked Iago.

"Montressor, you've been had," said the fool. "This is not amontillado."

"It's not?" said the senator.

"Tastes perfect to me," said the merchant.

"No, it's not amontillado," said the fool. "And I can see from your face that you are neither surprised nor disappointed. So while we quaff this imposter—which tastes a bit of pitch, if you ask me—shall we turn to your darker purpose? The real reason we are all here."

The fool drained his glass, leaned on the table, and

rolled his eyes coyly at the senator in the manner of a flirting teenage girl. "Shall we?"

The soldier and the merchant looked to the senator, who smiled.

"Our darker purpose?" asked the senator.

"Tastes of pitch?" asked the merchant.

"Not to me," said the soldier, now looking at his glass.

"Do you think me a fool?" said the fool. "Don't answer that. I mean, do you think me foolish? An ill-formed question as well." He looked at his hand and seemed surprised to find it at the end of his wrist, then looked back to the senator. "You brought me here to convince me to rally the doge for you, to back another holy war."

"No," said the senator.

"No? You don't want a bloody war?"

"Well, yes," said the soldier. "But that's not why we've brought you here."

"Then you wish me to entreat my friend Othello to back you in a Crusade, from which you all may profit. I knew it when I got the invitation."

"Hadn't thought about it," said the senator. "More sherry?"

The fool adjusted his hat, and when the bells jingled he followed one around with his eyes and nearly went over backward in his chair.

Antonio, the merchant, steadied the fool, and patted his back to reassure him.

The fool pulled away, and regarded the merchant, looking him not just in the eye, but around the eyes, as if they were windows to a dark house and he was looking for someone hiding inside.

"Then you don't want me to use my influence in France and England to back a war?"

The merchant shook his head and smiled.

"Oh balls, it's simple revenge then?"

Antonio and Iago nodded.

The fool regarded the senator, and seemed to have difficulty focusing on the graybeard. "Everyone knows I'm here. Many saw me board the gondola to come here."

"And they will see a fool return," said the senator.

"I am a favorite of the doge," slurred the fool. "He adores me."

"That *is* the problem," said the senator.

In a single motion the fool leapt from his chair to the middle of the table, reached into the small of his back, and came up with a wickedly pointed throwing dagger, which caught his eye as it flashed in his hand before him. He wobbled and shook his head as if to clear his vision.

"Poison?" he said, somewhat wistfully. "Oh, fuck-stockings, I am slain—"

His eyes rolled back in his head, his knees buckled, and he fell face-forward on the table with a thump and a rattle of his blade across the floor.

The three looked from the prostrate Fortunato to each other.

The soldier felt the fool's neck for a pulse. "He's alive, but I can remedy that." He reached for his dagger.

"No," said the senator. "Help me get him out of his clothes and to a deeper section of the cellar, then take your leave. You last saw him alive, and you can swear on your soul that is all you know."

Antonio the merchant sighed. "It's sad we must kill the little fool, who, while wildly annoying, does seem to bring mirth and merriment to those around him. Yet I suppose if there is a ducat to be made, it must be made. If a profit blossoms, so must a merchant pluck it."

"Duty to God, profit, and the republic!" said the senator.

"Many a fool has found his end trying to resist the wind of war," said Iago. "So shall this one."

Two
The Dark

"What are you doing?" I asked.

"I'm walling you up in the dungeon," said the senator, who crouched in the arched doorway to the chamber in which I was chained to the wall.

"No you're not," said I.

Indeed, it appeared that he was walling me up, but I wasn't going to concede that simply because I was chained, naked, and water was rising about my feet. Cautious, I was, not to instill a sense of confidence in my enemy.

"I am," said he. "Brick by brick. The first masonry I've done since I was a lad, but it comes back. I was ten, I think, when I helped the mason who was building my father's house. Not this one, of course. This house has been in the family for centuries. And I think I was less help than in his way, but alas, I learned."

"Well, you couldn't possibly have been more annoying then than you are now, so do get on with it."

The senator stabbed his trowel into a bucket of mortar with such enthusiasm that he might have been spearing my liver. Then he held his lamp through the doorway into my little chamber, which he had already bricked up to just above his knees. By the lamplight I saw I was in a passageway barely two yards wide, that sloped downward into the dark water, which was now washing about my ankles. There was a high-tide line on the wall, about the level of my chest.

"You know you're going to die here, Fortunato?"

"Pocket," I corrected. "You're mad, Brabantio. Deluded, paranoid, and irritatingly grandiose."

"You'll die. Alone. In the dark." He tamped down a brick with the butt of his trowel.

"Senile, probably. It comes early to the inbred or the syphilitic."

"The crabs won't even wait for you to stop moving before they begin to clean your bones."

"Ha!" said I.

"What do you mean, *Ha?*" said Brabantio.

"You've played right into my hands!"

I shrugged, as best I could, at the owl-horking obviousness of his folly. (Shrugging comprised my entire repertoire of gesture, as my hands were chained through a heavy ring in the wall above my head. I did not hang, but neither could I sit. If I pulled the chain to its exact balance point, I suppose I could have flapped my hands at the end of their shackles, but I had no story to go with the flapping.)

The senator chuckled and resumed troweling mortar for the next row of bricks. "We're below the level of the lagoon. I could torture you to death and no one would hear you scream. But I prefer to go to my bed and fall into slumber wrapped in the sweet dream of your suffering in the dark, dying slowly."

"Ha! See there. I thought myself dead when I drank your poison, so for my money, I'm ahead of the game."

"You weren't poisoned. It was a potion from farthest China—brought overland at great expense. It was already in your glass." He reached into his robe and held up a small red-lacquered box.

"Not poisoned?" said I. "A shame. I was enjoying my resurrection. I had hoped to come back taller, but then tall as well as roguishly handsome would be gilding the lily, wouldn't it."

"Would you like to wager on how long you might last? Two—three days, perhaps? Oh, that's right, you can't wager, can you? You have nothing."

"True," said I. "Yet you see a victory in what is a simple truth for all of us, is it not? We have nothing, we are nothing." The truth was, I had been nothing, felt nothing but longing and grief, since news of my sweet Cordelia's death from fever had reached me three months ago. I did not fear death, nor even pain. I'd never have come to Brabantio's palazzo if I had. That last moment, when I thought myself poisoned, I'd been relieved.

"Well, *you* are nothing. Would that you realized that before you brought ruin upon my daughter."

"Portia? Oh, she's not ruined. Bit sore, perhaps— might be walking a bit gingerly for a day or two from the rug burns, but she's far from ruined. Think of her not as ruined, but simply as well used."

Brabantio growled, then, red faced, he thrashed his head in the portal like a dirt-eating loony. (I thought he might burst a vein in his ancient forehead.) He seemed unable to form any retort but steam and spittle, which I took as cue to continue.

"Like a new pair of boots," I said, Brabantio's potion having made me especially chatty. "Like new boots you might wear into the water, so that even while enduring the squish and slop of them for a while, they cure to a perfect fit, molded, as it were, by experience, to receive you and only you. At which point you have to throw them over a chair and have raucously up the bum!"

"No!" barked the senator, at which point he flung a brick at me that would have taken a kneecap had I not quickly pulled myself up by the chains. The brick thudded off the wall and splashed somewhere in the dark.

"The strained-boot metaphor what sent you round the bend, then?" said I, a jolly jingle of my chains for levity. "You're short a brick now, you know? You've bollixed up the whole bloody edifice over a smidge o' literary license, thou thin-skinned old knob-gobbler."

"Tis my eldest, Desdemona, that's ruined," said the senator, pressing his point by placing a brick atop the wall.

"Oh, well, yes, but I can't take credit for that," said I. And I was, of course, lying about his younger daughter. I'd never so much as been alone in a room with Portia. "No, Desdemona's downfall is all Othello's doing."

Another brick joined its red brothers in line. Only the senator's face was visible above them now.

"And but for your interference, he would be gone—or condemned, if I'd had my way. But no, you were in the ear of the doge like a gnat, making a case for your precious Moor, talking of Venice's debt to him, spouting rhymes of how he was some noble hero instead of a sooty slave reaching beyond his station."

"Nobility and courage being frightening and foreign qualities to you—you piss-ant merchant, twat." The senator was sensitive about his nobility, or lack thereof. Venice was the only city-state in Italy, nay, the only state on the continent where there were no landed nobles, largely because there was no land. Venice was a republic, all authorities duly elected, and it rankled him. Only in the last few months had he convinced the doge and the council to allow senate seats to be inherited. And because he had no sons, Brabantio's seat would go to the husband of his eldest daughter. Yes, the Moor.

"Strictly speaking, he didn't really ruin her. I mean, she's married to a general who will someday be a senator of Venice, so really, a step up from her bloodline, which I think you'd have to agree is as common as cat piss."

He growled and flung another brick through the portal. This one took me on the front of one thigh, which should have been more painful than it was. Considering it, I suppose I should have been more concerned for my fate. Perhaps the Oriental powder had made me giddy.

"That's going to leave a mark, Montressor."

"Damn you, fool. I will silence you." He went back to his masonry with a fury that was making him breathless. Soon he was down to the last brick, just a square of yellow light from the port.

"Beg for mercy, fool," he said.

"I will not."

"You won't be able to drown yourself, I've made certain of that. You shall suffer, as you have made me suffer."

"I care not. I care for nothing. Finish your bloody business and be off. I'm tired of listening to your whingeing. Give me my oblivion so I may join my heart, my love, my queen." I bowed my head, closed my eyes, waited for the dark and what dreams may come. I don't suppose it occurred to me that I could be both heartbroken *and* dead.

"Your queen did not die of fever, fool," said Brabantio, a whisper now in the dark.

"What?"

"Poison, Fortunato. Formulated by one of Rome's best apothecaries to mimic a fever, slow and deadly. Put into place soon after you arrived as emissary and spoke your queen's strong opposition to our Crusade. Sent to Normandy on one of Antonio's ships, and delivered by a spy recruited from her guard by Iago. We may not have landed nobles, but he who rules the sea, rules trade, and he who rules trade, rules the world."

"No," said I, the truth of it burning through the haze of the potion and grief like a fire across my soul. Hate had awakened me. "No, Montressor!"

"Oh, yes. Go join your queen, Fortunato, and when you see her, tell her 'twas your words that killed her." He scraped the trowel around the opening, then fit the last brick and tamped it into place, plunging me into darkness as the water rose around my knees.

"For the love of God, Montressor! For the love of God!"

But the tapping had ceased and my last call on the senator's conscience was drowned by his laughter, which faded, and was gone.

Three
A Spot of Bother

Aspot of bother, innit: walled up and chained in the lightless, lonesome cold, seawater rising to my ribs, silence except for my own breath and a steady drip somewhere above my head. Then a slight scraping from the other side of the new wall. Perhaps Brabantio gathering his tools.

"Brabantio, thou treacherous coal-souled wank-weasel!" said I.

Was that cackling I heard beyond the wall, or just the fading echo of my own voice? The chamber had to be connected to the lagoon, somehow, but I could not hear even a distant lapping of waves. The darkness was so complete that I could see only the phantoms that populate the back of the eyelid, like oil on black water—"cracks in the soul," Mother Basil used to tell me before she would lock me in the cupboard at the abbey at Dog Snogging, where I was raised. "In the dark may you contemplate the cracks in your soul wherein leaks wickedness, Pocket." Sometimes I would pass days contemplating the cracks in my soul until the dark and I made peace. Friends.

Recently I had thought I might make a friend of Death as well, meet its feathery oblivion with a soft embrace. My sweet Cordelia's death had cleansed me of fear, of self-regard, and after weeks of drinking, of anger and control over most of my fluids. But now I was wide awake with both anger and anguish that my actions might have brought an end to my queen.

"Thou wretched pillar of syphilitic pheasant-fuck!" said I, in case the Montressor was still listening.

At least the water was warm. It being August, the lagoon had saved summer's heat, yet I shivered. A drip of cold water tapped my left hand with the regularity of a ticking clock, and as soon as I would think of it, it would sting like a needle of ice. I found that if I stood straight, took my full weight upon my feet, I could rest my arms on a ledge of brick at the level of my shoulders, where the wall met the rounded vault of the ceiling. In that posture I could take the weight of my arms off my shackles, and the cold drip of water would splash harmlessly on the chains. But if I fell to a position where I might rest, put my weight on my back against the wall, let my hands go slack in the chains in the manner of a praying saint, the cold drip would again vex me like a tiny frost-pricked fairy, humping away at my joints, jolting me awake when I would drowse. I could not know then that the cruel sprite would hold the key to my very life.

But I *did* drowse, after a while, hanging in the warm water, dreams washing over me both pleasing and horrific, wrenched from the company of my loving Cordelia by the claws of a voracious beast, waking breathless in the dark chamber, wishing it had been real, relieved that it was not, until the full weight of the darkness would descend on me again.

"Pocket," she had said, "I think I shall send you to Venice, to speak to them my mind on this Crusade they propose."

"But, lamb, they know your mind. You've sent them a bundle of letters, royal seal, Queen of Britain, Wales, Normandy, Scotland, Spain—do we still rule Spain?"

"No, and *we* do not rule any of them. I rule."

"I was using the royal *we*, wasn't I, love? Bit of the old God-in-your-pocket plural fucking *we* you royals use when being just a singular enormous twat will not suffice." I tilted my head and grinned, jingled a bell on my coxcomb in a manner most charming.

"You see, that's why I must send you."

"To convince them that you're an enormous twat? I was speaking figuratively, love. You know I adore you, including and especially your specific lady bits, but I respect the awesome twattiness with which you wield dominion over the realm. No, I say send them another pound of royal seals and wax, with a resounding 'Fuck off' to the pope, in Latin. Signed Queen Cordelia, Britain, France, et cetera, et cetera, and after lunch I can try to impregnate you with a royal heir."

"No," she said, her delicate jaw quite set.

"Well, fine then," said I. "We'll send the letter, skip lunch, and go right to siring the heir. I'm feeling full of tiny princes, bustling to get out into the world and start plotting against one another." I thrust my cod at her to show the palpable urgency of our progeny.

"No, that's why I must send you," she said, ignoring my eloquent gesture of prince pumpage. "No letter, dispatch, or herald can be even remotely as annoying as you. Only you can shame them for just how badly they bollixed up the last bloody Crusade. Only you, my darling fool, can convey just how ridiculous—and bloody inconvenient—I find their call to battle."

"*Moi?*" said I, in perfect fucking French.

"*Toi, mon amour,*" said she, in the teasing tongue of the frog. She kissed me lightly on the eyebrow and danced across our bedchamber to a heavy table where lay paper, ink, and quill.

"The kingdom is going to shit. I need my loyal knights here as a show of strength against those who would usurp me. You need to make it clear to the Venetians that I have no intention of joining yet another holy Crusade, nor will anyone from any of my lands, or, if I can manage it, our allies. And I want you to wear your motley. I want my message to come from a fool."

"But I am your king."

"No you're not."

"The royal consort?" I ventured.

"I have, in my weaker moments, shagged a fool," said she, her head bowed in shame.

"And married the same," said I.

"I don't think we should dwell on that, love. Go to them. Speak my mind. Dwell in their palaces, drink their wine, learn their secrets, and leave them flustered, frustrated, and insulted, as I know only you can do."

"But, lamb, sending a fool to the pope—"

"Oh, bugger the pope!"

"I think he already has someone to do that."

"No, you needn't worry about Rome. It's Venice that's behind this. Genoa has just kicked nine shades of shit out of them and they need to raise money. They think a holy war will rebuild their navy and reopen the trade routes they've lost to the Genoans, but they'll not do it on the fortune of Cordelia. Go to Venice. And take Drool and Jeff with you."

"Salting the earth of *all* decorum, are we then?"

"Yes. Take your great drooling ninny and your monkey and your acid wit and inflict them upon the court of the doge. They dare not turn you away. And when you return, we will make an heir."

"I am your humble servant, milady," said I. "But we've still an hour before lunch, and—"

"Cry havoc, and let slip the trousers of most outrageous bonkilation!" said the queen, throwing off the sash of her gown and stepping out of it. "Off with your kit, fool!"

I so adored her when she let her warrior-queen armor fall and came silly and giggling into my arms.

I heard footsteps on the other side of the newly bricked wall, heard them clearly, then the sound of a bucket dropping with a thud. So I *could* be heard down here. I don't know how long I had been in the dark, but the tide was still high, reaching to my chest. Perhaps Portia had returned from Florence, or a servant had come down to the cellar to retrieve some wine.

"Help! I've been walled up here in the dark by the bloody lunatic senator!" But what if it was Brabantio himself, wracked with guilt, returned to set me free? I gentled my discourse. "And by lunatic I mean a nutter of supreme refinement, exquisite taste, and—"

Before I could finish shouting my flattery, there came screaming from the other side of the wall—screaming so piteous and animal that even in my dismal state, I shuddered. It was the sound of slaughter, no doubt, and not a subtle blade slipped under a rib. Someone, a man, was suffering, calling unto God and the saints between howls of pain pitched with terror that crashed into a low wail, then were silent. I heard scrambling sounds like dry sticks snapping, then just the steady drip in my dark chamber.

I dared not call out. I did not want the attention of whoever had been on the other side of the wall, for I was sure that no rescue would be forthcoming from there. So tuned was I for a sound from the other side that even the dripping water became a distraction, an annoyance amid devastation.

Time passed. An hour maybe. Perhaps only minutes.

Then a splash—inside my chamber.

I screamed. I jumped, pulling myself up by the chains as something in the water brushed my naked thigh, something heavy and alive, sinuous and strong. I stopped breathing, willing myself to become invisible in the dark, trying to become part of the wall. I felt a wash of current on my legs, as if driven by a large tail or fin. Perhaps there was enough slack in my chains that I might flip over, spread my legs into a split and find purchase with my heels on the ledge. I *am* an acrobat, trained and practiced for many more years than I was a pampered noble.

I threw my arms out to my sides as far as they would go; my feet lifted from the floor, assuming the posture of one being energetically crucified. I pulled my feet up behind me, scraping my heels and my bottom on the wall as I went. My feet encountered the vault of the ceiling, then I spread my legs and lowered, lowered, and finally my heels caught the ledge that a moment before had been at the level of my shoulders. The shackles were cutting into my forearms, and my arms trembled with the strain, but I was out of the water, my face only inches above it. At my fittest, I might have been able to hold the posture for a quick chorus of "Ale House Lily," but now I was only a handful of breaths from doom. I opened my eyes wide so they might drink in any wayward light wandering in the room, but caught only the sting of my own sweat, which rolled down and dripped off my nose.

If only the Moor had let me sink in the Grand Canal and suck my own murky death when I had been ready . . . I would have gone, then, gladly shrugged off this mortal coil and stepped into dark oblivion. Then he'd made himself a pest of gallantry, but now, more desperate in hate than sorrow, I wanted to live, dammit.

Something broke the surface of the water, just in front of my face, I could feel it there.

"Take my head then, thou tarry devil! Choke on it!" Whatever was in the water licked the drop of sweat from my nose.

CHORUS: *In Venice did a fool turned emissary find himself, and he, a royal consort—a prince by penetration, as it were—was invited into the senate, and into the homes of all the most high, where he did speak his lady's displeasure at the pursuits of Crusade by the Venetians and the pope. And to his lady's will, he, with utmost lack of decorum, did jape, joke, and jibe at the expense of all of his hosts, much to the amusement of himself and a few others. Thus did Pocket of Dog Snogging gain the favor and ear of the doge, Duke of Venice, leader of the senate, while among others prodded by his wit, enemies bubbled, conspiracies boiled, and grave threats were made upon his head. (The last upon the occasion of his monkey Jeff biting a senator's wife on the nipple.)*

*So it came to pass that on the evening that the
fool received news that his lady, Queen Cordelia of
Britain, France, Belgium, et al., had perished of a
fever, he was in attendance at a ball at the palace of
a senate councilman on the Grand Canal and
received no comfort from the Venetians at court
except wine and silent scorn. Overcome with grief,
the fool cast himself in the canal to drown, but was
yanked out by the scruff of the neck by a
soldier . . .*

He lay there on the pavers for a long time, in a
puddle of canal water, weeping, great gasping sobs
at first, then commenced a breathless trembling, as if
breath itself was born of a pain he could not bear. A
thread of crystal drool ran from the tragedy of his face,
shimmering in the torchlight as if the only thing keeping his soul tethered to earth. The Moor, in his fine
blouse of golden silk, crouched over the fool, saying
nothing.

A breath finally squeaked out of him, a whisper as
weak as a fly dying on a windowsill. "She is dead. My
love."

"I know," said the Moor.

"You don't know love. Look at you. You're a soldier—a hard, scarred, killing thing—a weapon. You've

had an alehouse whore or the odd widow of the conquered, maybe, but you don't know love."

"I know love, fool. Love may not be mine, but I know it."

"You lie," said the fool.

The Moor looked at torchlight reflecting on the canal and said, "When a woman looks upon one's scars with wonder, and sees not the glory of battles won, but sheds tears for the pain of injury suffered, then is love born. When she pities a man's history and wishes away his past troubles with present comforts, then is love awakened. When that which makes a warrior hard is met with beauty offered most tender, then can he find love."

The fool said, "She sees past your handsome exterior to the dark, twisted, broken beast that your years have made of you—the libidinous little creature that you are at heart—when she takes you not in spite of, but *because* you are the cheeky monkey, that is love?"

"I'm not saying that, I—"

The fool rolled to his knees before the Moor and took him by the front of his shirt. "You *do* know! Tell me, Moor, if you know love, true love, then why will you not let me drown, stop the pain? If your love was taken from you, I would hold your sword so you could run upon it and I would hold your head while you twitched in your own heart's blood. I am kind that way. Why do you not do me the same kindness?"

"Because you are drunk."

"Oh, do fuck off. You Muslims and your aversion to drink. Fucking slaughter the greater part of the Western fucking world in Allah's name, but someone wants to toast to your health and suddenly it's all piety, prayer, throw out the pork, and let's put draperies around the women."

"I am not a Muslim."

"Well, a secret Muslim, then. Same thing. You have the curvy sword and the earring and you're black as Satan's scrotum, aren't you?"

"Tomorrow, when you are sober and the drink is out of your head, if then you still wish to drown yourself, I will help you tie a stone to your ankle and throw you in the canal myself."

"You would do that for a poor, heartbroken fool?"

"I would and I shall, but not tonight. Tonight I shall see thee home safely, little one."

The Moor picked the fool up as if lifting a child and threw him over a shoulder.

"Think not of robbing me, Moor, I have no money left. Not much, anyway. I will have to live by the largesse of the doge and I fear that may be running out."

"I know."

"You'll not have your way with me. I'm not one of you soldier types, ready to bugger anything that moves to relieve boredom between battles. Not that I blame you, I *am* fit—somewhat of a prize, really. I was a king for a while."

"If words were wealth," sighed the Moor. "A king among kings you would be, but now you are only small, damp, and loud."

"True, I am drunk, and small, and damp, but mistake not my moistness for weakness, although there's an argument to be made for that, as well. I'm armed, you know?" said the fool, squirming, trying to look back over his shoulder at his abductor. "Don't think that as soon as we're out of sight of the palace you can make your move. I have three daggers at the small of my back."

"Only a soldier or the doge's guard may carry a weapon in Venice," said the Moor.

"I am outside the law," said the fool.

"As am I, I fear," said the Moor.

"What did you mean, that you know love, but it may not be yours?"

"I will tell you tomorrow, when I come to see you drown."

"Tomorrow," said the fool. "Over the bridge, then go right."

The Moor walked up the stairs of the Rialto Bridge, which even in the evening was bustling with merchants, hawkers, and whores.

CHORUS: *And thus was friendship formed.*
Two outsiders, outside a palace in the night,
found fellowship in their troubles, and there
one's problems became the other's purpose.

"Who is that?" asked the fool.

"I don't know him," said the Moor. "Is he following us?"

"No, he's just yammering on about the bloody obvious to no one. A nutter, no doubt."

"I cannot carry him, too," said Othello.

Four
How Much for the Monkey?

Iago was a pillar of leather and steel among the silks and rich brocades of the Rialto merchants. They flowed like anemones in the surf—bargaining, bickering, lying politely and expansively—plucking profit from the flow of goods and services all around. You could buy anything from a pomegranate to a shipping contract on the Rialto. Notaries had set up their desks among the booths to record transactions, whores wagged their rouge-tipped tits from balconies above.

Iago stood with his hand on the hilt of his sword as commerce swirled around him, the odd merchant looking up and wincing as he passed under the soldier's scowl. Before long, a circle cleared on the pavers around Iago, an eddy in the current.

One of the whores, looking down, said, "That one must have a right stink about him, the way they're all movin' away."

When Antonio stepped out of the fray flanked by two young fops in finery too heavy for the heat, Iago did not offer his hand.

"You're late," said the soldier.

"Business beckoned. You didn't give me much notice," said Antonio. "Iago, these are my friends, Gratiano and Salarino—they have been trying to coax me from my melancholy with good cheer."

Iago nodded in turn to each of the two, both taller and more stout than the soldier. Well fed and well kept, he thought. Soft, he thought. "Gentlemen, please do bugger off."

"Pardon?" asked Gratiano, startled, his floppy hat falling over one eye.

"For a bit," said Iago.

Antonio stepped between Iago and the youths. "See here, Iago, these gentlemen are—"

"Business," interrupted Iago.

"Antonio's affairs are our business as well," said Salarino.

Iago shrugged. "Brabantio is dead," he said to Antonio.

"Oh," said Antonio. To his friends: "You two need to bugger off."

"Just for a bit," offered Iago, as the two backed into the crowd, looking more liberated than insulted.

Antonio took Iago by the shirt and hurried him to a nook between the booths of two spice merchants. "Brabantio is dead? When?"

"They found his overripe corpse this morning. Servants followed a foul smell to the cellar. I was brought word by my man, who was on the island. He uses one of Portia's maids on occasion."

"Portia has returned from Florence, then?"

"Just yesterday. The Montressor has been missing for two weeks—since the Assumption. The servants at Villa Belmont thought he'd gone to Florence to join Portia, or perhaps to Corsica to retrieve Desdemona from the Moor. They found him so deep in the cellar that the smell hadn't even risen to the wine cellar."

"Deep in the cellar? I wondered why I had not heard from him. Then he's been there since that night, with the fool."

"Undoubtedly."

"Do you think the fool awakened and attacked him?"

"No. I went to Belmont as soon as I heard, right after I sent word to you to meet. There were mason's tools by the body, a bucket with mortar and tools hardened in it. The Montressor had built a wall shortly before he died. He must have been planning what he would do even before he brought us into his plan. I believe he walled the fool up in that deep chamber where we carried him. Left him there to die."

"And in building the wall, Brabantio collapsed. He *was* very old, feeble of body, if not of mind."

"He was eaten," said Iago, and he smiled at the horror that crossed the merchant's face.

"Rats?" said Antonio. "If he'd been dead that long, I'm not surprised—"

"Yes rats, after, but something ripped his head from his body, ate his hands, his liver, and his heart."

"So not rats?"

"His arm bones were splintered. I've seen a man's hand twisted off by a runaway anchor chain. The bones looked like that." Iago reached into his belt and held forth a long, wickedly curved black tooth, half the length of his thumb. "No, Antonio, it was not rats. This was in what was left of his buttocks."

"His arse was eaten?"

"A bite."

"And Portia saw this?"

"The servants had warned her off. They feared what might be in the dark. I was the first to look at him. I wrapped him together in his robe before anyone came. I told them he had fallen and was eaten by rats. I secreted the mason's tools in a deeper chamber. No one will question it."

"Then you think the fool is still walled up in the cellar?"

"The wall was intact. You sent away that great simpleton who attended the fool, did you not?"

"I sent a forged note from the fool sending for him the next day. My protégé Bassanio arranged to put the giant and the fool's monkey on a ship to Marseilles and paid their passage. You think the natural* could have done this?"

Iago stroked his beard. "No, he is strong enough, but what was done to the senator requires a savagery beyond that of a simpleton enraged, even if he'd had a weapon of tooth and bone. It was an animal."

"The monkey, then?"

"Yes, Antonio. The senator's head was torn from his body and his liver eaten by a tiny fucking monkey in fool's motley."

"Jeff," said Antonio.

"What?"

"The monkey is called Jeff."

---

*A natural was a jester who came to his profession by way of a physical or mental anomaly—a dwarf, a giant, Down syndrome, etc. Naturals were thought to have been touched by God.

"Forget the monkey! What is this fascination you have with the monkey? Why didn't you just keep the monkey?"

"I needed to make the fool's departure appear genuine, didn't I?" said Antonio. "No one would go away without his monkey. Besides, I am a respected merchant of Venice. I cannot have a monkey, it would seem frivolous."

"Psssst, beg pardon, signor," said one of the spice merchants, leaning out of his booth. "But I might be able to procure a monkey for you."

"Oh for fuck's sake," said Iago.

"Very discreet, signor," said the spice seller, affecting a conspiratorial whisper. "You can keep it, or just have it for the night, if you'd like. My man will come take it away in the morning."

"No," said Antonio. "I have no need—"

"How much did you hear?" Iago said to the spice man.

"I know nothing of Antonio's desire to fuck a monkey." Innocence blossomed on the spice seller's face, blissful ignorance gleamed in his eye.

"I do not—" Antonio had taken off his floppy silk hat and was fanning himself with it, sweat having suddenly leapt out onto his brow.

"Beyond the monkey fucking, what heard you?"

"Nothing of a headless senator," said the spice man.

"Pay him," said Iago to Antonio.

"I don't want to—"

"Twenty ducats?" Iago raised his scarred eyebrow to the merchant.

The spice seller shrugged, as if perhaps, in some land, a land where his children were not hungry and his wife was not so demanding, twenty ducats might possibly be enough to make him forget what he had never really heard, but here, in Venice, now, well, signor, a man has expenses, and—

"Or I can kill you now," said Iago, dropping his hand to the hilt of his dagger.

"Never was there a more perfect price than twenty ducats," said the spice man.

"Pay him." Iago kept his hand on his knife and continued to regard the spice man as Antonio dug into his purse for the coins.

"And if word of what was said here passes your lips, your life is forfeit, as are the lives of your family."

"How do I know you won't kill me anyway?" said the spice man.

"Because Antonio has given you twenty ducats," said Iago. "And Antonio is an honorable man."

"I am," said Antonio. He counted the coins into the spice man's palm. "An honorable man with no interest in monkeys."

Iago draped his arm around Antonio and led him to another corner of the square.

"He may require killing, anyway."

"If you're going to kill him anyway, I might have saved twenty ducats."

"Twenty ducats is your fine for being shite as a conspirator. 'Twas foolish to meet on the Rialto."

"How was I to know you were going to speak of murder? Why must I always be the one to pay?"

"Money is your charm, Antonio, one which we may well need in abundance to purchase the power we've lost with Brabantio. Another senator of the council of six."

"If I commanded the wealth to purchase a senator, I wouldn't need a war to pad my fortune. And none of the existing five council members favors our cause; they were all stung by the defeat to the Genoans. I fear our cause is lost."

"Not if we can retain Brabantio's seat."

"Perhaps a year ago we might have put a candidate up for vote, spread our bribes around, but when the doge declared senate seats inheritable, our chances were lost. Brabantio's seat would go to his eldest son, but since he has no son, it will go to the husband of his eldest— Oh my." Antonio ducked out of the soldier's embrace and backed away.

"It goes to the Moor," said Iago. "Brabantio's senate seat will go to Othello."

Antonio looked around, hoping his friends might magically appear out of the crowd to rescue him from Iago's wrath, which the soldier wore in a hardened scowl. "If you'd like, you can go kill the spice merchant, now. I'm not much for killing, but I'll make a splendid witness."

Iago held up a finger and Antonio fell silent. "If the first daughter's husband will not do, we must make the second daughter the first."

"Portia?"

"Aye, she knows us. She trusts us, she would do our will."

"But she is not married, and Othello and Desdemona are even now on Corsica. Surely the doge will call them back."

"Call his general from the field? We shall see. But word will be sent with a trusted lieutenant. Can you find a suitor to Portia to be our senator?"

"I know someone—the young man I mentioned, Bassanio, would be perfect—he has his eye on Portia already. He is handsome and controllable, and he owes me."

"Good, arrange it. I will see to Desdemona and the Moor. I am off to the doge, then I'll arrange the journey to Corsica."

"But how do you know the doge will send you?"

"Did I not tell you, Antonio, that my own wife serves as one of Desdemona's ladies?"

"No. You sent her there?"

"When the Moor chose Michael Cassio as his second in command over me, I had to keep friendly eyes upon them."

"Well planned, Iago. What will you do in Corsica?"

"Do not ask, good merchant, if you wish to stay a clean and honorable man."

"Oh, I do. I do."

"Then I'm off to the senate, with the news," said the soldier.

"Wait, Iago."

"Yes."

"If money is my charm, and you have none, and power was Brabantio's offer, and you have none, what do *you* bring to this enterprise to justify a third of the profits?"

"Will," said Iago.

"Well, get on with it, thou shit-breathed carbuncle! I don't have all day."

When you start shouting at things in the dark, you've essentially given up, haven't you? You're more or less saying, "Well, I know I'm fucked six ways to doom, and I'm frightened out of my wits, but I'd prefer we get this over with quickly and with as little pain as possible."

But the thing in the water did not snap off my head, and my arms began to tremble until I could hold myself no longer. I let loose a great scream, relaxed my arms, and fell onto the slack of the chains like a plunging marionette, nearly wrenching my shoulders from their sockets and the skin from my wrists when the shackles went taut.

I continued to scream until my voice broke and what breath I had came with a desperate animal yowl that filled the chamber, the darkness, the very reaches of my imagination. All life became the instant before the bite, the slash, the sting from the thing unknown.

Nothing.

I hung slack in my chains and the water settled, a low wail drooled out of my lungs—hope hissing away. I would die now.

Water droplets tapped on the ledge by my hand and echoed like slow, distant clapping—Charon at his oar, applauding the pathetic efforts of his next fare to the underworld.

Something—a fin, perhaps—brushed my foot and I resumed my scream, kicked at the thing, which enveloped my legs, holding me fast, moving around and up my knees, thighs.

My bladder let go, and for the first time since I was a boy, I prayed. "God, save me, thou pompous great prick!" (Did I say I had not been on speaking terms with God for some time? Only polite to acknowledge our mutual resentments, innit?)

The creature, while bear-bonkingly strong, was not spiny, nor was its skin rough like the sharks I had seen at the Rialto fish market, but smooth—slick—it slipped around me as if I were being strangled by a great, slippery cord. I began to lose consciousness, some dreamy flowing of the mind from the terror—vestiges perhaps of the creature's poison. Off I drifted, welcoming oblivion, as a set of barbs pierced my hips and the monster fastened itself upon my man-tackle.

Five
Ladies of the Lagoon

In the sumptuous Villa Belmont did Portia Brabantio abide, a fair-haired, newly orphaned lady with the ripening of twenty-two summers upon her bosom, a wit as sharp as a dagger, and a beauty that had been praised on all the islands of Venice, particularly by those signors hoping to gain access to her knickers. Waiting upon the lady was her maid Nerissa, a raven-haired beauty half again as clever as her mistress, and as good a friend as money could buy. The two had been together since they were little girls, and so loved and hated each other like sisters.

"By my troth, Nerissa, my little body is weary of this great world." Over her hair Portia wore a net of gold punctuated with pearls, which she picked at as if they were opulent lice.

"Well, buying shoes can be taxing, especially when you have only one maid to carry your parcels."

"Not from buying shoes," said Portia, lifting her gown to check that she was wearing new shoes and that all the travel and her father dying while she was gone had not been in vain. "I haven't been sleeping well since we returned from Florence. I wake thinking I hear screaming deep in the bowels of the villa—the sound of someone suffering, but when I sit up in bed, I hear nothing."

"Perhaps if you did something during the day, milady—lifted a finger, maybe two, in care of yourself—exhaustion would pleasantly overtake you and your slumber would be filled with sweetest dreams."

"Dancing?" ventured Portia. "I do so prefer dancing to suffering, don't you, Nerissa?"

"You speak as if one must choose one over another, but as any gentleman who has turned you around a ballroom can attest, dancing and suffering can be partners in step."

"Oh, sweet Nerissa, I shall miss your loving snark when I am married and you are safely installed in a nunnery giving good service to priests and pirates, or in a brothel bearing the gentle jumps of rascals."

"Would it were so, but I fear I shall ever be here at Belmont, blowing dust and clearing the cobwebs from milady's nethers, your father's puzzle having verily assured your spinsterhood."

They tittered through gritted teeth, then Portia flung her needlepoint off the veranda as if it were a pie made from leprosy, then plopped down on a marble stool by the table, her legs askew, elbow to thigh, hand cradling a troubled chin.

"Oh balls."

"Milady?"

"You're right, of course," said Portia. She scowled at three jewel chests that were laid out on the table. "I know you're right. No man is going to pay the bride price and pass Father's sodding test. Three thousand ducats? It's absurd."

"Your father set the price and the test to see you married better than Desdemona."

"And yet she shall have Belmont, her Moor shall have Father's seat on the senate council, and I shall have one of our shoddy estates on the mainland— and for my bed, some rich old prat who's good at puzzles."

Nerissa walked around the table, running her hand over each of three jewel chests: gold, silver, and lead. "Perhaps once your suitors have proved they have the bride price, you can pick the one you fancy and we will steer him to open the right chest."

"That's just the point, I don't know which chest holds my picture, and therefore the right to my hand. Father's wax seal is on each of the locks, we cannot test them. I might have to marry the first man with three thousand ducats who chooses a key, or I may hand the key to the man I favor, only to have him pick a chest that holds some false treasure. Father vexes me from the grave. How did he think that such a test would lead me to a better man than wed my sister when the game is so bloody random?"

"He thought to guide your choice himself, while seeming to show no favor. I heard him say that he thought Desdemona married the Moor as much to defy his will as for any love of the general. With the bride price, he could assure that your suitors would be gentlemen of means, then with the chests he could steer the one he favored to the right chest, without spurring a rebellious spirit in you."

"A fine plan, I suppose, had he lived. I might have at least guided his choice."

"It was all properly drawn up by lawyers."

"Father and his lawyers. Who was it that said, 'First, kill all the lawyers'?"

"I believe it was the little English fool so favored by the doge."

"Oh, well, it's true anyway."

"Then he said, 'And after the lawyers, a proper thinning of you poxy nobles.'"

"So annoying."

"Yet comely, in his jittering way."

"You know, Nerissa, that enormous codpiece he wears is stuffed with scrap silk."

"That is not how he carries himself."

"Bowlegged, you mean?" Portia giggled.

"No, like he fears nothing. The fool stands steady among merchants turned jelly-spined for fear a wrong word might affect their fortunes. Steady anyway, before he was struck down by grief. Oh, to be loved so much that a man might ruin himself for my loss. That, milady, is a lover."

"He's an insolent fool, Nerissa, and tiny, too; I forbid you to fancy him."

"I don't fancy him, but I admire his boldness. Well, I admired it. They say he left in the middle of the night, took his monkey and his giant simpleton, and sailed back to France on a merchantman. Is that the bell at the dock?"

Portia stood, composed herself, and looked over the railing at where her needlepoint might have sailed. She turned and looked surprised as the doorman entered.

"Madame, Signor Antonio Donnola, a merchant of Venice, with two associates, Signors Gratiano and Bassanio, to pay their respects to the lady."

"Oh, I remember Signor Bassanio," said Portia, a crinkle of a smile sparkling in her gray-blue eyes. "Fetch refreshment, and bring some flowers for this dreary table. And, Nerissa, fetch those three daggers in their leather harness we found among father's things. Antonio will know which of Father's friends left them."

"Yes, madame."

CHORUS: *And so, chained in the dark, naked and bedeviled by a hellish creature unknown, after five changings of the tides, the fool went mad.*

I am not mad!

CHORUS: *Fear did twist the jester's tiny mind— stretch it past the limits of sanity until it snapped—and shivering and pale, he went mad.*

I am not mad!

CHORUS: *Stark, raving mad. Bonkers. Drooling, frothing, barking mad.*

I am not bloody mad, you berk!

CHORUS: *You're shouting at a disembodied voice in the dark.*

Oh, fuckstockings. Good point. Well, a bit knack-ered, perhaps, but not bloody mad. Although who could blame me, really, if I had taken a stroll down Barking at the Moon Lane, what with the poisoning, the thirst and starvation, the wounds, the pervasive darkness, and the fearsome creature lurking in the water, waiting to rend me to bloody shreds, and so forth. Enough, really, to put even the most sturdy bloke off his regimen, and I, a wan and wispy crafter of japes, what chance did I have to cling to sanity's silken tether?

I kept my mind busy during low tides, like now, by plotting intricate tortures and revenges upon my captor, between sobbing and moaning piteously over my lost Cordelia, my freedom, and my exile from light and warmth. Between bouts of soul-crushing despair, I busy myself slurping sips of water from my arm. A small triumph, the steady dripping from above that clapped on the ledge by my hand, like the tick of my life's clock running down, has turned out to be my life blood. It is freshwater, you see, no doubt leaking from some cistern above, and if I am determined, and I position my chains just so, I can drink enough as it runs down the chains and my arm to quell the thirst. Sometimes I busy myself by singing a song, or shrieking until my voice breaks. But when the tide is high and the chamber fills with warm seawater, then she comes, and this dark hell is a different place.

I do not know how long I have been here. I counted the changing of the tides for a while, but with no way to mark them, I lost count. It seems a lifetime, but it could be only days. I try to imagine Brabantio and his family moving in the manse above me, and I think I can hear voices, or the ringing of a bell, but I can't be sure. The sounds I hear in my head, the voices of the dead, are as real to me as anything I might hear from outside.

I talk to them, the dead, who come to me in the dark, and if I squint, I can see them, those phantoms of my past, blue-gray against the blackness. Lovers, friends, enemies, tossers, walleys, lick-spittles, catch-farts, slags, hags, and bum-snipers. People who I don't remember ever having seen before pass by, pause, look at me, their eyes as black and empty as everything else. I don't know if I dream them, or if I even sleep. The tide takes the weight off my chains and I drift. Just drift.

I always scream when she comes, sliding in by my knees, around the chamber, back behind my legs. Even if I have been waiting, anticipating, even if I am aware of her in the chamber, in that moment when she touches me, I am startled, terrified, and I can hear my pulse pound like a battle drum in my neck. My chains rattle and I fall, crucified in my shackles before her.

She will not harm me, until she does, but I am given to that. That first time, when the Montressor's poison and fear were still high in my blood, I felt it was a shark or a great eel in the room, saw in my mind's eye the saw teeth tearing pieces from me. And when claws or spines fastened into my loins and something soft—ever so soft—like honey in water, wrapped upon my manhood, my mind could find no picture to put on the creature. What thing of the vasty deep was soft, gentle, yet strong, spiny? I had seen octopi alive in buckets of seawater in the fish market in Venice, and a fishmonger had dared me to touch one, and yes, it was soft, and disgusting, little more than a tripe with a purpose. "You fucking Venetians will eat anything the sea pukes up, won't you? This looks like something shat out by something too disgusting to be allowed near a kitchen, and I am from a race of avowed offal eaters." The fishmonger laughed.

This thing in the water, in the dark, was not an octopus, though. What did I know? But it worked away at me and after some time settled, curled around my feet, and stayed there. If it was to kill me, so be it. My legs were constrained, wrapped in coils of unrelenting strength up to my hips. I could not fight it, nor kick at it, and I had used all of my breath in shrieking at it. I fainted or surrendered, or was constricted until I choked, I don't know, but when I was conscious again, the tide was out and I was alone in my chamber.

When thirst moved me to try to arrange my chains to channel water down my arm, my hand landed on something alive and I shrieked. (Yes, I do a lot of shrieking here in the dark. There is little else to do between the terror and the suffering—perhaps the disembodied tosser voice is right. Perhaps I have gone mad? Oh, well, how can you tell in the dark?) But it wasn't alive, what was on the ledge—recently alive, perhaps. I ran my hand over it gently, feeling the spines, the fins, the eyes—a fish. Dead, but recently so—as long as my forearm and as big around. And the flesh had been scored, I could feel the cuts through the scales. I assumed the posture of prayer, where both of my hands could meet, and I ate the fish's flesh, willing myself to slow down, not to swallow the scales or bones. It was the finest food I had ever eaten, and I felt my very being envelop it, making it part of me as if I were absorbing nourishment from the very dark itself.

The creature in the dark had left the fish for me, scored it for me, saved me from hunger if not delirium. What rough beast knows charity? What shark's cold eye shines with kindness? None! These are human things, but even as a man can act a beast, can a monster show the character of a man? A woman?

She came to me on the next high tide and I yipped when roused from my reverie, but I did not kick at her as she brushed by me, again and again, rubbing against me as she passed, the way a cat will. Then, again, the creature wrapped around my legs, and I waited, again, for the bite that might take my leg, as the great slick coils of muscle constricted me. The claws came again, piercing my haunches. I shrieked, but these were not the tearing slashes that had scored the fish, but only just broke the skin, then the pleasant drift and I felt her soft parts begin to assail my manhood.

It was that second time that I realized what was in the water, was able to put a picture in my mind's eye to the sensation, began to think of the creature as female. The calm drifting feeling that overcame me was not exhaustion, or terror, or the residual effect of the Montressor's poison, but the venom of the mermaid. Had I not seen a hundred such sirens portrayed in signs of alehouses and on the prows of ships? The mermaid was as common as the lion of St. Mark in the statues around Venice, and here, in my dark chamber, open to the sea, I had been seduced by one.

I let the venom and the passionate attentions of the mermaid take me until I was spent, then I collapsed into a floaty daze of a briny after-bonk, the mermaid curled around my legs, taking my weight off the chains.

And so, once again, as when I was a boy locked in the cupboard, I made friends with the dark. The tide would come in, and with it the mermaid, her dreamy venom then a sea-frothing shag and a slippery cuddle to wake to a breakfast of raw fish, sometimes two. Drink water and drowse in the dark until the tide comes in again.

What magical creature, what wonder had found me there, in my most desperate time? Why had no one written of this, why was this tale of the mermaid not told? Did she—did they—only come to the doomed? Perhaps I am already dead? Perhaps I am a ghost, bound to these chains to haunt this dark chamber evermore, and be tortured by the bawdy ministries of a fish-girl.

You know there's always a bloody ghost. Perhaps I am he?

When you think of ghosts wailing and suffering, you don't think of it as constant and eternal, do you? Bit of wailing around midnight, chain rattling and a cold breeze, grab an ankle on the stairs now and again to really get them shitting themselves, then you're on about your day, aren't you? Floating about, lots of naps, perhaps some tennis—stop by the abbey to have a laugh at the vicar's expense, wouldn't you? You don't really think about bloody eternity chained to a damp wall, revenge grinding at your conscience like a rotten tooth, regrets and grief and shivering filling in the mean-times. There *is* the shrieking, which, as I said, I do a fair amount of. Composing the occasional song lyric of a thousand couplets or so, to make sure you've not gone bloody barking. The future gets rather abstract for a ghost—revenge fantasies really more of a mental game you play to keep yourself busy. But I don't think so. There's an end. I can feel it. Maybe not far on.

She's more fierce each time she comes to me. Her claws, or spines, whatever they are seem to go deeper—she veritably ravages me, and I've been nipped on other parts of my body, although not, thankfully, on my manly bits. I've awakened from the venom's stupor to feel blood running down my legs from the wounds she makes on my flanks. If she does not kill me outright, I fear I may succumb to weakness from blood loss or infection of my wounds. Sometimes crabs find their way into the chamber and I can hear them scuttling around in the dark. I kick them away when they get close, but what will happen when I can't? I actually prefer the future when it's more abstract, I think. Dark. Yes, I've made friends with the dark. More than friends. I've learned to fuck the dark. We are one.

And now, she comes. Past my legs, around the chamber, a splash from a fin or tail, the water swirls with her gravity. Behind my legs—she seems bigger, wider, the picture in my head changes, and it's harder to hold the winsome, flaxen-haired maiden perched on a rock in my mind's eye. She is power, she is the dark.

She slides up the front of me, smooth, slick, and I brace myself for the claws. This is the worst of it, before the venom takes me away, when I'm still sore and raw from the last high tide. I try not to scream but scream I do and she works her claws in, like a fisherman setting a hook.

"Fuck's sake! Easy, Viv!"

I've named her Vivian, after some poxy English legend of the Lady of the Sodding Lake. It didn't seem polite, her having me off every turn of the moon, me not knowing her name.

But she doesn't ease into the sex like usual. She's pulling at me, yanking at me. Her mouth or whatever soft part of her that does me, locks on, hard, the suction hurting. I'm pulled straight out from the wall, the chains taut. My wrists are ripped against the shackles, then my shoulders feel as if they will come out of the sockets. There's crackling noise from the wall. The chains slip, and slip again, each time my wrists are scored, her claws sink deeper. Her tail is thrashing the water in the chamber so violently I can barely hear myself scream, and I scream and I scream, and the chains let go—

CHORUS: *And so, his chains ripped from the ancient wall, the mad fool was dragged by his hellish lover down—down into the dark depths of the Venetian lagoon.*

Six
The Players

Antonio hurried from the Rialto as the bells of St. Mark's tolled for the noon prayers. He was followed by an entourage of four young protégés dressed in business finery, a certain uniformity to their dark togs that identified them to others as members of the merchant class, but each wearing a swath of brightly colored silk, a broach, or a bold feather in his cap that advertised his specialness. "I am one of you, maybe one better" was the message. They tumbled along behind Antonio like puppies after a mother hound with her teats on the move.

"Why the urgency?" asked Gratiano, the tallest of the four and as broad shouldered as a dock slave, as they were about to mount the Rialto Bridge. "If it were important business, we should be headed to the Rialto, not to lunch, should we not?"

Antonio turned, and was about to point out, once again, the youth's talent for ignoring context and often the blindingly obvious, when he collided with a short, gray-bearded man in a long coat who had been thumbing through a folio of documents as he descended the steps of the bridge.

"Jew," said Gratiano, stepping around Antonio, and grabbing the old man by the arm, hoisting him up on his toes.

"Usurer!" said Salarino, the oldest of the youths—beginning to go to fat, forever at the flank of his friend Gratiano. He took the Jew under his other arm and at the same time smacked the yellow hat off his head.

"Antonio," said the Jew, coming out of his flinch, eye to eye with the merchant now.

"Shylock," said Antonio. What now? The two young dolts in coming to his defense were forcing action. Senseless. Profitless.

"Pardon," said Shylock, bowing his head but raising his eyes in entreaty. He knew Antonio.

Antonio kept himself from sighing, but instead feigned anger. "Jewish dog!" He barked, and spit on the Jew's long beard, then brushed Salarino aside and strode up the bridge stairs with purpose.

"Shall we throw him in the canal?" asked Gratiano.

"No, leave the cutthroat dog to his damnation," said Antonio. "We have no time. Come."

They dropped the Jew to his feet. Gratiano slapped the sheaf of papers out of the old man's hand. "Watch where you're going, cur," he said, as he turned and hurried after Antonio, catching Salarino's sleeve to pull him along as he went.

Bassanio, who was the most handsome of Antonio's retinue, sidled past Shylock as if afraid he might get something on his shirt if he passed too close, and tossed his head furiously to Lorenzo for him to come along. Lorenzo, the youngest of the crew, scooped up Shylock's papers from the cobbles and patted them awkwardly into the old man's hands, then snatched the yellow hat worn by all Jews (by decree) from the stairs, placed it on Shylock's head, and patted it several times while Shylock looked up at him, then stepped back, adjusted the hat, and patted it again. Only then did he meet Shylock's gaze.

"Jew," he said, nodding for approval.

"Boy," said Shylock, nothing more.

"All right then," said Lorenzo. He adjusted Shylock's hat one last time.

"Lorenzo!" said Bassanio between his teeth, an urgent and stressed whisper.

"Coming." Lorenzo ran up the stairs and joined his friend as they passed over the apex of the bridge.

"Why?" asked Bassanio. "A *Jew*?"

"Have you seen his daughter?" said Lorenzo.

Antonio kept a whole floor of rooms in the top of a large, four-story house on the Riva Ca di Dia, not far from Arsenal. His quarters were not in the most fashionable part of the city, and they were much farther from the Rialto than he would have preferred, but he had taken them when his fortunes were at an ebb and from his parlor he could see the ships sailing in and out of the Venetian lagoon and so he stayed there, even when his fortunes turned, telling his friends that he liked to keep an eye on his business ventures.

Iago was sitting with a younger man at Antonio's table.

"Your maid let me in," said Iago.

"And showed you to the wine, I see," said Antonio.

"This is Rodrigo," said Iago. "The one who brought me news of Brabantio's unfortunate passing."

Rodrigo stood and bowed slightly. He was as tall as Gratiano, but much thinner, and both his hair and his nose were longer than fashionable, the latter quite straight and thin, a fleshy blade protruding from his face. "Honored, sir."

"And these are Gratiano, Lorenzo, Salarino, and Bassanio." Each bowed his head as his name was mentioned.

Iago rose and went to Bassanio, offered his hand. "Then you're the one we need to speak with." He led Bassanio to the table as if leading a lady to the dance floor. Over his shoulder, he said, "The rest of you can fuck off now."

"Iago!" said Antonio. "These gentlemen are my friends and associates, some of the most promising young merchants in Venice. You can't keep telling them to fuck off."

"Ah," said Iago, his hand raised delicately to his leather doublet. "I see," he said, taking dainty dance steps back to the three youths, his eyes averted: the embarrassed maiden aunt. "A thousand pardons, gentlemen. I hope you can forgive me." He tiptoed around behind them, ever more the tiny dancer, his long sword in its scabbard brushing Lorenzo's shin as he passed by. He put his arms across their shoulders, and his face between Lorenzo's and Salarino's ears, and whispered, "I am a soldier, the son of a stevedore, sent to war when I was much younger than any of you, so my manners may seem coarse to you of the merchant class. I hope you'll forgive me." He rolled his eyes up at Gratiano, who craned his neck to see around his friend.

"Apologies," Iago said. Another roll of the eyes.

"Accepted, of course," said Gratiano.

"Of course," said the shorter Lorenzo and rounder Salarino in turn.

Iago broke his embrace of the younger men and pirouetted to Antonio. "Apologies, good Antonio. Noble Antonio. Honored Antonio. I would not offend thy friends."

"It's nothing," said Antonio, feeling suddenly very warm and itchy around the collar.

"Oh good," announced Iago. "Now that we're all friends, you three, do fuck off."

"What?" said Lorenzo.

"You, too, Rodrigo. Go, make the merchants buy you lunch. Fuck off."

"What?" said Rodrigo, rising from his chair.

"Fuck," said Iago, then a deep pause and a breath— "OFF! All of you."

"What?" said Gratiano, wondering what had happened to his new and gentle friend.

Iago looked to Antonio. "Am I being overly subtle? I'm seldom in the company of such distinguished young gentlemen."

"You want them to piss off?" asked Antonio.

"Exactly!" said Iago, turning back to the rabble, his finger raised to make the point. "I'm accustomed to soldiers doing what they are told under threat of the sword, thus I thought I might be mumbling. Gracious gentlemen, Antonio and I have business to discuss with Bassanio, so I will need you all to fuck right off."

"Oh," said Rodrigo.

"Now!" Hand to sword.

They tumbled out the door.

"Rodrigo!" Iago called after them. "Return in an hour."

From the stairwell: "Yes, Lieutenant."

"You others?"

"Yes?" Gratiano answering.

"Stay fucked off."

Iago closed the door, latched it, and turned back to Antonio. "That was entirely your fault."

"You brought your friend along, too."

"Rodrigo is not my friend. He is a useful accoutrement, an implement."

"A tool, then?"

"Exactly. As is this handsome young rake." Iago brushed Bassanio's hat back on his head. "Aren't you, lad?"

"I thought we were here to discuss Portia?" Bassanio said to Antonio, as if Iago were not in the room.

"Indeed," said Antonio. "But there is a problem."

"What problem? He's of good family, he fancies the girl, and he's fine and fit—too fit for my tastes. I'd see him locked down in marriage just to keep him out of my own wife's bed." Iago turned to Bassanio to explain. "She's a bit of a slut, I suspect. Not your fault you're pretty."

"Bassanio is not the problem," said Antonio. "It was obvious in her presence that Portia fancies him, but the late Brabantio has put conditions upon her marriage that bar our young lovers from finding bliss together."

"Conditions?"

"To avoid another calamity of the Othello and Desdemona stripe, the old man composed a puzzle. Each of Portia's suitors must choose one of three caskets: gold, silver, or lead. He is then given the key, and if the casket holds Portia's portrait, they may be married, but if not, the suitor must go away and never return. The entire process is overseen by Brabantio's lawyers, who hold his estate in balance—that part of the estate not willed to Desdemona, that is."

Iago backed into his chair and sat down; his sword hand hunted down and trapped his half-filled goblet of wine. "How did Brabantio think such a test might save his daughter from marrying a rascal? Picking a metal casket?"

"He thought to oversee the process himself—use the caskets to give the girl the illusion that he had left it to chance."

A vein had begun to pulsate on Iago's sun-browned forehead. When he spoke, his voice came measured and he watched young Bassanio for signs that he might be frightening the youth. "Then even Portia herself does not know the contents of the caskets?"

"Nor any of the lawyers. Brabantio sealed the locks himself, with his own seal. Only he knew which casket holds the prize."

"That miserable demented old tosser!" growled Iago. Then to Bassanio, gently: "May God bless him and have mercy on his soul."

"Amen," said Bassanio, bowing his head. "May God rest his soul, and my own when I join him in death's dark country. Deprived of my Portia's love for want of three thousand ducats, I shall drown myself."

"Seems dear," said Iago, scarred eyebrow raised. "I'll drown you for half—nay—a third of that."

"He quite fancies her," explained Antonio. "The three thousand ducats is the price a suitor must pay to open one of the caskets."

"Just for the opportunity," wailed Bassanio.

"We'll solve the puzzle before he attempts it," said Iago. "Even if it means we have to persuade some lawyers with metal less precious than gold. Give him the money, Antonio."

"I don't have it. All my fortunes are at sea. It will be months before I can collect my profits."

Iago's broken eyebrow rose and fell like the wings of a hunting bird flaring to land. "Remind me of what it was that you were to bring to our venture?"

Bassanio caught his head, weighted with woe, in his hands. "Some rich old man will have Portia and I shall drown myself at their wedding."

Iago rose and moved behind Bassanio, took the youth by the shoulders, and lifted him from his chair with a hearty shake. "Thou silly gentleman!"

Bassanio, now firmly in the grasp of Iago, looked to his friend Antonio. "Is it silliness to live when living is torment?"

"What love is not torment when a man knows not how to love himself? Talk not of drowning, but attaining your heart's desire by action: Put money in thy purse."

"I know it's folly to be so fond of her, knowing her as little as I do, but she is radiant, and I am helpless."

"And so, like helpless kittens and blind puppies, you will drown yourself? Nay, I say! Put money in thy purse. Give in to your passions and they will lead you to the most preposterous conclusions—passions make a fool of reason. Rather let reason find a path to passion: Put money in thy purse."

"But even the chance—"

"Make money, young gentleman. Sell your lands, your treasures, call in your debtors, take your lady, your fortune, your future, your fate—for fate favors the truest love, surely, when it is pursued with reason. Put money in thy purse."

"But I have no treasure, no lands."

"Oh for fuck's sake. Really?" Iago, his sails suddenly gone slack, glared at Antonio, who nodded sadly.

Antonio put his arm around Bassanio's shoulders and walked him out of Iago's stiff embrace. "But you have friends, and so they shall come to your aid. My ventures at sea are worth more than twice the bride price. Go, Bassanio, into the Rialto, and see what my good name and credit will provide. I will see you well furnished to fling woo at the fair Portia."

"But I already owe you more than I can repay—"

"Your happiness, loyalty, and love will be my payment."

"Yes," said Iago, now steering the youth out of Antonio's arms and hurrying him to the door. "Have I not said, put *Antonio's money in thy purse*? Now go, find fortune in the Rialto, and send Rodrigo back, we would have words with him."

Bassanio hurried out the door, then turned. "Oh, Signor Iago, do not forget your daggers at Belmont. Portia holds them for you."

"Go now, put money in thy purse," said Iago, closing the door. He turned to Antonio. "My daggers?"

"Portia found them among Brabantio's things and asked me about them. I would have claimed them, but as only a soldier may carry weapons openly, I told her they were yours."

"Well, the bloody fool didn't carry them openly, did he? You might have just shoved them under your doublet and we'd be done with it. You should have worn them out that night with the fool's motley."

"Just send your man Rodrigo to fetch them and we will be done with it. You said he goes to Belmont."

"Rodrigo knows that throwing daggers are the weapons of a cutpurse or a circus clown, not a proper soldier. I will go myself. Let us hope Brabantio didn't keep other souvenirs of his revenge. I would wear a hand of steam if I could slap the old man's ghost for his pigheaded plans and puzzles."

"Puzzles that seem too clever to solve. Even if Bassanio beats the lottery of the chests, how do we know we can bring the rest of our plan to fruition?"

"You're right, he does seem a bit thick, even if only to be a senator."

"That's not what I meant. I mean even if he succeeds in marrying Portia, she does not inherit as long as Desdemona's husband stands in her way. And when we conceived of this plan, you were to be general of the navy, but with Cassio as Othello's second in command, even that ambition is far-reaching."

"Then Othello has to go, and Cassio with him. The Moor would not be general at all, but for the stunning defeat of Dandalo, his predecessor, so shall I ride the Moor's defeat to my command."

"You would have Othello lose a war so you can take his place? There is so little left of the navy that another loss will give you nothing to command."

"No, I'll not use weapons of war to take down the Moor, for even as I know I am Cassio's better as a soldier, so does Othello's skill exceed my own. No, the weapon to bring down Othello comes presently up your stairs."

There were footfalls on the stairs, a single man ascending the floors.

"Rodrigo?" Antonio went to the door and held the bolt. "But he's an idiot!"

"Hold your base slander, Antonio. Do I disparage *your* friends?"

"Well—" Antonio threw the bolt and swung the door wide for Rodrigo. "Yes."

"Come, come, good Rodrigo," said Iago. "I was just telling Antonio of your affections for the lady Desdemona."

"You told him? I still wear the shame of it." Rodrigo shielded his face from Antonio's gaze with his hat.

Iago took the taller man's hat and tossed it in the corner, then put his arm around Rodrigo's shoulders. "Antonio is our friend. And there is no shame where there is no defeat, good Rodrigo. I tell you, you shall yet have your Desdemona."

"But she is married to the Moor, and they are away in Corsica; by what means can I win her now? I am lost."

"He says he's lost," Iago said over his shoulder to Antonio. "Yet even now Portia's maid Nerissa dotes on him and grants him her charms, and she is more than lovely for a serving girl."

"I met her when I was trying to court Desdemona," Rodrigo explained.

"And Desdemona shall you have. I promise it."

"But how?"

Iago grinned at Antonio, then pulled Rodrigo close. "By the means which you take command of your fate, good Rodrigo. By the means that reason satisfies passion, young stallion. If you seek Desdemona, first you must put money in thy purse."

"Truly?" asked Rodrigo.

"Really?" said Antonio, who was asking a completely different question.

"Aye, lad, put money in thy purse. Sell your lands, your treasures, call in your debtors, and when your purse is full, we are for Corsica and beautiful Desdemona. I tell thee truly, put money in thy purse."

"Is there any more wine?" asked Rodrigo.

"I told you," said Antonio.

ACT II

The Watery City

This thing of darkness I acknowledge mine.

—Prospero, *The Tempest,* Act V, Scene 1

Seven
La Giudecca

CHORUS: *Come now to a serpentine island south of the central districts of Venice called La Giudecca. Separated from the city not by a canal, easily bridged, but by a wide water avenue called Tronchetto–Lido di Venezia that must be traversed by gondola or ferry. Here, in sight of the Basilica of St. Mark, live all the Jews of Venice, and here, only, are they permitted to own property.*

On this soft September morn, the beautiful Jessica, only daughter of the widower moneylender Shylock, has found upon the cobbled boat ramp before their house a small, pale, and naked man, who was coughed up by the lagoon with the night tide.

"Oh my! He breathes!"

CHORUS: *Secretly, Jessica is overjoyed, not only because the flotsam fellow lives, but because she has been wishing for just such a delivery: a slave of her very own. While many well-to-do Venetians own slaves, the practice is forbidden to Jews and so Jessica is tasked by her father to keep house, cook, and perform other duties that a less tightfisted father might hire to have done.*

But alas, here comes the old Jew now.

"There you are, Jessica. I am off to the Rialto."

"Farewell, Papa."

"Girl, why do you squat on the boat landing?"

"Having a wee, Papa."

"In front of the house? Just like that? When I have had built a perfectly good privy in the house?"

"I didn't want to disturb you. See, my skirts are around me. No one can even see."

"That your mother cannot see you thus—peeing on the boat landing like a dog—for that I am grateful. I will return at noon for lunch. Do the washing-up."

"Yes, Papa."

CHORUS: *So, Shylock thus disposed, Jessica turned her devices to preparing her new slave for presentation later to her father, which would*

require some scrubbing, removal of his chains,
and perhaps restoring the jester to consciousness,
but even though her slave was slight, she found she
was not strong enough to drag him up the ramp
and into the house by herself.

"I'm not strong enough to get him up the ramp."

CHORUS: *She said with great superfluity, as the*
narrator had only just pointed out that selfsame
thing.

"I was talking to Gobbo, you knob. No one likes you, you know? Skulking about in the margins acting as if you know everything."

CHORUS: *And, indeed, with uncommon stealth and*
no little sneakiness, the blind old beggar Gobbo
had tapped his way down the walkway to pause at
the top of the boat ramp, thus surprising the
narrator, who is seldom underinformed about such
goings-on.

"Signor Gobbo, help me get this fellow into the house. I'm not strong enough to move him."
"What fellow?"

"This poor fellow who is nearly drowned, and has washed up on the boat ramp."

"Do you think it could be my son? My boy, long lost?"

"Fine. Your son. Help me get *your son* into the house, Gobbo."

"Well, why didn't you say so?"

CHORUS: *So, with the help of old Gobbo, Jessica was able to move the battered and sodden fool to the house, but as they pulled him up from the ramp, she heard what sounded like a small fish jumping, and spied, out by the end of the gondola docks, a sleek shadow moving beneath the jade green water of the lagoon.*

———————

CHORUS: *And so, while the fool slept the sleep of the dead, the beautiful Jewess snipped off the tip of his willy.*

"What!" said I, somewhat emphatically, when I awoke from my premature burial and submarine mermaid bonking. "Unhand my willy, young woman!"

"Settle down, slave, I just need to snip a bit of the tip off so Papa will let me keep you."

She was a lovely thing, wild dark hair and blue eyes; strong high cheekbones; and a long, straight nose like the desert princesses adorning the pillaged Egyptian obelisks that stood in the piazzas of Rome. Truly told, I didn't notice her features at the time, as she was holding the tip of my willy with two fingers of one hand, while in the other brandishing, with great concentration, a butcher knife the size of a rowboat. "He'll never let me keep a Gentile slave. I've seen the *mohel* do this simply dozens of times. Easy peasy. Now, hold still."

Lest you think me a cad, let me say I have never struck a woman—except for the playful taps delivered in passion, and relished by ladies of more decadent tastes—but I have never struck a woman with the intent of doing harm (unless you count poisoning as striking, which I don't really think it is)—but in that moment, a strange tart with a blade trained on my manhood, my years of training and natural instincts as a warrior became my spirit, and drove me to action. In a wink I snatched the nipple of her right breast between my thumb and forefinger and gave it an urgent twist.

"Ouch!" said she, jumping back and cradling the offended orb with her willy-wagging hand. "That hurt. Bad slave! Bad!"

I had retreated to the corner of the cot I'd been lying on and assumed a defensive crouch. "Where am I? How did I get here? Who are you? Why were you about to lop off my knob?"

"I wasn't. I was just confirming your covenant with God with your foreskin."

"Look, you mad tart, I have a covenant with God, which is: I don't mention that he has stocked the world full of villains, walleys, and madwomen, and in return he keeps his bloody hands off my willy. It's a strained relationship, but it works, with the exception of—" And then I was on my feet, confronting the girl despite her knife. "Say, you're not the mermaid made human again, are you? I've heard the bloody stories." I grabbed the hem of her skirt and threw it up to reveal her tail.

"Oh," said I. Having found no tail in evidence, I dropped her skirt and backed away. "Well, even if you're not a mermaid you should wear knickers about the house. People will think you wanton."

I was suddenly light-headed and fell back upon the cot, swooning.

"You're going to make a shit slave, aren't you?" she said.

"I'm knackered, love. Put away the knife and let a bloke rest. Some toast would be lovely. I've had nothing but raw fish for—" I felt my chin. I had more than a bit of a beard. I must have been chained in the dungeon for a fortnight at least.

She seemed to look at me, really, for the first time, and I could see her eyes widen in alarm. She put her knife on a side table, pulled back the covers at the other end of the cot, and nodded. "In you go."

Even though it was warm in the house, I was shivering, so I did as I was told, and she propped me up on some pillows. "You do look like you could use a meal. I'll fetch you some bread and cheese—maybe some sweet wine if we have any left. I'm going to have to keep you hidden here in my room until you're well enough to present to Papa, so you're going to have to be quiet."

"Quiet," I repeated.

"You look like you've been in the water for a long time. Were you shipwrecked? Escaped galley slave what went over the side in despair? They wash up now and then, but usually not still breathing."

I thought it best, at this point, to not reveal that I was ambassador from a kingdom that no longer existed, a former slave to the king of Britain and royal consort to his daughter, late queen of nearly a third of Europe. "I'm a troubadour. Traveling to England. Our ship hit a reef and sank."

"I didn't hear of a ship sinking."

"Well, it was far, wasn't it. Thus explaining why I was in the water for so bloody long before I washed up—where am I?"

"You're on the island of La Giudecca, at the home of Shylock the moneylender. I'm Jessica, his daughter."

"And I'm your father," said a tower of lint in the corner of the room.

"Holy Flaming Fuck-Moses! What's that?" You think that you have run out of fear, that you are beyond surprise. As it turns out, no.

It moved.

"Oh, that's the blind beggar Gobbo," said Jessica. "He helped me get you up here. Borrowed a chisel and hammer from the smith to break the chains off you."

I began to make out the shape of a bent old man who was uniform in color from head to toe, where covered by rags and where not, a shade I can only describe as, well, filth.

"I knew I'd find you," said Gobbo.

"I'd never have rescued you if it hadn't been for old Gobbo recognizing you as his son and lending a hand." Jessica raised her eyebrows and nodded for me to go along with it.

"Charmed," said I. "Didn't think to intervene during the circumcision, then, Da?"

"What circumcision?"

"Can't imagine why your son abandoned you," I said under my breath. Then to Jessica: "Bread and cheese, you said? Wine?"

"I'll fetch some. You'll need some salve for those scrapes on your wrists and gouges on your bum, too, or the wounds will fester."

"Fine, but no touching the willy. I'm grieving and I've been used roughly, so I'm in no mood for sport."

"Fine, we'll simply have to pass you off as Hebrew, but you'll have to put on some trousers or something before I show you to Papa. Besides, I want nothing to do with your scrawny willy. I am in love with the most wondrous man called Lorenzo."

"And a lucky young Jew, indeed, is this Lorenzo."

"Oh, he's not a Jew, he's a Christian. He is a merchant, learning his trade under Signor Antonio, one of Venice's most prominent traders." She rolled her eyes to the ceiling and hugged herself at the thought of her beloved Lorenzo.

"Antonio? Antonio Donnola?"

"Yes, you know him?"

"No. But I know of him." Had I gone so far, through so much, to end up in the nest of one of my murderers? For surely as far as any of them knew, I was dead.

I feigned a yawn and sat back on the pillows. "Dear Jessica, if I am going to be a proper Jew and slave before your father, I will need to eat and then sleep. But let's not tell anyone how you came to find me, or that I am here at all. In thanks for my rescue, I will serve you, but as a new Jew, freshly hatched. Agreed?"

"Smashing! Yes, yes, agreed," she said. "With you to do my chores I'll be able to sneak away to see Lorenzo more."

"Lorenzo, especially, must not know how you found me."

"But it's so exciting, I simply must—"

"I'll tell him I woke to find you fondling my naughty bits."

"Well, fine, then." She pouted. "What about him?" She tossed her head toward Gobbo.

"Gobbo," I called.

"What? What?" said the column of rags. "Who's there? Have you seen my son?"

"He'll be fine," said I.

A fever came upon me and I was five days hiding and recovering in Jessica's bedroom before I was ready to reemerge upon Venice's stage. When Jessica brought me her hand mirror I scarcely recognized myself and I had little doubt I could pass through the streets of Venice without being recognized, especially as Brabantio had stripped me of my trademark motley and bells. I have always been thin, but now my cheeks were drawn from my time in the dungeon and the fever that followed, and a mossy brown beard shaded my face in wisps. Still, I would need more disguise than time's wear and tear to move among mine enemies, and I would need Jessica's help to obtain that.

Jessica sat across the room by the window, preparing some sailcloth sailor's trousers she had bought for me at the docks.

"Jessica, love," said I. "You might hold up on the sewing for a tick."

"Bollocks, they're a good foot too long. You want to trip and break a leg so you can't do any chores, don't you?"

"Not at all," said I. "I am prepared to be your faithful servant, but before you present me to your father, there's something you should know. I haven't been entirely honest with you."

"What, you're not the deposed King of England, what once shagged a holy woman through a hole in a wall?"

I had shared some of my history with the girl, much of it while in the delirium of fever, but nothing about my previous tenure in Venice. Well, I didn't know her, did I? A gentleman does not begin a conversation with a young lady he's just met by saying, *"Oh, well, I've been having it off with the fish girl while buried alive in the senator's cellar, and you?"*

"No, that bit's true," said I. "But I am not, actually, a troubadour who was shipwrecked while on my way to entertain the seventh Earl of Bumsex."

"You don't say? That would explain the chains we chiseled off you, then? Why, yes, that makes sense, now, doesn't it?" She scratched her head and looked out at the sky, as if receiving a revelation from the heavens. As lovely as she was, sarcasm did not wear well on her. Still, she was a bright girl, and in our short time together we had built a bond of petty resentments that usually takes a lifetime to develop. She turned to me then. "Pocket, I am inconsolable in my disappointment."

"And there are men in Venice who would do me great harm if they knew I was alive."

"Is it because you're a shit?"

"I'm not a shit."

"Then why do they want to do you harm?"

"I have been unfairly judged."

"Over what have you been unfairly judged?"

"I know not, for many have said that I am charming and kind."

"Really? Many have said that?"

I nodded, woe sloshing heavily upon my brow. "Unjust suffering and horrendous hardship have been inflicted upon me, for little to no reason."

"I know, I know." She patted my hand. "It brings water to my eyes when you talk of your dear Cordelia. I hope that my Lorenzo loves me that much someday. So why do these fellows want to hurt you?"

"For merely doing what I was tasked to do by my queen."

"It's because you're a shit, isn't it?" Still a compassionate tone and the reassuring pat on the hand.

"No, it's—I—the evil that men do—" Oh bugger all. "Yes, it's because I'm a shit."

"There, there, Pocket."

"But a shit in the name of the crown!" I added, queen, country, and St. Bloody George implied in my voice.

"Though a shit nonetheless."

"The only difference between a pirate and a privateer is a flag, you know?"

"Do you have a flag?"

"Don't be literal, love, people will think you're simple. Venice's own general, Othello, was little more than a privateer when the city found him, and now he is a hero of the republic."

"Yes, and when you save the city from total destruction, you, too, will be regarded as a hero, which will—and I'm only guessing now, as I'm just a Jewish girl and know little of the sophistications of the ruling class—require you to wear some sodding trousers."

"Well, that's what I'm getting at, pumpkin. Have you a pair of chopines?"

Chopines were the wooden platforms that Venetian ladies, and even some gentlemen, wore strapped to their shoes to hold them above the mud, muck, and flotsam that filled the streets during rains or a high storm tide. Some ladies, to ensure that their gowns, made of the finest fabrics available from the most distant and exotic ports in the world, remained unsullied by street sewage, wore chopines longer than their own shins, and required a footman on either side to balance them, so they could walk to a ball or humble themselves at mass each Sunday. Taller chopines tapered from the bottom of the foot to save weight, then widened into a false foot where they met the ground. A nimble fool and skilled acrobat, trained and practiced in the use of stilts, might, with trousers properly tailored, pass for a foot taller than he was, on a proper pair of chopines.

"I have a smaller pair. None so grand as the senators' wives wear."

"Perfect. Bring them." I would meet my enemies in Venice eye to eye this time.

"And then I can ready your trousers?"

"Almost. I'll also need three throwing daggers and a cracking-huge codpiece."

"Not bloody likely, thou fluffy puppet," she scoffed at me. Scoffed!

"Ill-tempered nymph. Don't your people have a red tent they send you to when you're like this?"

"I'm not like that. You are annoying."

"Your compassion hasn't the endurance of a mouse fart?"

"Nourished by charm, it has wasted away since your arrival, puppet."

Eight
A Pound of Flesh

"I don't think you should be in the house when he comes home," said Jessica. "No one is supposed to be in the house."

We stood on the walkway in front of Shylock's house. I wore Jessica's chopines strapped to my feet under my newly tailored sailcloth trousers and I now stood a bit taller than the girl. I walked around on the cobbles and found I quickly was able to affect a natural gait on the platforms, which were only three-quarters of a foot high.

Except for soldiers and sailors, most Venetian men wore leggings under a long tunic, after the Byzantine style, sometimes belted, but my sailcloth trousers would attract no attention, as not much of them showed under a long, moth-eaten wool gabardine Jessica had liberated from her father's closet. With my floppy yellow hat, I looked every bit the unkempt Jew.

"Here he comes," said Jessica. Two men had rounded the corner a dozen houses away, and were coming up the walkway, both wearing garb similar to my own, the dark gabardine and yellow hats, and sported long gray-streaked beards.

"Father is the shorter one," said Jessica. "That's his friend, Tubal, with him. He lives down the way."

Indeed, as if she had cued it, the two stopped, and after exchanging smiles and nods, the taller man went into his house. Shylock continued down the walk, not looking ahead enough to notice us yet.

"Is that you, son?" came a voice from behind us. I turned to see Gobbo tapping his way toward us.

"It's the old blind loony," I whispered furiously. "Quick, push him in the canal before he cocks every-thing up."

"My boy? Is that you?" said Gobbo.

"Humor him," said Jessica. "There's no time."

"Top of the morning, Da," said I. "Thou stumbling stump of stink."

"Pocket!" scolded Jessica.

"Well, for fuck's sake, girl, he's blind in a city where the streets are full of water—how is it he hasn't stum-bled in for a bath in the last half century or so?"

"Boy?" said Gobbo. "My, you sound like you've grown. Let me feel your face."

He blundered toward me, his long cane dangling from a lanyard on his wrist, his hands waving in the air before him like the antennae of a crusty lobster.

I stepped aside, deftly I think, and said, "Touch me and I will hold you underwater until you dissolve." I was feeling much better, and strong enough, I thought, to properly drown a feeble blindster.

Bumbling past me, Gobbo's left hand found a perch on Jessica's breast, while his right settled on Shylock's face.

"Well, boy, you've got your mother's knockers but— Lord loves a joke—my face."

Jessica gathered Gobbo's arms down to his sides and herded him over to the wall. "Signor, Gobbo, please rest here in the shade while I tend to my father's business."

"What is this?" said Shylock, waving from Jessica, to me, to Gobbo, in a tight, repeated succession. "This? Them? In front of my house? My house. Daughter, what is this?"

Gobbo safely deposited against the wall, away from the water, Jessica approached her father, head bowed. "Oh, Papa, such good news, this is, is what this is. This young Jew has agreed to be our slave. He will clean and fetch for us, carry our burdens, perhaps we can even buy our own boat and he can row you to the Rialto."

"Shalom," said I, exhausting my Hebrew in two beats.

Shylock leaned in close and looked me in the eye. "What is your name, boy?"

Realizing, somewhat late I'd say, that we should have thought of this before, I improvised. "Lancelot," said I.

"Really?" said Jessica, letting her features drop as slack as a curtain.

"Lancelot is not a Jewish name," said Shylock.

"He's not been raised with the traditions," Jessica said, recovering. "Only his mother was a Jew."

"She was?" said Gobbo. "And that minx always pretending she was buggering off to mass. Aye, lad, your mum was a love, she was."

"Jews do not own slaves," Shylock said.

"But that is the beauty of it, Papa." Jessica stepped between Shylock and Gobbo. "The law only says that we may not *buy* or *sell* slaves; we are not buying him. He's delivering himself to us."

Hearing it out loud, I realized it was a rubbish ploy, but I needed a place to live, to hide, and I needed to get back into the city under-cover to find out what had happened to my apprentice, Drool, and my monkey, Jeff.

"Well, Signor Lancelot Gobbo, Moses did not lead our people out of slavery so we could bind one another in slavery. Good day."

"Not a slave, signor," said I. "Who said slave? Silly girl. I would be your employee. But I could do all of those things, plus more. I could help you with your accounts. I know maths and I can read and write."

"You know maths and you can read and write? Well . . ."

"Latin, Greek, and English, plus a smattering of Italian and fucking French."

"Fucking French, you say? Well . . ."

"*Oui,*" said I, in perfect fucking French.

"And what would you wish to be paid for such services, Signor Lancelot Gobbo?"

"Only room and board, signor. A roof over my head and a hot meal."

"A slave works for only room and board."

"And a farthing."

"A farthing? Room and board and a quarter of a penny would be your pay? Well . . ."

"Per week," said I, pressing my terms. I saw a light flicker in Shylock's eye, for although he would not be a slave owner, he could not resist a bargain.

He nodded, as if doing the figures and approving them in his head. "Well, then, Signor Lancelot Gobbo,

I shall retain your services for a week, as a trial. You shall accompany me to the Rialto this afternoon—carry my box of papers, inks, and quills. I wish to purchase a cask of wine as well. You can carry it home for me. For this and like services, you shall receive room and board plus one farthing for the week. Are we agreed?"

"Oh yes, signor," said I. I bowed.

"Meet me here after lunch." Shylock pushed past Jessica and went into his house. "I would have my lunch, daughter," he called over his shoulder.

Jessica whirled on me and whispered furiously, "*Lancelot?* Where did you get bloody *Lancelot?*"

"I thought it would explain away my English accent."

"We all have English accents, you knob."

"I know," said I. "And in an Italian city. Don't you find that strange?"

She shuddered with frustration. "Well, you're in, at least. You'll have to sleep downstairs in the kitchen now, though." She reached into her bodice and retrieved a parchment, folded tightly and sealed with wax, the sign of the menorah pressed into it. "When you are on the Rialto, slip away and give this to Lorenzo. He will be with Antonio and his other partners. Ask about, everyone knows him. Give him this note. You must not fail."

"I'll need a year's pay in advance," said I. "I'm going to buy me ol' da some lunch."

"Ah, what a good boy he is," said Gobbo. "Bread and fish will have to do, though. Can't find a banger in this city to save my life. It's like all the pork's floated off, innit?"

"He doesn't know where he is, does he?" I whispered to the girl.

She shook her head. "Walked off a ferry two years ago and has been wandering around the island since, thinking he's in Venice proper. No one's had the heart to tell him. We keep him fed."

"Did it occur to you that his real son might be in Venice, actually missing him?"

"Oh bugger," said she. "I never thought of that. Well, he's your bloody father, you help him."

An hour later I'd fed old Gobbo and on a series of fine paving stones by the dock had managed to hone a razor's edge onto an old fish knife I'd nicked from Shylock's kitchen. It was shit for throwing, with its thin blade and heavy oak handle, but it would thread through a man's ribs in a pinch, open an artery if deftly flicked, and more important to my purpose, razor the seal off a letter with such subtlety that it could be replaced and leave the intrusion undetectable. I'd resealed Jessica's letter with the tip of my blade heated on the food-seller's brazier, leaving her seal still pristine in the wax, but its content still troubled me. There would be no time to craft clever speeches and complex plans to undo my foes. I would have to find revenge on the fly, make action my eloquence.

"Come, Lancelot Gobbo," said Shylock, waving me out of the stripe of shade where I reclined against the front wall of his house. "I go to make a loan and secure the bond of the esteemed Antonio Donnola, merchant of Venice. Come, boy, carry my papers. Come and learn business."

Into the very nest of vipers I'd only recently escaped. So be it.

I followed Shylock out into the afternoon, carrying a carved wooden box that held parchment, ink, and quills. As it turned out, with age Shylock had lost the close vision to read and write his own contracts, so had to have Jessica do it at home or pay a notary. My ability to read and write gave me value. I thought it best not to inform him that across the lagoon on the glass-making island of Murano, they had begun to make small lenses, called spectacles, that rested in a frame across the bridge of the nose, which might correct one's reading vision.

We crossed the island through a narrow path, where the buildings were so close that they were buttressed over the alley on their upper floors with oak arches.

It was cool in the alley, and the breeze off the Adriatic washed the city smell away, so stepping out into the sun on the city side of the alley, filled with the activity of boats and traders, was an assault on the senses. And I, disguised in the long dark gabardine, felt sweat blossom and stream down my back. The heat and humidity of the Venetian summer made me long for the green, rain-swept, sheep-flecked hills of England. At least there are no horses in Venice, and the sewage drops through the floors of homes and is washed away with the tides, so as salty and fish befouled as Venice can be, it is less odiferous than Paris or London on a summer's day.

Shylock led me across a dock and into a gondola and gestured for me to sit across from him as the gondolier ferried us across the wide *tronchetto* toward the entrance of the Grand Canal. The water had a cloudy blue-green translucence that made it look as if it were lit from below. I saw something dark moving beneath the water, too deep to make out, perhaps it was just the shadow of the gondola, but before I could ask the gondolier about it, Shylock drew my attention.

"So," said he. "You are English?"

"Aye, signor. Born and raised at Dog Snogging on Ouse."

"I see. But old Gobbo, your father, he is Venetian?"

"Mum was English." She was. Drowned herself when I was but a babe, but as English as St. George himself, although I thought it best not to mention that to the Jew, as the Hebrew pantheon has sod all in the way of saints.

"An English Jew, then. Well." He stroked his beard. "You know about our people in York? The townspeople of York borrowed money from the Jews, then when the crops failed, blamed the misfortune on our people. They locked all the Jews in the castle keep and burned them."*

"Oh, right, I was sick that day, if I remember correctly. Sad." I looked into the well of the boat, sadly, I hoped.

"It was a hundred years ago," said Shylock with a shrug. "They do not allow our people to own property, but they hate us for lending our moneys at interest to make our way."

"Well, Yorkshire, county of gormless† gits, innit? Arsehole of all Blighty‡ for my money." Dog Snogging was bang in the middle of Yorkshire of course, so if Yorkshire was the arsehole of Britain, then I, born and raised there, was—well—being less than sincere.

---

*This actually happened in York in 1190.
†Clueless.
‡Great Britain.

As the gondolier swung the boat into the mouth of the Grand Canal, which swarmed with small boats, something hit the gondola and our oarsman was knocked off his feet. He caught himself on the oar before he went in the drink, but once righted he looked around for the offending craft, but it had not been another boat that had jostled our vessel.

"Did you see?" he asked me.

I shrugged. "Rock?"

"There are no rocks in the canals."

"Dolphin?" said Shylock.

"We see dolphins all the time," said the gondolier. "I've never heard of one hitting a boat."

"Well, they're the most spiteful of the large fishes, aren't they?" said I, with the great authority that comes only from countless years of knowing fuck-all about fucking fishes. I did not think it a dolphin.

"Jews," said the gondolier, spitting into the canal, dismissing our silliness.

There you have it. Taken as one of the tribe without so much as a bug's knuckle trimmed off the willy. I'd throw that in Jessica's face when I saw her again—well, so to speak.

"Does a Jew not pay you?" said Shylock, evidently not enjoying my induction into the tribe as much as I.

The gondolier was suddenly very intent upon navigating to the dock by the Rialto Bridge.

"Does my Jewish money not spend in the market?" Shylock stood up in the boat and faced the gondolier, trying to get him to meet his gaze. "Would you have me give your fee, my Jewish coin, to a beggar at the dock rather than have it befoul your Christian hand? What say you?"

"No offense was meant, Shylock," mumbled the gondolier as he churned the long boat in between two tall mooring poles. "You are my most steady fare, signor."

"Good day, then," said Shylock, tossing a copper coin to the boatman as he stepped off. "We will find another way home this evening."

"Just going to wander till then," said I, stepping onto the dock with my wooden box. "Just two Jews. Wandering." I felt a song coming on. "Wandering Jews." I suppressed the urge to rhyme. "Two Jews amused." Somewhat suppressed.

"Stay close, boy," said Shylock.

I hurried up the dock to join him in the bustling square of the Rialto, keeping my head down, my face hidden by my floppy yellow hat. As someone used to attracting attention to himself, wearing bells, and carrying a smugly profane puppet, the anonymity was more difficult than I anticipated. There was irony and mirth lurking everywhere, and it was my holy duty as a fool to point it out, nay, chase it out of the corners and poke it until it giggled.

I caught up with Shylock. "That bit with the boat-man was rather Old Testament," said I.

He wheeled on me, stopped, and assumed the posture of one about to lecture. I had seen it before. Everywhere. "Since the time we were first chosen, Lancelot, suffering has been the lot of our people, but still, we must take our lessons from the prophets. And what do we learn from the story of Moses confronting the pharaoh? When Moses did call down the ten plagues upon the Egyptians? What do we learn from this, young Lancelot?"

"As plagues go, frogs are not so bad?" I was raised in a nunnery. I know Testaments Old and New.

"No, what we learn is, *do not fuck with Moses!*" He patted my arm. "Come."

I found that suddenly I quite liked the old Jew. I felt bad at the suffering that was about to befall him, even, perhaps, by my hand. By keeping it to myself, was I turning on my tribe?

A handsome young merchant wearing a purple cravat hailed Shylock, waved him to come into an arch-way where a group of men were gathered.

"Bassanio," said Shylock. "He came to me as an agent for Antonio, who would borrow money. You know this Antonio, Lancelot?"

"I know of him."

THE SERPENT OF VENICE · 115

"Ah. Yes. Know this. I do hate him with all my being and I would have him undone. Does this shock you?"

"No, signor," said I. "I am sure he has given you reason for your ire." *Having somewhat to do with his being a massive festering twat!* I hastened to not add, lest I reveal my own substantial prejudice. Still, it appeared that Shylock and I were, indeed, brothers in arms, even if he did not know it.

We followed Bassanio into the arch, where Antonio held court with a group of young men. All seemed too tall or too light of hair to be Jessica's Lorenzo. The merchant was dressed in higher finery than his companions, silks and damask—higher finery, I thought, than appropriate when about to ask an enemy for a loan. I kept my eyes to the ground, my hat covering most of my face. If discovered, I could make no escape on the chopines, and I'd never be out of them in time to elude Antonio's entourage, but by God's cloud-cushioned balls, I would slash the fish knife across the inside of Antonio's thigh before I went down, and he would watch his fine hosiery spoilt as his life ran between the pavers in red rivulets. But there were three men to undo, three on whom to wreak revenge, so better the knife stay nested in its sheath of rags in Jessica's boot, which I wore as well. (Yes, I have small feet. The rest is myth. No one finds you clever.)

"Antonio," said Shylock, with a nod. "You do not borrow. I heard you say it when you denounced my business."

"I never do, Shylock, for myself. But I break custom to supply the ripe wants of my friend. Did he tell you the amount?"

"Aye, three thousand ducats."

"For three months," marked Antonio.

"Yes, yes, for three months. I had forgotten. But word is on the Rialto that all of your fortunes are at sea. You have an argosy bound for Spain, another in the Black Sea, and a third bound for Egypt. All subject to the temper of the sea and attacks from Genoans and pirates. I should bear your risk without reward? Yet you have called my charging interest evil."

"Charge what you will. My ships and fortunes shall all be returned within two months, a month before my bond is forfeited."

"Three thousand ducats; tis a good round sum," said Shylock, stroking his beard in thought.

"Tis a sick elephant's shitload," I whispered. "Are you daft?"

"Shhhhhh, boy," said Shylock.

"Sorry," said I. They'd all looked to me when I spoke, even Antonio, and there was no spark of recognition in his eye, nor did he see the fire in mine. His gaze stopped at the shore of my outfit and "Jew" was all he saw. Unworthy of a second look. I began to fancy my yellow hat.

Shylock said, "Signor Antonio, many a time in the Rialto you have berated me about my moneys and my usances. Still, have I born it with a patient shrug, for sufferance is the badge of all our tribe. You call me misbeliever and cutthroat dog, and spit upon my Jewish gabardine, and all because I use what is mine own."

Shylock threw his arms out as if receiving a revelation and continued, "Well now—now it appears you need my help. You say, 'Shylock, we would have moneys.' *You* say this. *You,* that did spit upon my beard and kick me as you might kick a stray dog in your threshold. What should I say to you? Should I not say, 'Hath a dog money? Is it possible a cur can lend three thousand ducats?'

"Or should I bend my knee, and with the bated breath of a slave, say to you, 'Oh, fair sir, you spit on me Wednesday last. You spurned me another day. Another you call me dog, and for these courtesies, allow me to lend you moneys?' Should this I say?"

Antonio had been backed against the wall as Shylock spoke, as if the old Jew was pissing on his shoes the whole time he spoke and the merchant avoiding the stream. Now he came forward.

"And I am likely to call thee dog again, to spit on thee again, to spurn thee again. If you will lend this money, lend it not as a friend, but to an enemy, and should I break my bond, take relish in exacting your penalty."

Shylock smiled and waved his hand as if dismissing the whole exchange, even as if Antonio's anger was a gnat born of imagination. "Listen to you, how you storm. I would be your friend, good Antonio." Another smile, as if the hatred hurled between them had been but a vapor. I relaxed in my own anger for a moment, for it was apparent, even if only to me, that Shylock was the master of this deal. "I will loan you your three thousand ducats, for three months, and take no interest for my moneys, and you may say that I have forgiven your offenses and shown you kindness."

"There *is* kindness in his offer," said Bassanio.

"Yes," said Shylock. "Now, go with me to a notary and there seal your bond. My servant has my papers here. And for merry sport, to mark our friendship, if you do not repay me on a certain day, let us say that you shall forfeit—"

"His Johnson!" said I, somewhat surprised I had spoken.

"A moment," said Shylock, holding up a finger to mark his place. "I would have words with my servant." He put his arm around me and walked me away.

"Are you mad?" whispered Shylock.

"Saw off his knob with a dull knife while he screams for mercy," said I, rather more loudly than Shylock's conspiratorial tone suggested was appropriate. This bit was not so surprising to me, but in for a penny . . .

"You, boy, will be silent and carry my papers and let me do my business."

"But—"

"I know you are not who you say you are," whispered Shylock. "Would you have me tell *them*?"

"Proceed," said I, bowing and waving him back into the fray.

"Ha!" said Shylock, returning. "The boy can be simple. I employ him as a kindness to his poor blind father. Now, Antonio, as I was saying, my moneys, with no interest, for three months, but as a jest, should you not repay me upon the date, let us say that I, take, uh—" Shylock again spooled his hand as if trying to reel in an idea floating above. "A pound of flesh, cut from your body, from a place of my choosing." The smile.

Antonio laughed, threw his head back. "Yes! I'll seal such a bond, and say there is much kindness in the Jew."

"No!" said Bassanio. "You shall not seal such a bond for me. I'd rather do without the lady."

"Fear not, my good friend." Antonio squeezed Bassanio's shoulder and his hand lingered there as he whispered, but loudly enough for us all to hear. "I will repay the debt a month before the bond is due and we shall all have a good laugh at the Jew's frivolity."

"Yes, boy," said Shylock. "What value is a man's flesh to me? Surely not that of a beef, or goat, or mutton. There is no profit in this for me, but only a gesture of good faith from Antonio. How say you, good Antonio?"

"Yes, Shylock, I will seal unto this bond. Lead on."

Shylock grinned, then quickly assumed his visage of serious business and trudged away, Antonio behind him. The entourage moved away from the wall in turn and I fell in beside the tallest.

"Tell me, friend. Is one of you gentlemen called Lorenzo?"

"No, Jew, but Lorenzo is a friend of ours. Why do you seek him?"

"I have a message for him."

"We are meeting him tonight at Signora Veronica's. You can tell me."

"Oh no, I couldn't," said I. "I must give the message only to Lorenzo in person."

"I am Gratiano, close friend of Lorenzo. Ask anyone, they will tell you that we are as brothers."

"I cannot," said I.

Gratiano bent in closely and whispered, "I know about Lorenzo and the Jew's daughter."

I nearly stumbled and fell off my chopines. "Fuckstockings, can no one keep a bloody secret in this steaming piss pot of a city?"

Jessica was not going to be at all pleased with her new slave.

Nine

Two Thousand Nine Hundred and Ninety-nine Golden Ducats

I followed Shylock down walkways along narrow canals to the landing at St. Mark's Square, where we would catch a ferry home, across the *tronchetto*. Since we'd left the notary with Antonio's signed bond, Shylock had not said a word about knowing who I was. I was carrying a small cask of wine, and although it was not terribly heavy, keeping balanced on Jessica's platforms was some challenge.

"So," said I. "Just chopping random bits off a bloke, something you Jews do a lot then?"

"It was your idea to take his manhood, *Lancelot Gobbo*. No man would agree to such a bargain. An arm, a leg, a random pound of flesh, yes. I merely made salvage of your folly. I am surprised that Antonio would put his bond to it. His need exceeds appearances."

"Why does he need to borrow funds from you? He said it is for his friend?"

"For the young man Bassanio, who proposed such a loan to me on the Rialto this morning. He says he would use it as a bride price for the lady Portia of Belmont, and Antonio staked him to it. I do not care about Antonio's reasons, only that they have put me at advantage over him."

"Portia? Brabantio's daughter Portia? Brabantio is one of the richest senators in Venice, and Antonio is his partner in most heinous ventures. He would give him three thousand ducats for the asking?"

"You have not heard, then? The Montressor is dead."

I meant to inquire when? How? But Shylock held his finger to his lips to signal silence. We had reached the ferry, which was fitted out to carry narrow hand-carts across the channel. It was clear that Shylock did not know the ferryman as he had the gondolier from earlier, whom we were spurning by walking in the heat and taking this shit flat boat.

As we crossed the wide green channel, I looked for the dark shadow I had seen beneath the water before, but there were only little silver fishes, wetly doing fish things near the surface.

Shylock did not speak again until we were across the channel and in the narrow alley that would take us to the seaside of La Giudecca.

"So, what is your grudge with Antonio, little one?"

"Little one? I'm taller than you are."

"I saw you were wearing Jessica's boots and platforms when we were crossing in the gondola."

"Well, this is a rubbish disguise." I balanced the cask on my shoulder with one hand and ripped off my stupid yellow hat with my other and cast it to the ground.

Shylock put down his box of papers and quills, picked up my hat and fitted it back on my head, then picked up his box and stood there, blocking the alley, which was only a bit wider than a man's shoulders. He raised a grizzled eyebrow at me. "What is your grudge with Antonio?"

"No," said I. "What is *your* grudge with Antonio, and how do you think it will be settled by giving him three thousand ducats?"

"I am your employer, and I did not reveal you to Antonio and his friends," said Shylock.

"Well, I have your wine and your daughter's shoes."

"I am a man of means and can buy more wine and shoes, but if you do not tell me, you will have no place to sleep tonight and no food to eat."

"Well, I'll have a bloody hogshead of wine to myself," said I.

"Fine, as the tailor said to the broke and naked knight, suit yourself." He turned and strode off down the alley.

Is that where that saying comes from? Seems I should have known that. Shylock receded down the alley. As he was about to go around the corner I blurted, "He killed my wife and he tried to kill me—left me chained in a dungeon to die. He does not know I survived."

Shylock looked over his shoulder. "Antonio did this?"

"He and two others."

Shylock nodded. "Come. Bring my wine."

"Now you."

"We don't call it a hogshead," said Shylock.

"What does it matter?"

"A Jew would not call it a hogshead. Mind your disguise."

"Why do you risk your ducats?"

"They are not my ducats. My friend Tubal will supply the loan."

"But to the point, your grudge with Antonio?"

"If I tell you that Antonio has earned my hatred, would you be satisfied?"

"It strains not my imagination that Antonio earns your hate, but for three thousand ducats you could hire a choir of cutthroats to remove him."

"Antonio hates me for my ancient faith, yet his pope makes wars to take Jerusalem from the Saracens. He makes profit on these holy wars, yet calls my thrift a sin. He mocks me for my interest, yet the law forbids me from owning property on which to collect rents. He laughs at me that I must pay to be ferried to and from the Rialto, because the law allows my people to live only on this island. He berates me for this yellow hat I must wear, because the *law* of his city dictates it. His city, Venice, that makes nothing, grows nothing but salt, does no other thing than trade, and is said to be the glory of the world because her laws treat all fairly. His Venice that has no king, has no lords, but is a republic, *a city of laws, a city of the people*, says he. A city built on justice, says he! Well, I will have my justice by way of the law. I will see Antonio's Venice condemn him, sentence him to pour his blood into the canals for his beloved laws. I would have my revenge by way of this so-just law."

Shylock's shoulders were heaving with breath, with his anger. I had been pummeled by the blundering angels of false justice as both slave and sovereign; I knew his fire.

"There is risk," said I. "What if he repays you in good time?"

"If any one of his three ships runs afoul, his fate is mine, and I will weigh his flesh on those same scales that Venice says do stand for justice. God will see to it."

"Well, I wouldn't wager a jolly jar of Jew toss for the God nonsense, but I'm in for three-to-one odds of undoing Antonio."

"Then you will not interfere with my plan?"

"Your revenge shall be my revenge," said I. *Unless it fails, then I will sculpt my own mayhem for Antonio,* I thought.

"Then home, and we shall drink to it," said Shylock. "But no word of this in front of Jessica. She is of a sweet and delicate disposition; I would not have her poisoned by her father's hateful strategies."

"Jessica pulled me from the sea—saved me," said I. "A right love, is your Jessica. If up to me, she shall never hear so much as the whisper of an unkind word."

But she would, she had, and I, undrowned for only days, was torn now by opposing loyalties.

"You scheming duplicitous harpy, why didn't you tell me?" said I to the gentle Jessica. "Your father says Brabantio was eaten by rats?"

"You didn't ask, *oh troubadour who was ship-wrecked on the way to England and therefore would have no interest in the politics of Venice.*" She *sang* the last bit, just to be annoying.

Shylock had gone to Tubal's house to assure that he could secure the ducats for Antonio's loan, leaving Jessica and me alone in the house.

"Making a point will not return you to my good graces." I could have crushed her paltry argument if I revealed that I knew the contents of her note to Lorenzo, although that would have somewhat undermined my own trustworthiness.

"You are the one who didn't do his job, slave."

"Lorenzo was not with Antonio. Would you have had me give your note to another of Antonio's scoundrels and hope he delivered it to your beloved? Gratiano wanted it, that egregious weasel—may as well give it to old blind Gobbo and have him orbit the island with it for eternity."

"Well, you must go back, then. Tonight. Papa and Tubal are sending a chest with the ducats to Antonio this evening. You will go with them and deliver my note to Lorenzo then. And wait for a reply."

"I will," said I, head bowed. And I would. And from there go to my old apartments to inquire after my monkey, Jeff, and my apprentice, Drool. I can't imagine the great ninny making do on his own for a month. True, he had nothing of value except for his great size and a preternatural gift for mimicry, but fate does not favor the dim, and I worried about him wandering around unprotected in a city whose streets were filled with water. He swims like a stone.

"Tell me, now," said I. "What do you know of this favor Antonio does for his friend Bassanio that would require he risk his very life for a loan? Do you know of it?"

"Oh, yes, Lorenzo told me of it. Bragged to his friends that he was so clever as to capture his lady love without risking his fortune like Bassanio. You know of the contest for Portia's hand and estate?"

"Contest?"

She explained the bizarre lottery Brabantio had left his younger daughter to be prize for: three caskets, sealed with wax and watched over by lawyers, three thousand ducats for the mere chance at the lady's hand. Oh, Othello, what a bitter mess you made of Brabantio when you married Desdemona. I thought that my murder was the limit of Brabantio's hatred for Othello, but apparently he was reaching out from the grave to torment his younger daughter as punishment to the elder.

Shylock had not known the circumstances preceding Brabantio having been eaten by rats. Perhaps his heart gave out while he was carrying away his bucket of mortar. The scream that night—I had some hope that his last thoughts might have been of me. Now, with my terror tamed, seems 'twas a sweet scream indeed, although not nearly long enough. But now, to have Brabantio's hatred spill out onto Antonio, well, perhaps the Fates were turning to favor a fool . . .

The Greeks believe the Fates are three sisters: one is *Order*, who spins out the linear thread of a life from the beginning; another is *Irony,* who gently cocks up the thread, marking it with some peculiar sense of balance, like justice, only blind drunk with a scale that's been bunged into the street so it never quite settles; and the third, *Inevitability,* simply sits in the corner taking notes and criticizing the other two for being shameless slags until she cuts life's thread, leaving everyone miffed at the timing. It seems to me that a nimble fool, possessed of a quick wit and passionate provocation, might have two sisters at once, and thus bring the third in to serve her purpose on his enemies as well. I would find my way to be fate's tool.

"What *are* you on about?" said Jessica.

"What?" I didn't know she was still there.

"About you shagging some sisters and being a massive tool?"

"I said that aloud?"

She nodded.

"Well, why are you lurking like a burglar in the dark, anyway?"

"I'm sitting at my own kitchen table. It's daylight. The window is open. Look, there's the sea."

"Fine, I was just having a loud ponder. If you did any thinking yourself you would have recognized it and excused yourself."

"I'll get you into Antonio's quarters, Pocket, so you can be the tool you yearn to be." She giggled.

CHORUS: *And so the bitter and shallow fool learns that it's not quite so funny when the soliloquy that is walked in upon is his.*

"For the love of God, shut the fuck up!"
"I didn't walk in. I was sitting here the whole time."
"Close the shutters. Maybe he'll go away."

CHORUS: *And thus, the shutters of Shylock's kitchen are closed, and many things in the house may transpire, unobserved by anyone of importance.*

Upon Jessica's urging, Shylock sent me to Tubal's house an hour before sundown, and I was met by two great hulking Hebrews dressed in the same dark gabardine and yellow hat as myself. Called Ham and Japheth, they were certainly the largest Jews I had ever seen.

"Ham, you say? Can't say our people lack a sense of irony, can you? Surprised your brother wasn't called *Bacon* or *Bangers*. Ha!" I amuse myself sometimes.

"We are named for the sons of Noah," said Should-Have-Been-Bacon.

"Of course," said I. "That's what I meant—great meaty blokes like you two in a city surrounded by water. Like Noah's sons."

They were young, just coming into their beards, it appeared, so they did not further question my balderdash. This is why we send youth to war: spotty lads possessed of passion but void of purpose will cleave to the most slippery species of bullshit. Ham and Japheth would make fine filler for the sausage grinder of war. But for now, they would do as guards for gold.

Tubal directed us from the dock in front of his house, where a broad-beamed boat waited with oarsmen standing at each end. He was still in his dark gabardine, but without his yellow hat he had a great explosion of curly black and gray hair that was broken only by a shiny white bald spot in its center, as if an albino turtle was hiding down a mine in the dark. "This boat will take you to the dock in front of Antonio's house, which faces the Lido, so you will not have to go into the canals of the city. You, Lancelot, Shylock says you have seen Antonio's men. Let the boatmen come into the dock only after you recognize them and confirm that they are ready to receive the gold. You jump to the dock and assure the way is clear all the way up the stairs to

Antonio's apartments and that he is in residence. Only then may Ham and Japheth leave the boat and carry the gold up the stairs to Antonio's apartments. Turn it over to Antonio himself, and offer to stay while he counts it. Then have him mark this receipt before you return. It must be signed or the law will not support the bond."

Tubal gave a rolled-up parchment to Ham, who tucked it into his gabardine.

"Go. Go, go, go," said Tubal. "They will be expecting you."

Ham and Japheth wrestled the heavy chest into the boat, which settled lower into the water with the weight of the gold and the two huge Jews.

The boatmen rowed us eastward around the outside of La Giudecca, around the island of San Giorgio Maggiore (the dot on the "i" of the long island of La Giudecca) and across the mouth of the Grand Canal, where even at dusk, the boats moved like a flock of confused ducks maneuvering for bread crusts thrown in their midst. The water of the lagoon had taken on a silvery sheen from the setting sun, which blocked the view beneath, but some small fish broke the surface perhaps fifty yards to our right, and I could see the wave of whatever large creature was below the water chasing them, moving parallel to our boat, toward Arsenal.

"Tuna," said Ham, catching my eye and probably seeing the alarm there. "Sometimes they come into the lagoon in the evening. Maybe a dolphin." He smiled and slapped my shoulder to comfort me and I returned his smile.

I did not think it was a tuna, or a dolphin.

"Relax, Lancelot," said Japheth. "The threat to our task will not come from the sea, but from such sharks as walk the land, and we are ready for them." He pulled aside the fringe of his gabardine and I could see a heavy oaken club hanging from his belt. I looked to his brother who grinned as he revealed an identical cudgel that he'd concealed.

I shrugged. "Say, what say ye, just for sport, instead of giving Antonio the gold, you two surprise him by bludgeoning him to pulp, perhaps a few of his cohorts, then we take the gold back to Tubal and have a drink and a good laugh over it?"

Really, what good was it to have two huge Jews with clubs if you couldn't use them to bludgeon your enemies to meaty paste? Granted, it wouldn't be the slow, ironic retribution that Shylock was hoping for, but I thought he might recover from the disappointment and would deal somewhat better with a more unpleasant surprise he was about to receive.

"That would be wrong," said Japheth.

"Wrongish," said I, making the sign of tipping scales with my hand. "Not like it's written in stone, is it?"

"Actually—" ventured Ham.

"Oh, all right—it's like sailing with an ark full of fucking lawyers with you two. Fine, we'll just deliver the sodding gold and leave Antonio unbludgeoned."

There were four men waiting in front of Antonio's house. The boatmen brought their craft into the landing bow first, allowed me to hop off, then backed off, as they had been instructed. I was agile on the tall chopines now, and only someone who was looking for it might have noticed my gait to be unnatural, less nimble than on my own tender feet. I nodded to the four, three I'd recognized from the Rialto that afternoon: Gratiano, the tallest; the handsome one, Bassanio, the one for whom the gold was meant; and two other shorter, rounder fellows who might have been the same person, if not twins, brothers, and although I had seen one of them on the Rialto, I couldn't have said which one.

"Lorenzo?" I asked the closest.

"Salarino," said he.

"Then you are Lorenzo?" I asked the other.

"Salanio," said the other.

I looked from one to the other. "You're joking?"

"I told you, Jew," said Gratiano. "We will see Lorenzo later."

"Right," said I. "I'm to check the stairwell for more scoundrels, then I'll be back down to signal for the gold."

"Top floor." Gratiano grinned and gestured to the doorway of the nearest building.

Off I went.

"Hey, what did he mean by *more* scoundrels?" said Salanio, or perhaps the other one, as I entered the building.

I was up three floors in two ticks, but the wooden chopines were making such a racket, I moved to the edge of the stairs and threw my weight on the banister before going up the last flight. Then I heard the voice.

"Don't worry, Antonio, if there is no one to collect your bond, you shall be free of it, regardless of the fortunes of your ships."

Iago. My body reacted with a shiver despite my resolve of spirit. I had had no such reaction to seeing Antonio, but then he had never seemed the dangerous one.

"We would just, well, assassinate the Jew?" Antonio sounded shocked. "Everyone would know."

"We are starting a war, Antonio. You can't run the whole thing on cynicism and profit. At some point blood *will* be spilled. There *will* be killing."

"I know, but I thought it would be far away, unpleasant, but removed, like a rumor."

"I will see your hands stay clean, Antonio."

"The gold is here," said Antonio.

He must have looked out on the lagoon and seen the boat.

"Rodrigo has been to Belmont," said Iago. "Nerissa says there is no way to discern the correct casket. Several of Brabantio's lawyers, as well as a senator, watch over the process. Suitors come in from many ports. Princes and dukes."

"We will find a way. The lady Portia yearns to be wed to Bassanio. She is her father's daughter; I have full confidence in her cunning."

"It will be on you, then. Rodrigo and I are bound for Corsica after the Michaelmas Carnival to see to the undoing of the Moor and Cassio. When next we meet, I shall be a general and you shall own a senator."

I listened for footsteps, and panic rose in my throat like a scream. Why did Iago engender such fear? I had lived a life infested with villains, Iago was no darker. Still, it was my very frame that shuddered, not my nerve.

"I wonder, Antonio, why do you not marry the fair Portia yourself, and *be* the senator, rather than *own* one?"

"I am too old for her, and I hold great affection for Bassanio. I would not stand in the way of true lovers."

"What a noble and poetic heart you have, good Antonio," said Iago. "And yet no wife with whom to share it. Enjoy Veronica's this evening."

Then the heavy boot heels on the floor and I was down the stairs, three at a leap, sliding on the banister where I could, until I came catapulting out the front door and across the cobbles, nearly plunging into the lagoon. The two Sals caught me, one on each arm.

"Come, come, it's all clear," said I to the waiting boatmen and the huge Jews. "Tell Shylock I had other business to attend to."

I was off the walkway and around the corner and down the lane called Fondamenta Arsenale into the city before Iago emerged from the door.

Onward to find my giant and my monkey! What elation I felt at the prospect of their calls of joy when they found I had rescued them. It had been some time since I had basked in the accolades due a hero, even from a monkey and a great drooling half-wit. They would be balm on my much-abused soul.

Ten
Intrigue Beneath the Bawd

"A horrible, shifty-eyed creature was that Pocket—a rascal of the lowest order, he was," said my former landlady, a nine-toothed crone of roughly nine hundred years in age, and a ghastly judge of character, assigned by the doge to care for dignitaries not housed at the palace. I had asked for separate quarters after Jeff bit the senator's wife and Drool wandered into the Cathedral of St. Mark next door, *sans* trousers, during high mass, his great dong swinging in time with the bishop's smoking thurible.

"A raucous, gutter-mouthed little libertine he was," the crone went on.

"Is that so?" said I, in my most courteous voice. "I heard that he was much loved in his native land, and the children sang songs of his kindness."

"Bollocks to that—'*the king of bloody Britain or France,*' he'd say, the lying cur. But the doge liked him, Lord knows why, so I had to put up with him. But I'll tell you my reckoning: I reckon, wearing that skin-tight silver-and-black motley, and that cracking big codpiece, I reckon that little one was a deviate. Never saw him with a girl, didn't even have a go at Signora Veronica's like the other men of his means, but couldn't say two words what it wasn't about bonking this and shaggin' that—I reckon he was havin' his way with the neighborhood cats in the night."

"Perhaps he was being faithful to his lady love," said I.

"No more constant than a fart on a hot skillet, was that one, just up and taking off one day, leaving the big ninny on his own, and what a state he was in. When the little fool went off, he come to my door three, four times a day lookin' for him, then asked to have a look at my tits before he'd go away. I'd give 'im a flash, outta good Christian charity, and he'd be on his way—have himself a tug in the courtyard, he would, then be back asking again an hour later. You know, a woman my age don't get that kind of attention much anymore. It was appreciated. That boy's as dense as a bloody doorknob, but really, just a big slow lamb. He kept that up for a week till they came and got him."

"They? The doge's men? Soldiers?"

"Nah, the doge dropped the little miscreant like a thorned turd once Britain's queen succumbed. 'Twas some merchants. Wearing fine silks. Young gents, three of them, two round and scruff, one quite tall and smooth. Said the little one had booked passage for the big one to Marseilles to join him."

"But he went of his own accord?"

"Happy as a duck in water, saying he was going to see his best mate, Pocket, monkey chattering on his shoulder."

"And are the fool's things still in his rooms?"

"No, the merchants took everything along, said they were sending it to Marseilles with the big bloke."

"Thank you, signora. This will help my master, who seeks the fool."

"You Jews livin' in luxury out on La Giudecca got no idea what kind of trash we have to put up with here in Venice proper."

"You haven't been to La Giudecca, have you?"

"I'm a proper Christian," she said, as if that was an answer. "But I hear you lot roll in your money and laugh like madmen. I'm told there's not a speck of good Parma ham on the island, though."

"Well, that last is true." I flipped her a coin. "From the little fool. For your trouble."

I began to walk away. "But this is a gold ducat," said she.

"Aye."

"I don't make this in two months."

"Perhaps you misjudged this Pocket."

She tucked the coin into her skirts then ducked into the courtyard and closed the heavy gate before anyone spotted the glitter of her gold. (I am a trained thief. One can't expect me to ride in a boatload of gold and leave it unmolested. One ducat. What is one ducat?)

Had they murdered Drool and Jeff? Surely if they had just drowned them, the old woman would have gotten word. It was fully dark now, a windless night, and Venice took on the feeling of a city paved with black glass, the odd lantern, torch, or candle reflecting in the canals like distant windows into hell, the crescent moon throwing silver scythes across the water where it could find its way between buildings.

I made my way along the cobbled walkways and over the narrow bridges from my old apartments to the Grand Canal, then down the wide promenade that lined it, past palaces and the closed market booths of the Rialto, to Veronica's, which lay down one of the more narrow canals on an open market square. The signora was a courtesan of the highest order, a Florentine, they said, who entertained the nobility of church and business in the sumptuous upper floors of a five-story building. The lower three floors were little more than a bawdy house with fine draperies, but it was patronized by the rich merchant and political classes, who sneered at tattered street harlots on their way to have their knobs gobbled by the broken bawds' younger sisters. Here Jessica's Lorenzo was supposed to meet his friends from Antonio's entourage.

A young blond whore stood in the arabesque arched entryway, her dress of bloodred silk rolled down to her waist, her nipples rouged and attending a chill I did not feel in the sultry night air. Only in Venice could a whore wear silk, a cloth rare enough to be reserved for royalty in other territories.

"Shag a virgin, five shillings. Sail you off the edge of the world for six,"* she called by routine, bored. The archway was lit by two oil torches, but she waved a small storm lantern as well, as if gondolas might have to navigate through the clear night to find her. "Hey there. I'm not supposed to service Jews, but it's a slow night, so I'll have you off on a stand-up around the corner for five shillings."

"The virgin price?"

---

* It's AD 1299. "Around the World" hasn't been invented yet.

"Why not? Was a virgin three times tonight already, innit?"

"Right, well done. You know Lorenzo?" I asked. "One of Antonio Donnola's men?"

"Lorenzo? Short fellow with the pointy black beard? He's fit enough but usually light a shilling or two for a shag, so stands about drinking. Right, he's inside with his mates, but you can't go in there with that yellow hat on."

"Would you fetch him for me?"

"What's it worth to you?"

I had only two pennies left from the bread money I'd begged from Jessica. I held the coppers forth, took off my hat, and bowed. "Tell him I've a message from Jessica, if you would be so kind, milady."

"I suppose," she said, taking the coins and making them disappear with the alacrity of a magician. "You know, you're not so bad. If you'd trim that beard and have a meal or two, I'd have a go at ya."

"For five shillings, of course?" said I, with a smile.

"Well, I'm not a bloody charity, am I, love?"

"I am honored merely to be considered," said I. Another bow.

"Watch my lantern. I'll be right back. Don't chase away any customers. And if you suck anyone off in the alley, it's three shillings, and I get half."

"A fair offer from a lady most fair," said I.

She winked, set her lantern on the step, then pirouetted, and off she went through the inner double doors, deeply touched by my charm. As I used to tell Drool, "Treat a whore like a lady and a lady like a whore and even a great stumbling dolt like yourself shall sail on the slippery seas of passion."

"So you can shag 'em in a boat, right, Pocket?" asked the oaf.

"Yes, it will work in a boat as well," said I, patient teacher to hopeful student.

"But not up the bum?" asked Drool.

"No, not up the bum, never up the bum, you great horse-cocked ninny. You could kill someone with that thing. Never up the bum!"

"Sor-ry," said he. Then, "Never up the bum!" he mimicked in my very own voice, a habit which I discouraged by batting him about his great empty noggin with my puppet stick.

After what seemed like a long enough time, I tucked my yellow hat into my coat, picked up the whore's lantern, and followed her path through the doors of the brothel, where a large arm, attached to a large sturdy ruffian, blocked my way.

"She forgot her lantern," said I, bobbing the lantern. "Uh, she—"

"Charity," the ruffian provided.

"Charity? Really? That's a salty sluice of shark wank," said I with incredulity.

"Charity's working the door tonight," said the ruffian.

"Yes, Charity," said I. "That's what I meant. She's asked me to bring in her lantern."

"Go then," said the ruffian, obviously chosen more for his size than his interrogatory skills. Where had the rubbish ruffian guards been when I was slinging intrigue in court and castle?

"Ta," said I, sallying forth, through a bacchanalian crush of traders and tarts in the throes of debauchery over cushions and couches, across the main rooms and even up the great marble staircase. I found Lorenzo in a parlor on the second floor, standing by a window, while Antonio and two of his friends sat side by side on a wide couch, being serviced by a trio of whores, whose heads bobbed in their laps like net floats in a choppy sea. The two younger men—Gratiano on one end and Bassanio in the middle—were completely lost in their pleasure, heads thrown back, eyes closed, arms over the back of the divan, wine goblets sloshing as the girls worked on them, Gratiano thrusted in the air in rhythm with the girl's movements, but Antonio, ah, Antonio was not floating away on his pleasure, but had his gaze trained on Bassanio, as if looking away might shatter a connection. His left hand was pressed against the younger man's chest, in his right he gripped a wine goblet as if it were a hammer at the forge. The young ginger tart might be the one doing the work, but Antonio's passion was focused on Bassanio.

The bloody obviousness of it all was embarrassing. How had I missed it? Of course. A rich, unmarried man keeps constant company with young male protégés who little assist him in his business—of course he was a pooft! Why he didn't just drag one of them into his apartments and bugger the daylights out of him was beyond me, but strange are the ways of the heart. Tragic, really, that he had to buy the boy a bride, rather than take her himself and reveal his tastes to all of Venice. Well, when he was revealed to be a most heinous scoundrel, he could rest easy about the revelation of his sexual tastes. I'll wager having an angry Jew carve out your sweetmeats before the court will take a bloke's mind off all manner of romance.

Lorenzo had noticed me watching his mentor and stepped away from his window, presumably to come to the gallant rescue of his friends' blow jobs, when I pulled the note from my coat and held it so he could see the wax menorah on the seal. "From Jessica," said I.

He stepped up to me, showing his back to his friends, and snatched the note from my hand.

"She said I wasn't to leave until I heard your answer. I'll wait for you downstairs, by the bridge to the left of the entrance." I looked down my nose at him in what I hoped was a haughty manner. I couldn't be sure, as I had not done much looking down my nose at chaps, but on the chopines, I was a full head taller than Lorenzo, so I was savoring the experience. Lorenzo was a handsome rascal, with his neatly trimmed, pointy black beard and his broad shoulders, but even if I were in my own shoes he'd stand only a hand or so taller than me. I would tease Jessica mercilessly about it when I saw her. Her little miniature merchant. Ha!

"Outside then," said I, as he broke the seal, and I turned and spotted Charity, the girl from the front door, who had been intercepted by a pair of ancient lechers who were pawing at her like palsied monkeys, which explained why she hadn't returned with Lorenzo in good time. I caught her eye and assured that she saw me set her lantern on a table, then made my way out of the brothel and off to the left to a stone bridge over the narrow canal that lay mostly in shadow. The lamps from the brothel and the windows above cast just enough light so I could see the landings cut into the stone at the side, a step down, where gondolas could load and unload their fares. In the dark, the landings below the bridge were perfect alcoves for conspiracy.

In a moment, Lorenzo appeared in the archway of the brothel. I whistled, waved when he saw me, and he quickly made his way across the courtyard and down the steps to the landing.

"Can I trust you?" he asked.

"She gave me the note, didn't she?"

"But you know not its contents." He had the note in hand and was waving it under my nose.

"You two are to run off together with a chest of her father's gold and jewels?"

He looked stunned, but nodded. "Then I will not write my reply. Tell Jessica I will come to her father's house on the night of the Carnival of Michaelmas. Her father will be out that evening, having dinner with Antonio, it is already agreed. There will be hundreds of boats in the lagoon and everyone will be in costume, so no one on La Giudecca will be the wiser. Tell her to have everything she needs ready, and to disguise herself as a boy. It will make our passage easier. I have secured our passage to Cyprus on a ship leaving on the morning tide."

"I will take her this message, but first a favor."

"You are Jessica's servant, you will do as you are told."

"Antonio knows, then, that you are running off with Shylock's daughter? Or shall I tell him?"

"Tell him. He will congratulate me on my cleverness."

"And Shylock knows?"

"Are you blackmailing me?"

"Yes, of course. Do keep up, Lorenzo. We'll never accomplish any proper skullduggery if I have to keep reviewing the bloody process."

I could tell he was scowling, even in the fractured moonlight. "What do you want?"

"I need to speak with Bassanio, now, here, secretly, and I need you to endorse my proposal to him, which does nothing but further his interest and my own."

"I cannot promise that he will go along. Why would he trust you? You're a Jew, aren't you?"

"Just like your Jessica. Go tell him that you met a man who can tell him which casket will win his lady."

"I know about the caskets," said Lorenzo. "You're talking nonsense. I've told him to find another rich girl." Lorenzo, evidently, was not party to Antonio's inner circle or the greater conspiracy with Iago. He might not even know about Drool and Jeff.

"Tell Bassanio," said I. "He will want to see me. I will wait for him here."

"Convey my message to Jessica and no word to Shylock, then?" said Lorenzo, letting a hand fall inside his doublet, from which he pulled the hilt of a dagger just far enough for me to see that he had it. Apparently, like most of the merchants I had met in Venice, to Lorenzo the law was a necessary restriction to facilitate trade, but beyond that applied only to the stevedores and tradesmen when it came to weapons or honor.

"Not a word to Shylock," said I.

Lorenzo marched up the stairs from the landing, across the courtyard, and back into the brothel, casting glances back my way as he went, as if he'd forgotten something. Which, of course, he had. He'd dropped his note to Jessica when he reached for his dagger, thinking, perhaps, he'd tucked it into his doublet. I picked it up from the cobblestones and was surprised by a gondolier who was poling his boat under the bridge, a lantern at its bow casting an orange sphere of light around it as it passed by. I nodded to the boatman, and he to me.

"*Buona sera, signor,*" said he, with a smile, seeing he'd startled me.

"*Buona sera,*" I said, pulling my hat from my coat and bowing over it. When the boatman saw the hat, the smile fell from his lips and I tucked it away again. "Aren't you supposed to be bloody singing?" said I.

"Marauding through the canals like a cutpurse, thou sneaky ship rat! Vermin!"

"Jew!" barked the boatman.

"That's not even a proper insult, that's just looking at something and saying what it is, thou pole-pushing wank-wally!"

I hadn't heard him coming at all, yet the Grand Canal from where he'd made his turn was a hundred yards away. This watery town could be right spooky at night.

"You asked for me?" came a voice from behind. I whirled around, nearly lost my balance on the chopines and had to grab the underside of the bridge to keep from going over into the canal. Bassanio stood on the cobbles at the top of the stairs.

"Oh, right," said I. I was either going deaf or these Venetian fish-floggers were taught stealth from a very early age.

"I know you," said he. "You're the small Jew who brought the gold to Antonio's this afternoon."

"Smaller Jew," I corrected. "Those were enormous fucking Jews I was with, you have to admit, so I am at least above average in size." It seemed pointless to be walking all over Venice on stilts if I was still going to be the tiny one.

"Lorenzo says you know something of the caskets at Belmont?"

"I know you will make a play for Portia's hand, and you've only the funds for one throw of the dice."

"That's no secret," said Bassanio. "Lorenzo says you have a way to gain advantage."

"I do," said I.

"And what would your price be for such advantage? You already know that the three thousand ducats at risk are borrowed against the life of my friend."

"Ah, but once you have won the fair Portia, and her dowry, then the ducats will be as a raindrop in a tempest of wealth, will they not? Only then will I seek payment."

"Payment of?"

"A thousand ducats."

"Very dear, a thousand ducats," said he.

"Not so dear to use as bait to catch a hundred thousand and such a beauty as Portia, whose value is beyond gold."

"No, not so much," he said. "How will you give me advantage?"

"The caskets are sealed with wax, and watched over by the senator's lawyers, are they not?"

"That is so."

"Have you seen them?"

"I have a comrade who has word from Portia's maid that they are on a high veranda, which is locked at night; from morning until dusk whenever the door to the veranda is unlocked, they are watched by Brabantio's lawyers, who confirm the wax seals and will reseal the caskets if a suitor chooses the wrong one. I'm at my wits' end. A prince of Morocco will make a try Wednesday, and my turn does not come until the day after, and if he chooses correctly—"

"Calm yourself, good Bassanio," said I. "He will not choose correctly, because the correct choice shall not be there for him. I will see to it."

"How?"

I held forth the note that Lorenzo had dropped. "This was given to me sealed, to bring to Lorenzo; I'm sure he gave testimony to my discretion."

"He said you could be trusted."

"I can be trusted if the price is right," I corrected. "And the price shall be one thousand ducats, after you marry Portia and take possession of her fortune."

"Agreed. How will you do it?"

Now the tightrope to walk, to reveal the special set of skills that I had acquired without giving up so much that should it get back to Antonio, who might suspect the royal fool was still among the quick. Had I boasted to Antonio of my training as a cutpurse and a burglar? And as a forger, trained by monks at the abbey at Dog Snogging to copy manuscripts? I couldn't remember.

Perhaps if I had done less drinking during my tenure in the sinking city . . .

I might have said, "I will scale the walls, climb onto the veranda, razor off the seals, discern the content, and report back to you which casket to choose." Which was, in fact, what I would do, but which also would require that I divulge details of a very unlikely past for a Venetian Jew, so I went with a more direct explanation.

"Monkeys," said I.

"Monkeys?" he repeated.

"Surely you've seen the thieving monkeys of Giudecca, at least heard of them? We Jews have been training them since the time of King David. How do you think we gain our wealth?"

"Monkeys?" repeated Bassanio, like some simpleton with a single word in his repertoire.

"Signor, I tell you, I have worked all my life in the training of the thieving monkeys, and I know they are equal to the task. They will ascend to the veranda, razor open the caskets with their clever monkey hands, reseal them, leaving them undetected, and report to me their contents, which I will report to you."

"How?"

"I just bloody told you, you nitwit, they'll scale the bloody walls—"

"No, how will they report?"

Bollocks. I hadn't thought out that bit. "Hebrew," I explained.

"Your thieving monkeys speak Hebrew?"

"No, of course not. You see, the Hebrew language, in its written form, was originally developed from a series of stamps made from monkeys' paws. The entire alphabet can be printed with a monkey hand dipped in ink. That's how they report. It has always been so. You should see the inner walls of La Giudecca, covered with their monkey profanities in Hebrew." I paused, breathless from my bullshit, and held forth Jessica's note again, pointing to the seal, which was stamped with a menorah. "See the four fingers on each side and the monkey thumbs on the side?"

"I do see," said the handsome, yet deeply stupid young merchant. "Make it so—what is your name?"

"Lancelot," said I, extending my hand. "Lancelot Gobbo."

"A thousand ducats, Lancelot Gobbo," said Bassanio.

"You shall receive a message before you depart for Belmont, revealing which casket holds the lady's picture."

"I will be at Antonio's."

"One more thing, Bassanio, now that we are partners. I require information."

"I've told you what I know of the caskets. I know Portia fancies me, what more—"

I raised my hand to silence him. "A month ago three of your friends went to the apartments of the English fool and took away the great simpleton and his monkey, do you know of this?"

"Aye, I sent Gratiano and the two Sals to fetch the giant and his monkey. They put them on a ship to Marseilles. Bought passage for them in the cargo hold."

"And your friends actually did that? The natural left Venice unharmed?"

"Well, yes, he *left* unharmed, but that was *the* ship."

"That was the *what* ship?"

"That was the ship taken last month by the Genoans at Curzola. All the passengers are in a Genoan prison being held for ransom. Word is all over the Rialto. There was a prominent Venetian merchant onboard with the other passengers."

"So the giant is in a Genoan prison?"

"He was listed as a hostage on the ransom demand that arrived with the news only a few days ago."

"Fuckstockings!" said I.

Bassanio left me on the landing, cursing in the night, still holding Lorenzo's note from Jessica.

Eleven
Siren Ascending

CHORUS:
Gondola knifes through vasty night
Past dying stars of lantern light
And distant cries of tart's delight
Ride drunken songs to bawdy heights.
Beneath a bridge doth stand the fool,
Crafting plans to free young Drool.
By stealth or guile or cutting throats,
No plots commence without a boat.

"Fuckstockings, I have no boat," I said to the night. And no money even to pay the ferryman to take me back to La Giudecca. I'd hoped to use the ducat I'd taken from Tubal's chest for fare and other expenses, but in a fit of bloody bollock-brained stupidity, I'd given it to the landlady to shore up the reputation of a poor, unjustly maligned fool.

Poor fool. Poor heartbroken fool. The fall from king to beggar was but a tender tumble compared to losing my love. Now, for lack of a penny, my reason to live, my revenge, would wither?

I think not! Bassanio could advance me coin for dirty deeds yet to be delivered. I made my way up the stairs from the landing, across the courtyard and through the entrance, where Charity had yet to return. I nodded to the ruffian at the door, now that we were mates, and spotted Bassanio holding court amongst a gang of his friends, Lorenzo and the two Sals among them.

"Need to have a word with Bassanio," said I to the doorman.

But before I could cross the room, Salarino, or perhaps it was Salanio—one of the two fat fucks—boomed, "So, Lorenzo, the Carnival of Michaelmas is the last we shall see of you? Off to Cyprus to father half-Jew babies?"

"Nay, I'll have the pleasure of her Jewish trim and her father's treasure, and be back in your company before a fortnight has passed."

"Have you seen her?" said Bassanio to the group. "But for her birth, Lorenzo's Jessica would be a treasure in herself. As fit in form and figure as any in Venice."

"She is like a swordfish flashing brilliant at the end of the fisherman's line," said Lorenzo, sloshing his wine as he pointed to a direction where he guessed the sea might be. "She is to be treasured only until she has been enjoyed, then cast back, just beak and bones, to the sea. And the fortune with which I am left will suit me to a wife of proper Christian birth, and a hundred whores to boot." Lorenzo had raised his goblet again to toast his own good fortune when he spotted me by the door.

"Bassanio seems otherwise engaged," said I to the doorman. Perhaps I would find my fee for the ferryman another way. I spun on one foot, a maneuver made easier by Jessica's chopines, and headed back out the door. I trotted across the courtyard pavers as fast as the stilts would allow, the wooden feet beating a clop-clop rhythm that echoed off the buildings.

I was halfway to the bridge when I heard the heavy footfalls coming behind me. I looked over my shoulder to see Lorenzo and one of the portly Sals breaking into a run after me. By habit, I reached for the daggers at the small of my back, but alas, they were not there. I cursed Brabantio's rat-eaten soul yet again.

I was good on the chopines, but not so good that I could escape the two young knaves. Just as I reached the arched bridge they each caught me under an arm and I was yanked back off my feet. Then Sal threw me against the rail. I might appear taller, but I was still slight, and half the weight of the stout Venetian who was manhandling me.

"What did you hear, Jew?" asked Lorenzo.

"Something about you praising Jessica as being as beautiful as a swordfish, or some rot."

"You're lying," said Lorenzo. He looked to his friend. "Hold him, Salanio."

"Well, good, we've cleared that bit up," said I, meaning at least I knew which of the Sals was attacking me. Perhaps Bassanio would intervene on my behalf, since I was the one, true master of the imaginary Hebrew thieving monkeys who would assure his betrothal. I looked back, but no one was coming out of the brothel to help me. No one was coming out at all.

Salanio put his forearm against my throat and bent me back over the stone railing of the bridge, then put a long fighting dagger to my cheek.

"You're not supposed to carry weapons," said I.

"And yet we all do," said Salanio.

"Jessica can't know about my plan," said Lorenzo to his fat friend.

"And so she shan't," said Salanio. "Die, Jew!" He loosened pressure on my throat to rear back for the blow, then thrust the dagger at my chest. I felt fire across my ribs, but my great gabardine coat had saved me. Just as the chopines made me taller, so the big coat made me look wider, and Jessica had padded the shoulders to make it hang so. He had but slain my yellow hat, tucked away, and grazed my ribs with the blade, yet I screamed as if murdered indeed, and bent over as if catching my spilling guts. Then, as the knaves backed up a step to survey their murder, I leapt into the air, knife in chest and all, turned a backflip over the bridge railing, and plunged feetfirst into the black water of the canal.

The water was still warm with summer's heat, and not terribly deep, but I knew if I should surface right under the bridge I would deliver myself into the hands of my enemies for the coup de grace. I am a good swimmer in better circumstances, trained by Mother Basil, the abbess at Dog Snogging, who would toss me in the Ouse River weekly to assure that I never met the same fate as my poor mother who drowned herself in that river.

I kicked, to level myself and swim underwater, far enough, I hoped, to surface by one of the stone walls of the canal, where I might escape in the dark. But even as I kicked, I did not move. The chopines were stuck fast in the mud on the bottom. I struggled to pull up one foot, only to have the other drive deeper, and the oversize gabardine, which had been pulled up over my head when I hit the water, was now sodden and constraining my arms as well. I bent and struggled with the straps that held Jessica's boots to the stilts, but they'd been tightened fast, and my chest was already beginning to convulse, trying to pull in air that was not there. Perhaps I could get my feet out of the boots? I pulled at them, even as the panic rose in my throat, and I spasmed three quick times before I let out a few bubbles, but willed myself not to inhale and suck in my doom. Even so, the strength fled from my limbs and I began to feel my mind close like an iris. I could see a single torch or lantern somewhere above the water, just a quivering orange dot that faded as I lost consciousness.

Then the claws bit into my sides and the last life's air that had been drooling out of my mouth exploded in a scream. It felt as if I were burning in the water, pain ripped down my sides, and I was moving, being dragged at such a speed under the water that my ears popped. *I'm being dragged to Hell,* was my last thought as my scream ran out to an airless croak and I was catapulted out of the water and up against a stone wall, which I slid down, settling into a human puddle on the landing under a bridge, nearly fifty yards from the one where I had been stabbed.

As I gasped in the air, which burned like ice-cold water in the belly of a heat-stroked sailor, I felt a pleasant wooziness, an almost drunken euphoria, fill my limbs. I heard voices, as if they were distant echoes, and looked down the canal to see Salanio standing at the top of the bridge, calling down to Lorenzo, who stood on the landing below.

"Do you see him?"

"No."

"Look for bubbles. There should be bubbles if he's drowned," said Salanio.

As I watched, the canal changed from a flat, black-mirror glass to a chevron pattern, a wave, caused by something moving just under the surface, something large and fast and certain. No churning, no wake, just the irresistible arrowhead of water, leaving its rays behind it to wash against the walls of the canal. I smiled, my head drooped, and I began to drift away. I had felt this lazy numbness before, in the dungeon, when her claws had pierced my flanks.

Then something broke the water underneath the bridge, like a waterspout, the great fountain that rises when a full barrel is dropped to the water from a tall ship and the sea leaps out of its boundaries. To me it was a blur of silvery black and wet motion, then Lorenzo was gone from the landing and the canal surface was settling around the spot where the violence had been born and returned.

"Lorenzo!" Salanio called. "Lorenzo!" He was leaning out as far as he could over the railing, but he could not see his friend. He ran down the bridge, around the railing, and down the steps to the gondola landing. "Lorenzo?"

He could see that something had disturbed the water there, he had, in fact, heard it, but it had been so fast he hadn't seen it. It had been so fast that Lorenzo hadn't had time to scream.

Salanio got on his knees and leaned close, trying to peer down into the dark water.

His face was only a foot from the water when the claw broke the surface and snatched off his head. Quick as that. His headless body, neck still spurting tarry trails of blood, rolled forward into the water and something dragged it quickly under.

I suddenly felt it prudent to be up, off the landing and onto the paved walkway—in fact, the second or third floor above the canal would do right now. I tried to climb to my feet, but could barely drag myself to the stairs, and all the time I watched the spot where Salanio had been dragged under. Then up it came.

The headless man—the meat that had been Lorenzo, I could tell by his doublet—was being propelled down the middle of the canal, half out of the water, a great wave driven before it. I scrambled to get up the stairs, away from the water, crawling, one step at a time, a burning returning to my ribs where the knife had striped them. I rolled onto my back, expecting, well, I don't know, what? Death, I suppose. Mad, panicked grasps for what I wanted to be my last thought, because it would come fast, so fast—but the body stopped, as if it had a second thought, and slowly sank. The water flattened, settled. I was not going to die tonight. Not here.

Oh, Viv. Thou venomous sea-wench. Thou wondrous, terrible force. Oh, Viv.

I could feel her, my mermaid, a presence there, under the water, even as I had felt her presence in the dungeon, I now realized, more and more as the time had gone by. Those strange blue visions, like phantoms in my mind, those had been her. She was not going to kill me. She had thrown me up on this landing, just as she had done in front of Shylock's house, to save me from drowning.

Oh, Viv, thou wicked, wicked thing. Thanks be to you, mermaid.

The chopines were gone from my feet, no doubt still stuck in the mud under the bridge, Jessica's boots still strapped to them. I tried to roll up my wet sailcloth trousers, but ended up cutting them off with Salanio's dagger, which had snagged in my coat. Once I could walk, I padded barefoot up the courtyard to the Grand Canal. Before I reached the Rialto Bridge I stopped and looked back at the water.

They must never be found. Never, I thought.

The blue-white images of bones underwater flashed across the black water, as if drawn on glass in front of my eyes. When I closed my eyes, I could see them clearly—two human skeletons, deep, deep underwater, lampreys and hagfish sucking them clean.

No, Lorenzo and Salanio would not be seen again.

CHORUS:
And so, the sodden and wounded rascal,
Now again as short of stature as of wit,
Friendless and heartbroken,
As poor in purse as he was in character,
Having betrayed fair Jessica's kindness,
And after gleefully fornicating
With an abomination of the deep,
The fool, Pocket, craven fish-fucker—

"I still have Salanio's dagger," said I. "And it's razor sharp, if you would prefer to narrate as a castrato for the duration."

CHORUS:

And so the noble fool, Pocket,
Did lay his plans to breach Villa Belmont,
And undo Antonio's plan for his protégé,
Then make way to rescue from prison
His companions, the estimable Drool and Jeff.

"Now you're just groveling, you pernicious lick-spittle," said I as I made my way into the square at St. Mark's. It was too late to find a ferry to La Giudecca, and too early to try to catch a ride with a fisherman, so I curled up in an alcove by the great cathedral and dozed, riding the dreamy waves of Viv's poison in my blood until the bells rang at dawn, calling the faithful to mass.

Gondolas had begun to arrive at the landing at the docks at St. Mark's, and I spotted the gondolier who had taken Shylock and me to the Rialto yesterday.

"Oy, boatman," I called. "Remember me? Shylock's secretary." To aid his memory, I put on my wounded yellow hat, which was stained with a bit of my blood as well as bearing its own stab wounds.

"Aye," said the gondolier, who was buffing his oar in an unsavory manner. "Wasn't you taller yesterday, though?"

"Rough night," said I. "Say, mate, could you give us a lift to La Giudecca gratis? The dice turned against me. I've not coin left to my name." I lifted my bare foot to show him that I'd lost even my shoes. It was a pitifully sad sight. Pitiful. I felt tears welling.

"Your master fired me, didn't he?" said the obstinate boatman. "I don't think any favors are owed."

I might have argued—convinced him of payment later and a return to Shylock's good graces, but I had no gut for guile or persuasion. "Look, I'll give you this smashing dagger. It's got a fake jewel in it."

The boatman eyed the dagger. It had a wide hand guard with jewels, probably colored glass, at the tips, as well as one set in the pommel. Rather garish, considering it was unlawful to carry unless one was a soldier, but as Salanio had said, shortly before his talking bits were detached from the rest of him, everyone had knives.

"A bloke would have trouble if a gendarme found that about his person," said the gondolier.

"Well, you can sell it to a cutthroat on the docks, can't you? Look at the bloody thing. It's like new. There're at least a dozen dirkings left in it, and that's not even counting stabbing the odd apple or orphan."

"Blimey, you've a gruesome tongue for a Jew."

"Aforementioned bad night, innit? Now, the dagger for fare to Giudecca, or you may hold it as security until I receive pay from my master, *and* I've another job for you tonight as well, for which you'll be paid ten times your normal fare."

The boatman pushed down on his oar and the blade breached the surface and dripped. "Ten times my fare? To where?"

"The Villa Belmont. You know it?"

"Everybody knows it. And any gondolier will take you there. Why ten times the normal fare?"

"We don't land at the dock. Back of the island. Midnight. No lantern or torches on your boat. You let me off, wait an hour, and bring me back. That's all."

"An hour? You burgling the place? I can't be part of that. Every time I row under the Bridge of Sighs I can hear the prisoners wailing. I couldn't take that. I've a wife, you know."

"No, no, nothing of the sort. You've heard the late senator's daughter is to be married?"

"Princes from all over coming to pay her suit, I hear."

"Well, before she's wed, she wants to shag a Jew, just to see what it's like. She's heard that the circumcised member is a sexual delicacy that will drive a lady to mad heights of ecstasy."

"That true?"

"'Course not. Tankard of turtle toss, that is, but I'm not going to be the one to talk her out of it."

"A fine lady like Portia's going to shag a scruffy little Jew like you?"

"Ten times your normal fare," I sang in an ascending scale.

"And I keep the dagger?"

"Cradled like a babe to your breast," said I.

"Deal!" called the boatman. "Hop aboard."

Astonishing, the level of complete bollocks a Venetian will buy for the promise of coin. Greed is a festering chancre on the merchant soul.

As the gondolier worked his oar, the sea breeze blew some of the fog from my mind. I would have to do my business at Belmont, then somehow find my way to Genoa and ransom Drool, and in the meantime there was Iago's undoing to attend to as well. I wondered if the soldier might not try to murder Shylock at Antonio's house on Michaelmas, before he left for Corsica. His intent had surely been to remove the Jew, to free Antonio from his bond, but would he do it so early in the intrigue, or perhaps wait to see the outcome of Bassanio's attempt to marry Portia and ascend to the doge's council? If he succeeded, and gained access to Brabantio's family fortune, the three thousand ducats would be as a star in the dusted heavens to what they stood to gain, but all was in the timing. And was I not going to see to Bassanio's failure myself? Was I hastening Shylock's assassination by pursuing my own scheme?

Clearly, I needed breakfast, then rest, if I was to storm Villa Belmont at midnight.

A group of Jews was waiting for the ferry on the docks at Giudecca. Among them I spied Tubal, and I hoped I'd be able to slide by him without notice, but the gondolier steered his boat into the very slip by which Tubal stood.

"Lancelot Gobbo," called the old man. "I would have words with you."

"A moment, signor," said I. I looked to the boatman. "Meet me here, at midnight, as the bells of St. Mark's toll." The gondolier nodded and patted the dagger he'd hidden under his shirt.

I jumped up onto the dock by Tubal. "Aye, sirrah!" said I, snapping to attention, bloody pert and nimble spirit of mirth that I am, despite being much abused and still slightly drugged.

"You left yesterday before the gold was delivered, and the chest was short the count by a ducat."

"Well, it was all there when I left. Did you ask the two huge Jews who were with me?"

Tubal stepped back and looked me over, from the cuffs of my raggedly cut sailcloth trousers to my now too long gabardine, to my impaled and bloodstained yellow hat.

He said, "Weren't you taller yesterday?"

"Ate a bite of ham and woke up badly beaten and a foot shorter," said I. "Bloody Torah's not fucking about on that bit—a bloke needs to stay off the pig if he knows what's good for him."

"It would appear. Perhaps, though, you're worn down from spending my gold."

"Oh, sod your sodding ducat, Tubal. If you were so worried about your gold, you should have never let it out of your sight, delivered it yourself instead of trusting me and the great Hebrew oxen brothers. Look at me: I couldn't look any more untrustworthy if I was wearing a pirate hat and being followed by a choir singing scoundrel songs. And them two—"

"Ham and Japheth are strong and take the risk to their persons even as I take the risk to my fortune. I have seen people of our tribe slaughtered over a rumor they carried plague, over being on the wrong side of a river at nightfall. A Jew does not get to be an old Jew by putting a three-thousand-ducat reward on his own head."

"But isn't that just what you've done to Shylock by funding his loan to Antonio?"

"Not so, he is protected by the law. If Shylock dies, the bond is due his heir, and since he has no sons, that would be his daughter."

It seemed that Iago, the soldier, did not know this subtlety of the law. Once he found out, the danger would not be only to Shylock, but to Jessica.

"I nicked your ducat, Tubal, used it for good deeds, and will see it returned to you presently with interest, but for now, do bugger off, as I've business to attend to."

"You—" Tubal had raised his finger and was shaking it to prime his lecture, but I ducked under his arm and was in the narrow alley across the island before the rant could commence.

Off to find Jessica. Another calamity threatened, another rescue to be attended to—what a bawdy bitch is fate when the best bit of a bloke's day is a brace of bloody mermaid murders.

Twelve
To Belmont and Beyond

"Hold still, thou squirming rat," said Jessica, cruelly stabbing me.

"Stop poking me with the needle, thou vicious harpy," said I.

By now Viv's venom had subsided and I could feel the stinging of the knife wound on my ribs and the claw punctures in my sides, as well as the needle being driven in me by the sadistic madwoman.

"Stop being such a coward. One more stitch and the wound will be closed."

"Coward, am I? I suffer great bodily injury to deliver your message and return with glad tidings and I am a coward?"

"I've made consideration for your glad tidings, which is why I am tending to your wounds instead of letting you die from fever when they fester."

How could I tell her that not only was she not going to elope with her beloved, but that he was quite headless at the bottom of the sea? It would be no comfort to her to know that he had been a scoundrel intent upon stealing her favor and her father's fortune. So, I had told her a different tale, and she was ready to sally forth into the arms of her bright and hopeful future. She had not been so gleeful when I'd first told her.

"Corsica? He talked of Cyprus. Why Corsica?"

"Lorenzo was quite insistent," said I. "And he insists I accompany you, to assist and protect you."

"But the whole reason I wanted a slave was so Lorenzo and I could run away together and not feel guilty that there was no one to take care of Papa; if you come with me—"

"We will bring your guilt as well. You wouldn't have escaped it anyway. It is a parent's gift. I was orphaned as a babe, yet carry the curse of my parents' guilt like a woodpecker around my neck."

"You mean an albatross. The curse is supposed to be an albatross around your neck."

"You're positive?"

She nodded. "Albatross."

"I was a very poor child. The nuns that took me in couldn't afford an albatross, so they just put a bit of string on a woodpecker the cat brought in."

"Well, that's not the same, is it?"

"An albatross is a crashing huge bird, innit? You can't just go garroting a small child with it, that would be heinous, even for nuns."

"But as a metaphor for guilt—"

"Well, quite right, as a metaphor, the size of the bird really doesn't matter, I suppose."

"Since you were lying outrageously anyway," she provided.

"Well, you may choose whichever guilt fowl you would like strung around your neck, but mine is a crashing-huge swan—with an eye patch."

"Fine, you'll have to book passage. I'll give you money."

"And Lorenzo said you are to disguise yourself as a boy," said I. "Cover your hair and, you know, your bits." I gestured to her more obvious bits.

"Well, as long as my Lorenzo will be in Corsica, so will I." She rolled her eyes and hugged herself in that dreamy, girlish way that lifted and accentuated her more obvious bits, and I felt the sudden weight of a one-eyed guilt swan for having to deceive her.

"Come here, sit," said she. "That knife wound won't heal if left open like that. It needs cleaning and some stitches."

"You can do that?"

"I can."

And so she had.

When she was readying to tie off the last stitch, she said, "Not much I can do for the puncture wounds on your sides. Clean and bandage them."

"Don't trouble yourself, then," said I. "They'll probably just poison my blood with madness and I'll die."

"Those are like the wounds on your bottom when I found you, aren't they?"

"Pish-posh, not at all, are you daft?" said I, as I tried to formulate some credible explanation for the claw marks. But alas, I was spared . . .

"Jessica!" came Shylock's voice from outside the door, the latch rattling.

"You may not be long for this world anyway," Jessica whispered to me as she went to unlatch the door, leaving needle and thread hanging from my ribs.

Shylock came through the door with great vigor and enthusiasm for a man of his years. *Great* vigor and enthusiasm.

"What? What? What? What? What?" said he, with what I really suppose, honestly, was more anger than enthusiasm.

"I sense a question coming—" said I.

"You! You! You! You! You!" said the Jew, waving a finger under my nose.

"And *there* is the answer," I replied.

"What are you? What kind of creature? What foul villain? You would eat of my food, live under my roof, and then you would steal from me? You—you—you— you—"

"And there he goes—"

"Philistine!" Shylock paused, trembled, his index finger doing a palsied anger twitch under my nose.

"Is that a good thing?" I asked Jessica, who had returned to my side on the bench where she'd been knotting the last stitch. She shook her head and looked back to her task.

"So, *no*, then," said I.

"You-you-you—*Philistines* are the ancient enemies of the Hebrew people. Goliath was a Philistine!"

"Oh, so they're tall?" said I. "Smashing!"

"No! Not *smashing*. Goliath was an enemy, a scourge on the Hebrew people, an evil giant!"

"Well, you don't know that, do you?"

"I know. Everyone knows. It says so in the books of the Kings."

"But what if he was just a normal-size bloke, and David was a more diminutive hero, like myself? A smaller fellow—with a huge *schlong*, of course." I nodded at the bloody obviousness of the last point.

"Goes without saying," added Jessica, nodding along with me.

Shylock repointed his twitching, accusatory digit at his daughter. "*You* do not say such things in my house. You—you—you—you—"

"Run along, love, it appears that Papa's been stricken with an apoplexy of the second person."

"I'm finished," said the lovely Jewess. She stood and breezed by her father and out the front door.

Shylock turned back to me. "What—"

I stood, and held my hand to Shylock's face to have him hold his tongue. "I sensed treachery afoot in Antonio's ranks, so knowing that their only loyalty would be to profit, I took the ducat to bribe one of Antonio's men. He arranged to meet me in a private place and told me that Antonio intends to assassinate you tomorrow night when you join him for dinner, so he will be released from his bond. After informing me thus, two of Antonio's men set upon me with knives, no doubt thinking I had more gold on my person, but certain with the intent that I would never return to you with this warning. So, I have bled for you and your gold, Shylock." I held my arms out so he could look upon the knife wound, the claw marks on my sides, the bruises on my back and shoulders where Viv had thrown me against the wall.

Shylock's rage ran from his face with what was left of the color. "But his bond will not be broken upon my death."

"But he does not know the law. Which is why you must go to his house with the two huge Jews, Ham and Japheth, attending you. Eat with him, and before you send your attendants away, share with him the circumstances of the bond—confabulate some outrageous legacy that goes beyond Jessica, so he will know that he may never be released by murder. Your bond over Antonio is the only reason he would risk venturing murder. He would only risk running astray of the law to avoid confronting it later, should you call your bond due."

"But surely his men have told him now of your escape. He will not expect me to come into his trap."

"His men will tell no tales. They are not the only ones who defy the law by carrying weapons. I took a wickedly sharp fish knife from your kitchen; you'll find it gone. Let us say the surprise of my having it was the last surprise for them. They will not be found." It was a serviceable lie. The fish knife was at the bottom of the canal with Jessica's boots, where I had sheathed it, but it was a serviceable lie.

"You killed them?"

"I acquired some skill with a blade before I washed up on your doorstep. Did I not say that your revenge would be my revenge?"

He took my hand and patted it as he shook it. "I apologize, Lancelot, for your pain and for doubting you. You shall be in my prayers—and my heart when I confront Antonio."

"Don't confront him, my friend, disarm him. Antonio plans his treachery with a cohort of scoundrels, as you shall see. You will disarm them with your own breath, by appearing fearless in their midst. Antonio knows you to be shrewd and will see that you would not expose yourself or your family to danger if your bond could be broken with the swipe of a blade. Hint that you considered his intent and dismissed it, knowing that he, too, would be too shrewd to think you'd leave your hold on him so flimsy."

"I shall."

"Good. Now, when Antonio secured the loan, he told you of each of his ships, the cargos, destinations, and the schedule for their return, did he not?"

"I knew them before he even asked. It is my business to know the business of the traders on the Rialto. I pay good moneys to stevedores and sailors at the docks for such knowledge."

"Then pray write them down for me, all those things you know of his ships and their schedules."

"I shall. What will you do with this knowledge, good Lancelot?"

"Trust," said I, trust being the shortest thread to the utter bollocks I might have spun. "I will use it well.

But now, good Shylock, I am wounded and weary and I need to rest."

And at midnight, on to Belmont.

"Do they have dogs?" asked the boatman.

We glided across the dark lagoon, gentle waves lapping on the bow like drinking dogs. Dogs? I didn't remember any dogs. But then, I had been very drunk when I'd arrived at Belmont on the night of my murder.

Dogs?

Wherefore dogs?

What ho, dogs?

Bloody buggering barking biting drooling bloody dogs?

"When we land, you go onshore to assure the way is clear, then, if no dogs, I shall debark."

"No," said the useless and shifty gondolier, stubborn and unmoving at his oar.

"Fine, I shall debark my own dogs," but even as I said it, I felt a twinge in my scalp and I saw in my mind's eye that *no*, there were no hounds on the island. She was there, under the oiled iron waves, under the gondola, and she was showing me that there were no dogs.

I leaned over the rail and stared into the water, trying to see below the inky surface. "Well, that's helpful, Viv, but you're a long way from providing bloody comfort with that bit about their being *delicious*." Then I pushed back from the railing, lest the siren snatch the head from my shoulders as she had my enemies' the night before. "Thanks loads, though, love." I shuddered.

"Bloody barking," said the boatman.

"No, there are no dogs," said I.

"Wasn't talking about the dogs, I was talking about you talking to the fishes."

"Just find a place you can land or let me off," said I. "I'm not swimming in."

I wore a pair of black wool tights and a black linen shirt that Jessica had tailored for me out of a trunk of Shylock's castoffs, over which I wore a wide belt pilfered from the lady's own closet. I'd knocked the heels off a pair of Jessica's shoes of soft leather and they fit me well enough I might climb in them as well as move on stone floors with stealth.

I'd managed to put together a kit of another fine filleting knife I honed myself to a razor edge for removing the wax seals, as well as a coil of rope and a padded grappling hook made from a gaffe that I'd bought from a fisherman with money from Jessica. In my youth, before I'd been picked to be the king's fool, I'd worked as a performer in a traveling circus, where the leader of the troupe, a vile Belgian called Belette, trained me, first as a cutpurse, and later as a second-story man, once he saw that I was agile enough to scamper up the side of a building, slip in through an upper window, and unlock the front door for my fellow thieves who waited outside. Jessica knew a goldsmith on the island who was happy to loan her a selection of his tools, which would provide me with lock picks fine enough for anything I might encounter. The locked veranda where the suitors' caskets lay, nor the locks themselves, would be little challenge.

I made the boatman circle the island twice to assure that the only servant on watch was a single man at the front dock, then he found a small swath of sand, barely wide enough for the gondola to knife its way between the rocks, where he was able to land the boat.

"Wait here. I don't know how long, but if the sky threatens dawn, go on without me."

"You said an hour."

"The bells of St. Mark's don't toll in the night. Pretend it's an hour."

"You're not here to shag Portia, are you?" asked the dim boatman.

I put a stack of coins on the raised deck where the gondolier stood. "Half your payment. The other half when you've returned me to La Giudecca."

"I'll wait," said the boatman.

I hopped out of the boat, scampered across the rocks, and across a wide strip of gravel into the gardens. Of course, Brabantio had a manicured garden, land being so dear in Venice, he *would* show the extravagance of having ornamental shrubberies, while the poor would paddle out to the most desolate of scrub islands in the marsh to dig out a root vegetable or harvest a few wild berries.

Belmont was Gothic in architecture, with pointed arabesque arches above the doors and windows, and little evidence that it ever had to be defended, as did most of the grand estates I had seen. With the exception of Arsenal, which was a formidable fortress, the Venetians seem to have always seen the sea and their barrier islands as their defense. Made it a piece of piss for even an out-of-practice thief possessed of inspiration.

The tower with the locked portico atop it jutted into the garden, with great carved marble railings that begged for the velvet thread of my padded grappling hook. Without so much as a clank, I had hooked the rope through the railings and was up the two stories to the portico in two ticks. A high, round marble table stood in the center of the portico, the three caskets—one lead, one silver, and one gold—each big enough to contain a deposed king's head, were set around the table.

While the fingernail moon was fine to creep and climb by, I'd need more light to do the delicate work of razoring the seals, so first I found my way to the double doors that led into the palazzo, and with a lever and the goldsmith's picks, soon I was inside. I found a small brass lantern with a candle near the still burning hearth of the great hall. With my lantern lit, I spied one of Brabantio's crests carved above the doorway that led to the central gallery and rage rose in me until I began to shake. That pompous prick and his cohorts had taken my heart from me—forget what they had done to me, or what lives they would ruin with their war—they had killed my Cordelia.

Dying in his cellar and being eaten by rats was not enough punishment for Brabantio. For the first time, I hoped that there was an afterlife and he could look up through the sulfurous clouds of Hell to watch me unwind his plots, drain his power, and extinguish the light of his legacy. Why bollocks about with caskets and seals when I could undo the cabal's plan with the flick of a blade on the snowy throat of a sleeping daughter?

I padded into the main hall and up the great marble staircase, as quiet as a cat. A row of heavy oak doors lined the mezzanine, no doubt leading to bedchambers that overlooked the gardens and the city beyond. With my lantern set against the wall to dim it, I pulled the fish knife from my belt and held it between my teeth, then palmed the heavy bronze latch so it opened without a rattle.

I had never killed a woman before, unless you count accidental poisoning, which I do not. I'd not have thought myself capable of it before I lost Cordelia, but accepting death folds the soul, tempers and layers it like a Damascus blade. When I'd thrown myself into the canal in grief, only to be pulled out by the Moor, I'd become colder, more durable. Again, when the mermaid dragged me under into the murky deep from the dungeon, I'd resolved myself to death, and awakened a harder, sharper thing. Even as my life bubbled away last night and I thought Viv's claws were hooks from Hell, only to find breath burning again in my lungs, my edge was honed, so fine and flexible now that I did not give two furry fucks for the life of fair Portia. I could hold my hand over her mouth and watch her life run red over the bedclothes and drip down on the head of her dead father and smile for the justice of it.

Such a creature had I become. Vivian and I, in killing were as one.

I pushed open the door to find no one—a room empty of people, but full of papers and maps, hand-copied books such as I had seen only in the scriptorium at the abbey where I learned to write. I carried my lantern into the room, and found there, laid out on the writing table, my throwing daggers. I had thought Antonio had worn them back to the city along with my motley, that long-ago night when I was walled in, but no, the old senator had kept them. Who, I wondered, had brought them up here, if he died in the dungeon on that very night, as was the rumor? Perhaps the puppet Jones, my jester's scepter, had survived as well. I strapped the leather harness with its three sheaths on the outside of my shirt. But alas, I did not find Jones. Not there.

My daggers in place, I was on to the next door, opening it to stream the yellow lamplight through the gap to fall upon the face of beauty, but masked in satin. Portia lay under the canopy of a high-poster bed, nested in rich silks and brocade. I slipped in and pushed the door shut behind me, leaving the room bathed in pale blue moonlight.

"I see you found your daggers," came a woman's voice from behind me. I jumped, straight up, about sixty feet, and came down turned toward the voice, my fillet knife in hand.

She lay back on a fainting lounge, in the shadows, just a silhouette against the wall. I looked over my shoulder at Portia, who snored softly on.

"Oh, don't worry about her," said the woman in the dark. "She puts beeswax in her ears and wears a sleeping mask. You could bang a bloody drum in here and she wouldn't wake."

"Who are you?" said I.

"I am called Nerissa," said she. "I'm the one that found your daggers, brought them up to the Montressor's study. You're the fool, right? The Englishman?"

"Possibly," said I, thinking that she really should be quite a bit more frightened, being as I was the very vision of a murderous nightmare creeping in the night to slit the throat of her mistress and whatnot.

"Were you the one in the dungeon, the one that did that to him?"

"Did what? I heard he was eaten by rats."

"He was torn apart, and not by rats. Pieces of him were gone—great bloody hunks of him—his buttocks were missing. I saw. I was called down there by a kitchen boy who was afraid to investigate the smell. Did you do that?"

I looked back at the sleeping Portia, then to the lady in the dark. "If you think I would do such a thing, why have you not called out?"

The shadow shrugged. "The Montressor was a right cruel old bastard, wasn't he? Deserved what he got, didn't he?"

"And what of what I am doing here, now?"

"Are you going to hurt me?"

"No." I remembered her now, through the haze of wine-soaked nights before my fall from grace. The dark-haired maid who attended Portia. Fit, she was, and quick of wit, I recalled.

"Then do what you will do," said she, throwing off her covers and rising from the couch. She moved to the door, slipped halfway out, then stopped. "Not wearing your cracking big codpiece anymore, then?"

"It was stolen," said I, somewhat bewildered. I was holding a knife, you know?

"Pity," she said. "There you go, love. Get on with it. Do what needs doing." And she slipped out the door.

And so I, the dark creeping thing I had become, did what needed doing, then slipped from Villa Belmont into the night and across the still Venetian lagoon as smooth and silent as a blade through milk.

Jessica met me at the dock the following dawn, dressed as a boy, and bouncing on her toes like an eager child before a sweets stand, a satchel slung over her shoulder and cradling a small wooden chest under her arm, filled, I presumed, with her father's treasure.

"Well, that won't work," said I, pulling off her yellow hat, releasing her dark curls to cascade about her shoulders.

"What? You said to hide my hair under a hat."

"Yes, but not a Jew hat, you ninny. We're supposed to be in disguise."

"I *was* in disguise. Now everyone will see I'm a girl."

I tossed her yellow hat in the water and fit my own floppy Venetian hat of brown silk on her head. "Tuck in your hair. And give me a few coppers so I can buy a new hat."

"Fuck off, rascal, you threw my hat in the water; get your own poxy hat."

I stepped back from her, somewhat surprised, and she grinned. She reached into the chest, came out with some coins, and handed them to me. "Having you on," she said. "My salty sea dog disguise, innit?" She bounced on the balls of her feet, looking for approval.

"Well done, then," said I. "But you may want to calm down just a bit. It's a long trip."

"But I'm so excited. I've never been to sea."

"Well then, close quarters on rough seas with you shall be a joy indeed."

"You're certain Papa will be taken care of?"

"Of course, I left him a pair of the new spectacles from Murano so he can see to do his own accounts, and I retained Tubal's huge Jews to look after him. They took an oath. Now wait here while I go buy a new hat."

Of course I had obtained no such oath from those huge Jews, and Shylock would be somewhat a wailing tragedy when he found his daughter and his treasure missing, but as the philosopher said, *"When rent by diverging loyalties, best to bugger off to an island somewhere."*

An hour later I wore my new hat as we stood on the rear deck of the ship watching Venice recede into the horizon.

"Why do they call it a poop deck?" Jessica inquired.

"I'll show you later," said I.

"We are going to be so happy, Lorenzo and I." She hugged herself and rolled her eyes dreamily.

"Don't do that, love, it's not manly."

I felt a pang in my heart for her, for her hope, and her joy, and the potential of a future she would never find. How could I tell her?

"What will we do in Corsica? Shall we stay at a seaman's inn? Go drinking and wenching?"

"I have a friend in Corsica. He will give us quarters."

"Who do you know in Corsica?"

"The Moor, Othello, he is a friend."

"The general? You are friends with the general of the whole Venetian Navy? How do you know Othello?"

"I did him a favor once, and he is forever indebted to me."

"You are a scandalous liar, Pocket." She bounced again, then leaned and rocked forward on the railing until I thought she might tumble over into the drink. "What will we do until Lorenzo arrives?"

And here I thought to at least put a path where a future had been pulled away.

"We shall have an adventure. We shall gather our forces at Corsica, then we will go to Genoa, to rescue another friend of mine. My apprentice."

She would need something, a purpose, when she found out about her Lorenzo. Here's the key, taught to me by a great grizzled warrior I once knew called Kent, who, when stripped of his lands, his family, and his good name, fought valiantly and against great odds to save the British kingdom. "Pocket," said he. "If you stop moving, the shroud of grief will overwhelm you and you will wither and die, so you've got to find your purpose and no matter what, keep buggering on." I did not revenge because I was incapable of mercy, or gratitude, or even joy, I revenged so I might live. I revenged for love. I revenged for my sweet Cordelia, who had sent me to Venice to show her contempt for their war, and by God's blood, I would stop their war, and if I had to, I would bring their soggy city down upon them to do it.

Poor Jessica, what purpose had she?

"Are you crying?" she asked.

"Wind," said I. "Salt air," said I.

"You're crying. You pathetic little girl."

She elbowed me and I winced.

"Oh my, it's your ribs, isn't it?" She was genuinely distressed. "I forgot about your wound. I can change the bandage for you. I'm sorry, Pocket."

"I'm fine, love. The wound is fine," said I. "It's just the wind in my eyes."

The ship turned into the sun, throwing the shade of the sails over us and behind the ship: the glare on the surface broken, I saw her shadow moving beneath the waves, following us.

Oh, Viv.

Who had terrified me.

Who had flayed me.

Who had taken my pain.

Who had used me.

Who had fed me.

Who had buoyed me up in the dark.

Who had pulled me down to the depths.

Who left me on the safe shores of light.

Who had stalked me.

Who had killed for me.

Who had given me life.

Oh, Viv.

On to Corsica.

ACT III

The Moor of Venice

Arise, black vengeance, from thy hollow hell!
—Othello, *Othello,* Act III, Scene 3

Thirteen
Bold and Saucy Wrongs

S he came to me in a dream. I'd been lying in for a
week after the Moor had stopped me from drowning myself, letting Drool and Jeff bring me wine, moving
off the sweat-soaked sheets only to hover wobbly over
the chamber pot before sinking back into my grief.

"Morning, love," said my Cordelia.

She wore the polished black-and-gold breastplate
of her armor with frilly knickers, which tipped me off
that all was not in order.

"Are you a dream, or a ghost?" said I, reaching out
to her, then catching myself before tumbling off the
bed.

"Which would better suit you?"

"Dream, I think. Less annoying rhyming."

"But then, there's always a bloody ghost . . ."

Cordelia's own mother had returned as such a spirit, resting only after her tormentors had been vanquished and her daughter settled in my arms.

"But you're fully dressed," said I. Her mum had been quite the tarty ghost. "In a manner of speaking."

"I'm not here to have you off, pet. Consolation and guidance, bit of spiritual direction, given you've fuck-all in the way of a moral compass."

"It *is* you," I sobbed then, bit of a nancy, I know, but fucking grief got the better of me, didn't it? "I'm broken without you."

"Oh, sweet Pocket." She cradled my cheek in her hand, but I could not feel it. "You've always been broken, love, it's the crux of your character. What would I have done with one of those fragile princes I was born for, his pride as delicate as crystal? You were like that lovely damaged doll a girl can bung down the stairs to see which limbs might come off, just for a laugh, just for the adventure of it."

"Or out a high tower window?"

"That was just the once, and you jumped."

"Being bloody gallant on your behalf, wasn't I?" I *had* jumped. To save a kitten. Cordelia's.

"Yes, as you have always been, and now must be again."

"Shall I dive out the window, splatter on the walkway, and join you in the Undiscovered Country? I'm quite ready, if you can help me to the window ledge."

"No, you need to help the Moor."

"Othello? Help him what? He's strong as a warhorse, rich, commands a bloody navy, annoyingly tall, and his—"

"His lady?"

"He is not married."

"His love?" said Cordelia. "Desdemona."

"Desdemona, the senator's daughter? She can't—well—he's a Moor, isn't he?"

"See to it."

"See to what?"

"You're clever, Pocket. Be clever. Help the Moor."

"Brabantio will never allow it. And I am but a wisp of a fool, drunk and weak, and vice versa, with no will to live."

"Yet you conquered a kingdom and handed it to me."

"Aye, but that was a piece of piss, wasn't it? Only had to wrench it loose from a feebleminded family of inbred deviants."

"*My* family, you mean?"

"Well, not *you*, obviously. But the rest of them. Point is, I am small and heartbroken."

"Yes, you are. Help the Moor."

"I've lost all influence in Venice."

"Not all. The doge still has some affection for you. You can still move in higher circles for a while. Help the Moor."

"Stop saying that."

"Promise."

"I promise to help the sodding Moor."

"And promise not to off yourself."

"You mean kill myself?"

"Yes."

"I promise."

"And don't shag the Jewess."

"What Jewess? I don't know a Jewess."

"You're a love, Pocket. Now wake up, you're about to wee the bed."

I awoke. Too late.

Two days after the dream, I pursued the task my Cordelia had set me: *Help the Moor.*

The priest was surprised that Othello answered his own door. The monkey and the great imbecile expected there would be sweets. The Moor wore a belted dressing gown of white linen and held his sword in its scabbard in one hand.

"Why, he's not dying," said the priest.

"He are black," said Drool.

"Moors are black," I explained to the ninny.

"You said he was dying," said the priest.

"Pardon, General," said I to the Moor. "The only way I could get him here was to tell him that you needed last rites."

"Pocket?" said the Moor. "You do not look well." He was surprised that I had arrived at his door at the supper hour with an entourage, but he was not angry.

"Get into some dressy togs," said I. "Bit of gold braid and a right fancy hat if you can manage; we're taking you to be married. One of those pointy Saracen helmets would be smashing, if you have one." I breezed past him into his house, which, although near Arsenal, was appointed more in the finery of a duke's home rather than the Spartan utility of a soldier's. "You three, stay out there."

The priest tried to address me around the Moor. "I'm not going to perform a marriage. You said last rites?"

"You'll do as you're told or I'll tell everyone your lot stole the bones of St. Mark from a temple in Egypt."

"That was four hundred years ago. No one cares about that. Tell them. I'm going home." The priest turned on his heel to leave.

"Stop him, Drool," said I.

The great oaf snatched the priest up by the cowl of his robe and made to lift him like a kitten by the scruff of the neck, but only succeeded in pulling the priest's robe up over his head until the scrawny padre stood bare from the waist down.

"Put him down, put him down. Just sit on him."

Drool dropped the priest's robe, pushed him to the ground, and sat on him.

"You can't do this! The bishop will—"

The priest closed his mouth rather abruptly when monkey Jeff squatted over it.

"Well done, Jeff. Don't let Drool suffocate him, and you, priest, you should wear knickers when you're out. People will think you wanton.

"Come, Othello, we shall have conference." I reached past the Moor and closed the door on my retinue.

"What are you saying about marriage? Who do you think I shall marry?"

"Why the fair Desdemona, of course. You love Desdemona, and you are confident the lady loves you, correct?"

"This I know better than anything I have ever known. But to take her from her father, without permission or blessing; I could not steal her away like a thief in the night."

"First, you are not stealing her, she goes with you freely, of her own will, and second, be not so disparaging of thieves in the night. Were you not a pirate before coming to lead the forces of Venice?"

Othello, and his twenty ships of pirates, had been hired as mercenaries to help the Venetian Navy in their war against the Genoans, to take down Genoan ships in the Black Sea. When word came that the general of the navy, Dandalos, had been devastatingly defeated at the island of Curzola, losing a hundred ships, Othello was tasked with protecting the Venetian homeland against a Genoan attack, to avert a siege and surrender. The Moor had performed brilliantly, turning back the entire Genoan Navy, and allowing Venice to rebuild her navy, which was put under the Moor's command.

"But I am a pirate no more."

"Why is that, Othello? Why bollix up your profession for Venice?"

"I like that there is something to do beyond pirating. Service. To sink a ship, plunder a cargo, these are deeds in service of self, where the prizes are wealth and power, but to save a city, spare the children, these are larger deeds, which serve the soul."

"And yet by saving the city you have attained greater wealth and power than ever."

"There may be flaws in my philosophy, Pocket."

"They're all selfish, underhanded, greedy twats, with no consideration for anything but their own comfort anyway, aren't they?"

"I think your misfortune has darkened your eye on Venetians. They are not all so bad."

"I was talking about humanity in general; wouldn't give a fetid firkin of fuck-all for the lot of them."

"And yet you are here, with a priest, to what end?" The Moor dazzled a grin at me, as if he'd scored touché while fencing.

"There may be flaws in my philosophy, Othello," said I. "And the bloody ghost of my wife entreated me to help you."

"Ah, I have oft heard it said that there is always a bloody ghost."

"Othello!" came a woman's voice from the stairs. "Who is it, darling?"

Desdemona rounded the balustrade and floated into the foyer, her gown flowing around her bare legs, her long hair down and playing about her shoulders and back. She was green-eyed and as fair as her sister Portia, but a bit more round of cheek, with a spark in her eyes that warned of a smile that might break out at any moment. She reminded me of my Cordelia, not so much in countenance as in bearing, strong yet gentle. Lovely.

"Thou squidgy tart!" said the puppet Jones, who had remained at my side, ever on the lookout for banality or the low-hanging fruit of comedy.

"Oh, it is the royal fool," she said, clasping Othello's arm. We had met at a ball at the doge's palace and I had twice been a dinner guest of her father at Belmont. She knew me. I had made her laugh. "Sir, I was so sad to hear of your queen. My deepest condolences, and if I or my family can offer any comfort, you need only ask." She turned her head and there was such sadness, such kindness in her pity for me, that I knew at once how the bold Othello, pirate and soldier—that hard, scarred, killing thing—had lost his heart. And beyond a doubt, I knew what had to be done.

"Othello, you must, with fearful vigor and utmost alacrity, marry this bitch."

"What?" asked Desdemona.

"He has brought a priest," Othello explained. "He is held hostage outside."

"I was going to bring Othello to Belmont, spirit you away to the garden, have the priest do his dread deed before your family knew the better of it, but now, here, it must be done."

"But my father—"

"What will your father do? You will be married, your union blessed by the church, to the man who saved Venice. Would your father, with all his power, dare challenge the church? The doge? You will have at once made your love your lord, and in the making, infuriated your father forever. Two birds, love. What say you, lady?"

The smile blossomed and she gripped Othello's arm. He looked in her eyes and fell to one knee.

"I am unworthy," he said. "But if you would so honor me—"

"Yes!" she said. "Yes! Yes! Yes! Yes! Yes! Yes! Yes! Oh, my sweet Othello, yes!"

"Fucking French call that the little deaf," said the puppet Jones.

"The little *death*, you Cockney knob," I corrected. "And I don't think that's what all the yessing was about."

"Sounded like she was having it off to me. Fine, let's fetch the vicar from under the ninny, there's bound to be sickening amounts of snogging in here soon."

I grasped the door latch, then turned back to them. "Lady, where does your father think you are now?"

"He thinks I've gone to Florence, to buy shoes."

"Clever. Then you have gold? To bribe the priest for his service—it's unseemly to force him at the point of a dagger, although I'm not entirely against the idea."

"I have gold," said Othello.

"Fetch it," said I. "I'll revive the priest. He looked weak. He'll have passed out by now."

"Stronger men have succumbed from being monkey-fucked in the nostril for this long," said the puppet Jones.

"Pardon?" asked Othello.

"He jests," said I, shoving the puppet stick down my back.

"I'll run put on some knickers," said Desdemona.

"I was going to suggest that," I called after her. "She's lovely," I whispered to the Moor.

I opened the door.

"I told you," said the puppet Jones.

"Jeff! Get off him. Bad monkey! Bad monkey!"

"Jeff were havin' a laugh wif the vicar," said Drool.

And soon after, in the witness of a noble fool, a nitwit, a monkey, and a puppet on a stick, were Othello and the fair Desdemona made man and wife.

CHORUS: *Two days did pass while the Moor and Desdemona enjoyed their wedded delights before word of their wedding spread from priest to soldier, to servant, to the ear of Rodrigo, and he, with heavy heart from having lost Desdemona, sought comfort in his friend Iago.*

"Then the Moor has ruined Brabantio's daughter?" said Iago, pacing about the officers' quarters with the heady vim of inspiration. "Ha! The council will surely have him hanged, now. These are glad tidings indeed! You have witnesses, of course? If not, we shall have to shape some from the most upstanding scoundrels we can afford. You have money?"

"No, that won't help," whined Rodrigo. "He has not taken the lady against her will, he has married her. Yes, she is ruined, but by her own will and consent, ruined only for me; in the eyes of God and the state, she belongs to the Moor."

"Oh balls." Iago ceased his pacing. "Married?"

"By a priest."

"The Moor and Desdemona married?"

"In front of witnesses. Signed into the city's record."

"Married? In front of witnesses?"

"Witnessed by a fool, a giant, and a monkey."

"Balls!"

"You said that already."

Iago now resumed his pacing, drew his dagger, and began drawing his plans in the air with the knife while Rodrigo flattened himself against the wall.

"It is not too late to make this marriage the Moor's undoing. When did this wedding take place?"

"But two days ago. Even now Desdemona hides in the Moor's house."

"And the Montressor does not know of it?"

"No, he is in his apartments near the doge's palace."

"Not at Belmont?"

"It was at Belmont I heard the news, from Portia's maid, Nerissa."

"The maid knows, but the master does not? I tell you, Rodrigo, women are a devious lot. Bed them if you must, but take their oaths but as cobwebs spun across a stable door, breaking with scant resistance to the next stallion to pass by."

"But, good Iago, do you not have a wife yourself? The fair Emilia?"

"Thus I know of what I speak. A bundle of deceit in a pleasant package is she, are they all. Woe to the man who thinks different and enables them with trust." Iago thrust his dagger in its sheath as if dirking Caesar. "Come, Rodrigo, we will rouse Senator Brabantio and see if we can loose deadly anger on the Moor before the full tale is told. Have men with weapons ready. Brabantio is old and will have his killing done by others."

Roused from my gentle slumber on the foyer floor of Othello's house, where I had landed after taking a tumble down the stairs, to settle in what appeared to be a puddle of my own sick, I went to the door to address whatever gang of reprobates was shouting and pounding and generally adding a rather grating edge to my newborn hangover.

"What?" I opened the door, expecting sunlight to drive spikes of regret into my forehead, but instead, in the night, stood Brabantio, and behind him perhaps two dozen men with torches, a few carrying swords.

"Montressor?" said I.

"Fortunato?" said the Montressor. "What are you doing here?"

"Confronting a bloody mob, evidently. What are *you* doing here?"

"We've come to seize the Moor, who has taken my daughter Desdemona and holds her under his heathen enchantment!"

A shout came from the rear of the crowd. "Even now the black ram is tupping his white ewe!"

"The Moor and Desdemona even now make the beast with two backs!" came another shout.

"Even now he doth do bold and saucy wrongs upon her!" shouted another.

"There's no spell," said I. "The Moor and your daughter are married. And your mob has no pitchforks. I've seen a crashing fuck-bushel of blokes dragged into the street by mobs, and *you* need pitchforks."

"But we have no horses," said a less enthusiastic voice.

"Nor cows, neither," said another.

"No need to shovel hay nor manure," whined a third.

"I could fetch a boat hook," suggested yet another knave.

"Send out the Moor!" demanded Brabantio.

"Montressor, your mob is shit," said I. "Come back when you've proper pitchforks and some coherent slogans. '*Beast with two backs*'? What did you do, just go from house to house asking for illiterate nitwits to come help drag the high commander of the most powerful military force in the land from his house without so much as a sharp stick? Shoddy fucking planning, Montressor." I slammed the door in his face and threw the bolt.

"What was that?" asked Othello, coming down the stairs in his dressing gown, his sword and scabbard in hand.

"Mob of knobs," said I. I held a finger up to hold a place in the exchange while I turned and chundered into the kindling bucket by the fireplace. I wiped my mouth on my sleeve and said, "Here to hang you, methinks. Oh, and Brabantio is leading them."

"Father?" said Desdemona, coming down the stairs behind Othello.

The pounding on the door and the shouting resumed, although it was mostly just "Hang him!" and "Black devil!" No one appeared to be crafting more hangnail metaphors after my scolding.

"I'll not have this." The Moor cinched his robe, then made for the door.

"Only let a few through the doorway at once," said I. "Keep their attack narrow. I'll dispatch any who get around the swath of your sword with my daggers." I drew one from the small of my back and flipped it so I held it by the blade. "Fate willing, we'll be knee-deep in corpses in two ticks, and you can call for sailors to mop up the blood and carry away the baskets of severed limbs."

Othello paused by the heavy door. I held my dagger ready to throw and drew a second knife from the small of my back with my off hand. Desdemona stood on the stairs, her hands clasped over her mouth as if capturing a scream.

"Perhaps I should address them from the balcony," said Othello.

"Excellent," said I. "Get the tactical advantage, innit? Desdemona, put some oil on the fire to boil, love. We'll scald the scurvy vermin before raining death and heavy furniture down upon them."

I turned and made to run past Desdemona up the stairs, then swooned with nausea, dropped my daggers, and caught myself on the banister. "Fuckstockings, I'm useless—"

"Or perhaps we could find out their grievances and in the understanding, calm them," said Desdemona, catching me by the shoulders and steadying me against another tumble down the stairs.

"Perhaps," said Othello.

He was past me on the stairs and out on the balcony before I could retrieve my knives.

"Put up your shiny swords, the dew will rust them," said Othello. "Good Senator, you shall command more respect with years than with your weapons."

"Oh thou foul thief," said Brabantio. "Where hast thou stowed my daughter?"

"Your daughter is safe."

"Damned thou art," said Brabantio. "No girl so tender and fair, yet so opposed to marriage that she turned away the most wealthy darlings of our nation, would find her way to your sooty bosom without you did bind her with spells. You, with your enchantments, hold her against her will."

"That I do not," said the Moor, rather more calmly than I thought appropriate.

"Back, you pack of dogs!" I called, pushing my way onto the balcony. "Before the Moor has all your heads bobbing on pikes." I reached down my back collar for the puppet Jones, who is a vivid example of the fate of the piked head, except miniature and more handsome than most, but Desdemona had asked me to put the puppet up during dinner, as she found his unbroken stare and resemblance to my own striking countenance "right creepy." Fine. "He'll have your guts for garters, will the Moor!"

"No he won't," said Desdemona from behind.

"No I won't," said Othello.

"He'll rain down death on you and all your families, ravage your women, and fit your children on spikes with frightful efficiency!"

"Set down your arms," said the Moor. "Were it my cue to fight I should have known it without a prompter."

"Oh for fuck's sake—"

The Moor pushed me back from the railing. "I will come down. Let us go before the doge and the council, and I shall there answer your charge under the law."

"Useless bloody sooty-bosomed toss-tick, that's what you are," said I. Othello had invoked the law, and Venice was a city of bloody laws, wasn't it?

"To prison with you, then," said Brabantio. "Until a fit time for a trial."

Then there came from below the cry of a new voice. "Hail, General, it is Cassio!"

I crept to the rail. At the edge of the mob stood an armed soldier in leather and light armor, and with him a cohort of six men-at-arms. Othello's captain, Michael Cassio, who I was yet to meet.

"The doge calls for you," said Cassio. "There is an urgent matter of strategy and the entire council is awake and waiting. The Genoans are moving on Corsica."

"Look," said I. "Your captain's brought help. We could slaughter these knaves and still be at the council within the hour."

"Stop it, Pocket," said Desdemona. "You're just trying to come up with new ways to off yourself to ease your grief."

"You mean *kill myself,* right?"

"Yes."

"Possibly . . ."

"I am coming down," said the Moor.

"Fuckstockings!" Out in the piazza, beyond Cassio and his men, I saw Iago crouching in a doorway, careful not to be seen by the other soldiers. How could I know that even then he was working his dread plot upon the Moor?

On the ship to Corsica the meaning of Cordelia's dream came to me . . .

"You're the bloody Jewess!" I exclaimed, coming out of a dead sleep and struggling to sit up in my hammock, which hung in our little corner of the cargo hold. We'd been at sea for two days; I'd spent much of it belowdecks, unwell.

"Rather undermines the disguise if you're just going to shout that out, Pocket," said Jessica.

"Right, sorry," said I. "But it's only now occurred to me that you're the Jewess I'm not supposed to shag."

"I'd have snatched your bollocks off and fed them to the fish if you tried, so probably just as well you remembered."

"You're still being piratey, aren't you?"

"I think I'd be terribly good at it, don't you? Maybe Lorenzo and I will go pirating."

"Yes, well, there's more to pirating than salty talk and not painting the decks with your breakfast every morning. There's throats to be cut, and some nautical bits to know, too, I'll wager. Plus, you're a sodding girl." This didn't seem to be the time to mention that Lorenzo would be somewhat impaired in his pirating by being quite dead.

"I can dress as a boy. I'm ever so clever at it. I was talking to two soldiers on the deck while you slept, and neither even suspected me to be a girl. One is even an officer—on his way to see your friend Othello as well. Called Iago. Looks a bit piratey himself. I didn't catch the other bloke's name."

"Iago? Iago is on this ship?"

"He said that's his name."

"Did you tell him you were traveling with me? With a companion? Or that I know Othello?"

"He didn't seem interested. He was rather distracted in lecturing his friend about money and how deceitful women are, which, overhearing, is how I found my way into their conversation. I was obliged to agree with him, given the circumstances. Excused myself when the two decided to have a communal wee over the side, so as not to reveal my manly shortcomings."

"But you told him nothing of yourself or me."

"It wasn't called for."

"Hand me your rucksack."

"You don't need any more gold. There's nowhere to spend it out here."

"I need to refashion my disguise," said I. "If Iago recognizes me, we are finished."

Fourteen
A World of Sighs

In Belmont did fair Nerissa curse the English fool when she rose to find her Portia quite unslain, her delicate throat quite unslit, and her musical voice still quite capable of barking commands to her servants, while intermittently whining about the sad path laid before her by her dead and arse-eaten father.

"Fucking fool," said Nerissa, under her breath, hiding a sour scowl behind her hand, as if a bite of lemon tart had bubbled up from below.

"Oh, Nerissa, I am beside myself with worry," said Portia. "Because he did not present his suit in time, Bassanio does not try for my hand with the caskets until tomorrow afternoon. Before him, in the morning, the Duke of Aragon tries, and today the Prince of Morocco, and he with as much the gift of chance as any. I dread him."

"Aye, mistress, but I hear the prince is fair-minded and generous."

"What does it matter if he has the condition of a saint, when he hath the complexion of a devil? Would you have me surrender my charms to his most dusky affections, even as my sister beslutted herself with Othello?"

"Rest easy, lady, no matter his choice, the prince shall be bound by bad luck, I'm sure."

"You're sure?"

"Absolutely," said Nerissa as she braided Portia's hair, preparing to fit it into a tiara for her appearance before the prince. While she worked, she mused, "Of course, if the fool *had* done the slaughter, *I* no doubt would be the one washing the body and scrubbing the blood out of the bedding, as the staff is composed of nothing but cowards and catch-farts, so perhaps the fool has done me service by leaving breath in your scrawny bellows."

Nerissa knew that as long as Portia fretted over her own fate, which was most of the time, she heard only the tones of her maid's voice and not the words, so Nerissa liked to take these opportunities to croon her resentment in a manner most melodious.

Portia said, "Perhaps we should fix my hair askew, muss my gown, taint my breath with garlic so the prince will find me unpleasant and go away without taking his chance at the caskets."

"Dear Portia, don't be silly, to thine own self be true; the prince will see through to your unpleasantness without the taint on your breath."

Before Portia could formulate a retort, a fanfare played from the dock and the two women looked at each other, eyebrows raised in surprise.

"He travels with his own trumpeter?" said Nerissa. "Perhaps you should reconsider, lady."

Portia led the way down the grand staircase to the foyer, where they were met by two of Brabantio's lawyers—bent-backed graybeards in black robes and mortarboard hats—escorting the Prince of Morocco and an entourage of six soldiers, all wrapped in white robes from head to toe, their faces as black as polished ebony, each wearing a scimitar in his sash, the prince's in a jeweled scabbard. The prince bowed, then held his bow so Portia might glide down the staircase as if presenting herself upon the stage before him, where she returned his bow. Nerissa, having played this scene out many times before, came bouncing down behind her mistress with such enthusiasm that her bosoms nearly escaped the top of her gown. The Moors were captivated.

The prince tore his gaze from Nerissa's décolletage and addressed Portia. "Lady, you are more beautiful than the stories that precede you. It is no wonder that the seas fill with ships bringing suitors from all the corners of the world."

"Thank you, kind sir," said Portia. She betrayed a sneer, which did not pass the prince unnoticed.

"Mislike me not for my complexion," said the Moor. "I am but the shadowed design of the burnished sun where I was bred. I would not change my hue except to steal your favor, my gentle queen."

"You stand as fair as any suitor I have looked on, but choice is not solely led by my eye. My father has set the lottery of my destiny."

One of the lawyers, longer and whiter of beard than the other, stepped forward. "He knows of the terms and has paid the price of his chance." The lawyer then made his way to the doors to the terrace, which he unlocked with a key on a chain about his neck.

"Condolences on the loss of your father," said the prince. "I heard only of his passing after we arrived in Venice or I would not have added the weight of my suit to the lady's grief."

Meaning, thought Nerissa, that his interest in Portia was the political alliance with her father on the council, not her legendary beauty and widely exaggerated cleverness.

Portia, too, caught the subtext of the prince's comment, quickstepped to the terrace doors, and drew aside the curtain.

"You must take your chance," she said. "Or not choose at all, but swear before you choose that should you choose wrongly, you must tell no one which casket you chose, and never speak to this lady afterward in the way of marriage."

"If so cursed, I will console myself with my other nineteen wives," said the prince.

Nerissa covered her mouth to stop from giggling, but alas, snorted a bit and drew the dragon's glare from Portia.

The prince made his way around the table, reading the placard on each of the caskets.

At the lead casket, he read: "*'Who chooseth me must live and hazard all he has.'* Why, this is more a threat than a promise."

He then moved to the silver casket. "*'Who chooseth me shall get as much as he deserves.'* But what a man deserves is not always that which he requires."

The prince stepped to the gold casket. "*'Who chooseth me shall gain what many men desire.'* Methinks that only a bed of gold would be worthy of fair Portia. I would have the key to this one."

The lawyer shuffled forward and drew a key from his purse and handed it to the prince.

"Take it," said Portia. "And if my picture lie there, then I am yours."

The Moor took the key, unlocked the casket, and pushed back the lid.

"Oh hell!" said the prince. "What have we here?" He lifted from the casket a miniature death's-head. A scroll protruded from the skull's eye. The prince replaced the skull in the casket, removed the scroll, unrolled it, and read:

" 'All that glitters, is not gold;
Often have you heard that told;
But my outside do behold;
Gilded tombs do worms enfold;
Had you been wise as you've been bold;
Your answer would be here inscrolled;
Fare you well; your suit is cold.' "

The prince stared at the parchment and let it snap back to form. "Then this is all? All of nothing."

"Make of yourself a gentle riddance," Portia said, with feigned disappointment, as she turned and looked out over the garden to conceal her grin.

The prince reeled with a flourish of his robes and walked off the terrace, his entourage in rank behind him.

"Draw the curtains, Nerissa."

"Bit harsh, don't you think?" said Nerissa. "Three thousand ducats for a death's-head?"

"Let all of his complexion choose so wrongly."

A fanfare played from the front of the house as the prince exited.

"I'm going after him," said Nerissa, hurrying to the door.

"Nerissa! I forbid you to fancy him."

Nerissa knew that as soon as Portia found the arms of her Bassanio, she'd be cast out on her own. Too many years had she acted as the gentle cushion to the suitors rejected by both Brabantio sisters (like Rodrigo, who evidently had buggered off to Corsica, still in pursuit of Desdemona) and Portia would never allow her more *accommodating* maid in proximity to Bassanio. Nerissa was going to need a cushion herself when Bassanio guessed the correct casket on the morrow. One of twenty wives of a prince seemed like a quite comfortable cushion on which to land.

"Sod fancying him, I just want to have a look at his sun-burnished trumpet."

"Thou art a hopeless slag, Nerissa."

"Not true, I am full of hope."

Jessica and I came down the ramp from the ship so close behind Iago and Rodrigo that I could almost smell the treachery coming off them.

Jessica had, by now, learned to walk without the slightest sway to her hips, while I had minced my steps more fitting to the humble shuffle of a nun, for so was I dressed, in wimple and veil, in such a nun suit as we had been able to fashion from the clothes in Jessica's rucksack. My beard now shaved and my Jew kit betrayed, the veil was a necessary accoutrement for my disguise; of leper or nun, I chose the latter.

We followed the two soldiers down the dock through the fray of sailors and stevedores resupplying the ships in the harbor. The Genoan fleet had been decimated by a storm on their voyage to attack Corsica. Othello easily turned the remaining force away and had fortified the harbor with archers, ballistas, and catapults ever ready on the breakwater.

Iago stopped at the street and hailed a soldier on horseback.

"Ho there, Sergeant, where might I find General Othello? I bring news from Venice."

"He is at the Citadel, Lieutenant," said the soldier, recognizing Iago's rank from the crest on his dagger. "The general's second, Captain Cassio, is just round the corner. I'll fetch him for you and he can take you to the general."

The soldier rode off and a minute later Michael Cassio stepped out of a white stucco building across the street and strode across the sunbaked pavers in his high boots to meet Iago. They exchanged salutes. Cassio was taller, younger, more handsome and clear of eye than Iago, the very model of a gentleman soldier, with such a bright and open nature that I shivered to see him standing guileless and unguarded before Iago, who, with the rise of his scar-broken eyebrow when he smiled, revealed the inner turning of gears grinding deceitful plots.

"Good Iago, you have news from Venice? Another attack on the city?"

"Nothing so dire," said Iago. "But I am tasked by the council to deliver my dispatch only to Othello and his lady."

"Desdemona," sighed Rodrigo, casting a wistful gaze to the clouds.

"His lady?" said Cassio. "Then this is not news of war?"

"You will know at Othello's discretion, Captain, but I am bound by orders."

"Quite so." Cassio tossed his head toward a great stone-and-plaster fortress that loomed over the town. "The Citadel is a short walk. I'll take you myself. I'll send a cart back for your things."

"Pardon, good captain," called Jessica, in her best boy voice. "Could you spare a moment for a word with this holy sister of mercy?"

I had retreated to the edge of the dock by a great mooring post. I peered out into the harbor, looking not at the ships and birds diving overhead, but for a shadow beneath the turquoise waves, and there, perhaps three hundred feet out, she swam. I closed my eyes and looked for the blue patterns of her thoughts, but there were none. *Spare this one. Leave him his head,* I thought. *Not this one.* Could she hear me? For Cassio's sake, I hoped so.

"Yes, Sister?" said Cassio, stepping up beside me.

"Act as if nothing is out of order. Iago must not see you react. I am simply asking for shelter for myself and the boy," I said in my own voice, undisguised.

"What?"

I stepped back from the edge so only Cassio could see my face, then raised my veil, winked, grinned, and held my finger to my lips to signal silence.

"You know me," said I. "I am the fool Pocket."

"You stood for Othello before the council."

"I am here to help the Moor again. I must see him, but on our lives, Iago and his friend cannot know my true identity. Do you trust me?"

He nodded, just a twitch.

"Fine then, old mother," Cassio called, rather more loudly than was required. He headed back to Iago. "You and the boy may follow us to the Citadel, give blessings to and receive alms from the lady and her retinue."

I thought back to when I had first met Cassio, on that night when Brabantio had led us through the streets of Venice to the palace of the doge, to accuse Othello of bewitching his daughter.

"I'm going to dive in and begin the killing," I told Cassio. "If I fall, stain the canals red with their blood until the city shatters with the cries of their widows and orphans."

"Or, if you'd put one of those daggers up, you can lean on me and we'll follow them to the doge's palace as Othello commanded."

"Well, yes, I suppose we could do that, too, if you're going to be a little nancy about it. But if I have to stop to be sick, carry on with the killing and the weeping widows."

By the time we reached the palace, many of Brabantio's mob had wandered off, having realized that the Moor was not going to be immediately hanged, and that, indeed, there were a half dozen well-armed men and a queasy fool with a quiver of daggers who would prefer the Moor remain unhanged.

We entered the main hall of the doge's palace, where the doge sat on a dais in the center of the Council of Six; one chair sat empty: Brabantio's.

"Ah, valiant Othello," said the doge as he stood and opened his arms to welcome the Moor into the hall.

"We must straight employ you against the Genoans, who have moved on to Corsica." The doge then spied Brabantio, who stormed into the room, robe flying, slamming a great walking staff into the floor as if he half-expected the earth to open and unleash Venice's wrath upon the Moor. "Welcome, gentle signor," said the doge. "We lacked your council tonight."

"And I yours, but I have been tending a broken floodgate of o'erbearing sorrows."

"What is wrong?" asked the doge.

"My daughter! O, my daughter!"

"Dead?"

"Tart," I answered. "Although a tasty bit of talent, to be sure."

"She is not!" protested Brabantio. "She's bewitched by this heathen."

"Tartish," I relented.

"Fortunato, what have you to do with this?" asked the doge.

"I speak for the Moor," said I.

"He does not," said the Moor.

"What have you to say of this, Othello?" asked the doge.

Othello addressed the group of them now. "Most potent and reverend signors, that I have taken away this man's daughter is true. I have married her."

"It's true," said I. "I witnessed the ceremony."

"Never!" shouted Brabantio. "Never would a maiden be so bold, to fall in love and marry something she feared to look upon. She would not have gone against her nature as such, without the Moor hid in her drink cunning mixtures to enchant her blood that wrought this imprudent judgment upon her. She's enchanted by magic, I tell you."

"Or his crashing huge cock!" offered the puppet Jones, who I had retrieved on my way out the door.

The doge said, "There is no proof of this."

"No, I've seen it," said I. "It swung out of his robe last week and nearly concussed the landlady's dog."

Another senator stood and spoke then. "Othello, speak, did you by indirect and conjured courses subdue and poison this young maid's affections?"

"I beseech you, signors, send for the lady at my quarters, and let her speak of me before her father. If, after hearing her, you find me in foul report, then take not only my office, but my life, for I would give both gladly if I had sinned so."

"Fetch Desdemona," said the doge.

Othello nodded to Cassio, who sent a brace of soldiers to fetch Desdemona.

"Until she comes," said Othello, "I do confess the vices of my blood, and that the lady doth dwell in my love, as I in hers, but not by enchantment. You know her father found favor in me, and oft did invite me to their home and question me for the story of my life. I spun it, even from my days as a boy, out to the room, and while Desdemona pretended to serve, she devoured my story with a greedy ear. Of moving accidents and hairbreadth escapes, of being sold into slavery, and my redemption from it, of my travels, from vast deserts to the mountains whose heads touch the sky, of cannibals and cutthroats, of battles I had fought, and pains that had been inflicted on me. My story done, she gave me for my troubles a world of sighs. She swore it was strange, 'twas passing strange, 'twas pitiful, 'twas wondrous pitiful, and she wished that she had not heard it, for with my story I had wooed her heart. She loved me for the dangers I had passed, and I loved her that she did pity them. This is the only witchcraft I have used."

"I think this would win my daughter, too," said the doge. "Good Brabantio, perhaps you should make the best of this situation—"

"Really, it was the storytelling and not the enormous willy?" I looked to my codpiece, which, under the circumstances, seemed a bit overstated. "Here she is," said I, seeing Desdemona glide into the hall. "Let's ask her."

Brabantio waved Desdemona forward. "Let her speak. Destruction on my head if she confesses her part in this wooing. Tell them, daughter, to whom do you owe obedience?"

"My duty is divided," answered Desdemona. "To you I am bound for life and education, and for those I give you honor and gratitude. I am, and shall always be your daughter, but Othello is my husband, and like my mother preferred you to her own father, so I must give honor to my husband."

I had heard nearly the same speech from my own Cordelia to her father, thus setting in motion the shifting of a half dozen kingdoms. Desdemona's spark and passion brought a lump to my throat.

"Then it is true. You have married him?"

"Under the church and the republic, as well as in my heart."

"It cannot be legal!" said Brabantio to the senate. "He is not Venetian, and under the law he would inherit my seat on the council. He must be Venetian born or the marriage is not legal."

The senators looked around at one another and finally the doge spoke. "We will have to consider your suit, Brabantio. The city's charter says nothing about a senator having to be a Venetian, only that he be elected by citizens of his district. It was you, yourself, that proposed the law that a seat could be passed down to heirs. It does not specify that a senator must be Venetian born."

"But when the law was passed, all senators were Venetian born, so it is implied in the law. When I go to the butcher to buy a duck, must I also tell him I want a bird? We know because it is a duck, it is a bird implied."

"He has a point," said the senator sitting closest to the doge.

"Oh bollocks," said I. I stumbled to the middle of the floor. "Complete bloody bollocks. If ducks are birds, then Othello is a Venetian by the same rule, because he is known as such."

"Fortunato—" The doge stood as if he thought he might direct me from the floor.

"Just listen, Your Grace. You all know how I came to Venice. Not as the wee broken fool you see before you, but as a diplomat, an emissary from the ruler of six countries. Spokesman for an empire."

"His queen is dead—," said Brabantio.

"Shut the fuck up, thou glistening dog knob!" said I, perhaps more sternly than was called for. "I have the floor."

The doge gave Brabantio a savage glare and the senator went silent.

"I traveled across Europe to come here, to speak my queen's will to Venice, because of one man: Othello.

O'er all the world, the legend of the Moor saving your city is prologue to the power of your empire. Who will ship their goods with Venice, send their soldiers to war with Venice, if Venice cannot protect her ships? The world knows that the spine of the mighty Venetian Navy is that brilliant general, the Moor, Othello, who saved them from the Genoans when he was five times outnumbered. In all the known lands, princes speak the name of Othello in the same breath with Venice, and see the city's esteem in his sword. Brabantio tells you Othello is not a Venetian, but I tell you that there would be no Venice without Othello. The Moor is a Venetian because he is the father of Venice—he gave it life. Even tonight, with wind of trouble on another sea, you call for the Moor to defend your city. Would you be so base as to boast of your city of laws, your republic that is *fair to all*, so *all* may be equal to trade here, and not accept this brave general into its bosom? I tell you, Senators, to the world, to those with whom you would trade, with those who you would call to war, Othello *is* Venice."

There was quiet around the room as the senators fidgeted. Brabantio's eyes burned with hatred for me. I had played his own card against him, the war. The bloody Crusade he had lobbied for, but had not been able to get passed by the council. I had thrown it on him: *Your daughter or your war, Montressor.*

"The fool makes good sense," said the doge to Brabantio.

The Montressor seemed to shrivel, from glaring rage to a beaten man—worn and exhausted. He shuffled to Othello and Desdemona, placed their hands in each other's and held them there. "God be with you. I have another daughter, this one is yours, and to me, is daughter no more."

Tears leapt from Desdemona's eyes and she turned her face into the Moor's shoulder.

The doge came down from the dais, took the newlyweds in his arms. "Venice blesses your marriage and declares Othello a Venetian, subject to and protected by all the laws of the republic." He released them and stepped back. "But we must save the celebration of your wedding, for now, brave Othello, you must quickly take forces to Corsica. We have word the Genoans intend to move on Bastia, our port there, and you must turn them back."

"I will go, Your Grace, but before I do, I would see that Desdemona is cared for in the manner to which she is accustomed."

"She is no longer welcome under my roof," growled Brabantio.

"Then perhaps Your Grace has room in the palace," said Othello.

Desdemona stepped away from the Moor, glared at her father, then addressed the whole chamber. "I would have a say in my future, if you please. I, too, am a Venetian, and I would be at my husband's side. It is true that he won me by tales of his battles, so I would be with him while he does these deeds that drew my affection. I would go to Corsica with him."

"But, beloved," said Othello, "I must leave on a fast galley tonight, a warship, which has no accommodation for a wife, and the need for haste allows no time for you to gather your things."

"I will see her to Corsica," came a voice from the back of the mob. Iago stepped forward.

"There will be new battles, Iago," said Othello. "You will be needed at Arsenal to fit men to ships."

"I will send my own wife to be Desdemona's handmaid, and see her returned to your arms in Corsica. You know her, Desdemona."

Desdemona squeezed Othello's arms. "I've met Emilia. She is of good character and will be good company."

"So be it, then," said the Moor. "Cassio, ready five fast ships. We are for Corsica on the tide." Then the Moor turned to the council. "Signors, I thank you for your faith, and for this lady; I will keep both on my life."

He offered his arm to Desdemona. As she turned to leave she mouthed "Thank you" to me and smiled.

I was left standing in the middle of the hall, hung a bit out to dry, I thought, so by way of exit, I pumped the puppet Jones in the air and marched out. "You ungrateful fucks!" I shouted. "If it weren't for Othello the Genoans would have sacked the city and you'd all be speaking bloody Italian."

"We *are* speaking Italian," said Brabantio.

I reeled to face him. "Can you imagine the pounding farewell shag Othello is giving your daughter even now, Montressor? I'll wager you can hear the moaning all the way to the Rialto Bridge."

In retrospect, given the walling up and whatnot, I might have been imprudently harsh with the Montressor.

So of course, Desdemona was overjoyed at seeing me when Jessica and I arrived at the Citadel. Well, not precisely when I arrived. We came in behind Iago and his friend.

"Your father is dead," said Iago.

"Oh, my lord," said Desdemona, who began to swoon. Othello caught her and held her fast to his chest.

"When?" asked Othello.

"A month ago, a little more perhaps. He died in the wine cellar—his heart—while the lady's sister was away in Florence. The servants did not find him for several weeks."

Desdemona sobbed on Othello's shoulder.

Cassio had been standing at the back of the room, a large chamber full of tables spread with charts and maps, from which Othello ran his command. The captain pushed Jessica and me forward.

"Lady, a sister of mercy has come to give you comfort."

I bowed my head and said, *sotto voce*, "Let us go to a quiet place to pray, child."

Othello nodded and gave Desdemona into Cassio's arms. Cassio embraced us both and guided us out of the room, Desdemona smothering her grief against my nunly bosom, Jessica following close behind. Once we were out of the command room and Cassio had left and closed the door between us and Iago, I threw up my veil and said, "Don't shed too many tears. Your father was a murderous fuck-toad, wasn't he?"

"Pocket?" Her grief turned to confusion.

"A right scurvy wretch, 'e was," said Jessica. "Not fit for shark chum."

"Don't mind her, love, she's just being piratey."

"She?"

"Aye," said Jessica. "I'm a bloody split tail in disguise, ain't I? Wench bits from stem to stern, innit?" She gestured to those spots where her various wench bits lay hidden.

Desdemona nodded slowly, as if she understood, when clearly, grief had made her loopy. "And you are now a purple-and-green nun?"

"Sewed his habit me-self," said Jessica. "Only had the purple and green to work with. Told everyone 'e's in order of St. Crispin, patron saint o' fried snacks."

"We heard you'd gone back to France," said Desdemona.

"Oh, that? That was a rumor started by that dog-fucking scoundrel Iago," said I. "No, lady, thanks to your father, I am quite dead. As will you and the Moor be if you do not heed my warning."

"I didn't know that Iago even liked dogs," said Desdemona, missing the point somewhat.

Fifteen
What Wicked Webs

CHORUS:
Plots in dark Iago's mind,
Like spiders' wicked webs unwind,
In every glance he finds a slight,
A mark for vengeful arrow's flight,
Schemes unveiled by waxing moon,
Reveal the knave a barking loon,
He vows by all that's Hell and night,
To bring this monstrous birth to light.

Once installed in their quarters at a local inn, Iago paced before Rodrigo as the innkeeper, who was quite deaf, swept the stone floor around them.

"Did you see him? Did you see him? Did you see him? Oh, the counting clerk, the arithmetician, the bookish theorist—no soldier is he?"

"Othello?" inquired Rodrigo, who was into the spirit of the rant, but not quite clear on the subject.

"No! No, not Othello—though the spirits know I despise him more—the Florentine Michael Cassio. Did you not see him, his arms wrapped round Desdemona like some tentacled monster?"

"He was giving comfort to the lady. You *had* just told her of her father's death."

"Oh, so says the most rejected suitor. I tell you, Rodrigo, Cassio is a base opportunist, comfort is his doorway, but lust his domicile—even now I'll wager the Florentine makes love's quick pants in Desdemona's arms. He is so disposed, you know? I suspect him of having done manly duty between the sheets with my own wife. Did you not see how she looked at him?"

"Really? Cassio? With Emilia as well? Is that why you're staying here at the inn and not in her quarters?"

"Oh, I do not pine over my faithless wife. Did you not see her let the Florentine bow over her hand like a rutting animal? Of all the ill will I hold for him, none is for his damp deeds with Emilia, for she is a devious prick-pull, like all of her sex. That Cassio took my commission, for this I hate him, but that he took my wife, and now takes Desdemona, for this weakness I am grateful, for we shall use it to our own ends and his undoing."

"How so?" asked Rodrigo. "Did you not see Desdemona treat me like a stranger today, even before she knew of her father's death? And after so much of my treasure that you have given to her to show my affection. Now Cassio stands in my way as well as the Moor?"

"Don't whinge, Rodrigo. Desdemona will never shag you if you whinge."

"Sorry. But all the treasure, and she knows me—I *had* called upon her at her father's house upon several occasions."

"*Several* was it? *Several* before you began bonking her maid?"

"Well, yes, but Nerissa has exquisite bosoms and . . . You're right, Iago, women are devious tricksters. Am I whingeing again?"

"Never fear, good Rodrigo. Desdemona is young and spirited, she'll tire soon enough of Othello, and the handsome Cassio shall be the bar we use to pry her from the arms of the Moor."

"How will that help? She runs from Othello to Cassio, and I am still out in the cold with no Desdemona and no money."

"Why, then we simply remove Cassio, and the lady, her marriage broken, shunned and ashamed, shall find comfort in your arms. The Moor, aggrieved from the betrayal of his slag of a wife, will need a second in command and I will have the position that was rightfully mine before the Florentine stole it."

"I'm not clear on what you mean by *remove* Cassio?"

"We will discredit him. Stage an incident where he shames himself, a fight. I know that having spent a little time in the field and at sea with him, he does not well hold his drink. I will persuade him to drink with me, as a brother-in-arms, in celebration of the recent victory over the Genoans and of Othello's marriage, then it will take little to push him into unwise action. Go now, find Cassio, but don't let him see you. Follow him. Find his nightly habits, and therein look for the trap that we will set."

"Find him? Where do I find him?"

"He is posted at the docks. Othello always has a senior officer at the docks to keep sailors and ships ready to launch at an instant. Remember the building from where he emerged to greet us? Find him there, and when his watch is ended, follow him."

Rodrigo stood, buckled his swash, and prepared to leave. Paused. "Some money for dinner, perhaps?"

"You have none?"

"I've given all to you for Desdemona."

"Very well," said Iago, flipping him a silver coin. "And, Rodrigo?"

"Yes?" said Rodrigo, tucking the coin in his belt.

"She shall be yours. *Adieu.*"

"*Adieu,*" said Rodrigo with a smile as he left.

Iago turned to the old innkeeper, who now busied himself stirring the contents of a great black kettle hung over the fire.

"Thus have I made the fool my purse—for without fortune, would I spend time with such a sniveling snipe? I think not! Of all of Rodrigo's fortune from his lands and his contracts called in, Desdemona has seen not a penny, but my own fortunes have been well-padded, for a time when I shall need finery that well fits my position: commanding general of Venice.

"Oh, the Moor will be undone, but my ascent to command is not assured with Cassio in my way. Rodrigo will clear him from my path by shaming him with a drunken brawl, thus will his downfall begin, and soon the Moor will follow him, dragged down by his darling Desdemona. Although Rodrigo is a dolt, he is a fair swordsman, and Cassio is of a steady nature and will not join a fight unless drunk, and therefore diminished. No, before the fight I will give Rodrigo some of the tarry potion that Brabantio used on the English fool—just enough to make him slow and dreamy, and if Cassio kills him, well, he will have served his purpose.

"The plan is engendered! My hatred takes life."

CHORUS: *And so did Iago yammer madly on into the night, oblivious to the innkeeper's deafness and complete lack of interest.*

"I need a ship," I said to Othello. We stood atop the fortress overlooking the harbor, I the vision of the perfect windblown sister of St. Crispin in my nun suit, he in the flowing white robes of his homeland, the waves of white fabric flowing off him as if he'd caught a catapult loaded with fresh laundry full in the face.

"You can't have a ship," said the Moor.

From the wall of the Citadel we could see Othello's galleys, out past the breakwater, practicing attacks on a large raft they had towed into the sea. Each of the smaller, faster galleys had a catapult on a *rambata,* a firing platform at the bow. Each ship would row in at top speed, a great drum beating rhythm for the oarsmen, then just as it came into range, fire would be applied to the missile, often a tightly woven ball of willow, saturated in oil and pitch, and the catapult would fire. The oarsmen on either side would stand and lean on their oars to bring the ship around, then a line of archers along the length of the ship would let loose a volley of arrows at the target while the ship ran back

and reloaded the catapult. One after another, like dancers in some great marine waltz, they charged, fired,
turned, and retreated just at the edge of the catapult's
range. In battle, the archers would duck beneath shields
until the missile had exploded on the deck, scattering
the enemy crew, then they would stand and skewer any
man who rose from cover to fight the fire or shoot back.
This was the tactic that had allowed Othello to turn
forces larger than his own. When most naval battle was
simply lashing your ship to another and hacking away
at each other until you were the only one left standing on a blood-soaked deck, Othello had perfected the
thrust and feint, nearly destroying an enemy's ship and
putting its men in the water before ever getting close
enough for melee combat. Today they were coming in
by oar *and* sail, then dropping the sail as they made the
turn.

"Like poking a bear with a stick and running, really,
innit?" said I.

"When I was a pirate, we used less fire," said the
Moor. "The catapults were loaded with stones. To save
the cargo."

"What do you do when there's a whole flock of
ships?"

"Fleet, not flock."

"What then? Some give chase, I reckon . . ."

"I have four tall merchantmen, like you came here in, only fitted for war. We tow them just out of range. They are too tall to easily board and too slow to attack, but the wide decks hold many archers and many catapults. If the enemy ships pursue, death is rained down upon them from above. If they attack the merchantmen, our galleys return to defend them."

"So your secret is that you practice?"

"We practice and I feed my men well. A man rows harder when he is fed and when he is paid. There are no slaves in my ships."

"I was a slave," said I.

"As was I," said Othello. "Chained to an oar for three years, was I, until my ship was sunk by pirates and I floated away, saved by the broken oar that I had been shackled to."

"Not so much rowing for me. Greasy fuckload of juggling and jesting, but very few nautical bits."

"I don't think you would do well at sea, friend Pocket. Men on a ship, unable to escape your chatter, might try to kill you. Have you heard of keel hauling?"

"Ha! I've been to sea and survived. And I was quiet the whole time, but for some retching and a wee bit of complaining."

"Why do you need a ship?"

"You remember my monkey, Jeff?"

"A horrible creature—"

"He needs rescuing. From Genoa. As does my enormous apprentice, but I thought Jeff would evoke more sympathy."

"And what of your puppet? Does your puppet not need rescuing as well?"

"Jones? You know he's not real, right? I give him voice. He's not a living creature, you know?"

"Yes, this I know," said the Moor, dazzling a grin at me that veritably shimmered with self-congratulation. "I was making a joke."

"Excellent point. I'll need a ship and a pilot and a crew."

"How did I make that point?"

"With your joke, I have seen my folly in thinking that I, an unskilled sailor, could take a ship to Genoa without help."

"It was a good joke," said the Moor.

"When it comes to crafting jape, thou art a soldier indeed."

"You think because I am a soldier and you are a joker that you can make sport of me, but I am a strategist, too, Pocket of Dog Snogging, and I know when someone feints, then tries to outflank me."

"If not for me you'd not have your Desdemona."

"If not for me you'd be drowned," said the Moor.

"That's not a fair trade. I am but a wisp of a fool, a used and broken one at that, with no reason to live but revenge. Desdemona is worth a hundred of me."

"She is my soul's joy," said the Moor.

"A thousand of me."

"You shall have your ship."

"And crew and pilot?"

"Yes, yes, but you cannot just sail into the harbor at Genoa. We are at war with them. The ship will have to put you into a longboat down the coast, out of sight, and you can row in. Do you even know where they are?"

"Yes. Well, somewhat. The Genoans are holding them for ransom. In prison, I reckon."

"With a fair wind it will take four days to sail there, half a day for you to row in. The ship will wait two days for you, then they will leave and you will have to make your own way. I cannot come rescue you, Pocket. The harbor at Genoa is the most fortified in the world."

"I'll be back in little more than a week." I slapped the Moor's shoulder by way of thanks; he scowled at me. Really, I preferred the grin, despite the dreadful joke that preceded it.

"What of the girl?" asked the Moor.

"She's waiting for her fiancé."

"Who is dead, you said."

I had told Othello of Lorenzo's demise, although I said he'd died by my blade in a fight, not that he'd been done in by Vivian. It was quite enough to run through the whole story, from my walling-up to Antonio and Iago's plot to take Brabantio's seat on the council so they could start a bloody Crusade for profit without adding the complication of a bloody mermaid having me off in the dungeon and murdering Jessica's betrothed.

"She doesn't know that. I'll take her with me to keep her distracted."

"You are going to have to tell her."

"I thought I'd just share in her dismay when he didn't show up."

"Take her, but tell her."

"She's forsaken her father and her home, now to find out that I killed her lover, even if he was an appallingly devious bastard, it would be cruel. I am all she has."

"You must be cruel to be kind.* You are all she has."

"That's a flaming flagon of dragon wank, if I've ever heard one. She'll be fine, waiting. When you're waiting the world is full of promise."

"Tell her, or no ship."

"I'll tell her, after we've rescued Drool. I may need her gold to pay ransom."

---

*Hamlet, Act III, Scene 4: "I must be cruel only to be kind."

"Promise you will tell her. Color it how you may, Pocket, but tell her."

"I will promise to tell her if you promise to throw Iago in chains."

"I will be cautious of Iago, but he has fought by my side in many battles and been true; I must see evidence of his betrayal before I take action."

"He killed my Cordelia, recruited the spy that poisoned her."

"So you say."

"So said Brabantio. Iago is a traitor, you night-browed ninny. You cannot trust him."

"I will keep my back to the wall in his presence and I will look for proof of what you say, but Iago is as clever as you in the way of words, subtle fool, and if I confront him on only your word, he will evade me and I will appear a tyrant. This force is mine to lead because I am steady, not rash."

"So I *don't* have to tell Jessica that Lorenzo is dead."

"You do," said Othello. "Do you know the names and routes of the ships that Antonio has at sea, the ones he used to guarantee his bond to Jessica's father?"

I pulled the parchment that Shylock had written out for me from my nun's habit and gave it to the Moor. "They are here, and a schedule of when they are expected to return to Venice. But these do not guarantee the bond. For that Antonio promised a pound of his flesh."

"Surely that was meant as a jest."

"That *is* part of the job, but no."

"Why are you still in nun's clothing? Without your motley and puppet stick, I forget that you are a deeply silly man. It's unsettling."

"I'd make a fit nun, wouldn't I? That's the problem, innit? You fancy me in this nun suit, don't you, you bloody great stallion?"

"You need to shave," said the Moor.

"But then, eh?" I winked, tarty teasing nun that I was.

"You are silly and you make a homely nun! I will go arrange for your ship. Watch the exercises; maybe you will learn something, thou irritant fool."

So I did watch, watched the great aquamarine slate of the Ligurian Sea laid out before me to the horizon, scored with the wake and churn of a dozen ships, but it was not the smoke and warships that drew my eye, it was that shadow just under the surface by the breakwater, waiting for me to return to the sea.

"Oh dear, Nerissa," said Portia. "I am so distressed, I've scarcely had time to think about shoes."

"And shoes surely wither with your neglect, lady, but the Duke of Aragon awaits. Shall we make our entrance?"

"I don't look too beautiful, do I?" Portia primped as if Nerissa were a looking glass and she would know when everything looked just right by the look on her maid's face.

Nerissa smirked. *Three thousand ducats just to have a go? You're a country villa and a lifetime of blow jobs short of being too beautiful, love,* Nerissa thought. But she said, "You are perfect."

They made their way down the stairs, Portia gliding ahead, Nerissa bouncing behind, as was their habit, to find the Duke of Aragon, a dazzlingly handsome young man with a waxed mustache and coal-blackened eyelids, waiting with a pair of manservants in the foyer.

The lawyers made their statements and Aragon bowed grandly over Portia's hand.

"Nerissa, please show the duke to the caskets."

As she passed, Nerissa whispered, "Fear not, lady, he may choose the same casket as did Morocco. The odds do not favor him as much as you suppose." If the duke did pick the casket with Portia's portrait, Nerissa might gain security by remaining at her lady's side and perhaps even relieve her of some of her wifely obligations. Aragon was no stingy republic or Islamic caliphate dripping with competitive wives; Aragon was a proper feudal kingdom, with an aristocracy, and an enterprising wench possessed of a royal bastard might find leisure there for life.

The lawyer unlocked the terrace door and bowed out of the way.

The duke walked slowly around the table, reading each of the inscriptions, squinting at the caskets' exteriors as if some of the promise within might be leaking from the seams. Finally, after several revolutions, when the lawyers had begun to cough, politely, the duke paused in front of the silver casket.

"'*Who chooseth me shall get as much as he deserves,*'" read the duke. "I would have the key to this one."

The lawyer came forth and handed Aragon the key.

The duke opened the box and stood aghast. "What is this? This is shit!"

"There will be a rhyme to explain it," said Nerissa.

"No, it is real shit," said the duke.

"But look, tis glitter sprinkled upon it," said Portia.

"Perhaps this means you have won your prize," said Nerissa, unable to help herself. "A symbol. The Montressor was ever so fond of symbols."

Portia growled, slightly, even as she grinned at the duke's misfortune.

The lawyers tittered and thought this might be just the sort of thing old Brabantio might do to a noble from whom he had just swindled three thousand ducats.

"It's a turd. Three thousand ducats, for a turd?" The duke was waving wildly at the offending object, and in doing so bent one side of his splendid mustache. "Three thousand—"

"You gave your word," said Portia. "Please do go, good sir, and make suit no more."

Humbled by his oath, the duke turned on a heel, tossed back his cape, and strode out without another word.

"Aren't you going to chase after him?" Portia said to Nerissa. "Flaunt your bosoms at him?"

"I would, but I'm curious about the rhyme your father left for this one."

Portia peered into the casket with its odiferous brown passenger, but saw no parchment like Morocco had found in the gold casket. She looked to the lawyers, who shrugged.

"There's no poem."

"Nothing rhymes with silver, does it?" said Nerissa.

Sixteen
A Nasty Piece of Work

"I am not so sure of this, Iago," said Rodrigo. "Cassio seems lovely."

"He is not lovely. When he drinks he is a devil, as you shall soon see. I despise him, I loathe him, I dislike him in the extreme. My hate for him is to hate as is hate to love. He is a pestilent and complete knave. You may not say he is lovely."

"I didn't mean lovely, but he seems a gentleman."

"A gentleman who will shag your Desdemona cross-eyed. What chance will a gangling hedgehog like you have with her once she's been with a handsome rascal like him? Now drink your wine to fortify you for the fight."

"But it tastes of pitch."

"Drink it. It will warm you against the night until I bring Cassio to you."

"Which will be where?"

"At the foot of the Citadel's walls, in the narrow alley there, you will see a lantern with a red lens in the window, the house of the courtesan Bianca. Wait in the dark, three doors from there. After he is well drunk, which will be a short time, I will put the notion in Cassio's head that Bianca has sent for him, and the rogue will stumble that way in search of her charms. I will follow behind, out of sight. Have your sword at the ready, but make a fight of it. Once you have engaged him, I will cry havoc and bring down the watch to witness Cassio's knavery and attest that he attacked you unprovoked."

"So I am to slay him?"

"If it happens, it happens, all the happier for us, but you must make a fight of it. Suffer a light wound before you deliver the killing thrust."

"A light wound?"

"Or if you fail, as your friend, I will wound you for appearances."

Rodrigo started to speak, then paused as the old innkeeper tottered by them with an armload of wood for the fireplace.

"Speak your mind," said Iago. "He's deaf."

"I think it best not to trust that he is as deaf as he appears."

"Ah, good thought. His gait is feeble, but there's a randy mischief in his gaze. I suspect him of doing the dark deed with my wife in my absence."

"Really? The innkeeper, too? Friend Iago, pardon if I speak out of turn, but you should have words with her."

"Later. Now you must find your place near Bianca's house. I have seen Cassio drink before, and after but one cup he will be wobbly and mad for a night's slippery adventure. Go, be there, and I will go to the officers' post at the harbor with a fresh jug of wine."

"I go," said Rodrigo, making for the door, hand on the hilt of his sword. He turned and took two steps back, as if drifting with his momentum. "I am heady for the fight, Iago. I move as if in a dream."

"Go!"

"I go!"

He went.

Iago was quickly up the stairs to hide the tiny, red-lacquered box taken from Brabantio's body that held the last of the tarry potion. Only a small bit remained, less even than they had put in the fool's amontillado, but he would save it. Use it on the Moor, perhaps, or better yet, Desdemona. It would be wasted on Cassio—for it was the one true thing he had ever told Rodrigo—Cassio would be nearly helpless after a cup or two of wine.

He polished the box on his sleeve, and the black serpent set in the red lacquer shone green-eyed under the lantern. A curious Oriental thing. He kept it tucked beneath a pair of gloves in his trunk. A most curious thing.

CHORUS: *Under a waxing crescent moon did two dark creatures lurk by the harbor's edge, one walked into the warm lamplight of the officers' station under the guise of friendship and good cheer, the other lay like an inky shadow among rocks at the shore, watching.*

Iago put the jug down upon the table where Cassio was seated, quill in hand, over a ledger.

"Come, Captain, fetch cups, I have a stout jug of wine and we have not celebrated our victory by storm over the Genoans and the health of gallant Othello and his new wife."

"Oh, not tonight, good Iago," said Cassio. "I have poor and unhappy brains for drinking. I wish courtesy would invent some other custom of entertainment."

"But they are our friends, for which we must celebrate life, and our enemies, whose deaths save our friends from peril. To life, one cup?"

"I have had one cup tonight already with supper and the figures dance on the page like scattering ants."

"One cup! One cup and I will tell you good news, a message, just for you, that will smooth the lines from your brow and draw them as smiles at the edges of your eyes. One cup, for a surprise."

"Fine, then, there are cups on the mantel. One cup."

Iago retrieved the cups, tall, heavy cylinders of green Murano glass, then plunked them on the table and splashed in the wine, staining the corner of Cassio's ledger as well. "Now drink with me. To Venice! To Othello! To Desdemona! Happiness to their sheets!"

"What?"

"Just fucking drink."

They drank, emptying their cups, Iago watching the captain over the edge of his cup, while Cassio winced as he drank and shivered when his cup returned to the table with a thump.

"Now tell me the good news," said Cassio.

"One more!"

"No, one more and I shall lose my wits, Iago. I tell you, I have no head for it."

"But when I tell you, you'll be glad of it. I promise."

Cassio squinted at Iago as if trying to spy the truth through the haze rising around him, and was suddenly taken with the purple color the wine made on his ledger when it mixed with the ink. "Balls," he said. Then, slamming the cover on the great leather book he said, "Fine, one more. Pour, good Iago!"

Iago poured.

Cassio stood and with a great flourish and no little spillage raised his cup in a toast. "To Othello, to Desdemona, to Venice, to Iago, to tits!—you've got to drink to tits, if you're drinking to happy things—to—"

"To Venice!" said Iago.

"Venice? What about tits?"

"Just fucking drink!"

"Right."

They drank, and the glasses came down on the table like twin gavels.

"One more!" declared Cassio.

"But your surprise. I must give you your message."

"God's blood, Iago, are you going to talk or are you going to drink? Pour!" Cassio held his cup out like a demanding beggar.

"Bianca, the courtesan, sent me to fetch you. She wants to see you tonight. Now."

"Oh. Bianca." Cassio pulled his cup to his chest. "She visits me here sometimes—flirty little tart. I think she fancies me. She's right fit."

"Aye. Beautiful."

"All right, then. Let's go! Onward! Come on, Iago. To the fair Bianca's." Cassio stormed out the open door.

As he went, his sheathed sword caught the doorjamb, spinning him around three times before he recovered, more or less looking out to sea.

"You really are a most outrageously pitiful drunk," said Iago, leaning in the doorway now.

Cassio paced his way back to Iago in great exaggerated steps, stopping just short of touching noses. "You are!"

"Bianca," reminded Iago.

"Right. Bianca. Ahhhhh!" The captain charged off into the dark.

"Cassio!"

"What?" Cassio stopped, turned. "What do you want, villain!"

"Do you know where you are going?"

"No fucking idea."

"Along the harbor, at the third lane, go right, then go to the end, all the way to the wall of the Citadel. You'll see the red light in her window."

"Right. Three lanes. Right."

"If you take a left, you'll fall into the harbor and drown."

"I will not, I am an excellent swimmer. You scoundrel!"

"Just the same, go right. She's expecting you."

"Aren't you coming?"

"I have other duties to attend to."

"Oh, right. Your wife. Emilia. There's a tasty bit of talent, there, innit?"

"Go!" Iago turned away, willing himself to not murder the Florentine. "I'll watch you from here to make sure you make the right turn."

"You are the best comrade a soldier could have, good Iago. *Adieu!*"

Cassio stumbled down the edge of the harbor. Iago waited for him to turn up the third lane, then followed, quickly, staying close to the buildings, in the shadows. The narrow lane wound up the hill to lessen the steep climb, but nevertheless the three-story stone-and-stucco houses had been built so tightly together on either side that except for a stripe of blue moonlit sky, walking it was like traversing a cave. Several blocks toward the Citadel, it became so dark that he lost sight of Cassio, but could hear him bumping into walls and swearing before carrying on. Rounding one severe bend, the lane opened and Iago could see the high Citadel walls looming above, and at the end, the red light, marking the courtesan's house. Silhouetted in the red light was a very tall, thin figure of a man having a wee in the street, turning as Cassio trudged toward him.

"I am surrounded by gormless gits," Iago whispered to himself. "Were I their general, would I be one of them, too? Do I want to be what I want to be?"

He heard something move behind him, but could see nothing there in the dark. Perhaps a cat. Then he heard movement above him, but there was no balcony. Another cat, on the roof. The smell of the sea was stronger here than even at the harbor, and he wondered if one of the fishermen might not have hung his nets from the window above and a cat was climbing there. The sound of ringing steel brought his attention to the fore: Rodrigo drawing his sword.

"Defend yourself, thou scurvy patch," said Rodrigo as he advanced on the stumbling Cassio.

"What?" said Cassio.

"*En garde!*" cried Rodrigo, raising his sword.

Cassio made as if to draw his sword, then stumbled back and fell out of the light with a crash. "I shall shout something French back at you presently. Hold there!"

Rodrigo advanced. *No, it has to be a fight,* thought Iago. *The watch has to find Cassio shamefully drunk.* Iago stepped out of the shadows, drew his sword, and was about to shout the alarm when the thought snapped in his head, *SPARE THIS ONE.* A foul and foreign thought, like the flash of a fever dream, *NOT THIS ONE.* A lightning white-blue image of Michael Cassio fired across his mind's eye, giving him an immediate, nearly blinding headache.

"Awake! Awake!" Iago cried. "Thieves! Mayhem! Murder most foul."

"Where?" said Cassio, trying to draw his sword but instead the blade stayed put and the soldier spun with the effort and fell again.

"Awake!" said Iago. "Murder! Alert the watch!"

Rodrigo advanced on the supine Cassio.

Then it came down from the rafters as if the shadows themselves had gone liquid—a black blur passed behind Rodrigo, flipping his legs out from under him. He fell, screaming, curled and clutching at the ragged wound where his calf muscle used to be.

Iago stopped, dropped the tip of his sword, the call for alarm caught in his throat. Rodrigo's scream rattled, broke, but went on piteously.

That darkness thrust again and the screaming stopped. Rodrigo's headless body sat up on the cobbles for a second, twin fountains of blood arcing from his neck, glistening black in the dim red light. The shadow moved again, puddled around the twitching lump of meat that had been Rodrigo, and Iago saw the eyes, green, like emeralds catching moonlight, swaying, then fixing on him.

A latch clicked to his right, a door opened, and an old man holding a candle appeared. "What's this?"

Iago dove through the open door, knocking the old man back as he did. He slammed the heavy door and threw the bolt, bracing his back against it just as something hit the other side with such force that he was knocked forward onto the old man, his sword rattling off into the dark. The bolt held, but something worried at the door with frenzied rasping blades on the oak, like a thousand rats trying to claw their way out of a burning barrel, the sound so terrifying Iago that he lay there for seconds atop the old man, paralyzed, until he realized that he was looking at the door by the light of his burning sleeve, set aflame by the old man's candle.

"No, defend *yourself*," came Cassio's voice from beyond the fury. "I will teach *you* a lesson in manners, you knave! As soon as I have cleared my sword of this sodding scabbard, I will. Don't just lie there, you rascal, stand up and fight! Pretending you don't have a head won't help you. Fight, I say!"

"I was not a very good child," said Bassanio to his friend Gratiano, who sat opposite him in the gondola on the way to Belmont. "When I say I was not a good child, I do not mean that I was not well-behaved, nor of good nature, but that I was not good at *being* a child. I did not care for childish things, and I was never the right size. In my clothes, I was often too large, in games too small—I was often the wrong speed, as well."

"Slow?" inquired Gratiano, turning his head so the garish feather in his hat would not be bent by the breeze.

"And sometimes too fast. And just when I began to master childhood, suddenly I was a youth, at which I was also undistinguished except for the growing of hair. As a man, I have been a disappointing son, a miserable merchant, a delinquent debtor, and a general disappointment to my friends and family."

"That is not true," said Gratiano. "We have very low expectations."

"Still, on this day, in this boat, with this chest of borrowed gold, I am certain of one thing, as if I have only just broken the seal on certainty itself: I shall be an excellent husband to Portia! And in so being, an excellent friend, in that I will cancel Antonio's debt before even one of his ships returns and repay all my back debts to the rest of you. I shall henceforth be an excellent trader, shrewd with experience forged from my myriad losses, and in my demeanor and wisdom, an excellent man overall, redeemed by the love of fair Portia."

"If you choose the right casket."

"It is all but assured, good Gratiano. For the message from Salanio brought me by the gondolier assures it."

"If, indeed, the gondolier was sent by Salanio, unsteady as he has been, buggering off to Cyprus with Lorenzo without notice."

"Oh, the message came from him most assuredly, for the gondolier had Salanio's jeweled dagger, given him to assure delivery of the message and affirm its authenticity."

"That dagger has no brothers, there is only one like it."

"You see," said Bassanio. "Here is the dock." To the men who guarded the dock at Belmont, he called, "You there, send servants to help us. We bear a chest of gold too heavy to carry without ungentlemanly grunting and sweating."

"Oh, for fuck's sake," said Gratiano under his breath.

When the lawyers had confirmed the amount of the gold, it was taken away and Bassanio and Gratiano were led to the foyer.

Portia made her traditionally grand entrance down the stairs, followed by Nerissa, but this time, rather than standing off and waiting for praise, when Bassanio bowed, Portia rushed forward and curtsied before him with great enthusiasm, lifting her skirts to show her newest and most fabulous shoes, the soles of which were as smooth and unscarred as Portia herself, and which slid on the marble floor as if on ice, depositing the lady in a position of the "full splits," from which she was not immediately able to rise.

"Oh, Bassanio," said she.

"Dear Portia," said he.

"The day, the time, the moment is upon us, and I have wished nothing but that you be here, with me."

"And I with you. Please rise, lady."

She did not rise.

Nerissa, still standing on the bottom step, looked over the head of the lovers to Gratiano, who she had not remembered as being quite so handsome. He smiled and returned her eye roll.

"I would have you know," said Portia, "if I were not bound by the legacy of my father, all that is mine would be yours, as would I, but these naughty times put bars between owners and their rights, for surely, without cruel lottery, my heart is yours already."

"And mine yours, sweet Portia. Arise!"

Nerissa now giggled, and covered her mouth coyly as she exchanged glances with Gratiano, his eyes following the twin moons of her rising décolletage, her gaze tracing the grand arch of the feather in his hat and falling to the hilt of the bejeweled dagger he wore in his belt. The game was afoot.

"I would have you tarry, extend the time we have together, a week, a month, even two," said Portia. "For once you have made your choice, should you not choose right, then bound by your agreement, we shall never speak again."

"Then let me choose, lady, for I wait as if stretched upon the rack."

"Very well, the gentlemen will show you to the caskets." Portia gestured for the lawyers to lead Bassanio to the terrace.

"You are coming, lady?"

"I'll be along. You go ahead."

The lawyers unlocked the door and led the two young merchants to the terrace.

Nerissa stood over her mistress, trying not to laugh. "You're stuck, aren't you?"

"These Florentine shoes are shit," said Portia.

"Are you not wearing any knickers?"

"Of course I'm wearing knickers. Do you think me wanton? I'm stuck because I haven't the strength to lift myself out of this position—now help me."

Nerissa looped her arms under her mistress's arms and pulled her to her feet, so they stood there in a rather awkward embrace.

"Even through silk, the marble *is* cold on one's ladybits, though," said Portia.

"Warmed soon by a handsome merchant husband," said Nerissa with a note of hope that was not altogether false. If she could charm Bassanio's tall friend, perhaps Portia wouldn't dismiss her out of jealousy after all.

"Oh, Bassanio is so handsome."

"As is his friend."

"Do you fancy him?"

"Do you jest? I was lucky not to be sliding on the slippery floor next to you."

"That is *not* why I slipped."

"Let us go join him, lady. There's rumor that he was given the secret to the casket that holds your portrait. You may be a bride by evening."

They glided to the terrace, hand in hand, like dancers, and were met by the smiles of the men, except for the lawyers, who never smiled unless actively fucking someone, as was the credo of their trade. Bassanio already held a black key in the air and stood before the lead casket.

"You've chosen already?" said Portia, surprised, yet pleased, yet anxious.

"Oh, lady, the world is deceived by fair ornament, by gaudy gold, hard food for Midas, or silver's pale shine, that common drudge that is passed 'tween man and man, when the weight of beauty is what must be measured. I choose base lead."

"Did he just call you fat?" whispered Nerissa.

"I think I'm going to be sick," said Portia.

Bassanio unlocked the casket and looked in, the lid obscuring the contents to all others except Gratiano, who stood beside him.

"What find I here?" Confusion.

"The picture is flawed," said Portia. "The artist had been drinking, I'm sure of it. I told Father we should do another—"

"A fool's head," said Bassanio. "A puppet." He lifted it from the chest with both hands, holding it as delicately as if he were cradling a baby bird.

"Look, there's a scroll," said Gratiano, who plucked it from the casket and read aloud.

"'The lesson of this cask of lead.
Taught by greed of a father dead.
Turns a lover into merchant's tool.
Who plays for love, but is made a fool.'"

"Oh, well played, fool," whispered Nerissa. "Well played, indeed." She left Portia to weep and followed them out to their gondola to make sure Gratiano knew that he, in particular, was not forbidden from returning to Belmont.

"Lady, I forgot to give you this," said I, handing Desdemona the tiny portrait of her sister, which had been painted on a marble amulet. We stood at the dock, ready to board our ship to Genoa, a small merchantman fitted for only eight oars, and a crew of twelve. It was the fastest, lightest vessel that Othello would trust to the journey.

"Oh, how kind," said Desdemona. "I shall treasure it. I do miss my sister. She must be terribly sad with Father's passing."

"Despite his being a wicked old scalawag, eh?" said Jessica. The Jewess had somewhere procured a pair of high leather boots, turned down on the thighs, and a wide belt with a brass buckle.

"Stop being piratey," said I.

"Arrrrrr," she arrrrrred.

"Fathers and daughters do often love with barbed embrace," said Desdemona. "The love is true, if sometimes untender."

Jessica swallowed hard. "That is well true, lady. Apologies."

"It's nothing," said Desdemona, patting Jessica's hand. "And we have a gift for you, Pocket." Desdemona stepped aside and Emilia came forward with a cloth bundle, tied with string. I dropped it to the dock and released the bow. Inside lay a black silk jester's hat with silver bells, and below it a doublet and tights of black satin and velvet argyle. It had been some time since I'd seen the *all*-black motley.

"It is as you were when you arrived in Venice," said Othello. "The *black fool* you said they had called you before you came to us. We had it made. Wearing your motley again should be enough to remind everyone of your incurable silliness."

"Well, I'll need a cracking big codpiece to be true to form."

"We've forgotten that, but a pair of soft boots with curled toes and bells are being made as well; they will be ready by your return. I am sorry, a puppet maker we were not able to find on the island."

"The puppet Jones yet perseveres, kind Othello. And I suppose I could have one of your codpieces enlarged. At any rate, my thanks, to you and most delicious Desdemona." I bowed over her hand. "I left another gift at the Citadel for you, lady. Emilia will fetch it for you from our quarters, I hope."

"And I will have a pretty dress for you when you return, Jessica," said Desdemona.

"Oh, lady, that is most generous. I would not have my Lorenzo see me thus transformed into a boy."

"Take comfort, love is blind, and lovers cannot see the pretty follies that they themselves commit. Your Lorenzo would be proud to see you so coifed in courage, coming to the rescue of a friend."

"Thank you." Jessica embraced Desdemona in a manner most unlike a pirate.

"Safe journey, black fool," said Othello. "My most skilled navigator will command your ship as pilot." The Moor gestured to an officer I hadn't met, tall, with a ginger beard, who clicked his heels. "Lieutenant Montano."

"But where is Cassio?" I inquired.

"Sad tidings," said Desdemona, looking at her shoes.

"Cassio is in the brig," said Othello. "Still drunk from last evening, where alarm was raised for a drunken brawl and Cassio was found standing over the body of Iago's second, Rodrigo, who had been beheaded and mutilated."

"Cassio a murderer?" I asked.

"I think not. His sword was clean and this killing was not the doing of a blade, but he is still too drunk to tell the tale and there is no doubt he was a part of the mayhem."

"Beheaded? Mutilated? This was by the harbor then?"

"No, just beneath the south wall of the Citadel."

I did not care to hear more. Of what had happened to Rodrigo, I had little doubt, until I learned it was not near the water. Had my mermaid grown legs? I shuddered at the thought.

"I'm sure, when he sobers up, you'll find him not guilty and as dull as dirt. We must be off. Come, Jessica. *Adieu*, my friends."

I scampered up the ramp and Jessica joined me at the rail as the pilot boarded and called to cast off.

"Why all the gifts and good wishes?" Jessica asked.

"Because they don't think we are coming back, love."

"Blast," said the dread pirate Jess.

"Stay back from the edge for a bit, would you, matey?" I watched the water for the deadly shade.

Seventeen
A Fool's Ransom

"Genoa," said Montano, pointing to an orange point of light in the distant dark that for all I could see might have been a sinking star or a bloody dolphin carrying a candle. "We can't take the ship any closer. There's a lighthouse on a point at the mouth of the breakwater. Steer for that light. Just beyond her is the harbor. Don't take your boat into the harbor if you can't stay with it, though."

"Aye," said Jessica. "Lest a scurvy bilge rat plunders it and takes the bounty in grub and grog, eh, me hardies? Arrrr."

"You know that's utter nonsense," said I. She'd been at it for the entire four days' voyage to Genoa.

"It is not. It's piratey," she said.

"We don't really talk like that," said one of the sailors, who was helping us get our gear into the rowboat.

"You're just common Jack Tars, ain't ya," said Jessica. "Not proper pirates."

"We were pirates under Othello, before we joined the Venetian Navy," said the other. "Same job, different flags."

"The lad's learning new languages," said I. Actually, I preferred her pirate nattering to the hope-filled fairy tales of her never-would-be life with Lorenzo. "Go ahead, say something in Hebrew, Jess."

"*Shabbat shalom*, ye scalawag salts."

"Look behind you, Pocket," said Montano, before I climbed down into the boat. "See those three bright stars? Memorize 'em. You leave from the lighthouse at dusk, two nights from now, we'll be right here. Steer for them stars, keep the lighthouse at your back. There's a lantern and flint and steel in the boat. Light a lantern once that lighthouse looks the same size it is now. We'll find you."

"What if it's foggy?"

"Well, you're right fucked then, aren't you? We'll come around again two nights after that. Go now, it'll be dawn by the time you get there."

"It's a good six hours before sunrise," said Jess.

"Aye, get to them oars, lad," said one of the sailors.

I climbed down into the boat and after they handed in the last of our gear, including the heavy leather bag that we'd transferred Shylock's treasure into, we pushed off. Jessica and I sat hip to hip on the seat, each with an oar, and we pulled and complained until our hands were blistered and our voices raw, then pulled and complained some more, yet I did not breathe easy until the rowboat was beached beneath the lighthouse and we stood on the narrow path atop the breakwater, watching the sun rise over the hills above Genoa.

I had not seen the mermaid's swift shadow for the entire journey, but I could feel her presence like the raising of the hairs on your arms before a lightning storm. Why Rodrigo? Why not Cassio, who was clearly there when the slaughter took place, although he couldn't remember anything but his shame? And if Viv could move out of the water, something I'd little suspected since I'd accused Jessica of being a mermaid changeling, why not tear into the city like a starving orphan into an unguarded larder? I'd assumed that Brabantio, found mutilated in his cellar, had tottered down another passage like the one he'd walled me up in, to the water, where'd she'd struck, but now I wondered if she might not have come in the front door.

"That there is the prison," I said, pointing to a cracking huge stone fortress that squatted over the harbor. Othello had shown me where it would be on one of the charts, but there would have been no missing it.

"A bit grand for a prison, don't you think?" said Jessica.

"Was a royal's palace before, no doubt," said I. "That's how it goes. Bit of a revolution, royalty gets imprisoned in the castle, next lot of royals comes along, doesn't want to live in a sodding prison, builds a grander castle down the way, the old one's turned into a prison, and so it goes."

So it had gone with the White Tower, where I'd first been made the royal fool to Lear, and later the royal consort and kind-of-a-king to Cordelia. Genoa was no London, though. She was a seafaring town like Venice, if Venice had been built up the side of a hill instead of in a bloody swamp. The masts of the ships in the harbor were as thick as bristles on a boar's back. And as Othello had said, the harbor was fortified: catapults and ballistas at the mouth of the harbor, arrow loops in the lighthouse tower, and a fortified battlement just below the lights; a massive winch that could raise a chain with links as big around as my leg across the harbor entrance that no wooden ship would be able to break. No, the prison had not been a palace, it had been a fortress, and could be pressed into defending the harbor at the sound of a trumpet. For all I knew, they had trebuchets that could be raised on the roof that could hit any ship trying to reach the harbor mouth. At the opposite side of the harbor lay a shipyard every bit as large as Arsenal in Venice; even at dawn, the hammer blows were rattling across the water in a furious tattoo, and a dozen war galleys were growing into tall wooden frames from which they would slide onto the seas. So this was the other side of the war for the seas that Venice had been fighting for fifty years?

"Othello defeated this lot?" said Jessica, taking it all in.

"Well, not entirely, but he sent them away licking their wounds."

"No wonder Desdemona turned away Venice's darlings for him. A hero, he is!"

"Yes, well, a common pirate who had a good day, innit? Annoyingly earnest, too."

"Speaking of, he told me that you had something you should tell me."

"Yes, well, for now we should set our sights on liberating Drool." We were nearly to the fortress; its main gate faced away from the harbor, toward the hill. I chose to approach a guard at a small portal in the side, who looked to be nearly falling asleep on his lance, but as we approached I could smell the soured wine stench coming off him as if he'd been painted in the blood of the grape.

"Shouldn't we find an officer?" Jessica inquired.

"Always bribe at the highest amount you are willing to pay, at the lowest level of command. Resentment is as good as gold when loyalty is being sold."

As we approached the soldier, the iron-clad door he guarded flew back on its hinges and a dozen armored men carrying spears and crossbows came through. The scruffy, hungover guard did his best to stand at attention while they passed, then slumped on his spear again. The patrol made its way around the fortress and out onto the breakwater from which we had just come. They were actually patrolling the bloody harbor on foot.

"Fuckstockings, our boat," I whispered.

"The boat's no threat to them. They may not even see it. Let's get your bloody monkey and go."

I nodded, then approached the sentry. "Beggin' pardon, yeoman, would you happen to know if there's an enormous simpleton with a monkey being held in here?"

"Might be, what's it to you?"

"Well, the nitwit is this poor boy's father, and we're hoping to bring him home."

"What's the monkey, his little brover?"

"Half. We are a poor family, and—"

"Four ducats," said the guard.

Jessica elbowed me with a great nodding grin and started to dig into her leather bag of gold. We'd expected a bit more resistance and a much higher ransom.

"But there ain't no monkey no more. I traded him for a jug from Giotto the wine seller on the piazza, a month ago."

"You traded Jeff for a jug of wine?" I was reaching into the small of my back for a dagger. Yes, admittedly he was an obnoxious creature, but by the tucked balls of St. Cinnamon, Jeff was *family*!

Jessica grabbed the wrist of my knife hand and held it steady in mid-draw.

"Please, sir," she said in her best boy voice. "If you could just fetch my old da, I'd be ever so grateful."

She opened her hand and the gold coins fanned on her palm, then she snatched them to her chest when the guard reached for them. "If you would, sir."

"Well, all right," he said. "But you can't tell no one I gave him to you. I'm going to tell the captain he died, so keep him out of sight."

He went through the iron door and closed it behind him.

"Are you daft?" said Jessica, throwing my knife hand away from her.

"He traded bloody Jeff for a jug. My people have suffered enough injustice."

"Here's a tip for you, oh, wise fool, do not dirk the man who is about to free your apprentice for a hundredth of what you expected to pay. Let the bargain be your revenge."

"You are indeed Shylock's daughter."

"Just don't be a fool—well, sorry—don't be foolish," she said. "We know *who* he sold your monkey to, and we know *where* to find him. So we go to Giotto the wine seller in the piazza, buy him back, then find an inn and lie low until tomorrow night when we make our escape."

"Lying low in Genoa with Drool might not be as easy as you think."

Just then the door opened.

"Holy ripened fuckcheese!" said the Jewess, dropping all pretense of her boy voice as Drool unfolded out of the door and she backed away. She had learned to properly swear since we'd been together. I was somewhat proud.

"Boy's happy to see his father," I explained to the guard.

"Pocket! My friend! My friend!" The enormous oaf swept me up in his arms and squeezed the breath out of me, while inflicting me with most slobbery affection.

"Stop licking, Drool. Put me down and go hug your son."

"Huh?"

I heard the coins clink into the hands of the guard and Jessica say, "Well, we'll be off then. Cheers!"

I took Drool's hand and led him quickly down the wall of the fortress and around the corner.

"You might have warned me," said Jessica.

"I told you he was large."

"I told you he was large," said Drool in my voice, mimicked note for note, exactly.

Jessica spun around. "What was that? What was that?"

"He does that, too," said I. "It's his gift, nature's way of compensating him for being an enormous, beef-brained child. He can remember whole conversations, hours long, and recite them back, word for word, in the voice from which they sprouted, and not have a fluttering notion of what he's been saying."

"Sounds bloody spooky to me," said Jessica, putting a bit more distance between herself and Drool.

"They took Jeff, Pocket," said Drool.

"I know, lad, we're getting him. Jess, you go to the piazza and buy Jeff from the wine merchant. I'll take Drool and the gold back to the boat to wait."

"The gold? You're not taking my father's treasure."

"Can't have a girl running about a strange city by herself with a bag full of gold and jewels, can we? Unless you'd rather stay with Drool while I go."

She looked the grand buffoon up and down and handed me the heavy leather bag. "You might pull the boat out a bit if the patrol comes by. I'll wave from the breakwater for you to come in and get me."

"The lad are a lass, then?" said Drool.

"Jess is Jessica, Drool," said I. "Bow proper to the lady."

"Milady," he said, bowing. "Not my son, then?"

"No, seeing as she's a bloody girl and not ten years your junior, she's not your bloody son." I forget at times just how impenetrably dense Drool can be. But I had missed shouting at him.

"Can I have a wee peek at your knockers then?" Drool asked the girl.

"Drool!" I scolded.

"Sor-ry," he sang. "*May* I have a wee peek at your knockers?"

"No, I don't have to prove anything to you."

"Oh, he's not asking for proof, he asks that of all the girls."

"Give me ten ducats from the bag," said Jessica. "I'll go buy your monkey back."

"Jeff likes to bite a lady on her bosoms," said Drool. "Sometimes the bottom."

I nodded as I handed her the coins. "Do be careful. Leash him, and don't let him at your hat. He has a weakness. We'll meet you at the boat, then Drool can row us up the coast and we'll sleep rough on a beach or something until tomorrow night. I don't think we'll stay safely hidden in Genoa with a monkey and this great drooling draft horse."

"I can't wait until Lorenzo comes and rescues me from you scurvy rascals," said Jessica. Then she turned on her heel and walked off to the city.

"Who are Lorenzo?" asked Drool.

CHORUS: *On the isle of Corsica, the port town of Bastia, the once captain, Michael Cassio, stripped of his rank, position, and favor of his general, did mourn his fate, and was sulking at a table in his quarters, when Iago visited him under pretense of offering comfort.*

"I've brought wine!" said Iago, coming through the door without so much as a knock.

Cassio moaned. "No, the devil drunkenness hast lost me my reputation, and in the doing made me despise myself. Never! I shall never drink again. I have lost that part of myself that is immortal, my reputation."

"I know," said Iago. "I was just fucking with you. I don't have wine. Ha, bruised reputation is a false and trifling injury, and one easily mended. The way you wail I would have thought you'd received a real, bleeding wound in the melee. You didn't, did you?"

"No, no injury. Truth be told, I remember a mass of things but nothing distinctly. I am aggrieved that your second, good Rodrigo, was slain, but it was not I that did the deed. Of that, I am sure. But even that I do not remember is an affront to my good commander, Othello, whose trust I have broken with a single drunken debacle, the damage of which I cannot repair."

"Good Cassio, as your friend, I wish that such misfortune had not befallen you, but it is not so dire that it cannot be forgiven, your honor and position restored. You did not kill Rodrigo, so what is your offense, a single drunken night? One night of riotous drinking and memory-clouded barking at the moon? Go to the Moor. Ask him, and he will restore you."

"I have gone, begged, but he denied me."

"Go to him again. Surely when the heat of anger has cooled and Rodrigo's true killer is found, Othello will restore you. Who is to say that you were not defending Rodrigo when he was attacked? In fact, say that. The Moor is a soldier, he knows that victory is not always the reward for valiance. Go to him."

"He will not see me."

"I see." Iago scratched his beard, and paced as if pondering, then snapped to, as if hit by the full impact of a weighty solution. "Othello has presented you with his hardened side, that part of him that is forged by war and by necessity, ruthless, turning away that side which we know to be just and compassionate. But of that side, he is not the commander, but has ceded that position to his lady. She knows you, has shown deference and respect to you."

"She knows me and has always been kind."

"Then go to her. Confess yourself freely to her, and ask that she appeal to that part of her lord who would forgive you, restore you, and lay faith once again in your abilities. Surely the loving kindness she holds for the world will mend the rift between you and the Moor. Go to her, in private, out of sight of Othello, so your case would appear pled by her unbidden. Be honest and true, forthright and contrite, yet stealthy and discreet, and surely the Moor will invite you back again into the fold."

Cassio had been nodding as Iago spoke. "I think you advise me well. A true kindness that you would counsel me so, when you have only just lost your friend. Thank you, good Iago."

"I do only what would any man for a good commander, what you would do for Othello. But I must be off to pay the carpenter to build the box for Rodrigo's burial. *Adieu!*"

"*Adieu,* Iago."

CHORUS: *Into the night went Iago, the gears of treachery grinding between his ears, works of an infernal machine, its brake broken, a runaway scheme engine gone awry . . .*

"Ha, who can say I am evil, when I have given such good advice? For what I told Cassio is true; the best way to win back Othello is through Desdemona, who has a sweet and forgiving nature and has precious influence over the Moor. Even now, I go to see my own wife, to assure the success of Cassio's suit. You call me villain? I, who have only just lost my dearest friend to some demon of the night? Poor, grieving Iago, a villain?"

CHORUS: *You said villain, not I. I merely wipe the mist from the mind's eye with simple descriptive strokes, no more.*

"If you think me villain, follow me into the dark, glib Chorus. Listen to my bones tremble as we are pursued by the dark nature I have conjured with my sins. Oh, it has taken form, and it turns on me, even as it took Rodrigo and nearly shredded an oaken door to get at me. If you would call me villain, face the dark thing that pursues me, that is born of my hate, my ambition."

CHORUS: *You think the creature in the dark is born of your ambition? After I've just constructed a perfectly lovely metaphor about your mind being a gristmill of bloody evil? A villain you may be, but a lunatic you are most assuredly.*

"Come with me, into the night, Chorus. Stay close. Comfort me."

CHORUS: *And thus the knave did think a humble narrator dim-witted enough to serve as decoy for the creature. Alas, as was most often the case, Iago was in thought, intention, and execution deeply fucking wrong, and off he went to find the fair Emilia.*

The rowboat that had seemed absolutely spacious when Jessica and I were rowing it in suddenly seemed small and inadequate with Drool's hulking form at the oars. It did not help that the lummox could not swim and so flinched at every wave. I'd had him row several hundred yards out from the breakwater to avoid the attention of the patrol, so we sat, pretending to be fishermen, I suppose, that is, sitting in a boat looking at the water, waiting for something to break the bloody boredom.

"Jessica are a fit bit of stuff, yeah?" said Drool.

"A half hour ago you thought she was a boy, now she's fit?"

"You have a go at her, Pocket?"

"No, I am still bereft from the loss of Cordelia, and Jessica is engaged, although that may be a bit of a false promise, but I have not had a go at her."

" 'Cause Lorenzo would be cross with you?"

"No, because I have promised the ghost of Cordelia."

"I shagged a ghost once. It were all right, until I got scared. You have a go at her?"

"No, I didn't have a go at her. I've been dead. Not really dead, but unwell. Injured. Betrayed, disparaged, much abused, and somewhat plagued by a sable-colored melancholy."

"Aye, she sounds fit. You have a go at Sable's Melon Jolly?"

"No, you nitwit, I've not had a go—" And so I spun out my story, from when I'd first gone to Brabantio's, to being walled up in the dungeon, of his confession to killing my Cordelia, of the fear and submission to Vivian, of my time in the dark, kept alive by the will to revenge and my worry over the dim giant's welfare. And though I know he did not follow it all, he would remember it, as was his way, and I needed to tell it, so I told him of my escape from the dungeon, my rescue by Jessica and her nursing me back to health. I told him of the plot to revenge those wrongs, my disguise as a Jew (although the only Jew Drool had ever known was Phyllis Stein, who ran the pawnshop in London and used to let him blow the candles out on the menorah every Christmas to celebrate the baby Jesus' birthday), so I explained that they were the people in the yellow hats. I told him of the attack by Lorenzo and Salanio and how Viv had saved me, followed me, and had no doubt slain Rodrigo.

And when I had talked for an hour, and brought us round to a rowboat outside the harbor at Genoa, Drool said, "Smashing, Pocket! You shagged a mermaid."

Which made me wish that I hadn't left the puppet Jones sans stick, in a box at Belmont, so I could pummel the enormous fool about the head and shoulders with it for missing the bloody point. I thought perhaps to press Jessica's bag of treasure into action in the puppet's stead, when the black shade moved under the boat.

"Oh no," said I.

Drool followed my gaze over the side, then followed the movement of the mermaid from one side of the boat to the other, causing the boat to rock precipitously.

"Pocket . . . ?" said Drool.

I leaned over the side, trying to follow her movement, as she swam out, perhaps fifty yards, then turned and came back toward the boat. "No," said I, to the water, trying to send the command to her with a picture in my mind's eye. "Not this one. Do not hurt him," I said.

"Pocket," said Drool, his voice rising in tremolo terror. He started to stand and I grabbed his shirt and pulled him down. "Pocket . . . ?"

"No, not this one. No!" I barked at the water, straining to send my thoughts at the creature. "He is a friend. A friend." Did this venomous creature of the deep even understand the concept? But I felt a response of sorts, a blankness, confusion, a question maybe, an image in the lightning blue I had seen in the dark.

Whatever she had received, the creature stopped, about five yards from the boat, then surfaced and stood out of the water half again as tall as a tall man, so black that she nearly soaked up the light. A thick, serpentine body, for she was a serpent, her head—jaws—wide and square, with long whiskers at either side, nostrils that snapped open and took breath, audibly, but gills down her neck. She had short arms, front legs, with web talons, and from the tip of each heavy black claw, each as long as the blades of my daggers, emerged a fine, translucent, needlelike claw that dripped a milky venom. She hovered there, held aloft by her rear legs paddling and a great tail swishing below the surface, looking at us, emerald eyes set back on the sides of her head glistening in the sun, set in the unscaled skin like the small whales the Venetians call the blackfish. She turned her head to the side so she might get a better look at us, then slid back into the sea and dove down until we could see her no more.

"Pocket?" said Drool, some of the alarm gone from his voice now.

"Aye, lad. Don't be afraid. She won't hurt you."

"Pocket, that weren't no mermaid."

"No, lad, I don't know what that was." Of course I knew what it was. I am English, am I not? I was raised in the bosom of the church, was I not? You couldn't count a half dozen church windows, tapestries, or altarpieces in all of Blighty that weren't emblazoned with St. George and his bloody dragon.

Then Drool spoke in a voice that I did not recognize. *"The Khan told me, on pain of death, I was never to speak to outsiders of the black dragons, who were gods to his people, and whose venom could be distilled into a black tar that made men's heads swim as if in the most pleasant of dreams. Yet as our caravan left the Khan's kingdom, I paid a village fisherman to catch me a very small, perhaps newly hatched serpent, which I was able to smuggle back to Venice in my rucksack, keeping it damp in a bundle of wet cloth even while crossing the wide desert."*

"What is that, Drool? Whose story is that?"

"Bloke what was in my cell with me. He was on the ship when they sunk it. He were the dog's bollocks, Pocket, told stories near good as you."

"Row, Drool. For the lighthouse."

"We gettin' Jeff and that girl what looks like a lad?"

"No, foolish fool, we are going to get your cellmate out of prison."

"Smashing! You can tell me mate the story of how you shagged a dragon."

ACT IV

The Green-eyed Monster

If any wretch hath put this in your head,

Let heaven requite it with the serpent's curse.

—Emilia, *Othello*, Act IV, Scene 2

Eighteen
Cloak, Dagger, Wimple, and Veil

Antonio Donnola, the merchant of Venice, looked out from his balcony, over the Venetian harbor, and wondered for a moment if the four-story fall to the pavers below would kill him instantly or if he might linger, bleeding and broken for a time, before he expired. He was not considering suicide, but considering how Iago might react upon his return from Corsica to find that his part of the plot to take Brabantio's council seat had gone horribly awry. There would be questions before the violence, and although he was not a man of great courage, he would allow Iago's wrath to fall upon him before sacrificing his beautiful boy, Bassanio.

"A fool's head, you say?"

"Aye," said Bassanio. "Like one would find atop a harlequin's scepter at Carnival, except there was no

302 • CHRISTOPHER MOORE

stick. I beg your forgiveness, Antonio. I was assured that it was the right casket. Salanio had found out and sent word through a gondolier."

"A gondolier?"

"He showed me Sal's dagger as proof the message was authentic. They must have changed the caskets after Sal and Lorenzo left for Cyprus." Bassanio joined Antonio on the balcony and squeezed his shoulder. "I will pay you back, I promise. I will pay you back."

He wouldn't, of course. Three thousand ducats? Bassanio would never see such a sum unless he married into it. He was a strong, handsome young man, and not entirely dim-witted, but he was a shit merchant. If not for Antonio's patronage, the boy would have been begging in the street years ago. Perhaps Iago had been right—he should have paid suit to Portia himself, taken the senate seat himself, not utterly bollixed up the whole process—threatened a lawyer or two, as the soldier had suggested. It was too late now. He no longer had funds to make suit himself. Oh, he still had weeks before his bond was due to Shylock, and at least one of his ships would return by then with the profits to cover the debt, but he couldn't secure another three thousand ducats plus the money to intimidate the lawyers. Iago would counsel for that, he was sure. Should he send word to Corsica? Declare their Crusade defeated before it started, take his three-thousand-ducat loss, and stop Iago's plot before it went too far?

He looked at the pavers below again. Perhaps it would be quick and painless. Perhaps he should go to mass, to get his soul in order, because if Iago returned to find the calamity that had befallen them, someone was going to die.

"The gondolier, do you think you would recognize him?"

"I would know him in a second," said Bassanio. "I thought him to be the messenger of my most happy future and so committed his face to my memory."

"Find him, then. Find out his name, and where he lives. Bring him here. Offer him a bribe if you must."

"Oh I will, good Antonio. I will."

Would Iago accept a gondolier as sacrifice?

"A fool's head, you say? Did you keep it?"

"No, I was so distraught and overcome with heartache that I threw it over the railing into the garden."

"Do you remember anything else about it?"

"It was a fool's head made of painted wood, like any other. Except instead of bright colors, it wore a black hat with silver bells at the tips."

"Go, find the gondolier. Take Gratiano or Salarino with you."

"I will, Antonio. Thank you. I will make this right, I promise."

"Of course you will," said the merchant.

He looked to the pavers below and imagined a sunburst of blood spread across the stones.

Despite being uncommonly pretty, like many working-class girls, Emilia had married the first fellow with a means of support who showed an interest in her. Also, like many poor girls, both plain and pretty, she found herself bound to a man who was, despite a handsome aspect and mercurial charm, a vicious scoundrel. She had hoped when the war with Genoa escalated that she might be mercifully widowed, but instead of doing the proper thing and perishing like most of Venice's forces at Curzola, Iago had the annoying luck to have been serving under Othello, defending the city, and had not only survived, but in his more grandiose moments (which were many) claimed that credit for saving the city had been stolen from him by "*that upstart crow,*" Othello. Then she thought fate had smiled upon her side when Iago volunteered her to serve Othello's wife, Desdemona, in Corsica, putting a sea between her and her husband, yet here he was, in her chambers, in need of a favor.

"I hope you are not here to ask me to do my bawdy business—the monkey has a nosebleed and the circus, sir, is closed."

"As it has been for three years solid, wife," said Iago.

"Fine, do your will, I'm sure you will be the one blessed man whose willy does not turn black and drop off after taunting the crimson curse. Don't mind my praying as you perform your disgusting deed."

"No, I am here to ask you to prevail upon Desdemona to speak with Michael Cassio, and to arrange that they might have a private place to speak—on Desdemona's balcony, perhaps."

"And why would you have me do that?"

"Because Cassio is a fine officer who has made a simple mistake, yet he is denied the audience to ask forgiveness of his general."

"You would have me prevail upon my mistress on behalf of the fine officer you have previously referred to as an *'addlepated accountant,'* that *'bum-brained bean counter,'* and that *'flouncing fucking Florentine'?*"

"He has flounced, upon occasion, but I have new, kinder eyes toward him, for all men, since the death of my good friend Rodrigo." Iago looked off to the corner in the way he imagined would a strong man trying to avoid tears.

"I am sorry about your friend, Iago. He will be missed."

"Oh yes, of course *you* will miss him," said Iago, shrugging off his grief as easily as an unpinned cape. "Miss him in your bedchamber."

"You're mad." Emilia sighed and started to walk away.

Iago grabbed her arm and spun her around. "I remember, you showed him favor, made eyes at him when you saw him before."

"Favor? I said he didn't seem to be a *complete* knob. That is not favor, that is just a kind comparison to everyone else with whom you keep company. Despite what you might think, Iago, I am not shagging every man I meet just because I am not shagging you. I am not shagging you because you are *you*, and I am not shagging them because they are not my husband. There is no sodding shagging going on."

"So you say."

"So it is. What do you want, Iago?"

"I need you to prevail upon Desdemona to receive Cassio."

"What's in it for you?"

"Nothing. A brother-in-arms."

"Bollocks. What's in it for me?"

"It would suffice as the wifely duty you would owe me in other ways."

"For how long?"

"For a month."

"Forever."

"Unfair."

"Well, fuck off then."

"Fine, forever."

"Have him here in an hour. I will show him to the lady's balcony."

"I shall. *Adieu,* foul harridan."

"Good-bye, husband."

It was well past noon, hours since she'd left us, when Jessica appeared on the breakwater and waved a red scarf, signaling for us to row in and pick her up. We'd taken the boat out several hundred yards and pretended to be fishing to avoid the Genoan patrols. She had a great cloth flour sack slung over her back and her hair was down in long curls.

"Where's Jeff?" I inquired, before the boat had landed. "And where is your hat?"

"Jeff is in the sack, having a go at my hat."

There did seem to be more than a bit of movement and chatter coming from the sack than would have been produced by a more contemplative monkey.

"Well, your disguise is completely useless without the hat. Even with the pirate boots and the blousy shirt it's clear that you're not a boy."

"I don't need a disguise in Genoa, as no one here gives a lazy toss whether I'm a girl or not. And besides, it was either let him have at the hat in the sack, or try to wear it while he was having at it; either way, some hat fucking was going to get done. This seemed more discreet."

"Yes, Jeff always had a taste for fine millinery."

"Jeff!" cried Drool. "Me wee mate! Oy, Jeff!"

"It was *my* hat," said I. "Perhaps he was just overjoyed at my scent on it."

"Oh, he's a right bundle of joy," said Jessica, holding out the bag, which was still twitching rather rhythmically. "I brought some bread, cheese, and wine, since you said we were going to stay on a beach tonight, so I hope you don't mind if Jeff is overjoyed all over your supper along with a fair flinging of rhesus feces."

"Well, come aboard then. You can sit up here with me to balance the load."

Drool rowed slowly forward until Jessica was able to catch the bow of the boat. She handed me the twitching flour sack, pushed us off, hopped in the boat, then sat down on the bench next to me.

"Which rather forces the question," said she, "of who the fuck is that fellow sitting at the back of the boat?"

"Neptune's salty balls! There's a stranger in our boat!" I exclaimed, then revealing what is widely known as my most charming and lap-dampening smile, I said, "Alas, I jest. That, my pretty pirate, is Drool's cellmate from prison. A Venetian, like you, Jessica." I was laying it on a bit thick, before I had to get to the bit about paying the ransom. "May I present the trader and explorer Marco Polo."

An hour after leaving Emilia, Iago was walking the high battlements with Othello, under the pretense that he would need to know the particulars of the fortress if he were to fill the void left by Cassio's banishment.

"Who is that on the balcony, there?" asked Iago. A man and a woman, her back to them, the man facing.

"It appears to be Michael Cassio," said Othello. "I will have him removed. There was no subtlety in my wishes. He was released from the brig on the condition I would not suffer his presence."

"But, my lord, Cassio is an obedient officer even in his shame, for it was your presence you forbade him, and this, like his presence at the murder of Rodrigo, is merely an accident. See there, he is here to see your lady."

"That is not my lady. Desdemona has no gown of that color. That is Emilia."

"Slut!" Iago spat out with urgent pressure, as if a bee had flown into his mouth.

"Beg pardon?"

"I mean, Cassio does not know my wife, and those *are* your lady's quarters."

"Emilia seems to know him now. Look how she titters and touches his sleeve like a coy maid."

A vein sprouted on Iago's temple, he felt it throb with the stress of his subterfuge. "Emilia merely receives the captain on behalf of your lady, I'm sure," he said. *Slut! Slag! Slapper! Prick-pull! Egregious hose-hound most foul,* he thought.

"Ah, it is so, for there is the spark of my soul, Desdemona, now."

At last. "I did not know that Cassio knew your lady, but for some fawning he did upon her at the dock."

"He knows her. In Venice he carried messages between us when our love was a secret."

"Ah, she knows him. Look, a friendly embrace. He kisses the air by her cheek in the manner of the Florentines. He kisses the tips of his fingers in salute to her perfection. Ah, he knows her."

"I *said* he knows her."

"And surely he has good reason to seek her counsel, now."

"You think his intentions not honest?"

"Honest?"

"Aye, honest? Forthright. Honest. Don't parrot what I say. Speak your thoughts, Iago."

"Please don't make me say, General. Cassio is an honest man, for the most part, so if my suspicions are wrong, and they probably are, I would wrong him to speak them. All men are subject to moments of weakness: Cassio said he did not drink, and for the most part, he does not. One slip. A single indiscretion. So may the case be here."

"A case of what, Iago? For I swear if I find you know something and do not tell me, I will throw you off this very wall."

"My wife, Emilia, she said that Cassio came to her, asked her to plead his suit to Desdemona, and ask that she would grant time alone with him. I'm sure his intentions are honest. I am suspicious by nature, sir, and I often see offenses where they do not exist."

"But Emilia is there, with them, as you can surely see."

"As you say. She *was* there. For me to speak full my suspicions would only destroy your peace of mind, and for what? I would not besmirch a man's good name on my habit of mistrust. A man's good name is the immediate jewel of his soul. He who steals my purse, steals trash, but he that filches my good name robs me of that which enriches him not, yet leaves me poor indeed."

"Cassio was found out of his mind with drink, vomiting on the mutilated corpse of your officer, Iago, with no recollection of how any of it had come to be. His reputation is ash. Speak."

"Well, he *is* very handsome, and there is a certain smooth charisma to him, and your lady is, well, young, and fair, as is he."

"Fair?"

"I'm not saying that his intentions are dishonorable, nor the lady vulnerable to his oily Florentine charm, but it is better to know, isn't it? Wouldn't it be? If I may suggest, watch your wife. Look for evidence that her attention is wandering. I have had to do so with my own wife—what soldier, in the field for months at a time, has not felt suspicion? But do not crush that gentle trust with accusation. Watch her, I say."

"You give me good counsel, Iago. That I will do. Let us finish the work and I will go to her, look for signs."

"O, beware of jealousy, my lord. It is a green-eyed monster which mocks the meat it feeds on. But better to know than suspect."

"Monster? Ha! Your infernal spinning of words gives power to enemies that are but specters of imagination, Iago. Let us finish our inspection and I will go slay your green-eyed monster with a single kiss from my sweet Desdemona." The Moor climbed to the highest wall and did not look back to see if his lieutenant followed.

"Not enemies," whispered Iago. What was Emilia doing laughing at the Florentine's jokes? And why was he joking, did he not know he was ruined? If not now, soon.

I contemplated a bold prison break, with many disguises, much bloodshed, and buckling of swashes, but as I am small, and had neither my puppet nor my monkey at hand but instead a cracking big bag of gold, I decided to approach freeing Drool's cellmate by means of ransom.

About the bit of paying the ransom: As it turns out, there is a good reason most kingdoms never turn the key to the treasury over to the king's fool. The reason is, of course, we are, by nature and training, foolish, and consequently cannot be trusted with money. A lesson Jessica would not have had to learn were it not for the besotted git who guarded the side gate at Fortress Genoa, and the blistering toss-toad who was his commanding officer.

The guard appeared to have sobered up some, since we'd ransomed Drool, but he was no less miserable.

"Can't do it," said the guard, holding his spear as if he was hiding behind it while he looked about. Drool was hiding just around the corner of the great fortress, as I could not convince him to stay in the boat, due to his fear of Viv and water in general. "Even at twice the price. This one's a real prisoner, a merchant and a gentleman, and a ransom demand's already been made to the family. The big one was just his servant. You want this one, you got to talk to the captain."

"I'll give you twenty ducats and you can just say the big one fell on this one when he succumbed, killing him. Or plague? You can't beat a good plague to explain mysterious death."

"I'll fetch the captain," he said. He disappeared through the gate and presently returned with an unctuous and overpolished young officer with the suggestion of a mustache, the downy promise of beard, and the willowy wan look of a boy who has never, and shall never, do a day of work in his life. He was too young to have earned his command—born or bought into it, no doubt. If this was what Genoa was putting into the field, it was no wonder that Othello had thrashed them like ripe grain.

"I am told you wish to ransom the prisoner Marco Polo?"

"That would be true," said I.

"Come in to the command chambers and we can negotiate the terms of his release. *Monsieur* Polo is an important prisoner."

"*Monsieur?* Are you speaking fucking French at me?"

"*Oui*," said Captain Fuzzcheek. He clicked his heels.

"Oh, *très* pretentious, signor. I presume you can take me to a proper officer now, so I don't have to trade terms with a mossy-chinned little wanker whose father bought him a jailer job to keep him from buggering the help?"

As it turned out, I *would* be dealing with the aforementioned wanker, who felt it was his duty, I suppose, to extract every grain of gold I had before he would release Marco Polo into my care, so insulting him had worked in my favor. *He* thought he'd won, of course, but since it was not my gold, I had bested him. Ha!

Thus the explorer collected his kit and we led Drool back to the boat to await Jessica's return. I agreed to row, as Drool wanted to sit in the bow of the boat and keep an eye out for Viv, while Marco Polo sat on the stern bench, levered upward somewhat by Drool's stonking density at the front of the boat.

"You seem rather well-kept for someone who has been in prison for two months," said I. He was a fit, sharp-featured Venetian of about forty, his beard starting to gray, with more lines and color to his face than most of his merchant counterparts. This one had done more than eat rich food and bargain on the Rialto.

"Except for the children playing in the harbor calling my name all day, it wasn't entirely unpleasant. The Genoans knew my family has means. I was confined to quarters that had once housed a duke. I just could not leave. I thought I would take the time to write my memoirs."

"Marco!" called Drool in the voice of a small boy. "Polo!" came the response in another child's voice, as if it were coming from a different spot.

"Yes, like that," said Polo, wincing at the sound. "I had discovered your friend's incredible gift before our ship was taken, and since our captors would not provide me with the parchment and ink I needed to write my tale, I told the Genoans he was my valet; he was brought to my quarters and I began to recite my story to him."

"Which kept him from being chained to an oar on a war galley?"

"Since there had been no response from Venice to ransom him, there was talk among the guards he would be sent that way, yes," said Polo.

"I thank you for that," said I. I really had been terribly worried about the great ninny, and kindness is so uncommon in these dark ages.

"It is more than repaid by your ransoming me. I have had the good fortune to encounter the miraculous in my travels, and I feel duty bound to try to preserve it."

"Yes, Drool's a bloody miracle, innit? You know he can fart the chorus to 'Greensleeves'?"

"I can give 'er a go, Pocket," said the dim giant, from behind me.

"No! Not necessary, lad." Three out of four tries, Drool produced a trumpeting raspberry of "Greensleeves," but every fourth time or so, he shat himself in the harmony. "I would like to know about another miracle you rescued on your travels. Drool said you brought a serpent back from the Orient. A dragon?"

Polo's eyes went wide. "I suppose I never thought about how that would sound when my story was heard. I wouldn't blame you if you thought I was a loon. They are rare creatures, even in China. But I wanted to show it in Venice, show people that the wonders of the Orient are real. It is no matter. The creature slipped out of my rucksack into the canal when I was climbing out of the boat at a dock near Arsenal. After surviving a trek across the great desert, too. A tiny thing, no bigger than my forearm it was. I'm sure it perished in the foul water of the canals. They live in the great rivers of China. I tried to draw it back to the dock using a balm they are attracted to, made from their venom, but it was no use. The creature was gone."

"Perhaps not," said I.

"Pocket shagged a dragon," said Drool matter-of-factly.

"I did not shag her. I was cruelly abused while chained in a dungeon."

Marco Polo raised an eyebrow. "Signor?"

"I was taken captive, as well, but in not so comfortable circumstances as you." So, for the second time in the day, I told my tale: of being drugged, chained in the dungeon, of the creature coming to me in the dark, doing the dark deed upon me, and its subsequent murders and mutilations. I left out the bits about being able to project my thoughts to the serpent, to receive what appeared to be return messages on the dark canvas of my eyelids, and my plans for revenge.

When I finished my tale, Polo said not a word, but dug into one of the two rucksacks the Genoans had allowed him to keep, and pulled out a small, red-lacquered Chinese box. He removed the lid and held it under my nose. It was full of a dark, tarry substance. "Smell. Was this the taste of your amontillado?"

"Aye," said I. "I remember it well. And when Viv sunk her claws in me, I would taste it in the back of my throat for hours afterward."

Polo closed the box and replaced it in his rucksack. "This is the substance the little dragon was attracted by. It has a dreamy effect on someone who eats it, a stronger painkiller than even the milk of the poppy."

"I know its effect," said I. "I very much know its effect."

Polo looked at the well of the boat, as if ashamed. "I sold another such box to a merchant on the Rialto."

"Antonio Donnola?"

"He said his father was dying with a tumor and was in great pain."

"His father has been dead for years."

"I am sorry," said Polo. "I didn't know."

"Not to worry," said I. "No way you could know. Nor that your creature had grown up. I expect we may be seeing her soon."

Polo shuddered. "Do you wonder why she didn't slay you?" Then, before I could answer, his gaze strayed over my shoulder. I heard a rhythmic slapping sound coming from the bow and I looked over my shoulder to see Drool standing in the boat, his back to us, twitching and laughing in a low, breathy giggle.

"Drool! What are you doing?"

"Havin' a bit of a wank."

"In the middle of your bloody rescue?"

"Just a wee one," said the oaf.

"It was a constant the whole time we were captive," said Marco Polo.

"You had yourself off for three months solid?"

"There weren't nothing to read."

"You don't know *how* to read."

"Yeah . . . ," said Drool.

I turned to Polo. "Why didn't you just tell him to stop?"

"In my travels I have learned to be respectful of other peoples' cultures."

"What culture?"

"Well, he's English, isn't he?"

"Nonstop wanking is not part of English culture."

"It helps if you tell him a story," said Polo. "Distracts him."

"It helps if you beat him about his great empty melon with a puppet stick," said I. "Drool, stop that and sit down. You'll fall in the water and Viv will eat you."

With an alarmed tremor, Drool sat down. "Proper threat works, too," I said to Polo.

"You're English as well, no?" asked the explorer.

"Full blood, noble-born bastard of Blighty, I am, at your service."

"Hard to tell with everyone having the same accent. I can row for a while, if you need a respite." Polo again raised the inquisitive eyebrow. "Some time to yourself . . ."

"That is *not* part of English culture!"

"Of course not."

"Oh, right, part of the national health, innit? *'Here's a leech and two tosses a day, and the bloody queen thanks you for your loyalty.'*"

"Apologies," said the Venetian. "I only know your apprentice, and he—"

"Look, there's Jessica on the breakwater," said I. "Drool, put that away and take the oars."

CHORUS: *The Moor, a storm of suspicion conjured in his mind by Iago, did burst into his lady's bedchamber to confront his enemy—fear—the fear of losing his love to another. And Desdemona, the only one who had ever brought that sweet, soft calm of love upon his warrior's brow, could only his solace deliver.*

"Lady! Desdemona!" said the Moor, throwing the door open and back on its hinges. "I would have words with you!"

CHORUS: *When he spied the veiled figure reclining on the bed, he screamed, a yip most manly and not*

at all like the sound that might chirp from a small
dog that's been trod upon. The general, in that
instant, hopped back through the door, his sword
rattling against the doorjamb as he went, and
became the very model of a man ready to bolt.

"Who are you?"

"Oh, brash general, I am but a helpless nun at the mercy of your rough barbarian ways."

"Desdemona?"

She tossed the purple veil back. "Well, who else would it be, silly?"

"What are you wearing?"

"It's Pocket's nun suit. He said you'd find it saucy." She put wrist to forehead and leaned back on the pillows in feigned distress. "Oh no, thou rough pirate, please do not ravage me and have your dread and disgusting pleasures on my nubile body." She squinted in fear, and thrashed her head in denial, while sneaking a bit of a peek to see how her nun bit was playing.

"I do not find this saucy. The fool knows nothing of my desires."

"Not wearing any knickers . . . ?" She pulled the hem of her gown up a bit. "Helpless nun, no knickers . . . ?"

"There are no purple-and-green nuns. The fool made that up."

"But the no knickers bit is true."

"No." Othello crossed his arms, resolute.

"Totally naked nun . . . ?" And in two deft moves, but for the wimple and veil, she was.

"No."

"Fine, then, what did you want to have words about?" She sat up, cross-legged on the bed, elbow on her knee, chin in hand. "Well?"

"I don't remember," said the Moor.

"Well, close the door and come to bed, love, you're tenting your robe, the servants will be scandalized. Emilia will be jealous."

"Jealousy!" said the Moor. "That was it! A green-eyed monster!"

"Oh no, thou raging lunatic, I am but a helpless nun," said Desdemona, quivering in her most naked distress, since apparently this was how Othello wanted to go with the bloody game.

Bested, the Moor shrugged, closed and latched the door, and went over to the bed.

"A green-eyed monster that mocks the meat it feeds upon . . . ?" Othello mumbled.

"Why not?" said Desdemona, taking her turn to shrug. "We can do that."

Nineteen
Well Met in Corsica Once More

Jessica stood at the rail of the poop deck in her white blouse, canvas sailor's trousers tucked into her high boots, and the red silk scarf she'd bought in Genoa tied around her head, her dark curls spilling down past her shoulders. I must admit, she made for the most fair and fit pirate I had ever seen, despite her surly mood. We were two days from landing back at Corsica and she had not spoken to me since we'd retrieved her from Genoa and she'd found out about my spending her father's gold.

I approached her cautiously, but not so quietly I would startle her. Truth be told, I did not like her standing so close to the rail, for although I had not seen her since she presented herself to Drool and me, I could feel the dragon out there, following. I'd tasked Drool to look after Jessica, and he had followed her around the ship like an enormous slobbering puppy. He sat with his back against the rail, watching her, his gaze as vacant as the cloudless sky above.

"It was my only recourse, Jess. Polo saved Drool, kept him alive, no doubt. And his family will repay you the ransom when he returns to Venice. It is little more than a loan."

"And will he repay my mother's ring, which I had to give for your fucking monkey? My father's turquoise wedding ring."

"To be fair, you are not blameless, you *did* steal the treasure first."

"What will I tell Lorenzo when he comes to Corsica? He may be waiting for me even now. That money was for our life together."

"Viv eated him," said Drool.

"What?" said Jessica.

"Nothing," said I.

"Viv eated Lorenzo," said Drool. And then, before I could stop him, in a perfect imitation of my own voice, the natural recited the story of how Viv had taken Lorenzo and Salarino, word for word as I had told the tale to Marco Polo.

Jessica turned to me, tears welling in her eyes. "What is this?"

"Well, the ninny has the story all wrong. He was wanking the whole time I told it."

She took me by the shoulders and shook me. "What is this? Where is Lorenzo?"

Tears poured down her cheeks and my heart broke again for her, for it was that hope in her eyes that I had so dreaded, that she was casting on me like the leaden yoke of the one-eyed guilt swan. Is it the fault of a girl bright with the light of romance that she falls in love with a rascal? Is the love any less pure? Any less heartfelt? Any less painful when lost? It would serve no purpose to paint Lorenzo as the scoundrel I knew him to be. "Drool has that bit wrong, love. Lorenzo is no more, but he was killed by his cohort, Salarino, while trying to save me from being murdered."

"Lorenzo is dead?"

I nodded, opening my arms to her.

"Why didn't you tell me?"

"Because of this," said I, brushing a tear from her cheek. I told my story again, for the third time in four days, except in this version, Lorenzo was a hero, and it was his love for the fair Jessica that spurred him gallantly and courageously to face down an armed assassin, to rescue a nameless messenger, simply because he had carried the words from his love. And after he fell, the serpent rose out of the canals and struck down Salarino in vengeance. She did not question the existence of the serpent, or my sanity for saying it was so, for she had tended the wounds left by the creature and they fit like puzzle pieces. She believed.

I sat there, at the rear of the ship, holding her while she wept, until the sun had boiled well into the sea.

Soon after, in Corsica, Iago found his wife in the Citadel's laundry, folding Desdemona's linen on a table near the great central cauldron, in which steamed a gigantic simpleton, rather than the usual load of shirts and trousers.

"I thought I was finished with you," said Emilia. "Or you with me. It was agreed."

"I need you to arrange for Desdemona to meet Michael Cassio in his quarters."

"Not bloody likely. But I'll arrange to meet Michael Cassio in *my* quarters anytime you'd like, though."

"Woman! You are here by *my* leave, and on *my* order, I can remove you—from the world of the living if I so wish it—and no one would look twice for you, thou worthless trollop."

"Bit of a knob, innit?" said the giant in the cauldron.

"Who *is* he?" said Iago. In Venice, Iago had never seen Drool. Didn't know he was the fool's apprentice.

"He works in the stable. The stable master said he smelt of shit and so sent him in here to have a good hot bath. Stand up, love."

The giant unfolded in the raised cauldron and great cascades of soapy water ran off him as he stood, naked, his enormous erect dong swinging in a wide arc at Iago's eye level like the loose boom of a sailing sloop.

Iago backed away from the swaying beam and looked at his wife. "Did you put him in that state?"

Emilia fluttered her eyelashes coquettishly. "Possibly."

"Emilia's got smashing knockers, she does," said Drool.

Iago raised his hand as if to backhand Emilia and felt himself suddenly yanked into the air by that selfsame hand—held high and squirming as he tried to draw his sword and Drool turned him so they were looking eye to eye.

"I fink you should fuck off now, sir." He dropped Iago, who landed in a heap on the slippery stone and struggled to roll over so he could get to his sword.

With the same meaty paw he'd used to lift Iago, the giant snatched up a boat oar the laundress used for stirring the cauldron.

"Would you like to bugger a soldier, puppet?" Emilia asked Drool.

"Yes, please, mum."

She crouched down until she was face-to-face with her husband. "You might want to do as the boy says and fuck off, *now*, husband."

Iago scrambled to his feet, snatched a handkerchief from the table, and ran out of the laundry, roaring with frustration as he went.

"He were cross," said Drool.

"He often is," said Emilia. "Impressive willy wagging."

"Fanx. Just a peek then?"

"Well, you've earned it, haven't you? But sit down first, love, you'll frighten the cats."

Shylock had spent a fretful two months with no word of his daughter, until today, when the two huge Jew brothers, Ham and Japheth, came to his door on a chilly winter morning with a message from his friend Tubal to meet him on the Rialto at noon. The moneylender donned a heavy, fur-lined cloak and hired a gondola with a closed cabin, and was an hour early for the meeting, so he stamped his feet and blew on his hands until he saw his friend ambling over the Rialto Bridge. Shylock rushed to meet him and was breathless from climbing the stairs when they met.

"Tubal, you have news? What of my daughter?"

"Shylock, you rush too much, maybe we should go inside, where it is warm, where you can sit down."

"I would know now. What of Jessica? Did you find her in Cyprus, as you thought?"

"The news is not so good. I spread the fingers of my sources from the harbor in all directions, with promise of silver for news, but the news did not come o'er the sea from Cyprus as we thought, but from travelers by land, from Genoa."

"Genoa? She is a prisoner, then?"

"No, but a prisoner she saw there, she bought there. Word is that for ransom of a prisoner she gave all of your treasure—two thousand ducats' worth of jewels and gold—all that she took. And in the square there, she did trade a blue and gold ring for a monkey."

"My treasure? My daughter? My ducats? Two thousand ducats? That ring—that ring was the turquoise my Leah gave me upon our wedding, I would not have traded it for a whole wilderness of monkeys. Tis a tempest of troubles. My daughter! My ducats!"

"And she was dressed as a pirate."

"My daughter, a pirate! Stick a dagger in me, I am finished. My ducats are gone and my daughter is a pirate."

"But there is good news, too; other men have had ill luck as well."

"Other men? Whose bad luck is my good news, unless you say those rascal friends of Antonio who stole my daughter are arrested."

"It is news of Antonio's bad luck I bring. Word came in the harbor that one of his argosies, the one bound for Alexandria, was wrecked, the cargo destroyed. His losses are beyond your own. The creditors say he can but break, now."

"Good. That *is* good news. I'll plague him in revenge for letting his men take my Jessica and make a pirate of her, my own daughter, against whom there can be no justice, no satisfaction, so the hammer of justice must fall on Antonio. Yes, good news."

"But alas, more bad news."

"Bad news?"

"The gold that you lent Antonio was mine. It will be due as well."

"Ah, I see good news for you, too, Tubal," said Shylock, poking a hole in the sky with his finger. "The sympathy you will get when you tell your wife how hard you had to work to hide your smile when you told me I am ruined. I have had better friends, Tubal."

"**You were** right," said the Moor. "They are trying to start a holy war. A Crusade, from which they will profit."

"So you've put Iago in chains and tortured him until he confessed?" I stood on a chair in the general's war room while a tailor made marks on my new motley with a sliver of soap. The fool suit was too big by a good measure. "Well done, Othello."

"I have no proof that Iago is involved."

"Other than he fucking told me, only when he thought I was going to be murdered."

"You are not always reliable, little one. Drink and grief can cloud a man's mind."

"How do you know, then?"

"My fleet in the south stopped one of Antonio's ships headed for Alexandria. It was loaded to the rails with great beams of French and English oak. The pilot confessed they were bound to be given to a Mameluke general."

"Firewood? Scaffolding? A bloody great wooden sphinx? Egyptians love their sodding sphinxes—lions with girl faces and bosoms—right degenerate if you ask me, but . . ." I considered my own experience with the rodgering of mythical beasts and reconsidered my hasty condemnation of the Egyptian sphinx shaggers. "So the lumber is for . . . ?"

"The oak is to build siege engines: catapults, ballistas, and trebuchets. There is no wood strong enough for such machines in Egypt, or in most of the lands of the Muslims. Antonio is selling material to Muslims to build weapons for a war that the Venetians are hoping to push the Christians into starting."

I looked at the top of the bald head of the tailor, then at the Moor. "Should we, perhaps, present a bit more of a challenge for any spies in your command?"

"He does not speak the language."

"I see," said I. To the tailor I said, "Leave loads of slack around the cod, tailor, I'll need lots of room to expand when your daughter's doing the nightly knob rubbing for all the blokes in the regiment."

The tailor glanced up quickly, then went back to his work, marking and pinning. The Moor raised an eyebrow as if to say, "Well?"

"He either doesn't understand or he's resolved to his daughter being a slut."

The tailor appeared to be finished. He smiled and stepped back, gesturing for me to take my kit off and give it to him so he could get to his sewing. He folded my motley and left the room with a bow to Othello and a grin toward me.

"So, a holy war would be on but for your late father-in-law shuffling off this mortal coil and a humble and handsome fool surviving their heinous fuckery most foul. A war setting the church against your own people, Othello."

"I am not a Muslim, Pocket."

"Well, you're not a bloody Christian, are you? And every druid I've ever known is on the snowflake side of pale, so I'd say you're a bit tar-tinted for that persuasion. You're not a Jew, are you? No, of course not, you don't have a yellow hat. Unless . . ." I engaged the Moor with a steely yet inquisitive gaze. "Othello, do you have a secret yellow Jew hat?"

The Moor laughed, a raucous cough of a laugh, then said, "No, fool, there are no gods in my philosophy. I learned my way of looking on the world from an old slave I was chained to on the galley. From the farthest east, he was. He taught me that as I suffer, so do all, and if any suffer, so do I, that we are all part of one, that in any moment my dark skin connects me to all things, light and dark, and all things, light and dark, are part of me, so to do harm to any man, any creature, is to be ignorant to my own nature, to do harm to myself and all other things. That is what I believe."

"Really? How did that work as a pirate?"

"Reality is oft uncooperative." He shrugged.

"Aye, well said, Moor!" I laughed then. I suppose his philosophy has served him as well as mine, which until Cordelia, after having been much maltreated during my childhood in the church, amounted to surrendering to being dragged trippingly through life by a savage willy, stopping occasionally to thwart injustice, rescue the distressed, or have a snack.

"So your mates sank Antonio's ship, eh?" I inquired.

"No, they reported that it is most difficult to sink a ship that is hold-to-rail filled with seasoned oak." The Moor dazzled his pirate grin then. "But I am told it was two days burning to the waterline and was still smoldering on the horizon when my ships departed."

"You don't think the doge's council might get their knickers in a knot about you sinking a Venetian merchant ship?"

"What can they say? The pope forbids Christian nations from trading with the Mamelukes, by threat of excommunication. My ships were enforcing a papal bull. Saving souls."

"Well, if that's not the duck's very nuts, pirate business by Christian bull? Jessica will be thrilled."

"Then for your part of our bargain, fool. You told the girl about her fiancé as you promised?"

"In a manner of speaking, yes. She knows."

"And she hates you now, I presume."

"I didn't tell her that he was a scoundrel, or that he was slain by my hand, but instead that he died gallantly defending me from his murderous friends."

The Moor considered it, looked at me askew, as if doubt was pushing his pointy beard to the door. "I think you have more affection for her than you would say."

"There's no room for that. My heart is full of grief for my Cordelia and a desire for revenge. She's an annoying reminder of the folly of having hope."

Othello went to a chair at the table and sat down, a heavier weight than commanding a navy seeming to fall on his brow all at once. He said, "I do not understand women, Pocket. I have these many years in the field come to understand the nature of men, but women are yet a puzzle. Desdemona confounds me."

"Ah, so she moors the Moor, so to speak. I had a tryst with a tart who confounded me, left me tied in a dungeon once for two days, starkers, without food nor water. Just ask her to loosen the ropes next time she confounds you."

"*Confound* does not mean 'tie up.' I mean she confuses me."

"Oh. Well, that's different, isn't it. But I have known many women—many women indeed, and it is in their nature to confound us, Othello. They are all by their natures lovely lunatics. But among them, Desdemona is more lovely and less loony."

"Is she so lovely if she is untrue?"

"Desdemona?"

"Yes."

"Untrue to you? Cheating with another?"

"Yes."

"Bollocks!"

"Yet I have my suspicions."

"You have no proof?"

"Others have made comment."

"If this is about the nun suit, that was my idea entirely."

"Not the nun suit. The nun suit was—"

"Smashing! I knew you'd like it. You should have her confound you while wearing the nun suit—say stern things to you in Latin while shagging your bloody brains out."

"*Confound* does not mean that!"

"Fine. So you would accuse your lady of being untrue—your lady, who did throw all of Venice away for you, stood up to the most powerful men in the republic, for you, Moor; *she* you would accuse, without any evidence but the comment of another, yet Iago, who you know to be a villain, a cutthroat, and a traitor—for him you need proof beyond my word? Respect my judgment in this, Othello, if in nothing else, or thou art a fool."

"I saw her on the balcony talking to Michael Cassio. She came to me, made a case for me to forgive him."

"That is because she is kind, and just, and forgiving, and has been wrongly judged for mere appearances, because she loves you, she wishes you to be kind, and just, and forgiving as well. You will have to get your own moniker, Othello, the *Black Fool* is mine, but thou art surely a fool."

The Moor let his head slip from his hands and his forehead thumped against the table. "I am a fool," he said.

"You can't switch sides now that I'm winning."

"No, you are right, I am surely a fool. I have wronged my love with my suspicions. I don't know what to do. I am a warrior, my speech is rough and not so polished as yours."

"You always say that, but I think we both know you could talk the tits off a tavern tart."

"I mean that asking forgiveness is not in my experience. What did you do when you wronged your Jewess?"

"First, she's not *my* Jewess, she's *a* Jewess, and I did not, strictly speaking, wrong her, although she *is* angry at me for delaying telling her about Lorenzo."

"And yet you were merely trying to spare her pain."

"Exactly! And she's still somewhat unhappy that I spent all of her father's gold."

"For which the Genoans freed an important prisoner."

"Which apparently does not hold the weight for her it does for you and me. Speaking of such. Let me fetch the Venetian I rescued." I went to the wide double doors.

"Forgiveness?" the Moor insisted.

"It's best to blame it on your monkey, if possible. Now, let me get the Venetian."

"Aren't you going to put on some trousers first?" asked the Moor.

"He's just outside, waiting on a bench with Drool."

"All this time he has been waiting?"

"Well, he's been in prison with Drool for three months, a few minutes on a bench isn't going to send him round the bend." I peeked out the door and called, "You two, come in. The general needs to see you."

Marco Polo came in first, followed by Drool, both rudely ignoring the presence of the high general of Venice, distracted, it seems, by the fact that I was naked. "Oh fuckstockings. Fine, I'll put on some trousers. I'm wearing my daggers, aren't I?" (I was. Little point having my fool suit fitted if I couldn't conceal my daggers underneath.) "A gentleman can't even discuss fucking philosophy without you puritanical twats casting judgmental glances at his tackle *d'amore*."

"'At's fuckin' French, innit?" Drool explained to Othello. Then as if seeing the Moor for the first time, he said, "The dragon Pocket shagged were black, too."

The Moor lifted his head from the table. "What?" He stood to receive the explorer.

"Ignore him, he has rabies. Othello, Marco Polo. Marco Polo, Othello," I said, hastily, as I pulled on the sailcloth trousers I'd removed for the benefit of the tailor.

The explorer and the general exchanged pleasantries, and acknowledged the reputation of each, then, before they began to trade stories of all the places they'd been and the people they'd seen, I said, "Polo, give me that lacquer box out of your rucksack. Othello, you must see this. I thought of the trebuchets you wanted to put on your ships."

Polo retrieved the red lacquer box emblazoned with the black dragon and I waved it away. "Not that one, the other one. Are you mad?" He handed me a black lacquer box, larger than the other, about the size of a large man's foot. I worked the top off, and from a padded compartment, I pulled four round paper packets, each no bigger than a fingertip. I threw one at the floor at my feet, and jumped when it snapped in a small explosion and a puff of smoke. Another I threw at Drool's feet, and he cowered at the noise and smoke. I did a backflip and snapped the last two to the floor as I landed, with a distinct and ear-ringing bang.

"They call it dragon powder," said Marco Polo. He looked at me. "Although it has nothing to do with dragons."

Othello watched, waited, said not a word. I brought the box to him and pulled up a pinch of the black powder from another compartment in the box. "Not impressive, I know. Just a few grains of this, in a packet with some fine gravel. When the gravel hammers the powder, it ignites with a snap. A magician's trick, right? But imagine a larger amount, contained."

I pulled from the box a small cylinder of paper, as big around as my thumb, Chinese characters drawn on the paper. From the cylinder protruded a waxed cord, impregnated with the black powder. "Now, just this amount, watch this."

I spotted a Turkish vase as high as my chest, in the corner, and from the bowl on the table I grabbed a melon. Then spinning it on my finger as I went, I lit the wick of the paper cylinder, which hissed and threw out sparks as it burned. I scampered to the vase, dropped in the sizzling cylinder, then fit the melon in the mouth of the vase and hastily backed away.

"Don't be alarmed," said I. "It will be loud. I was startled when Polo showed us."

"I weed meself," said Drool.

In a second there was a deafening bang and the vase disintegrated into shards that peppered the room, including us. The melon calmly dropped to the spot where there had once been a vase, but now there was but a sunburst of porcelain dust and a dented melon.

Othello shook his head, trying to clear his ears, as each of us tried to make some adjustment to the high-pitched ringing we were all hearing. "So," said I. "That is not, precisely, how I thought it would work, but you can see the potential. That was barely a spoonful of the powder, and compressed only in paper. If you were to pack it into a great steel or stone ball and fling it at your enemies with one of your war machines, I trust it might be days before the surprise was wiped from their faces."

"The Chinese send self-propelled tubes made from bamboo hundreds of yards into the air with it," said Marco Polo. "It could make a fearsome weapon for war."

"I see that," said Othello. "I would not want to fight an enemy who had mastered this powder first."

"Which is why no other soldiers in the West have yet seen it," said I.

"And the Genoans did not make you tell them of this?" Othello asked Polo.

"They did not know to ask. Only a few friends in Venice have ever seen it, and then it was only a novelty at a dinner party. The Genoans only wanted to know if my family had money and if they would pay for my return. Anything more I might have told them only Drool heard."

"It were lovely," said Drool.

"You were in prison, you nitwit," said I.

"Aye," said Drool, a dreamy look in his eye.

Othello went to the table and looked at the lacquer box, with its compartments, fitted the lid on it, then ran his finger around the edges of the box while thinking. "No city could stand under a siege armed with weapons made of this."

"No," said I. "Not for long."

"A general who has this has the lightning hand—if his cause is not just, he would be a devil."

"Aye," said I. "A general who wages war for a republic whose cause is not just would make devils of soldiers, and turn honor to evil."

"I think you are not so much a fool as I thought."

"And neither are you, milord."

"I think it's time for you to return to Venice, Pocket."

"Aye," said I.

"I will have a ship readied for you."

"Signor Polo, will you fetch Jessica and tell her to be ready? Bundle her up if you must. I suspect we'll sail on the tide. Drool, go to our quarters and ready our gear."

Othello nodded, exchanged farewells and thanks with Marco Polo, and wished them on their way, while I stayed behind.

"I'll be along presently," I called.

"Othello, have I told you about how the bishop of York ordered me hanged when I was only a lad, barely sprouting a beard?"

"No. A bishop, you say? How did you escape?"

"I didn't. I was hanged. And then freed to follow my fancy, find my fortune, and become a fool and a king."

"Because you were hanged?"

"The abbess at the nunnery where I grew up knew I would never escape the fate pronounced me by the bishop, so he put a heavy belt around my waist, rigged a noose so it appeared to go around my neck; but my weight was held by the rope tied to the belt under my shepherd's tunic. Then, in the morning, under the watch of the entire village, he had me hanged in the barn, with priests to witness that the deed had been done. When they left, Basil cut me down, gave me coin, and sent me out into the world a free spirit. Really, all that bollocks about resurrection had some sound fucking reasoning in it after all."

"Your abbess was a man?"

"Mother Basil, as sturdy a blue-bearded bloke as you've ever known, but he found life dressed as the nun in charge a much more pleasant way to pass these dark ages. He told me that he, himself, had died, in much the same way, which freed him to his avocation."

"And you tell me this why?"

"Because even now, I am dead to Venice, which frees me to find and free my apprentice, and avenge my Cordelia. You will only know your true enemies, Othello, when they reveal themselves by killing you. Because you are my friend, I would have you pick the time and the circumstances for your defeat. If I am wrong, then you can have a laugh at my expense."

The Moor took me by the forearm and slapped my back in the manner of comrade warriors.

"Good-bye, silly fool."

"*Adieu,* thou sooty-bosomed devil," said I.

Twenty
The Art of Persuasion

CHORUS: *With the fool's words still echoing in his ear, Othello did call to his chart room Iago, who thought the moment was upon him to take the command and position of the shamed Michael Cassio, but instead of promotion, he was met with the Moor's ire.*

"Iago, if thou slandered Desdemona only to torture me, and there is no proof of her betrayal, then never pray again for mercy, and never hold thyself safe from any violence, for the pain you have brought upon yourself cannot be more dire than the fate you have set if these doubts you raise be false. Am I plain enough in my speech?"

Iago reeled—*this*, after having thought this battle already won. "By my troth, my lord, I am not spinning tales, but merely adding facts like an arithmetician." He counted his points on his fingers. "She deceived her father, did she not? She turned down all the fairest young men of Venice for you, did she not? You have seen her meeting in secret with Cassio, have you not? Why, you can almost smell her rank and foul dispositions, her affinity for dark, unsavory pursuits in the bedroom, so depraved that even her father thought her bewitched. Mind you, I don't mean to say that she was always a degenerate strumpet, only that those who show such habits constantly would be considered so. Methinks she is only a *sometimes* slut. I worry that she only chose you over those pretty Venetians out of twisted rebellion against a father, and now, in comfort and boredom, might revert to her true *sometimes* nature."

"You've planted thoughts of my love's deceit, and you have no proof."

"Would you have me arrange for you to watch while they are at it? Can I give you that proof? Would I find them flagrantly fucking as drunken monkeys for you to watch, would you then be satisfied?" Iago thought himself well-suited to play the role of the wronged in this affair.

He went on: "Some nights ago, Cassio was down with toothache, so I did give him a potion for pain given me by the apothecary. It put him in a dreamy sleep; while I still sat in his quarters, he talked in his sleep, saying, 'Desdemona, we must hide our love from the world. Kiss me hard, love, and curse the Fates that gave you to the Moor.'"

"Dreams and delusions," said Othello. "Cassio babbles nonsense with his first flagon of ale, much less a pain potion."

"Tell me, then, have you seen a handkerchief with strawberries embroidered upon it?"

"I have. Such a cloth was my first gift to Desdemona, a legacy of my mother."

"It looked like the favor of a woman. Today I saw Cassio wipe his beard with such a handkerchief."

Othello spun on his heel and spoke as if calling out to an inattentive god. "If it be so, then killing the Florentine once would not be enough, for I would slay him a thousand times and not quell the hurt in my heart. My love turns to anger, my anger calls for blood. Oh, arise black vengeance from thy hollow hell, thy hate is become the tongues of venomous serpents."

"I felt a selfsame darkness rise within me, for what man betrayed by his wife can feel any other way. But hold thy vengeance, Othello. Have patience. Let me be your sword, good General."

"So shall you be, but on your honor, report to me within three days that Cassio no longer lives."

"I will do so, sir, consider Cassio dead, but I beseech thee, let Desdemona live. She may yet be innocent."

"Damn her, lewd minx! Oh damn her, damn her! I spare her now. I withdraw now, but find me a means of swift death for her before I again see you, and surely, for this service to honor, you shall be my captain."

"I am your own forever. You shall have your proof, then your will be done."

CHORUS: *Thus Iago went from fearful suspect to gleeful celebrant and his greatest enemy became the laugh he had to fight down as he hurried from the command room. Much relieved, he left the Citadel directly to arrive, hat in hand, his most gallant and gracious false face on display, at the door of the courtesan, Bianca.*

She answered the door in a plain linen gown, hair disheveled, the unapologetic yawn of a day sleeper forced to have discourse with deranged people who inexplicably preferred morning at the beginning of their day rather than, properly, at the end. She was tall, dark of hair and eye, with a fine jawline, lips that evinced a bit of a pout, even in her smile, and a delicate thin nose.

"What?" she said with another yawn.

"Good day, lady, I am sorry to rouse you at the very crack of noon, but I am here on behalf of my friend Michael Cassio."

At the sound of Cassio's name she shook off her torpor and fixed her robe. "Cassio? I have not seen him for a week. I heard of his troubles—on his way to see me, I was told."

"Indeed, indeed. And I fear he did not want you to see him in his shame, but his talk of you is constant, and I know he has purchased a small gift for you to show his affection, but as I said, he is taken with a melancholy that will not allow him to venture to your door."

"Oh my. My poor Cassio. I wondered."

"I know he will be in his quarters tonight, lady. Perhaps if you could visit him there, allow him the joy of giving you this token of his love, and perhaps use your own charms to help break the lock of his despair. To speak truly, lady, he needs you."

Her breath stopped and her fingertips went to her chest as if to test that her heart had not stopped.

"He needs me?" She had been wanted, often, constantly since she was a girl, as had many a beauty, but needed?

"Aye, lady. But you must not tell him I was here. Go there, as if drawn only by your affection."

"I will. Oh, I will."

"Eight o'clock," said Iago.

Alas, once more I feel as if I am on the edge of a very precipice, at the edge, almost, almost, almost, and yes, I sneeze," said the Moor. "Choo."

Desdemona had been brushing her hair at the mirror when Othello came in. She turned, regarded him. "My lord, I've never known a man more brave, nor more manly in body and demeanor, yet your sneeze concerns me, for when I heard such a sneeze last, it was in the gardens of Belmont, and belonged to a weak and soon to be deceased squirrel."

" 'Twas a strong sneeze," said the Moor.

"Aye, a mighty, heroic sneeze, my lord. The ship-sinking tempest blushes with shame at the blustering destruction of thine most magnificent and not at all sickly squirrel sneeze!"

"You mock me?"

She tossed her long hair over her shoulder. "I do, my lord."

The Moor held his hand over his nose. "I would not offend thee with my squirrelish rheum, then. Bring me a handkerchief."

Desdemona quickly retrieved a handkerchief from the chest by the bed and handed it to the Moor, who held it as if it were a foul, dead thing. "Not this one," said he.

"But it is clean."

"Have you the handkerchief I gave you? The one with the strawberries embroidered upon it?"

"I know not where it is, my lord."

"I would have that one, with the strawberries. The one I did give you as my first favor. Given to me by my mother, who received it from an Egyptian charmer who could almost read the thoughts of people. She told my mother that as long as she kept it, it would subdue my father completely to her love, but if she lost it, or made gift of it, he should hold her loathed, and his spirits should hunt after her new fancies. She gave it to me as she was dying, and made me promise I would give it to my wife and she should make it the darling of her eye."

"Really? You've a handful of snot, and a perfectly good handkerchief, but you would prefer to hold out for the one with the strawberries on it?"

"Tis true, there is magic in the warp and woof of it. A prophetic sibyl did weave it, and the worms that spun the silk were blessed, and the thread for the embroidery was colored with dye made from the hearts of mummified virgins. I would have that handkerchief. If you be true to me, lady, and not a wanton strumpet, I would have that handkerchief now."

"Well, if it was so sodding sacred, my lord, you shouldn't have soiled it as you did."

"What?"

"I sent it to the laundry because you used it after you had me in the nun suit."

"I am a soldier, Desdemona, and not refined in my ways. It was you bade me use it."

"I told you not to wipe your knob on the curtains, I didn't tell you to use the mystical bloody handkerchief and then storm in here and throw a wobbly over my being an adulteress because it got lost in the laundry."

"It is true," said Emilia, emerging from behind a dressing screen. "I am witness to it."

"Ah!" said Othello, somewhat surprised that there was someone else in the room. "You saw me wipe my knob on the handkerchief?"

"Oh look, Emilia," said Desdemona. "You've embarrassed him. He was the one in the nun suit at that point. Such a charming, impassioned lad is my Moor. Such a love."

"No, General," said Emilia. "I took the handkerchief to the laundry, where your lieutenant, Iago, absconded with it after being frightened off by the fool's giant apprentice."

"Iago?" said the Moor, dropping his arms as if the puppeteer had cut his strings.

"Aye, good sir," said Emilia. "Iago."

Desdemona went to her husband and squeezed his strong shoulder to steady him in his confusion. "You'd better tend to that sneeze, love. We can't have the high general of Venice marching about the castle with crusty dragons perching in the caves of his noble nose."

"Even the most powerful move to my will," said Iago, to no one in particular. "Not by force or by threat, but by wit and guile. Othello is not so much caught in my net as he throws it over himself and comes along, thinking he is the fisher. As my own evils came alive as a dark killing creature, so will I with cleverness conjure the Moor from night-faced devil to cuckolded beast eating its own tail.

"I have instructed Othello to tell his wife that he will be out late, inspecting the vessels in the harbor until well into the night. Over a flagon of wine at the alehouse, I will fill his mind with vision of misdeeds and betrayal until he is enraged like the caged tiger taunted with sharpened rod. Then will I bring him to Cassio's house, listen at the window while the Florentine does his dread deed with Bianca, who is well known for her lustful howling. And what husband, when so enraged, can distinguish the moans of one woman when he expects it is his own? And when I see the Moor's temper has well come to a boil, then shall I call Cassio to the door and stand aside as the infuriated Moor murders him. Cassio, although a Florentine, is a darling of Venice, and the council, led by Antonio's young senator, will depose Othello and appoint me to head the Venetian forces. First will come power, then, with our Crusade, will come wealth."

CHORUS: *And so, mad Iago, his vision as shallow as his intellect, his strategies as weak as his character, did draw plans for his own undoing.*

"But alas," said Iago, "perhaps there is a flaw in my plan that, because of the strength of my will and the breadth of my ambition, I am yet to discover . . ."

CHORUS: *So beguiled by hate is the soldier, that he does not realize that the Venetians would never prosecute Othello, the son-in-law of a Senator, the heir to a Council seat himself, for what would look to be a well-justified killing of the man who wrongly used his wife. No working man at the docks would be undone for such a deed, so a general, a national hero, will not even stand trial.*

"Oh bugger," said Iago. "There is the ring of truth to it, isn't there?"

CHORUS: *Dazzlingly obvious to all but the most profoundly thick.*

"Of course, Cassio is already failed as an officer, his murder serves not my purpose but for the pure pleasure of it. It is Othello who must fall before the Florentine's sword. Yet, as Cassio is a skilled swordsman, though not from battle but from dogged disciplined practice, so is the Moor dangerous with his scimitar. I will have to slow his hand, as I did Rodrigo's, with the Oriental potion. And if the darkling beast forms from the shadows and kills Othello, too . . . ? Well, he would have done well not to have trifled with my loyalties. You, Chorus, say nothing of this. I will see the Barbary horse dead this night, and I will not by your meddling be undone."

CHORUS: *A humble narrator is but a flourish in the scenery, no instrument of Fate is he. The watch bell tolls seven, and villains and heroes are called to put in motion their plots.*

"'Tis justice that on his last night the general waits in a common alehouse. It shows his kind were not meant for command. I am away."

Marco Polo stood beside me at the rail on one side of the ship, while Jessica looked out over the sea on the other. "She is still not speaking to you, then?"

"Holding fast to her anger," said I. "Not like telling her about Lorenzo sooner would have made anything better. She's seen the world, met new friends, and learned to swear like a pirate—if she'd gone off with Lorenzo her gold would still be gone and her carcass would probably be feeding the fishes off some poxy Greek island."

"What of your other lady, Pocket? The darker one?" The explorer bounced his eyebrows as if he were party to some bawdy secret, nudge, nudge.

"I haven't seen her since we left Corsica, which is just as well. You keep that potion of yours capped, Polo. She might have been cute as a kitten when you last saw her, but now she seldom shows up without there's a trail of gruesome gore and grieving survivors."

"Except for you. She doesn't harm you?"

"I am a tenderhearted fool, so I suffered bruised feelings when she used me roughly and left me hanging there in the dark, but not mortally, no."

"Why do you suppose that is?"

"My roguish charm and clever wit, no doubt."

"No, that's not it. Maybe you just taste bad. English food . . ."

"Marco!" I cried, fixing the explorer with a critical gaze.

"Polo!" Drool answered from another part of the ship.

"Marco!" I repeated.

"Polo!" called Drool in the voice of a child.

And that continued for quite a while until the adventurer admitted that it is an accepted fact among monsters and giants of all stripes that Englishmen are delicious.

It was of no little concern to Iago that Brabantio's potion had not made the Moor quick to anger, yet slow to move in a fight, as planned, but instead, agreeable, sentimental, and not a little sloppy. Iago crouched there, under Michael Cassio's window, with the high general of Venice, listening to the sounds of lovers wafting through the shutters.

"The fiend!" said Iago. "He uses her like a base strumpet, listen to them."

"I knew a caulker's mate in Barcelona who played the base strumpet as we supped each evening," said Othello dreamily. "Ballads as sad as a lost calf lowing for its mother."

"A strumpet is not a musical instrument, my lord. Cassio uses your lady like a common whore."

"And who could blame him?" said Othello, tilting his head as if listening to a sweet melody. "She is the soul of beauty, the very heart of kindness, the soft bosom of most soothing touch—and has a bottom to launch a fleet for—go to war over."

One hopes, thought Iago. Thinking now that he might have better served his plan to just cut Othello's throat in the dark and blame it on Cassio, rather than use this unpredictable potion.

A rhythmic feminine yipping beat into the night from the window, counterpoint to low masculine moans.

The Moor's eyes rolled back in his head and from his crouch beneath the window he rolled back onto his back on the cobbles until he was staring wide-eyed at the sky. "A bottom so fine as to make the lovers' moon hide its silver face in shame and never shine again."

The Moor closed his eyes and went limp.

"Oh, for fuck's sake," said Iago. "My medicine has worked too well."

"He dead?" said a fisherman who had been out casting his nets by lantern light and had come up the street with annoying stealth.

A shutter creaked open two floors above, spilling lamplight into the night. Out popped a boy's head. "Oy, zat the Moorish general you kilt? Oy! This bloke kilt the Moor, and I only just seen him for the first time."

Suddenly shutters clattered back on their hinges, lamps were lighted, and Iago found himself crouching over his commander under an audience of dozens.

"He kilt the Moor!" said a woman from her window.

"I did not kill him."

The door of Cassio's house opened and the onetime captain stepped out wearing a robe.

"Iago? What is this? You've killed Othello?"

"No, he's fine. He's having an epilepsy. A fit. It is his second in two days."

"He's not having a fit. He's grinning like a lunatic."

"Eyes that sparkle so that all the constellations would tumble from the skies to be within her sight," whispered the Moor to the sky.

"What is he on about?" said Cassio.

"I don't know. Help me get him to a physician," said Iago.

When Othello awoke he found himself on a small bed in a small room, with Iago sitting by his bedside. "Where am I?" said the Moor. "How did I come to be here?"

"You are in my quarters at the inn, my lord. I brought you here myself, with the doctor, when you fell into your apoplexy at your lady's betrayal."

Having completely failed to get Michael Cassio to kill Othello, Iago had amended his plan to goad the

Moor into doing something so outrageous that Venice couldn't help but reject him, despite what the Chorus said.

"Apoplexy? Betrayal? I remember only that we were going to Cassio's house to find my handkerchief, but after that all is in fog."

"Oh, you went to Cassio's house, and found your handkerchief under the lovers, Cassio doing dreadful animal things to your lady, who yowled like a cat in heat, and screamed for him . . . Oh, I cannot say."

"No, say. It would be an excellent idea for you to say."

"She did call for him to shag away the memory of that black monster's touch."

"Monster, was it?"

"Yes. And then Cassio called you a twat."

"Cassio did? While he was atop Desdemona?"

"Didn't even break rhythm. Just, 'eek, eek, eek, you twat, eek, eek eek.'"

"He said that? 'eek, eek, eek'?"

"No, my lord, but his bed is squeaky, and thus I spoke how it squoke as he pounded your wife like the slut that she is."

"Well, that must have angered me indeed?"

"Indeed it did. You were so overcome with anger, and heartbreak, of course, that you fell into a fit of apoplexy and twitched upon the ground like a beheaded chicken."

"Like a chicken? I don't remember ever having been so angry. So you have dealt my wrath upon Cassio."

"As soon as the physician arrived, yes. He is deeply dead, but for the actual killing bit."

"Good man, Iago."

"I am thy sword, my lord. But it was not on me to kill the wanton bitch that is your wife. That is your right as a husband wronged."

"And so I shall."

The Moor still seemed more than a little dazed, and although the words he was saying fit Iago's plan, there was a listlessness about him and again Iago thought it might have been better for everyone if he had just dirked Othello in the dark and cried bloody murder at Cassio's door.

"Go now, my lord. Before she is able to gather her things from the Citadel and flee."

"I am for her, and surely she is as doomed as she is damned. Where is my sword?"

"Here it is, my lord. Go, and do not let her say a word in explanation. Hear not a word of her pleas for mercy, for she has wormed her way into your heart and you will lose your resolve. Choke off her lying words as you choke the life from her lying body."

"I will!" And the Moor sat up, wheeled on the bed until his feet were on the floor, then stood, snatched his sword and scabbard from Iago, and with a bit of a wobble strode out the door.

Iago, now quite amazed by how well that had gone, thought it might be better if he were far away from the Citadel when the Moor killed Desdemona. He could enter the castle a short time later, pretend to be shocked at the carnage, then amid the panic and despair, be the calm presence of command, summon the entire watch and arrest the Moor, with a great show of compassion and justice, and fit his feet most naturally into the general's shoes. The confirmation from Venice and the council would be only a formality. And if the Moor resisted, if he raged beyond his lady's bedchamber, well, a half dozen guards with spears would take down even the finest Moorish swordsman.

For now, he would go to the harbor and pretend to inspect some ships, ask about rigging and weaponry, make himself enough of a nuisance that everyone would remember where he was when the Moor made his murder.

He headed out of the inn and had not passed four doors down the lane when he came face-to-face with a cohort of Venetians, the one most formally dressed in purple silks and a hat with a long ostrich feather trailing it leading them in determined stride.

"You, soldier," he called. "I saw you come out of the inn. We were told we would find General Othello there. Have you seen him?"

He was from the senate, no doubt, just the way he dressed and spoke, and so, so far away from Venice, his stylish pomposity made him look quite the clown, Iago thought.

"I am Othello's lieutenant, signor. Iago DiFuretto, at your service. Othello was here earlier, but he left some time ago. I would look for him at the harbor. I'm going there myself. I can lead you if you'd like."

"We've just left the harbor," said the Venetian. "I am Lovichio, senator of the fifth district, cousin to the general's wife. Othello is ordered back to Venice and I am to appoint Michael Cassio provisional governor of Corsica."

"Cassio? Governor?"

"Yes, governor. Do you know where we can find *him*?"

"I think, signors, you need to follow me to the Citadel."

As he led the Venetians to the Citadel, Iago thought that this might be the best way of all to find his place at the head of an army: stand with a senator and his attendants to look on the Moor, his dead wife's perfume still fading on his hands, crazed jealousy still in his mad-dog eyes. Iago would take command, make the arrest, in witness of a senator, and take his prize without even having to plead before the council. Had not the Moor found his own position by turning the Genoan fleet? So he, Iago, would turn the man who had turned the fleet.

But as they entered the castle wing where Othello kept his private quarters, Iago's own wife, Emilia, rushed out of the great double doors, screeching, her hands and the front of her gown painted in blood.

"Thou pernicious evil devil! This is your doing, you cur, you knave! Your lies have done this!" She held her bloodstained hands like palsied claws, trembling them under his face. "You have spilled this noble blood with your lies!"

"Go home, wife," said Iago.

"I will not! Go, look upon what you have done. Yonder lies my lady, strangled by her lord, Othello, who did stab himself in the heart while still kneeling over her. This blood is on them both, on you!" She leapt at him and wiped her bloody hands down the front of his shirt. Iago grabbed her wrists, threw her aside, and drew his dagger.

"You would draw your blade on a woman?" The senator and his attendants had backed away from the screaming woman into a bunch, forming a phalanx of dread from which they had been watching. "This is your wife?"

"Aye!" said Emilia. "But whatever evil I did to deserve a curse such as this, only heaven would know. Cursed!"

"Signors," said Iago, awkwardly trying to pretend that he had not raised his dagger over his wife's breast and instead had somehow accidentally found it in his hand: a foreign thing magically appeared. Forward with the plan. "Othello has been wronged, and although luck has favored him on the battlefield, he is not the master of his temper."

"He's bloody dead, you git!" said Emilia. "And he would have never harmed a hair on my lady's head, even spoken an unkind word to her, had he not been driven by your lies."

"What of this?" said the senator, emboldened now by Emilia's complete lack of fear in the face of her husband's dagger.

"Good sir, this woman, who I took as my wife out of pity, for she was a simpleton and so had shared her favors with many wanton boys in her neighborhood—even though she was such spoiled goods, out of charity, I took her in, but her mind has never been right."

"Thou mendacious fuckweasel," said Emilia, almost spitting it, disgusted now rather than hysterical.

"Methinks the lady doth protest too much," said Iago.

"Methinks the lady protests just the right amount," said Emilia. "Methinks the lady is just getting fucking started protesting."

Iago blazed on, ignoring her. "Even last evening, when I was at his side, Othello went to Cassio's house, and heard the young captain rutting with Desdemona."

"That was me," said Emilia.

"What?" Iago lost his train of thought and looked to the Venetians as if they might give him a hint of what to say next. "Then"— he paused, trying to find some way to stitch this calamity back into some advantageous order—"then the Moor went mad, hearing his beloved wife making the howling of the beast with two backs—"

"Also me," said Emilia, a smile crossing her lips now, pure triumph between her teeth.

"She is mad. She does not make that sound in bed."

"I do when I'm being done right. Ask any of the boys in my neighborhood, you berk."

"I tried to calm the Moor, but Cassio's betrayal, and his wife's, was too much for—" He turned to Emilia. "What of Bianca? Wasn't she supposed to—I mean . . ."

"She was there. I gave her the bloody handkerchief you promised her and sent her away."

"She did," came a man's voice from the hall. Michael Cassio came through the doors, his sword drawn, and put the blade between Emilia and Iago. "Signors," Cassio said, nodding to the Venetians. "Sheathe your dagger, Iago, or lose the hand that holds it."

Iago thought for a second, just a second, that he might fight, but he knew the Florentine, alert and sober, would go through him like a hawk through a spiderweb.

"I confess, signors," said Iago, dropping his dagger and raising his hands to yield before Cassio. "I am the instrument of a plot laid by a great and powerful Venetian—following his instructions. I am only doing the business of the council. No one could foresee the Moor would act in such a rash and tragic manner." Live to fight another day, he thought. Throw it all on the backs of Antonio and Brabantio—let them condemn their own kind. "I shall say no more," he said.

"You will have your opportunity to make your case before the council," said Lovichio.

Cassio put the point of his blade under Iago's chin as he relieved the traitor of his sword. "Chain him in the hold of the next ship bound for Venice."

ACT V

A Pound of Flesh

Come not between the dragon and his wrath.

—King Lear, *King Lear*, Act I, Scene 1

Twenty-one
Savage Puppets

G ratiano and Salarino were strolling through
St. Mark's Square on their way to the Rialto when
they spied the Jew walking, head down, hunched into
the wind, carrying his box of papers under one arm
while he held his yellow hat in place with the other.
Despite it only being noon, the young merchants were
half drunk and fully fascinated with the sheer fabulous-
ness of being them, and so did not notice the cold.

"Look, it is the Jew!" called Gratiano. "Shylock, we
heard you were on the Rialto, crying of your bad fortune."

"Oh, my daughter! My ducats!" mocked Salarino.
"My ducats and my daughter are gone! I know not
which is worse!"

Shylock stopped and squinted at them over his new
spectacles. "She is not my daughter. She is dead to me."

"She's not dead to our friend Lorenzo," said Gratiano. "He enjoys her and your ducats even now on Cyprus."

"Unless he is done with her already and passed her over to my brother," said Salarino.

"*Then* they'll throw her in the sea and live off your ducats." Gratiano laughed. "Oh, your ducats, your daughter!"

"Laugh at my misfortunes, young man, but I am not the only one who has suffered withering loss."

"Ha!" said Salarino. "We know you sent a Jew to Belmont to rig the boxes for Bassanio's try for Portia's hand. We talked to your gondolier, he has no loyalty to you. He was the same one my brother hired, he had his dagger."

"You know this, do you?" said Shylock, nodding. "He had your brother's dagger, did he? I see. Well, it is strange that you know these things when I know nothing of them. I have no gondolier, and I have no interest in who Brabantio's daughter marries. You know all these, which are not true, and not important, but you do not know what is word on the Rialto this morning, because you have been in an alehouse, drinking to your good fortune and my bad, no?"

"Say what you will, Jew."

"Word on the Rialto is that a second of Antonio's ships is lost. Taken by pirates off Gibraltar. The crew were stranded on the Moorish coast and the ship scuttled offshore while they watched. One of the sailors, who was picked up by a Spanish ship, returned this morning. Tell me, did I do this? Do I, because I am a Jew, control storms and pirates that cause Antonio's misfortunes? There is one week left, young brigands. Tell your master to look to his bond."

The two young men, suddenly sobered and drained of their hubris, looked to each other, not sure of what to do, what to say. As Antonio's fortune went, so went theirs.

"Go, go," said Shylock. "Off to the Rialto to confirm my story for yourselves. You know how we Jews lie."

Like scolded puppies, the two hurried off to the Rialto, desperately hoping to find that the Jew was lying.

It was true. It was true. They had actually spoken to the sailor from the sunken ship. But now, how to tell Antonio? They found him in his chambers, sitting with Bassanio, the two drinking wine that had been warmed by the fire, on the table what was left of a simple luncheon of bread, cheese, and thin slices of Parma ham.

"Come, join us," said Antonio. "There is enough left for a meal, and I'll wager you two haven't eaten yet today."

374 · CHRISTOPHER MOORE

Gratiano and Salarino hurried to the table, but neither sat down. They stood.

"Friend Antonio," said Gratiano, the tallest.

"Good Antonio," said Salarino, the roundest.

"Good friend Antonio," said Gratiano.

"Are you two going to sing?" said Bassanio, the handsomest. "I'm in no mood for your singing."

"Noble, most generous Antonio," said Gratiano.

"What?!" said Antonio. "What? What? What is it?"

"Another of your ships has been lost," blurted out Salarino. "Sorry."

Antonio set his goblet on the table and pushed back, his eyes closed, as if he was letting a wave of nausea pass through him before he spoke. Then he said, "Where did you hear of this?"

Gratiano looked to Salarino, who looked back. Should they say they had first heard it from the Jew? No. "It was passing on the Rialto," said Gratiano. "But we found a sailor from the lost ship."

And so the two took turns telling small bits of the tragedy, so at any time, when Antonio's brow began to show a shadow of hatred or anger, the other would take the next fragment of the story to attract his attention.

When they were finished, Antonio pushed back in his chair yet again and spoke with head tilted back, eyes closed. "I have one argosy yet to deliver its goods and return safely to port, and with it I will pay my bond to the Jew."

"But there is only one week," said Bassanio.

"Yes, there is only one week, and the ship is overdue by two weeks already, so you must go to your Portia, who has still had no one pass her father's test, and ask her if she will help you. I ask you to do this, Bassanio, as your dearest friend, who loves you most. You must do this."

"I will, Antonio. I think she has no access to the family fortune unless her sister, who is away in Corsica, relents, but I will ask her to show her pity for you as if it were for me, for in my heart it is."

"You two," said Antonio, still not looking up. "You must find Shylock, in the city, not on the Jewish island, and you must make a plea to him to meet with me. Not here, and not on the Rialto. Someplace private, down one of the streets where there are no windows."

"What will you say to him?" asked Salarino.

"I will say nothing, as I shall not be there. Instead I will be at Signora Veronica's, where many witnesses shall see me. But you two shall ask the Jew to give me grace, more time to make my bond. Two months, a month, a week even."

"And what if he says no?"

"Then you will kill him and dump his body in the canal. Be quick, be quiet about it, and leave quickly in different directions. Do not come to see me until the next day, where you will find I have made a drunken spectacle of myself before passing out in the brothel."

Salarino looked to Gratiano, who looked to Bassanio, who shrugged, as if to say, "I have my part to do, you must do yours." They did not answer, did not jump to be agreeable and frisky at the prospect of helping their friend. Yes, they were arrogant and strutted and bullied their way around Venice, and they had drawn blades in fights, even drawn blood. But they were not killers. Salanio and Lorenzo, they had been the cruelest of the crew.

Antonio let his chair fall forward and when the legs touched the floor he came out of it with a violent fist to the table that made the wine splash and the bread jump. "Do you have questions? Friends?"

"Um," said Gratiano, "we are most willing and able to do what you ask, but shouldn't it be done by proper ruffians? We are gentlemen, and surely not suited for such dark doings."

"If you hire ruffians, then you will have to kill the ruffians to eliminate the ruffians. You see, a proper gentleman is efficient in his business. What would you rather do, face off with two experienced cutthroats, or take down one feeble Jewish dog?"

"The Jewish dog," said Salarino with a pout.

"But if Shylock dies the bond passes to his daughter, then a cousin from there," said Gratiano. "The Jew told us this himself."

Antonio sighed. "And they will have to *find* his daughter, which will buy me time, and if they find her, then you can hide her again, at the bottom of a canal."

"Are there Jewish dogs?" asked Bassanio. "I would think that it would be hard for them to keep to the kosher diet? I've never known a dog that wouldn't eat a pork rib when given it."

"Ah, my beautiful Bassanio," said Antonio, shaking his head. "Go see your lady. I need to have a lie-down in the dark."

For two days Gratiano and Salarino watched Shylock from a distance and memorized his ambling clockwork movements. Two days in which they hoped that news of Antonio's third argosy, now the ship of his rescue, would arrive in port, and indeed, after two days, the word fell like angry hands slapped against their ears (with pain, an unsteady step, and a residual ringing): The wreckage of the ship had been found floating in the Black Sea with no sign of the crew. They would have to go to the Jew and ask for mercy, and if denied, deny it in kind and kill him.

"I'm not so sure," said Gratiano, as they made their way to the Rialto toward the end of the day, "that we shouldn't be exceptionally friendly. Perhaps we should approach the Jew in an expansive and laughing manner—slap his back like the good fellows that we are—assure him that all is well. Say, 'What is a few weeks among friends?' and he may relent. Perhaps we should take him a pie. Do Jews eat pie, I wonder?"

"Unless it has pork," said Salarino. "Or prawns. And they have some rule about milk and beef in the same pie. Oh bugger all, I don't know what goes in a Jewish pie, let's just fucking kill him. He's not going to believe we're his friends, we've been horrid to him."

"Well, we were being horrid on Antonio's behalf, not our own," said Gratiano defensively. "We were obligated by friendship to be horrid."

"Quite right," said Salarino. "Loyalty is virtue, and we were being virtuous indeed."

"Indeed. And he *is* a Jewish devil."

"Well, yes. Who slew our Lord and Savior."

"So, really," said Gratiano, "we are obligated by friendship and faith to be horrid bullies, provoke Shylock to deny any grace to Antonio, and then take just revenge for him and our Lord and Savior by dirking the Jew and throwing him in the canal."

"Well, I feel better," said Salarino. "Our time tracking him won't have been wasted. And I did sharpen my dagger."

"I'll hold him and you can stab him, then. I'm taller and can catch him around the neck so he can't scream."

And then they saw him, doggedly making his way toward the narrow alley he used as a shortcut that he took every day on his way home, where he would come out on a canal that had a walkway on only one side, and make his way past several bridges until he came out to a wider street that led to the dock at St. Mark's. The shortcut didn't seem any shorter to Gratiano and Salarino, but it was out of the wind, which perhaps is why Shylock took it, but perfect for their purposes, as it was very sparsely traveled. Only two doorways opened onto it, and those were back doors, so unless someone had their window open—and who would do such a thing on a cold winter evening—they would have a few moments of complete privacy, and a few moments was all they needed. They had discussed it.

"How now, Shylock," said Salarino, stepping onto the walkway from the recess of one of the doorways. "What news today among the merchants?"

Shylock pulled up, startled. "If you want the news, go to work on the Rialto as an honest merchant would. Maybe you would know as much about your master as you do about my daughter."

"It is about Antonio that we are here," said Salarino. "To make a proposal."

"We?" said Shylock, backing away from the portly man.

"Aye, we," said Gratiano, coming around the corner a few yards behind Shylock.

"What is it you want?"

"Time, Jew. Only a little time. Antonio, who is the most kind man in Venice, the most generous, the most gentle, asks only for a little more time on his note."

"Antonio sends you? Like a beggar who will not show his face on the Rialto. Tell him he has four days to look to his bond."

"What if he forfeits?" said Salarino. "I'm sure you would not take his flesh. What is it good for?"

"To bait fish with . . . ? I care not. If nothing else, it will feed my revenge. Antonio has hindered me in my business half a million ducats over time. He has laughed at my losses, mocked my gains, scorned my nation, thwarted my bargains, cooled my friends, heated my enemies—and what is his reason? That I am a Jew."

"Well what do you expect, you *are* a Jew," said Salarino.

"I think we're all in agreement there," said Gratiano, moving closer.

"Hath not a Jew eyes?" said Shylock, pointing to his eye in the manner of the Turks. "Hath not a Jew hands, organs, dimensions, senses, affections, passions? Are we not fed with the same food?"

"Do you eat pie?" asked Gratiano. "We were thinking of bringing you a pie."

"Are we not hurt with the same weapons?" continued Shylock. "Subject to the same diseases, healed by the same means, warmed and cooled by the same winter and summer as a Christian is?"

"I'm going to say yes, on the weapons," said Salarino.

"Counting on that one, really, since we didn't sort the pie part out," added Gratiano.

"I didn't know there was going to be a bloody quiz," said Salarino. "We're woefully unprepared for it."

"If you prick us, do we not bleed? If you tickle us, do we not laugh? If you poison us, do we not die? And if you wrong us, *shall we not revenge*? If we are like you in the rest, we will resemble you in that. If a Jew wrong a Christian, what must he endure for the wrong? *Revenge*. If a Christian wrong a Jew, then how should he endure it, by Christian example? Why, *revenge*. The villainy you teach me, I will execute, and it shall go hard but I will do better than your lesson. *Revenge!*"

"Well, if that's how you feel," said Gratiano, "I suppose that the pie ploy wouldn't have worked anyway."

"Might just as well have put ham in it and eaten it ourselves," said Salarino, as he glanced around and began to draw his long dagger. "What is that?"

A soft jingle sounded from down the canal behind Gratiano and the tall man turned just in time to see a monkey dressed in black, bounding down the walkway behind him, little bells jingling on its tiny jester hat as it approached. It leapt into the air, landed on his shoulder, slapped him with a tiny monkey paw, grabbed his hat, then jumped to the ground and made for Salarino, tossing a tight parchment bundle in the air as it passed Shylock, who clutched the paper to his chest.

Salarino drew his dagger to intercept the simian if it leapt for his face as it had Gratiano's, but instead the monkey ran by on its hind feet, wiping its paw on Salarino's boot before scampering down the canal, then up a drainpipe until it disappeared over the roof.

"A monkey?" said Gratiano, stunned and hatless.

"Ha!" said Salarino. "He wiped shit on your face."

"Well, he wiped shit on your boot."

"He gave me a letter," said Shylock.

Gratiano swiped at his face, which was smeared with a dark brown streak. He sniffed his fingers. "It's not shit. It's sticky. Smells of pitch."

Shylock broke the seal and did not notice that there was a menorah pressed into the wax. "I don't have my spectacles," said Shylock. "I can't read this. What does it say?"

Salarino snatched the parchment away from Shylock and held it out to catch the last of the twilight. "It says, *'Don't be afraid. You are safe.'* " He tossed the letter into the canal. "Well, that's a load of monkey bollocks, because you are most definitely not safe. Grab him, Gratzi."

Gratiano had taken one step toward Shylock when the serpent came out of the canal right below Salarino's feet and rose as if she was climbing through water, her front claws stripping the muscles from his arms like gloves while her rear claws sliced his thighs down to the bone before he could fall. The scream Salarino was composing was cut off as the serpent's tail slashed his throat back to his spine.

Without a tick she flowed with the fountain of water that had erupted from the canal with her, fifteen feet up the side of the building, describing a great arc as she bounded along the wall over Shylock's head and dropped, jaws wide, on Gratiano, who was just turning to run. She caught his entire head in her mouth and twisted in the air like a great fish on the line as she fell back into the canal, dragging Gratiano beneath the water's surface with her. Salarino collapsed into a lumpy puddle of meat and bone and oozed over the edge of the walkway into the canal. A second later, a razored talon broke the surface and pulled the corpse under.

Shylock stood, shivering, covered in blood and freezing water, watching the canal settle as the red stain spread to the other side.

"Pie would have been good," he said to the empty air.

He kicked Salarino's dagger into the canal and hurried on his way, keeping his eyes wide open to dry in the cold, afraid to close them lest he see again the thing from the canal in the dark of a blink.

Antonio found morning stretching deep into the afternoon as he tried to shake off the hangover from his night of debauchery and alibi at Signora Veronica's. Bassanio had retrieved him from the brothel in the morning and had trundled him home to his apartments, but light, sound, air, and regret were still painful, and they had not yet heard from Gratiano and Salarino about the Jew's answer for a plea of grace.

Bassanio had kept the fire going and was boiling all the hope out of a chicken, in promise of some curative soup from a recipe concocted for him as a boy by his nursemaid, but for all his fretting and contrite fussing, he was only making his failure to attain financial rescue from Portia more annoying.

She had said: "I would pay double, treble, three thousand ducats for a friend of this description, Bassanio, but until I marry the man chosen by the dreaded caskets, I have only the allowance to maintain Belmont. Unless I appeal to my sister, who is away in Corsica, and as you need the ducats in less than a week, word could not even reach her in time. For you, for your friend, I would do all, but I cannot offer a fortune that is not mine."

Bassanio looked up from stirring his soup. "Perhaps the Jew will relent. Maybe he has learned to be more kind since his daughter ran off."

"Mercy might be more forthcoming had she not run off with our Lorenzo," said Antonio from under a blanket, where he sat enshrouded on the divan, hiding from the light and other harsh realities.

There came a light knock at the door.

"There," said Bassanio. "That might be Gratiano and Sal now."

"Because they are known to always knock timidly before entering," said Antonio, but the sarcasm was lost on his young protégé.

Bassanio opened the door.

"There's a monkey at the door with Gratiano's hat."

"A monkey?"

"He says his name is Jeff."

"He says that?" Antonio liked monkeys. He almost looked. "The *monkey* says that?"

"Well, no, there's a collar around his neck, and on it there's a brass tag, and *it* says '*Jeff*.' Oh look, there's a letter in his hat. Not the monkey's hat. Gratiano's hat."

"What's the letter say?"

"What's the letter say?" Bassanio asked the monkey.

"No, Bassanio, *read* the letter, don't ask the monkey."

"Oh, right. He probably only reads Hebrew."

Antonio pulled the blanket off his head and said, "What in the name of Saint fucking Mark are you talking about?"

The monkey screeched and bounded off down the stairs.

Bassanio closed the door and turned slowly to his friend, the letter in hand. "I didn't want to tell you, since they failed so miserably . . . but I hired the thieving Hebrew monkeys of La Giudecca to fix the caskets to win Portia in marriage. See here, the menorah pressed in the sealing wax, that is their sign. Funny, he didn't have on a yellow Jew hat, but a little black harlequin's hat. Perhaps it's a Jewish holiday."

Antonio hadn't thought his headache could worsen. But yes. "Break the seal, Bassanio. What does it say?"

Bassanio unfolded the letter and read:

"'Four friends have been taken
To Death's savage pool.
No pound of flesh flayed
Shall appease a wronged Fool.
Condolences.'"

Bassanio looked over the edge of the parchment at his bedraggled friend, whose eyes had gone wide. "Ha! The last line doesn't even rhyme. What does it mean?"

"It means that the gondolier with Salanio's dagger lied. He did not receive the dagger from Sal to carry the message to you, and it was not a small Jew he took to Belmont in the night. And Salarino and Gratiano are not going to come through that door with good news."

Twenty-two
No Shit, Shylock

S hylock did not see us there, in his house, when he entered, so intent was he upon closing the door behind him and locking it, putting a hefty slab of oak between him and whatever was in the outside world. He leaned his forehead against the door and stood there, shivering and out of breath. When Jessica came behind him to wrap a towel around his shoulders, he screamed, and she jumped back.

"Papa," said she.

"Look!" said I. "I've returned your loving daughter. Go ahead, give the girl a proper cuddle."

"I have no daughter," said Shylock, his back pressed so firmly against the door that I think it was the first time I had not seen him hunched over. Jessica clutched the towel to her bosom and backed away, trying to squeeze back tears.

"Thief!" he said to me. "Where are my ducats?"

"Look, I've brought Marco Polo!"

"Where is my turquoise?"

"And I've brought this monkey called Jeff. Look at his little fool's kit."

"What of my other jewels?"

"And look at this great drooling nitwit. Bigger even than Tubal's two huge Jews."

"Charmed," said the ninny.

"I have seen this monkey," said Shylock.

"Jeff," provided Drool.

"He gave me a letter not an hour ago."

"I know," said I. "I sent him with the letter."

" 'Don't be afraid,' it says. 'You will be safe,' it says. Then that thing, that creature, that monster—"

"That were the dragon Pocket shagged."

"There was no dragon shagging."

"Beggin' pardon, sir," said Drool, conspiratorially behind his hand, as subtle as a war hammer. "A gentleman don't talk about his dragon sextool adventures, so as not to compromise a lady's reputation."

"That is *not* what I taught you."

"Sor-ry."

"She was a mermaid when she shagged me—I *thought* she was a mermaid. And I was chained up. I'm not even sure it was a proper shagging. Could have been either end, although having now seen the toothy end, I will say she's not without her amorous skills—"

"'And even a homely girl can be beautiful when she bears a generous spirit in the dark,'" Drool quoted me in my own voice.

"Deviate," spat Jessica. "Dragon shagger!"

Shylock's eyes widened. "What is this? What is this? What is this? Consorting with monsters that tear the flesh from a man's bones like he would take off his socks? What *are* you?"

"Just the pert and nimble spirit of mirth, at your service," said I, with a dance step and a bit of a jingle on my hat bells, as Shylock had not yet seen me in my official togs.

"He *did* rescue you, Papa," said Jessica. "They *were* going to murder you." The first unstern, ungrowling thing she had said to or about me since she'd learned of Lorenzo. "But he *is* a thief, and a rascal, and most assuredly a fool."

"Look," said I, trying again for a distraction. "Marco Polo, famed Venetian explorer, under your roof."

"Signor," said Polo, with a slight bow. "Your daughter and Pocket gallantly rescued me from a Genoan prison, when even my own family had been unable to negotiate the terms of my release. I regret that they had to use your treasure, but my family will gladly restore it

to you, *with interest,* as soon as I am able to arrange it."
He really did know how to pour oil upon the churning
waters of an angry temper with his bearing. *With interest,* that simple phrase calmed Shylock, not because
he was greedy, but because he thought it was the one
thing that allowed him, as a Jew, to participate in this
oh-so-sophisticated republic of merchants, and Polo,
somehow, had known that. Perhaps years in the courts
of mad and murderous Oriental despots had taught him
how to best keep his head atop his shoulders.

"You are welcome in my house, Marco Polo," said
Shylock. Momentarily, the rest of us were not in the
room. "My daughter will bring you some wine." He
turned to Jessica.

"You have no daughter," she said. "Get your own
wine."

"Respect! Daughter! You take my gold, run off with
this Christian, this scoundrel Lorenzo—"

"I ran off with *this* scoundrel," she said, gesturing in
my general direction.

"Viv eated him," said Drool.

"Stop saying that," said I. "That is not right."

"Sor-ry," said the oaf, hanging his head. "Viv *ate* him."

"He said that before, Pocket," said Jessica. "He may
not be able to find the round side of a barrel, but he
does remember what is said, disturbingly well."

"Well, I am glad you were not with this Lorenzo, even if it means that you return wearing trousers with this—this—abomination," Shylock said, waving in my general direction.

"*Abomination*? I take your daughter out for a spot o' sailing, and in the mix rescue a national hero, teach her to speak pirate, and save her from a bloody murder plot, then return her in better than new condition, and I'm an abomination? What ho, respect, Shylock? Wherefore respect, Shylock?"

"What murder plot?" asked Jessica.

"Lorenzo was going to use you, take the gold, and cast you in the sea," said Shylock.

"No, that's not it," said I. "I mean the one that culminated a bit ago with Viv somewhat eviscerating Antonio's other minions. They would have killed you next to try to break your father's bond on Antonio." I frowned *my dire frown of truth,* I liked to call it, but as I did my hat bells jingled, undermining the dire sincerity of my lie.

"That's a wandering wagonload of Jew wank," she said, looming rather largely over me for a girl of her size.

"You know excessive use of alliteration is a sign of madness?"

"Antonio's ruffians were boasting of it days ago," said Shylock. "I thought you lost."

Jessica stormed up to me, her teeth gritted, her nose only a hairbreadth from my own. "You knew about Lorenzo all along, yet you didn't tell me?"

"I was afraid you'd be cross. It's easy for Shylock, you're always cross with him."

"Well, I'm bloody well cross with you now."

"Red tent?" offered Shylock with a cough.

"Like I've been living under one for months," I replied under my breath.

"It's not a bloody red tent!"

"So to speak," said I.

She screamed then, loudly and somewhat protractedly, frightening some of us more than others.

"If you're quite finished," said I from my nest, cradled in Drool's arms where I had leapt. "I have things I need to attend to."

"Well, the dragon's already fed, so you can tick that one off," said Jessica, a begrudging smile finding its way to her lips. Sometimes, methinks, a lass just needs to have a proper enraged scream.

"I need to catch a boat to Belmont, Shylock, if I could prevail upon you for coin for the fare."

Shylock shrugged and began digging into his purse.

"You're going to give him *more* money?" said Jessica.

Shylock shrugged. "He saved you, and he saved me, and I will charge him interest. I will write this up, fool."

"Ah, writing your own loans again. How do you like the spectacles?" He had fetched them from his desk and fit them on his nose.

"They are serviceable." He also betrayed a weak smile, a rare gem upon the surly Jew. "But you will do nothing to deprive me of my revenge."

"Good Shylock, have I not told you before, I'm but the weapon of your revenge?"

"Aye, he's a wickedly dangerous marauder, cradled like a frightened lamb in the arms of his great lummox," said Jessica. She tweaked my nose and turned on her boot heel with a flourish. "I'll bring us some wine, Signor Polo," she said. "Then Papa and I will take you home to your family."

"You cannot go out in those clothes," said Shylock. "A good Jewish girl does not wear pirate—"

Jessica reeled on him with the same fierceness in her eye she had shown right before the scream.

Shylock turned away and pretended to have something important to do in the opposite direction. "Fine, fine, dress like a pirate. I am just glad your mother cannot see you thus . . ."

"I'm telling you, Iago, the fool is alive. Even if the note had not mentioned a fool, the monkey was called

Jeff. How many monkeys called Jeff, dressed in motley, can there be in Venice?"

Antonio paced his apartments while Iago sat calmly at his table, cleaning his fingernails with his dagger. They'd let him out of irons after only two days at sea. The sailors whose job it was to keep him had been persuaded that their prisoner might, indeed, become their new commander. With Othello and Desdemona dead, and Cassio burdened with his duties in Corsica, no one could even figure out how the council could prosecute the charges. By the time they'd reached Venice, he'd walked off the ship with his weapons restored, and only the promise that he would appear before the council on the appointed date.

"I don't believe it. Calm yourself, Antonio, I control the orbit of the spheres of fate. With Othello dead, we may yet see your protégé as senator and our plan will go forward."

Antonio had always been frightened of Iago, his rough certainty and willingness to violence was out of place in the genteel world of commerce, where battles were metaphors and triumphs measured in profits, but now, after his time in Corsica, Antonio also feared the soldier had gone quite mad.

"They found pieces of Salarino and Gratiano in the canals today," said the merchant. "Pieces of them. And the note came due the day after they were to remove

Shylock. I have to answer Shylock's suit before the council tomorrow. He's going to cut out a pound of my flesh."

"Gentle Antonio, the Council of Venice will never allow the Jew to collect his bond. A Jew? No more than they would prosecute me for actions against the Moor. We are Venetians, they are outsiders. Justice favors the favored sons. If it comes to it, I have a plan for your trial that will play for both our interests. You cannot imagine the force that has come to my aid, the creature conjured into being by my hatred for the Moor."

"Yes, yes, so you've said." Antonio had, without intent, been moving away from the soldier the entire time they had been talking, until he was nearly standing with his back at his own door, the stairwell being the only way to find further distance, short of leaping out a window. "But you said, too, that Brabantio had been eaten as if by some creature, and this—thing—this thing of darkness, it killed your friend Rodrigo. You saw it."

"I was going to kill Rodrigo anyway. My hatred simply anticipated my desires. Ah, perhaps it was such with Brabantio as well—the imp of my ire anticipating the need to have the old man out of the way before I even knew it myself."

Antonio put his hand on the door latch before he answered. "Because the *imp of your ire* couldn't have thought of a better way to bollix up our entire venture than by killing the essential partner? I tell you, Iago, the little fool is alive, and he works, even now, against us. My good sense tells me that your tale of a creature is a false vision, a hallucination brought on by handling that infernal sticky potion of Brabantio's, but a false vision did not put ragged pieces of my friends in the canal. A hallucination did not put a fool's head in the casket at Belmont to thwart Bassanio's marriage to Portia. Your grand and powerful hatred did not send a note ticking off my dead friends like so many sausages on a shopping list. I tell you, Iago, the fool lives, and he works his revenge against us."

Iago sighed. "Well, we shall just have to kill him again."

"His will is done now. Tomorrow I have to stand before the court and answer Shylock's bond with a pound of my flesh."

"Then Shylock shall have to be removed as well."

"But you have no men, no forces, and neither have I. I cannot send Bassanio to do such dread deeds. It is not in his nature. He is already distraught at the deaths of his friends."

"Calm yourself, merchant. This is my business. I still have some of Rodrigo's fortune cached away at Arsenal, and between his gold and my will, forces will come to our aid before morning."

"Oh, Nerissa, I am beside myself with worry." Portia fussed at her dressing table while Nerissa arranged her shoes into mismatched pairs in the closet. "I sent Father's lawyer, Balthassar, to Padua a week ago with a letter to our cousin, Bellario, who is a doctor of law, and I fear he will not return with the response before the morning. If he does not, I know not how we will aid Bassanio in saving his friend Antonio."

"How would we aid anyway? All the funds of the estate are out of your reach, lady. And even the funds by all the suitors have stopped coming with rumors that there could be no winner among the players."

"We shall help them by pleading the case, Nerissa. As a doctor and clerk of law."

"But, lady, only men may be doctors of law."

"That is so, and so shall we be men. We shall dress as men, with jeweled daggers at our waists to show our authority, and great empty codpieces, where the court thinks our brains and abilities reside. I will turn feminine mincing steps into a manly stride, and speak with a voice that breaks like one passing from boy to man. And I'll wager, when we appear as men, I'll be said to be the prettier of the two." She giggled.

"No doubt, sweet Portia, and your brash nature and unfounded self-confidence shall further convince all that you are the better man."

A servant appeared in the doorway then, and cleared his throat.

"Lady, a visitor at the door for you. He asks that you meet him at the servants' entrance."

"A gentleman?" said Portia. "Well, show him into the foyer and I will make an entrance."

"No, lady, not a gentleman, and the caller is for Miss Nerissa. He is a clown."

"A clown?"

"Yes, mum. The visitor wears the motley of a fool. He would not give his name."

"I'll be right down," said Nerissa.

She was gone for perhaps half an hour, in which time Portia noticed that she was having a particularly difficult time choosing shoes for dinner.

When she returned, tears streaked Nerissa's face. "Portia, oh lady, I'm so sorry. Your sister."

"What? What, Nerissa?"

"Desdemona is dead."

———————

As the gondola from Belmont glided up to the landing at Shylock's house, I could see one of Tubal's huge Jews, I know not which, eclipsing the doorway. Not alarming in itself, except I could see his heavy club dangling from a lanyard at his wrist, and we had approached at such an angle that I could see the other huge Jew poised at Shylock's side door, ready to shoulder through it.

"Not a word," said I to the gondolier. "Throw my bundle on the landing after me." I plopped a coin down by his feet, and ran the length of the boat, leapt, and landed on the cobbles, coming up from a roll with one of my daggers in hand just as Jessica was opening the door.

I sent the dagger flying into the back of the thug's knee, and when he bent over in pain, I sailed feetfirst over his back, into the house as Jessica stepped back in alarm. I had landed on my hip on the table, which I slid across, drawing another dagger as I landed on my feet.

"Drool! Side door!" I called, just as the side door exploded inward and banged back on its hinges. I sent the dagger straight to the oaf's thigh and he tumbled into the house, leading with a long butcher knife. Drool had been sitting by the fire and now stood over the huge Jew as surprised as if he'd just discovered a live snake in his breakfast porridge.

I turned to face the attacker I'd wounded at the door. My friend Kent had taught me that, as a rule, with men of great size, it was more important to stop them first, rather than try to kill them in one blow.

I held my third dagger by the blade, poised to throw. "This one in your eye, boy," said I. "Do twitch and I will send thee to a porkless Hebrew hell with stunning swiftness."

He stopped struggling to gain his feet and froze on the spot; good fortune, for I was not sure that I would hit the mark, so long out of practice I was. If I'd missed, he might have bludgeoned us all to death. I heard Jessica's intake of breath as she looked over my shoulder toward where the other huge Jew had fallen and was rising.

"Drool, hit him!" I called.

I took my eyes off my own huge Jew just long enough to see Drool smash a heavy, three-legged stool across the knife-wielding brother's head, showering the room with splinters, kindling, and a fine spray of blood. The downed brother went limp on the floor, quite unconscious, perhaps dead.

I held my dagger fast. "Drool, fetch my dagger from that chap's thigh. And come get the other one from this one's knee."

"Jones!" said Drool, noticing that I was again in possession of my puppet stick, which I'd shoved down the back of my jerkin for the gondola ride. "Me wee friend."

"Get the knives, you great slobbering dreadnought," said the puppet Jones, a bit breathless from the tumbling and whatnot.

Drool went around the table, a bloody knife in one of his hands, and regarded the huge Jew who stood in the front door. "It will hurt when I pulls out the knife," Drool said to the huge Jew with no menace whatsoever. "Sor-ry."

The huge Jew seemed as disturbed by the sight of a man-shaped creature larger than himself nearly as much as he was by the blade in his knee.

"He and I will both kill you if your club hand moves, Ham, so be brave lest you be twice slayed."

"I'm Japheth," said the giant Hebrew.

"I don't give a jostled jeroboam of monkey jizz, you yellow-hatted buffoon. If you move, you die."

Japheth gasped as Drool pulled the knife from his leg. Drool stepped back just as Jessica came around from the side with a half-full wine bottle, which ended its arc by bouncing off the huge Jew's forehead, unbroken, sending him back a few steps from the door.

"Well done, love," said I. "Can't account for the thickness of his hat nor the density of his great noggin, but a normal bloke would've been right well brained."

She smiled and curtsied, despite that she was still shaking a bit from the adventure.

"Take your brother and go home," said I to Japheth. "Tell Tubal what happened here and that there are no more layers between him and his mayhem. If two hours pass and he is still on La Giudecca, he and his whole family will be floating dead in the canal by morning, and you two with them."

Japheth, limping pitifully, made his way around the outside of the house and dragged his brother out the door. Ham groaned as he was moved, so evidently Drool had not killed him.

"Ta," said Drool as Japheth carried his brother away.

"Drool, there's a bundle of clothing out on the landing; would you fetch it before the tide takes it, please?"

"That were smashing, Pocket."

"Go, lad. We'll need that bundle."

Shylock stood in the middle of the room, unmoving, where he had been when I'd sailed sideways into the room.

"So," said I. "Marco Polo found his way back to his family?"

"Yes," said Shylock, still a bit dazed. "He returned my ducats with interest."

"Lovely. And he left the boxes for me?"

"Yes," said Jessica. "As you asked."

"Tubal has been my friend many years. And he sent these boys to kill me? He would not have done this for spite. He must have been paid."

"No shit, Shylock," said I. "It was business."

"You are more agile than I thought," said Shylock, nodding to himself sadly.

"Treated by a wizard with *syrup of cat,* he was, givin' him magical quickness," said the puppet Jones.

"Really?" said Jessica, her eyes wide.

"Nah, havin' you on. I'm just a wooden-headed ninny," said the puppet, tapping the Jewess on the bottom with a jingle of his hat bells.

Twenty-three
The Trial

CHORUS: *When war makes commerce and commerce is law, profit rules prudence and justice is flawed. Behold now, the court of Venice, a grand edifice on the Grand Canal, and among the lawyers, senators, citizens, and those seeking justice, stand foreign traders and dignitaries, here to see the rule of law in action, the backbone of the republic, the insurance of their fair trade with the watery city-state. And here, too, amid costumed fools and cross-dressed maids, Shylock seeks to satisfy sweet revenge dealt by a sword forged of irony.*

"Who are that?" asked Drool. We stood with Jessica in costume at the very back of the court.

"Just a grandiose nutter who can't help himself bursting through the fourth wall like a great dim-witted battering ram," said I. "Pay him no mind."

A bailiff was calling all to order at the front of the room, where the high council of six senators sat on a dais, with the doge at the center, wearing a grand gold-and-silver robe and a hat that looked more than anything like a white, gold-trimmed codpiece inverted on his head.

"Is Antonio Donnola the merchant here?" asked the doge.

"I am here," said Antonio, coming through the great arch behind us, flanked on one side by Bassanio, and on the other by Iago. Iago? What was Iago doing walking about free like a roaming plague in boots? And armed, for fuck's sake.

"I am sorry for thee," said the doge. "You come to answer a stony adversary, an inhuman wretch incapable of pity, void and empty of any measure of mercy."

Well, that seemed a somewhat prejudiced portrayal of Shylock—if I were one of the foreign merchants watching this for a taste of Venetian jurisprudence, I would think, *"Well, you don't want to wear a yellow hat to trial, or these fucks will most certainly throw you to the dogs."* The puppet Jones twitched under my costume, begging to be allowed to shout it out.

"I have heard, Your Grace, he is resolved to his course, and I have no lawful means to carry me."

"Call the Jew Shylock," commanded the doge.

"Shylock," called the bailiff, and Shylock trudged through the door in his normal dark gabardine and yellow hat, his appearance differing today only in that by his purse, at his belt, hung a long carving knife in a leather sheath.

"Let him stand before me," said the doge.

Shylock passed one of the many bronze braziers lit around the room to warm it on this bitter day, to a spot before the dais.

"Shylock, the world thinks, as do I, that you pretend this cruel malice, and in the last moment, you will relent and show mercy. All believe, despite your protestations, that you will be touched with human gentleness and love, and forgive not only a pound of this merchant's flesh, but a portion of the principal, taking pity on his recent losses, which would ruin even the most royal merchant, and would spur mercy from even the rough hearts of the most stubborn Turks and Tartars. We all expect a gentle answer, Jew."

Shylock cleared his throat and stood straight for only the second time I had seen him such. "Your Grace, I have stated my intent, and by your holy Sabbath I have sworn to have the forfeit of my bond. If you deny it, let danger light upon your city's charter, for the law is your foundation—your only surety of value to offer these merchants from all nations who trade with you. If you ask me why I would have a pound of carrion flesh, I will not answer, but instead ask you, why do some men lose their urine at the sound of bagpipes?"

"Cracking non sequitur," I said to Jessica. "That should send the doge to scratching his knobbish hat."

"That's a bollocks reason!" shouted Bassanio.

"I am not bound to please you with my answers," said Shylock.

"Do all men kill the things they do not love?" asked Bassanio.

"What, wouldst thou have a serpent sting thee twice?" said Shylock.

At this last answer, it was not Bassanio, nor even Antonio who reacted, but Iago, who had seemed bored with the proceedings until now, who suddenly whipped his gaze around to Shylock, his features locked in disgust, as if they'd been frozen in place by a Gorgon.

I grinned. *Well done, Jew.* They knew, at least Iago knew, what had happened to Antonio's cohorts. Antonio looked to be in a daze, like a man who has been stunned by the sight of a massacre, or the rescue therefrom.

"Very well, then," said Bassanio. "For three thousand ducats, here is six." From behind us, two servants carried in a casket of coins as big as a man's chest and set it on the floor before Shylock with a heavy clink.

"*Take it, take it, take it, Shylock.*" I thought I was chanting in my head, but someone shushed me, so perhaps I had been thinking aloud.

"Not for six times six thousand," said Shylock. "I shall have my bond."

"How should you ever hope for mercy, having shown none?" asked the doge.

Or sense? thought I.

"What mercy shall I need, having done no wrong?" said Shylock. "You have among you many a purchased slave, which you work like your dogs and your mules, and keep in quarters fit for animals. Shall I say to you, 'Let them be free. Let them marry your heirs. Let them live in your houses, eat as well as you, let their beds be as soft as yours.' And you say, 'They are our slaves, we will do as we will.' And so I say to you, the pound of flesh which I demand is *mine*. It is bought and paid for dearly and I will have it. And if you deny me, there is no validity in the decrees of Venice, and the city and her trades cannot be trusted. I would have justice. I would have my answer."

I whispered to my right, where Jessica stood dressed again as a boy, her pirate kit somewhat subdued by a long, unadorned cloak. "Your father is so stubbornly unmovable he would make stones gloat at their ability to dance."

"Why do you think I was going to elope?" she whispered back. "But he is not so different from you in your own revenge, except he would have his witnessed by all of Venice."

"Upon my power," said the doge, "I would dismiss this court, unless Bellario, a learned doctor of the law I have sent for, comes to determine this."

The bailiff spoke up: "My lord, a messenger from Padua arrives with a letter from Bellario."

"Read the letter," commanded the doge.

The bailiff unfolded a parchment and read, " 'Your Grace shall understand that I am very sick, and cannot heed your call, but when your summons arrived, I had as my houseguest a young doctor of law from Rome, called Balthassar. I acquainted him with the case between Antonio and the Jew, and he is furnished with my opinion, bettered with his own learning, the greatness of which I cannot commend enough. Let not his youth be an impediment, for never have I seen one so young with such a body of knowledge.' Signed Bellario." The bailiff folded the paper.

"Where is this doctor?" called the doge.

I heard steps behind us and turned to see Portia, dressed all in black, the robes of a lawyer, a false beard and mustache fixed upon her face, followed by Nerissa, who was dressed in similar clothes, wearing the hat of a clerk, and carrying a secretary's box, much like I had carried for Shylock in those early days.

The duke held his hand out to Portia, and she bowed over it as stoutly as any boy. When Nerissa had told me of their plan, I thought it would never work, but I would have believed Portia a young man if I did not know better. Fine of features, to be sure, and Nerissa had disguised her girlish curves by draping her robe and having her wear high boots so the curve of her calves did not show.

"You know the case, and Bellario's judgment?" asked the doge.

"I do, Your Grace," said Portia. "I am informed thoroughly of the case. Which is Antonio and which is the Jew."

"I don't know, love," I whispered to Jessica, "perhaps the one wearing the bloody bright yellow Jew hat who is sharpening his knife on his boot."

Jessica giggled, far too girlishly for her disguise, and I was forced to elbow her in the side, at which she giggled more, but silently, as she elbowed me back.

Before I could respond, Nerissa shoved into the space between me and Drool. "You look fetching," she said, making no effort whatsoever to sound like a young man.

"As do you," I whispered. "Smashing beard. Strapping down those bosoms seems sinful, like hiding your light under a bushel, innit?"

"Shhhh," she shushed.

"Is your name Shylock?" Portia asked the Jew.

"Shylock is my name. Murray Shylock."

"Murray? Bloody Shylock's Christian name is *Murray*?" I said to Jessica, who shushed me from that side.

"Not really his Christian name, though, is it?" said Nerissa.

Jessica shushed us both.

"Of strange nature is this suit you follow, Shylock. Yet Venetian law cannot impugn you as you proceed." She turned to Antonio. "You stand in his danger, do you not?"

"Aye, he says so," said Antonio.

"Then must the Jew be merciful," said Portia.

"On what compulsion must I?" asked Shylock, now honing his knife on the leather sheath with great flourish.

"The quality of mercy is not strained," said Portia, pacing as if lecturing a class. "It droppeth as the gentle rain from heaven, upon the place beneath. It is twice blessed. It blesses him that gives and him that receives. It is an attribute to God himself, and earthly power does show most like God's, when mercy seasons justice. Therefore, Jew, consider this: All of us pray for mercy, and that same prayer teaches us all to render deeds of mercy. So must *you* mitigate your plea with mercy, or this strict court of Venice will render the full sentence against the merchant."

"I crave no mercy, my deeds fall upon my head," said Shylock. "I crave the law, the penalty for my bond." Two swipes of the knife on the leather sheath.

Portia nodded. "Is he not able to discharge the money?"

"Yes," called Bassanio, "I tender it for him in court. Yea his bond plus twice the sum, or I will be bound to pay ten times over if need be, or forfeit my hands or my heart. Anything to curb this cruel devil from his will."

"Shylock should love that," said I to Jessica. "The way you people love lopping off body parts." Then to Nerissa I said, "How did Bassanio come to have six thousand ducats suddenly?"

"Nine thousand," said Nerissa. "When news of Desdemona's death came, the lawyers released the gold that had been paid to the estate to Portia for the lottery for her hand. She married Bassanio last night in secret."

"Well, so much for the three caskets."

"Did you shit in one?"

"Moi?" said I, in perfect fucking French.

"You left a turd in one of the boxes, didn't you?"

I shrugged. "Not ungarnished. I took my knife and scraped some gold leaf from a table leg over it."

"You are a most wicked rascal, Pocket."

"Me? *You* wanted me to cut her throat."

"I was feeling melancholy."

"Red tent?"

"What?"

"Jewish thing."

"I will stab you in your poxy little ear, Pocket," said Jessica.

"Shhh," I shushed them. Bitter harpies. Jessica did have a knife, though.

"It must not be," said Portia to Bassanio. "There is no power in Venice that can alter an established decree. It would be recorded as a precedent, and many errors will be forced on the state by its example."

"Oh, wise judge," said Shylock. "Oh, much honored young judge."

"Let me look upon the bond." The bailiff handed it to her; she unfolded it and read. "Shylock, there is thrice thy money offered thee. Will you not accept it and let me tear up this bond?"

"An oath. I have made an oath in heaven and will not perjure my soul. No, not for Venice."

"Then this bond is forfeit," said Portia. "And lawfully the Jew may claim a pound of flesh to be cut off him nearest the merchant's heart. Shylock, take thrice thy money, and bid me tear the bond."

"Take it, you muleheaded ninny!" came a shout from alarmingly close by and was followed by a great rise across the crowd of similar calls.

I looked at Jessica, who had her hands over her mouth, her eyes wide with dismay. "Slipped out," she explained.

"'*Honor thy mother and thy father*,' doesn't it say in your book?" I said.

"Aye, a full chapter after the first lesson of the Bible, which is 'Don't shag the bloody serpent,'" she said.

"Fair point, well made," said I.

"Who is that?" asked Nerissa.

"She are Shylock's daughter," said Drool.

"She looks like a boy."

"Aye," said the oaf. "She's a apprentice pirate."

"What are you?"

"Apprentice fool."

"She's the voice you'll use, Drool," I whispered to the giant.

Out on the courtroom floor, Shylock pressed on: "No, Your Honor, you know the law and appear a worthy judge; proceed to judgment. By my soul, I swear, there is no power in the tongue of man to alter me. I stand here on my bond."

"Idiot," I whispered to my retinue.

Antonio stepped forward, jaw set. "Most heartily I beseech the court to give judgment, no word of man will turn the Jew."

"So be it," said Portia. "Prepare thy bosom for his knife."

"Wise judge," said Shylock. "Oh, excellent young man."

"Bind him," said Portia.

Antonio then seemed to lose whatever resolve he had found, because he began to faint. Iago and Bassanio caught him. Bailiffs brought in a chair, which was set in front of the dais. Gasps and shouts ranging from "Show mercy!" to "Damn the Jew devil!" rang through the crowd.

"Have you a scale to weigh the flesh?" asked Portia.

"I do," said Shylock.

"And have you a surgeon to stanch the blood so he does not bleed to death?"

"I thought I'd just carve and see how it went," said Shylock. "My daughter, she could have married a surgeon, and I would have one here. But no—punch in my heart—she is of her own mind. And so no."

"So it is *my* fault if Antonio bleeds to death?" Jessica said. "That's a squirming stein of squid spooge."

"I adore you," I said.

"Yeah, right, bugger off," said the pirate Jess.

"Proceed then, Jew," said Portia.

Bailiffs took Antonio and bound him to the chair, while he went on about loving Bassanio and how the boy shouldn't feel bad that he was going to die, nor blame himself, that it was other forces, and his own doing, that caused it. Honestly, I wasn't paying attention.

"What is Portia up to?" I asked Nerissa.

"I think she'd hoped to talk Shylock out of his revenge."

"I'd say that plan has gone solidly tits up."

"I think she overestimated the persuasive abilities she honed bargaining with shoe salesmen. Truth be told, though, she *is* talented. They'd all be barefoot if the trial had gone in that direction."

Shylock stropped his knife two more strokes on the leather sheath, then moved up on Antonio to lay the blade across his bare chest.

"Wait!" said Portia.

"Wait!" said Bassanio.

"Wait!" said Iago.

"Wait!" said I.

"You go," said Portia to Bassanio.

"After you," said Iago to Portia.

"Go ahead," said I. Actually, I was just going to request that Shylock dull the knife a bit so it would be more painful. For all his noble civility, Antonio had been complicit in murdering my Cordelia and me, not to mention giving the order to kill Shylock, and no doubt Jessica if he'd had the chance. But it appeared that the others would draw it out.

"Antonio," said Bassanio. "I am married to a wife which is as dear to me as life itself and all the world, but I would here sacrifice her and all to save you, my friend."

Portia threw out a hip, betraying her womanly shape beneath the man's clothes. "So, you would offer up your wife to Shylock in place of your friend, Bassanio?"

"Not for the pound of flesh part, just for the night, I thought."

Even Shylock looked at Bassanio like he'd lost his mind.

"She is most beautiful and smells of rosebuds," added Bassanio.

"I'm cutting him," said Shylock.

"Wait!" said Portia. "While this bond gives you a pound of flesh, it allows you no blood. So you may take your pound of flesh, but by the laws of Venice, if you spill one drop of Christian blood in the process, then *your* life will be forfeit and all of your lands and goods shall go to the state."

"This is the law?" asked Shylock.

"It is," said Portia.

"Then I'll have the nine thousand ducats, and let Antonio go."

"No!" said Portia. "The Jew shall have all justice, and only the penalty."

"Fine," said Shylock. "I'll take this fellow's wife for the night."

"That is not part of the bond. Even Bassanio may not have his wife for the night. For several nights."

"That is the law?" asked Bassanio.

"It is," answered Portia. "So, Shylock, prepare to cut off the flesh, but shed no blood, nor take thee less than one pound by even a jot, nor more by the weight of a hair, but one pound exactly."

"Exactly?" said Shylock. He looked to the doge. "The young judge is just making this up as he goes along. Give me my principal and let me go."

"I have it ready, here," said Bassanio.

"He has refused it in open court," said Portia. "He shall have his bond, and nothing more, to be taken at his peril."

Shylock dropped his knife, the clang of which echoed in the marble hall. "Then the devil give him the ducats. I'll no longer stay in question."

"Tarry more, Jew," said Portia, holding her hand before Shylock to stay his exit. "The law hath another hold on thee. If it be proved against an alien that, by direct or indirect attempts, he seek the life of any citizen, the party he contrived against shall receive one half of his goods, and the other half comes to the state. The offender's life lies at the mercy of the doge only."

Shylock fell to one knee, breathless, stunned by the pronouncement. Jessica grabbed my biceps, digging her nails in.

"What," I shouted, "if the one conspired against was himself a traitor to the state, murdered the queen of one of Venice's allies, caused the death of the high commander of the navy and his lady, and planned to kill and replace the doge? What then?"

Portia—no, everybody—looked to the back of the room where I stood. Of course they couldn't see me, because I'm dogfuckingly small, aren't I, but they looked at Drool and gasped.

"Well, that would be different then," said Portia.

"Who spoke there?" said the doge. "I would hear him."

"Wait!" cried Iago.

Twenty-four
The Verdict

I minced, I tiptoed, I blushed, I tittered and tee-heed behind a fan as I made my way to the front of the court, ever the shy girl, dressed in one of Portia's fancier gowns. Behind me, Drool, dressed in a gown fashioned from three of Nerissa's dresses, minced, tiptoed, blushed, tittered, and tee-heed as well, his voice note for note, tone for tone, the exact copy of Nerissa's.

"Who is this?" asked the doge.

"It is I," said I. "Portia of Belmont, daughter of Brabantio."

The color and expression ran from Portia's face as if someone had turned a spigot under her false beard.

"With my maid, Nerissa."

Drool curtsied, ever the enormous, delicate, donkey-donged flower of femininity.

There were various expressions among the crowd of awe and dismay at the sheer crashing magnitude of Drool in drag.

"Why, that's the biggest woman I've ever seen," said one onlooker.

"And the ugliest, too," said his companion.

"I'd have a go at her," said another.

"How much for the big girl?" came a woman's voice from the back.

It was Signora Veronica, who ran the brothel, and knew by experience that there was no creature on earth so vile that some punter wouldn't pay to shag it.

While we had tarted Drool up more than somewhat for his disguise, he still made for a child-frighteningly unattractive woman. Myself, however, in the guise of a fair and ambling nymph, could have tented tights and broken blokes' hearts across the land, as long as I kept a close shave on.

"This is highly irregular," said the doge. "Women are not permitted to speak before the court."

"Yes, Your Grace, but as I am the only voice of my family still among the quick, allowances are due, don't you think?"

"We are sorry to hear about your sister, lady, and I suppose—"

"It shall not be so!" barked Portia. "A woman shall not speak before the court unless a case is made against her."

"Thank you for your condolences, Your Grace. I was very close to my sister. It seems like only yesterday that we were but girls blossoming into womanhood, sharing a bath, touching each other in the most delicious—"

"This woman is an imposter!" shouted Iago.

"Yes," said I, turning to the soldier, pulling my fan aside, fluttering my eyelashes at him, and Portia, in turn. "Do go on, you handsome ruffian."

Portia turned to Iago and tried, with a shake of her head, to subtly signal for him to shut the fuck up, but all eyes in the court that were not still captured by the horrific grandeur of Drool in skirts saw her move.

Iago stepped back in rank with Bassanio. "Excuse me, Your Grace, I am mistaken."

"Fooled by the bloody frog of war, innit?" said the puppet Jones from under my skirts.

"The *fog* of war, you Cockney knob," said I.

"Your Grace, if I may. Before you unbind Antonio, I think the solution to the dilemma stated by the young judge is simple. Shylock need only lay his knife in one of these braziers until it is red hot, then make his cut with the glowing knife, thus cauterizing the wound as he cuts. Not a drop of blood shall be spilled. Once the blade is quenched, he may heat it again, then make his next cut. He'll have his pound of flesh and Antonio will not have lost a drop of blood. There may be some discomfort, as the surgeons say, but it will satisfy the law. Such a method is often used on the field of battle to cauterize wounds, is it not, Iago?"

Iago, now retreated to join Bassanio, seemed as if he'd rather not venture an opinion.

Antonio was dazed now, having lived his terror, his rescue, and now his return to jeopardy, all while still tied to a chair.

"Iago," said the doge. "Why are you here? Are you not to come before us in two days?"

"Yes, Iago," I said. "Please explain why you are here—why after all but murdering your commander and my queen, and conspiring with the enemies of Venice—why are you early?"

Shylock picked up his knife from the floor, took a few steps, and stabbed the blade into the coals of the brazier closest him, at which point Antonio appeared to faint.

Iago stormed over to me, loomed over my helpless and womanly figure. "This, this, is not Brabantio's daughter, Your Grace."

"He's right, Your Grace," said Portia, having gathered her wits, I suppose. "This woman is an imposter." She strode to me and snatched the fan from my hand. "Behold!" she said.

I snatched off her mustache. "Behold," said I.

She grabbed the front of my gown with both hands and tore it down the front, revealing my black motley beneath. "Behold!" she said.

I took her poet's shirt, and tore it down the front, revealing that she was wearing nothing whatsoever underneath. "Behold!" said I.

"Them are smashing," said Drool, reaching under his skirt.

Portia, suddenly aware of the draft upon her bosoms, clutched herself and ran screaming from the room in a manner quite unmanly, but to her credit, inspiring great cheers from the gallery.

I pulled off the veil and stepped out of what was left of Portia's dress, to many gasps and exclamations of surprise. I pulled my puppet stick from the pile of skirts.

"Drool, run along and see that Portia is out of distress."

"Portia?" said Bassanio.

"Yes, she's your wife, you bloody nitwit. You go, too."

"Fortunato," growled Iago, now trapped on the floor before the court.

"Fortunato?" said the doge, surprised, but pleased, I think. The other senators seemed less so.

"No one calls me that," said I.

"We thought you had returned to France," said the doge.

"Aye, which is what these two scoundrels wanted you to think, along with their partner, Brabantio."

"He is mad," said Iago. "You know how the fool drinks!"

"I was mad for a bit, Your Grace. When these two, with Brabantio, walled me up in his cellar, leaving me there to die, all because I was sent here by my queen to oppose the prosecution of a new Crusade, yes, madness was with me for a spell."

"That's ridiculous," said Iago. "I am a soldier. I have no say in the politics of war."

"But you would, if you took command, wouldn't you? Appointed by Brabantio."

The doge stood now. "What are you saying, Fortunato? Brabantio was a beloved colleague and member of this council."

"But he was not doge, was he?" said I.

Antonio had come out of his haze to see me standing before the doge. "I knew he was still alive. I told you!"

Iago winced, and turned a lens of hatred toward the merchant. "Of course he's alive," said the soldier through gritted teeth. "Why would he be other than alive?"

"Your Grace! My bond?" called Shylock. He was drawing his knife, which was now as red as the coals, from the fire.

"Wait, Jew." The doge conferred with the other five on the council, Brabantio's seat still unfilled, and after a bit of nodding, said, "The bond on Antonio by the laws of Venice is dismissed, and he is free to go. As the young doctor of law stated, you, Shylock, an alien, have broken the laws of Venice in pursuit of your bond, so it is invalid."

"You know," said I, "I presume, Your Grace, that the young doctor was *not* a doctor of law but a *young lady.* And by the way, that gigantic slapper with the erection that followed her out *was not,* in case you were further confused."

"I would have justice," said Shylock. "If not my bond, the gold."

"You forfeit the gold as well," said the doge. "The council has determined it."

"One moment," said I. "Where were you born, Shylock?"

"I was born here, on La Giudecca, where I have lived all my life."

"And where do you make your living?"

"On the Rialto, as any merchant. I make my living where business is done in Venice."

"How, Your Grace, is Shylock, who was born and raised in Venice, an alien? Does Venice determine the alien at its convenience, so that traders from other lands may not be protected upon the whim of the city?"

There was a lot of whispering going on in the gallery, I presume among the traders from many nations who were in attendance.

The doge looked at his brethren on the council, then cleared his throat. "Shylock is an alien in that he is a Jew, and does not pay homage to the church and our Lord. Such was shown in his refusal to grant mercy to Antonio, as mercy and forgiveness are the instruction of our Lord."

"Well, yes," said I. "The Hebrew God is a great, vengeful twat, isn't he? Wiping out whole races of people on a whim, storming around in jealous rage, while your Christian God ponces around with, 'Oh, by your leave, good sir, allow me to turn the other cheek and wash your bloody disgusting feet. Have some loaves with them fishes?'

"Oh, that one time he did throw a wobbly with the money changers in the Temple, which, not to herniate the bloody metaphor in this little scenario, would be you fucks, and for it, you, you bloody Italians, nailed him to a tree. Shylock is a Jew, but you papists use your

Jesus like I use my bloody puppet stick here." I bobbed Jones before them.

"You lead in with his *suffer the little children come unto me,*' when it's convenient, but the whole time you got your vengeful Old Testament God right behind, like a wicked dagger hidden in the small of your back, ready to smite the first flailing fuck that works against your interests." I drew one of my daggers, as quick as a cat, and made as if I was dirking some imaginary foe.

"Did you just compare yourself to the Holy Trinity?" asked one of the council indignantly.

"Don't be literal, Senator, people will think you thick. But in a word, *yes.* And you would be well advised not to ask to see the Holy Ghost in my trinity, as she's got two sides, and one of them is a wet nightmare of dark destruction that makes your Othello look like a bloody parade princess."

Only then, in front of the council, Iago and Antonio constrained, did it occur to me, why, exactly, Vivian had not attacked me like all the others.

"So Shylock may be a vengeful, greedy bastard," said I. I grinned at Shylock to assure him I was on his side. "But not because he's a Jew, any more than the lot of you are shiftless, greedy tossers because you are Christians. You all share the same god: gold. Your faith follows fortune, and would deny him fortune for his."

"Yes! Yes!" said Shylock, coming forward now, leaving Antonio still tied to his chair, straining to turn to watch the proceedings. "I am deprived justice because I am a Jew? Hath not a Jew eyes? Hath not a Jew hands?"

"Hath not a Jew shoes?" said the puppet Jones. "If you count them, are they not two Jew shoes? If you dye them blue, are they not two blue Jew shoes? If they, too, make the sound of a cow, are they not two blue Jew moo shoes?"

"That is not what I am saying!" said Shylock.

"I thought we were just asking about Jew kit. Proceed," said Jones.

"If you prick us, do we not bleed?" said Shylock. "Ouch!"

"That would be a yes," said I.

"Why did you poke me?" Shylock held his arm where I'd barely touched him with my dagger.

"Hardly worth toting three sharp daggers about if you can't use them during question time, is it? To the point, Your Grace, you use your faith as a tool to exclude this Jew, the same way these two scoundrels and Brabantio were going to use it to foment war. A Crusade. They poisoned my queen, they told me their plan because they thought I would never live to tell anyone."

"He has no proof," said Iago. "You have no proof."

"That Antonio sits bound there now," said I, "is proof. The three thousand ducats he borrowed from Shylock was to finance his protégé Bassanio's marriage to Portia so he could influence the council."

The council members whispered among themselves.

"Is this true, Antonio?" the doge asked.

Antonio had returned to us during my rant, although he'd gone pale and seemed he would faint again at any shock. "It is true that I borrowed the money to finance Bassanio, but because he loves Portia, and I wanted him to be happy."

"So out of kindness you put yourself in peril for a friend," said the doge with the hint of a smile. " *'Greater love hath no man than this, that he lay down his life for his friends,'*" the doge quoted to me. "Release Antonio from his bonds."

The bailiffs moved quickly, released the merchant, and restored his shirt to him.

"I see," said I, nodding, watching Antonio rub the blood back into his wrists. "You have lovable friends, indeed, Antonio. I have recommended them to a dark lady I know, who very much enjoyed their humors. Oh, and your friend as well, Iago—I think you saw her flirting with your friend Rodrigo in Corsica."

Whatever Antonio was going to say, he stopped before it left his gob, and he looked at Iago as if the soldier would have some explanation.

"The fool is mad with grief," said Iago. "Who knows what drunken depths he has sunk into since we last saw him? Pray, let us end this his raving, dismiss this court, and send good Antonio on his way."

"Aye," said I. "Let justice be done, let us get on with our day. Let Iago's treason to his commander and Antonio's treason to the church and the state be forgiven, as is your way, and let them get on with bringing you into a bloody war that the Venetian people neither want, nor can afford."

"What war?" said the doge. "Even if there was some plot, as you describe, a single member of the council could not bring us to war, nor the general of our forces."

"But they don't know that, Your Grace. These two nitwits, in all their conspiring, didn't know the one part of the plan that their dead partner knew.'"

I pulled a parchment from my jerkin and handed it to the bailiff. "I found this, in Brabantio's study at Belmont."

"What is it?"

"It is a very detailed receipt of an order for a hat, Your Grace."

The bailiff looked over the paper and nodded, handed it to the clerk, who also nodded.

"Tell me, Your Grace, does anyone else wear a great gold-trimmed codpiece on his head like you?"

"The ducal *corna* may be worn only by the doge, and each is buried with him."

"Then why do you think Brabantio was having one made?"

The doge looked to the others on the council. "Did you know of this?"

They were all innocent babes tumbling out of the bulrushes with surprise.

"Your clerk can confirm that is Brabantio's hand, I assure you. In his study you will also find a bill of lading for the cargo on Antonio's recently lost ships. Oak from France and England, slaves from above the Black Sea, steel and finished blades from Toledo. All bound for Alexandria and Damascus. To the hands of the Muslims."

"There are no such bills," said Antonio. "Brabantio had nothing to do with my cargo."

There weren't, of course, but if need be, I could forge some quickly, as I had the receipt for the hat. A crown, which would be made by a Jewish goldsmith, who had been happy to tell me and Jessica what the specifications should be.

"All of Venice was almost excommunicated once for selling weapons to the Mamelukes during a Crusade, wasn't it?"

One of the senators stood now. "Antonio, where were your argosies bound and what was their cargo?"

"Don't forget to ask Iago about killing the Moor, as that's a stonking-huge part of the plan."

The gallery had become very quiet now that the attention had turned from Shylock's suit.

"It was all Brabantio's doing, Your Grace," said Antonio. "We acted at his instruction, thinking it the will of you and the council."

Iago winced, only slightly, when Antonio had used the term *we*.

"Then you *were* trying to draw all of Christendom into a war with the Muslims?" asked the doge, more concerned now that his assassination might have been part of the plot.

"I'm sure they would have poisoned you in a manner that made it appear like a fever, as they did my queen, Your Grace."

"The fool is right," said Iago. "We were trying to start a war. And Antonio is right, we knew nothing about any attempt to usurp or harm Your Grace. We are guilty."

"I'm not," said Antonio.

Iago walked to Antonio and put his arm around the merchant's shoulders.

"We two, brothers-in-arms," said Iago. "For Venice, we thought to bring a war to end a war, for the Genoans would not dare attack us once our ships were flying the flag of the pope. Peace would come with Genoans, and money would flow into the coffers of Venice, as it did in the last Crusade, from all the barons of Europe. And at the end of that Crusade, after we had built a hundred ships with their money, the ships belonged to Venice."

"Until they were all lost at Curzola by the last doge's son," said I.

Iago laughed and waved me off like an annoying insect. "There was no greater time for Venice than when all of Christendom was united against a common enemy. We wanted that glory again for Venice. War is the lifeblood of this merchant republic. Every ship we build expands the influence of our ideals, takes the thought of our way of government and free trading to the heathen parts of the world. Every sword forged feeds the children of the armorer, trains his apprentice, gives tithes to the church, which feeds the poor, pays the baker, the fisher, the farmer. Raises them up from hunger, gives them purpose and glory, serves their souls and blesses the nation and its markets. There is no greater act of kindness, than war. There is no higher act of love for the republic, than to make war. For this, Antonio and I are guilty. *Mea Culpa, Mea Culpa, Mea Culpa.* Upon your good mercy, gentlemen." Iago went to one knee and bowed his head, Antonio, a second late, followed his lead and dropped to one knee.

"Well, that's a bloody great bundle of bull bollocks!" said I. "You love your wars for the coffers, but for the warrior and the widow, the orphan and the owned, you've not two dry fucks to give."

"Quiet, Fortunato," said the doge. "Let us confer."

The doge and the council huddled together, there was much whispering and nodding, until a few minutes had passed, and Shylock looked forlorn that his red-hot knife had cooled off.

The council took their seats again and they signaled to the bailiff to mark his words. "We find these men to have acted, although unwisely, in the interest of Venice, therefore, the suit against Antonio is dismissed, and the republic awards him the nine thousand ducats to rebuild his business. The failure of a merchant of Antonio's stature is the failure of our nation, so he must not be permitted to fail. As there is no evidence that Antonio traded with the Muslims, as forbidden by the holy father, he is free to procure ships and trade with the full protection of the Venetian state. You may go, Antonio."

Antonio thanked them, then scrambled away more quickly than I thought possible, although he was looking for someone to help him carry his gold.

"Iago," the doge continued. "It is recognized that you, too, have acted to further the interest of the state, and there is no evidence that you have disobeyed your general, even when he sank into madness. While we will hold our judgment on what your position is to be in our service in the future, you are absolved of any charges and are free to go. Fortunato and Shylock are to be arrested by the guard for carrying and brandishing weapons in public, and are to be taken to the prison adjacent to our palace."

"Oh for fuck's sake," said I. Four guards, bearing spears, advanced on me from the rear doorways. Another pair from either side of the dais moved in as well. Shylock had fallen to his knees, dropped his knife, and was shaking his head in disbelief.

I ran straight for one pair of guards, then faked toward the other, then when they had leveled their spears I ran and jumped upon the table before the doge and whipped two paper packets to my feet, which exploded with a loud pop, sending two of the council over backward in their chairs. The guards paused, but as the smoke rose, resumed their advance. I threw two more of the paper bombs at their feet, and they leapt back. The four guards from the rear doors had reached the floor and I cast two more bombs right at the breastplates of the lead two. The explosions so terrified one that he dropped his weapon and fled; the other, blinded by the flash and smoke, screamed and pounded at his chest.

"If I could have your bloody attention!" I shouted to the room. The gallery was trying to clear, and was clogging the doorways to exit. "Magic powder from the Orient," I explained to the doge. I flipped off the table, landed a few feet from Iago, and grinned up at him as I lit the fuses on two of the paper cylinder bombs. I ran at two guards who had backed away to the side, and barked at them. They jumped out of my way and I slammed two bombs into the mouths of two great wine amphorae that had been set by the walls for decoration. I skipped by Iago, the council, the now very uncertain guards, and lit two more of the paper cylinders and slammed them into amphorae at the other corner.

"Dragon powder, they call it," I pronounced. "Brought to Venice by Marco Polo, rescued and ransomed by, of all people, the alien Shylock. Pardon," said I. I raised a finger to mark the place in my oratory, then put my fingers in my ears just as the first two amphorae exploded, peppering the room with shards of pottery, sending great silver mushroom clouds of smoke to the vaulted ceiling. Terrified shouts filled the hall, onlookers dog-piled on each other to get through the doorways. The council was on their feet, but didn't appear to have an idea what to do beyond standing up. "But a thimbleful," said I. "And two more." The second two amphorae exploded with a fury similar to the first pair. Even Iago, hand on the hilt of his sword, flinched

"Thimbles full, Your Grace. Yet even now, loaded into catapults and trebuchets on a fleet of warships, are hundredweights of dragon powder, packed into great steel and stone balls to be launched on your city by Othello."

"Othello is dead!" shouted Iago.

"Is he, Iago? Did you see him fall? Did you see his body?"

Iago's eyes danced at the edge of their sockets, trying to search his memory.

"Blood!" said Iago. "My wife—"

A trumpet sounded outside, echoed from the harbor and Arsenal. The bells of St. Mark's began to toll.

"A call to prayer?" I asked. "At this hour?"

"The signal of arrival of the fleet," said the doge.

"Well, as you said, Your Grace, Iago acted for the republic. When he betrayed Othello, he was acting on behalf of the city, and now brave Othello, vengeful

Othello, the alien, the Moor, with a hundred ships armed with dragon powder will rain deadly hellfire down on your beloved city until it is little more than flaming rubble and a distant memory. Venice, Your Grace, is no more. This was the test. You have failed."

"Fortunato," the doge pleaded. "We did not know about your queen."

"You know now, and I'm off to your prison. Quickly now, while you still have walls. A thimbleful." I held up one of the paper cylinders I'd tucked in my belt.

"Plead mercy to the Moor. We did not know. We made him our general."

"Arrest Iago," I said.

"Arrest him!" said the doge. Guards moved on Iago and as he reached for his sword I held one of my daggers at the ready to throw. "I will kill you where you stand, you villainous wretch." He let the guards take his arms.

Now the onlookers had calmed in their escape and had turned back to watch.

"Issue pardon to Shylock, and restore his fortune."

"It is so decreed," said the doge, the council nodding like pecking chickens. "The nine thousand ducats are so awarded to Shylock, and he is absolved of all charges. Now, please, Fortunato, go to Othello, plead mercy for Venice."

"Don't call me Fortunato."

"Pocket, please! Mercy."

"Antonio has already taken the gold," said Shylock.

"We will call him back," said the doge. "He conspired with Iago, he will be arrested, now go. Save the city."

I turned to run out when a familiar voice boomed through the gallery.

"Your Grace! Senators!"

The crowd parted and Othello strode through, fully draped in golden-and-white-striped silks, a great golden silk veil trailing from a bronze Saracen helmet, his jewel-sheathed scimitar in a yellow silk sash at his waist.

The doge came around the table and fell to his knees.

"Oh please, Othello, General, please spare the city, Venice is and shall be true to you. Do not destroy the city. We did not know." The doge bent until his stupid hat touched the ground.

Othello looked at me. "Fool?"

"Moor," said I. "Smashing togs."

"What are you up to?"

"Stay the dragon powder, Othello," said the doge. "Please, spare the city."

"Oh, that?" said I. I sheathed my dagger. "Just having you on. We only had what I carried with me today. I have to go catch Antonio. Ta!"

Twenty-five
Arise! Black Vengeance!

I ran out the door, under the eye of many confused onlookers. I spotted Drool, towering above the fray near the canal, and Bassanio helping Antonio load the chest of gold into a gondola.

"Drool, stop them!" I cried, but the ninny took too long to see the target of my instruction. Bassanio was pushing the gondola away from the walkway, Portia pulling him back toward the court as the boat moved away. Antonio stood amidships, grinning at me.

I shouldered my way through the crowd, drawing a dagger and plunging the pommel into my purse as I moved. When I reached the edge of the water, clear of the crowd, I flung the dagger.

It whistled over the water and thunked into the wooden seat by Antonio's feet.

"You missed," he said.

"Yes," said I. "Blast and damn. Toss that back, would you, mate?"

Antonio bent down and worked the dagger out of the wood. He smiled rather smugly as he stuck it in his belt, confident he was out of knife-throwing range, but then looked at his hand. "It's sticky."

"Yes it is, innit?" I called. "Ta!"

The wave moved in a chevron up the center of the Grand Canal's chilly water.

"Wot's that?" said one onlooker, pointing to the dark missile moving under the water at the apex of the wave.

The others gathered and watched. Antonio followed their gaze and saw the thing moving at him. He looked around, looked at the gondolier, realized there was nowhere to go.

I will give him credit, he wasn't the nancy-boy coward I'd thought him to be. He drew my dagger from his belt, crouched, and faced the oncoming wave.

She was like a column of silky tar erupting from the water, her skin shining where the sun hit it. She took his knife arm at the shoulder in her jaws and rolled him over backward into the water, his bones audibly snapping and her front claws disemboweling him before they hit the water on the other side of the gondola and he was carried down in a blossoming red stain in the green water to be seen nevermore. There had been no pause, no break in her momentum; she went through him in the leap as if she might surface again a few yards away and take another merchant, then another, as fluid and natural and irresistible as the sea—an elegant terror—a beautiful monster.

The gondolier had dropped to a crouch on his platform as the gondola lurched sideways with the dragon's impact, then righted itself. He stood and stared at the red stain in the water, like all of those on the shore, not believing what he had just seen.

"You'll want to paddle in this way, mate," I called to him. "Before she comes back." He leaned into his oar and the gondola shot toward us.

I looked around, caught Shylock's eye. "Drool will help you wash the blood off your gold and carry it home."

I turned to look for Jessica and saw Bassanio, hiding his face in Portia's shoulder as she embraced him. I went by him, squeezed his shoulder. "He loved you, lad. Truly. He was a bloody villain, but that was the one true bit about him."

The crowd gave me a wide berth for some reason, and I moved through them until I spotted Jessica, sneering at me from under the boy's hat she was wearing to hide her hair.

"Bit gaudy, innit? I suppose that wet and shiny type has a tawdry appeal to certain lowlifes." She grinned.

Iago could hear another prisoner down the corridor moaning and shouted for him to shut up.

They'd put him in one of the cells in the Bridge of Sighs, which linked the doge's palace to the prison, three stories above the canal. He was chained to the wall, but by only one leg iron, the chain long enough to allow him to pace his entire cell. The chain was unnecessary, he thought. There was only one small window above the level of his head, too small for a man to fit through, and then a cupola with four vent windows at the center of the arched ceiling, large enough for a prisoner to fit through, but entirely too high for even an unfettered man standing on another's shoulders to reach.

When, on his third day of incarceration, the guard announced that he had a visitor, he half-expected it to be Othello, there to curse him in person, perhaps even one of the men of his barracks, but when a pretty dark-haired woman appeared outside the cell, her green silk gown a respite for the eye in this gray stone world, he was taken aback.

She carried a basket, the neck of a bottle of wine protruded from a nest of linen, and the smell of freshly baked bread was tall in the air.

"I know you," said Iago. "You were at Belmont the day they found Brabantio in the cellar."

"You remembered," Nerissa smiled. "I had been seeing your friend, Rodrigo."

"Oh yes, of course. Nerissa." Iago's mind was a blaze looking for fuel. How could he use this to his advantage?

"I do not know you, signor," said Nerissa. "But Rodrigo always spoke highly of you, and how you had helped and advised him."

"Ah, Rodrigo, a good mate. He is missed."

"Well, I thought I would bring you some food, comforts from the outside. And because of Portia's favor with the doge, they allowed it."

She looked to the guard who had been standing by. He unlocked the door and let Nerissa hand the basket in.

"Don't get your hopes up," said the guard. "There's no blade concealed in there, and when the wine is finished you'll hand that bottle back through the bars before this door opens again. Weren't for the command of the doge, we'd not allow that nonsense."

"You are very kind, lady," said Iago. "Rodrigo was a lucky man to have earned your attention."

"I was very fond of him," said Nerissa.

The guard signaled with a nod that it was time for her to go and she smiled. "I do hope you enjoy this. The wine seller said to drink the wine last. He says it will somehow best complement the cheese and sausages in that way."

"I will, lady. Again, thank you."

Iago retreated to the stone platform that served as his cot, and searched the basket. As the guard promised, there was no knife, only a wooden paddle for spreading soft cheese on the bread. The bread and salt, sausages and cheese, dried fruit and fish tasted of the outside, of freedom, which he had never craved before, not knowing he had enjoyed it. All of it reminded him of defeat, of shame, of infamy, and all brought about at the hands of the annoying little fool.

As the light through the windows turned pink with the sunset, he pulled the seal from the wine. The cork was flared and could be removed by hand, but had been sealed on with lead foil, which he tore off with his fingernails. Even so, the thin lead clung to the bottle, adhering to the sticky resin that smelled of pitch. No matter, he wiped his hands on his trousers, flung the cork to the corner of the cell, and drank. The wine was fortified, strong, and warmed him going down, smoothing the jagged edge of his anger, but sending him into a morose self-pity as he drained the bottle.

He was dozing when he heard the rustling on the roof. His head ached and his mouth tasted of tar, the cell was cold and he reached for the wool blanket they had left him. Shadows were breaking the cold blue moonlight streaming in from the cupola and he looked about for the source of the noise.

His mouth tasted of tar. The wine bottle had smelled of pitch . . .

He watched as liquid night filled the window, then slid down into his cell.

CHORUS: *Piteous screams did fill the night, out the windows and over the canals, for no quick death was gifted to Iago with his basket. The screams were ignored, as always were the calls of fear and sorrow that give the Bridge of Sighs its name. She lingered there, in the cell, much of the night, toying with him like a cat with a mouse, careful to keep him active by not using her dreamy venom, eating one part of the scoundrel and then another, slowly, until just before dawn, her belly full, the serpent of Venice slipped out the cupola window, down the wall, into the canal, and away.*

In the morning, when the guard came, he found
only Iago's high boot chained to the wall, his foot
and leg to the knee still inside, and nothing else
but a great red slick and a serpentine smear of
blood painted up the wall and leading out the high
windows.

Drool and I were sleeping on the floor in Shylock's great room, before the fire, when she came to me. I had no doubt, this time, whether she was dream or ghost as I felt her touch on my cheek. My Cordelia. Her hair was down and she wore a silver-and-black silk shirt from my motley, nothing else.

"It's you?"

"Well done, fool," she said.

"You from the start, wasn't it, pulling the strings with Viv? Directing her, keeping me safe."

"You know what they say, 'There's always a bloody ghost.'"

"You're wearing my shirt."

"The symbolism is bloody ominous, innit?" She grinned, giggled.

"But you've no knickers on."

"Imagine that. Do you think me wanton?"

"Not for me to say, but one hopes."

"Oh, that's right, you've never shagged a ghost, have you?"

"Well, a few who would go on to be ghosts, but strictly speaking, no."

"Then get your kit off, fool. Queen Cordelia is going to have her otherworldly way with you."

"If you insist, but we'll have to be quiet so as not to wake up Drool. Ghost bonking unsettles him."

"This will be good-bye then, puppet. I've ticked everything off my spirity list."

"I've missed you. I miss you. I am inconsolable."

"Just as well then that I'm not here to console you, but to shag the bells off of you."

"I'll always miss you."

"I'll miss you, too, love, but you can carry on now. You've got Jessica."

"But you said don't shag the Jewess."

"I didn't want her to distract you while you were avenging me. She's lovely. Take care of her."

"Then you don't mind?"

"Jettison the codpiece, you rascal, there's squishy haunting to be done!"

Twenty-six
Off Jolly Rogering!

We stood at the dock, duffels full of gear at our feet, a longboat with sailors at the oars waiting to take us to the ship.

"My daughter cannot marry a Christian," said Shylock.

"I'm not a Christian," said I. "Heretic of convenience at worst."

"I'm not marrying him," said Jessica. "We are simply sailing off to do dread deeds and have drunken debauchery beneath the mizzenmast. I'd not marry such a small and irritating pest of a man."

"Despite my puckish charm and enormous knob?" said I.

"Both soundly imaginary," said Jessica.

"You agreed yourself, in front of this very father of yours, that I had an enormous knob."

Shylock moaned and cradled his head in his hands as if it might explode any moment.

"I thought I was agreeing that you *were* an enormous knob," she said.

"Oh, well then, now you've hurt my feelings," said I. "I'll be in the longboat, sulking, when you are ready. Farewell, Shylock. I will take good care of her, despite her sour disposition."

"This is a punch to my heart," said Shylock, by way of a good-bye.

"Well, don't blame me, you're the one that raised her. Might have added a soupçon of human kindness to all the guilt and kvetching if you didn't want her to run off to be a pirate."

"You, you, you, you, you—you do not talk this way of my daughter. You give me my ducats, but you take my daughter."

"I am *not* taking your daughter. Your daughter is seeking her own adventure."

"Pocket," said Jessica. "Please, wait in the boat. I'll be along in a bit."

"*Adieu,* Shylock," said I. I took my duffel, went to the end of the dock, and handed it down to the sailors.

There was much embracing and many tears and when Jessica finally joined me in the longboat, Shylock stood and watched us until we were all the way out into the harbor, and his dark figure, topped by his yellow hat, was still there, even as we raised anchor and set sail.

Drool was standing at the bow, letting the wind wash the stink off his hulking frame, and Jeff was cavorting in the rigging, chattering and shrieking with glee that he had been so sly as to have tricked us into building all this smashing monkey-climbing equipment for him. Nerissa had decided to join us on our travels, and she stood by the helm with Montano, whom Othello had appointed as our captain and pilot.

After he took his seat on the council, the Moor had given us the ship and crew in thanks for our service to him and Venice. Desdemona, as mistress of the estate, had rescinded her father's instructions and saw that half of Brabantio's fortune, along with the villa at Belmont, went to her sister, Portia, on the one condition that she never let her handsome, yet terribly thick husband, Bassanio, manage the money.

In Corsica, after an appropriate half-hour of mourning upon finding out she had been widowed, Emilia married Michael Cassio, and was now installed, quite comfortably, in the Citadel at Bastia, the new Baroness of Corsica.

"I worry about Papa," Jessica said.

"He will be fine. He has his spectacles, so he can do his own accounts, and that widow Esther is taking care of him at the house. She has a healthy laugh and won't put up with his bollocks. Shylock had nearly smiled when he met her. The possibilities are as dazzling as they are disgusting." Tubal had hired the woman to look after his friend. It turned out that it had been Iago who had hired the two huge Jews to kill us, not Tubal, and the two old moneylenders had resumed their friendship with new frontiers of resentment and envy to help it along.

"Can you even get to China by sea?" asked Jessica, as we stood at the rail at the rear of the ship, watching Venice recede into the horizon, and the shadow of the black dragon following behind just below the surface of the water.

"No idea. I thought we agreed when we decided to go pirating that you will learn the nautical bits and I will compose bawdy songs of our legendary adventures. Marco Polo says it may be possible, but he also said that we may have to take her overland to get her home."

"Montano thinks there may be a river to China from the Black Sea."

"If not, we can sail back the other way."

"South," she provided.

"If you say so. We will get her back to her own kind, if there are any left, even if we have to sail the *Serpent of Venice* o'er all the seven seas together. There are *seven* seas, right?"

"It's a shit name for a ship," she said.

I'd had the name of our ship emblazoned on her stern in great gilt letters, and an effigy of Vivian carved in ebony graced her bow.

"Well, we aren't going to call the ship the *Dread Pirate Jessica.* That, my dear, is a shit name for a ship."

"Arrrrr," she arrrrrred.

Afterword

I'm sure, by now, you've thought, "I've read *Othello* and *The Merchant of Venice,* and try as I may, I do not remember the part about a fool knobbing a dragon; perhaps I should give them another look." If you decide to go in that direction, and there are certainly worse ways to spend your time, you may be somewhat disappointed to find that Shakespeare left that part out. *The Serpent of Venice* was inspired by and draws upon three works of literature: *The Cask of Amontillado,* a short story by Edgar Allan Poe, and *The Merchant of Venice* and *Othello: The Moor of Venice,* by William Shakespeare. Also, there is no little contribution from Shakespeare's *King Lear,* which was the inspiration for my previous novel *Fool,* in which Pocket, Drool, and Jeff first appear. I've also quoted or paraphrased lines from about another dozen or so of Shakespeare's plays; right now I couldn't tell you from which. Trying to reconcile a story built from so many diverse sources, while also trying to accommodate history, can lead, I'm sure, to some confusion, so I hope I can clear up a few details about history, characters, and attitudes here . . .

HISTORY

As the preface states, *The Serpent of Venice* is set in a mythical late thirteenth century. This was necessary to continue Pocket's story, which ends in the same period in *Fool,* so I set *Serpent* several hundred years earlier than the source materials. *Othello* is set during the time when the Venetian Empire is at war with the Ottoman Empire, which was throughout much of the sixteenth century. In the play, Othello is sent to Cyprus to thwart an invasion by the Turks (Ottomans). The Turks took Cyprus from the Venetians in 1570, so I assume that Shakespeare is working in a time contemporary to his own. It's estimated that *Othello* was written around 1600–1601. *The Merchant of Venice* (approximately 1596–1598) is also set in a time contemporary to Shakespeare's, and one assumes that the conventions and mores of his time would at least resonate with his London audiences. (More about that later.)

The Serpent of Venice is set around 1299, when Venice's dominance of trade in the Mediterranean was still being established, and the city-state had, indeed, been at war with Genoa for most of the last part of the century, a war over maritime superiority that would continue through most of the fourteenth century as well. I moved the action taken from *Othello,* from the island of Cyprus, which was strategically valuable to the Turks in the 1500s, to the island of Corsica, which is almost literally in Genoa's backyard, in order to facilitate the travel to Genoa and back in a time frame that would fit the story. Here the story was driven by history, as much as by the influence of plays or stories. *The Cask of Amontillado* specifies no particular time, but one infers that it takes place sometime in the eighteenth century, easy enough to reconcile, since Carnival time in Venice seems to have remained constant for hundreds of years.

Venice had been established on an archipelago of islands in a salt marsh in the Adriatic Sea by refugees from Tuscany who were fleeing the invading forces of the Lombards and later Attila the Hun. Protected by a natural moat on the land side, and barrier islands, called the Lido, on the sea side, Venice grew into a powerful trading city with a representative republic as its government. The senators were elected by the neighborhoods, and a doge, or duke, was elected by the senators, and was advised by a council of six senators who ascended by seniority and election of their peers. (Different sources I found said the number of the council varied from six to twelve at different times, so I chose six for the story to give the position more power.) This representative republic was maintained in various forms until 1287, when Doge Giovanni Dandalo proposed that eligibility for the council be limited only to those whose fathers had been on the council. By 1299 it had become law and the republic became more of an inheritable oligarchy. This is the law that Iago and Antonio attempt to exploit by trying to arrange the marriage of Bassanio to Portia and eliminate Othello, who, by the circumstances I have created in the story, has been awarded Brabantio's seat on the council. Venice, despite the attempt in the thirteenth century to turn it into an oligarchy, did remain, in some form, an independent city-state until it was overthrown by Napoleon in 1797.

It should probably be noted that Venice had, indeed, profited greatly by being the transport hub for soldiers and supplies during the Crusades, particularly the Fourth Crusade, when they were paid a hundred thousand ducats to build ships and transport knights, horses, and supplies to the Holy Land to take the city of Acre, and eventually, Jerusalem, from the Mameluke

Saladin, who had beat nine shades of shit out of the occupying Crusaders a few years before, basically expelling them from the holy city. The Venetians would use their influence, and the Crusader soldiers, to attack their trade competitors on the Dalmatian coast (Croatia now) and take the Christian city of Constantinople, for which the pope would eventually threaten to excommunicate the entire city. (Venice also maintained some trading relationship with the Mamelukes, a practice forbidden by the pope—as with Antonio in *Serpent*, Venice sold materials to build war machines.) In all cases, Venice built the ships that were paid for by the crusading nobles of Europe, but were also able to keep the ships, as well as the fees they contracted for the transport. The Crusades, despite the war with Genoa, were the glory days for the Venetians, and established them as a world power, despite the carnage, suffering, death, and destruction their actions facilitated.

To the specific 1298 battle of Curzola, all but twelve of Venice's ninety-five galleys were lost to Genoa. The admiral, Dandolo (who was the son of a doge), committed suicide in shame. Among the prisoners taken was a Venetian merchant called Marco Polo, who was imprisoned in Genoa. In *Serpent*, this is the battle from which Venice barely recovered, which puts Othello, a mercenary, in the position of saving the city.

While in prison, Marco Polo would dictate the tales of his travels to another prisoner, called Rusticello. It was easy enough to make this prisoner a beef-brained ninny with the gift of perfect recall, thus Drool becomes the author of *The Travels of Marco Polo*. In Polo's book, he describes vicious, man-eating reptiles that live in the Chinese rivers. It's fairly obvious to us now that he is talking about crocodiles, but at that time he does not use the term, and he also describes a bird large enough to "seize an elephant with its talons, and lift it into the air." So who is to say he didn't smuggle out a baby dragon in his rucksack?

CHARACTERS

More than thirty-four named characters appear in *The Merchant of Venice* and *Othello,* as well as the four characters I carried over from *Fool,* and the two characters from *The Cask of Amontillado.* Most have Italian-sounding names and some of the characters even have identical names (i.e., there is a Gratiano in both plays). There are far too many characters to include them all in a single comic novel and not lose the thread of the story, already made somewhat complex by marrying the three source works. Further, it was an annoying reality that Shakespeare named two of Antonio's associates Salarino and Salanio. A modern novelist would never do this, as the eye confuses the two similar names almost by habit. (They teach that on the first day in author school.) And in *The Merchant of Venice,* the two serve exactly the same function and appear to share a personality. One transcription of the play I found even added a third, Solanio, because it just wasn't confusing enough, I suppose. Thus, I tried to kill off one of the Sals as soon as possible. It should be noted, however, that Shakespeare wrote the plays to be performed and not read, and each of the Sals would have been distinguished by the actor who played him, so having like-sounding names wouldn't have presented as much of a problem in the theater.

I chose *Merchant* and *Othello,* obviously, because they are set in Venice. Early on, as I dissected them to see what parts I could stitch back together to make the abomination that became *The Serpent of Venice,* I started noting that characters in each of the plays perform similar functions, and although I did not research it, I suspect the parts were written for the same actors. Portia and Desdemona are obviously similar, both smart and beautiful, by the descriptions from the other characters, of high birth, and each with a controlling father (Portia's, however, deceased). Bassanio and Cassio could be the same character, as could Rodrigo and Gratiano, Lancelot Gobbo and the Clown in *Othello*, although Gobbo has a much larger part. The Duke of Venice appears in both plays, as well as members of the council; Shylock and Othello, although very different in disposition, are both outsiders to Venetian society. Iago and Antonio are both antagonists to the outsiders. Emilia and Nerissa are both lady's maids, and Nerissa is more of an attending "lady in waiting," but they serve similar functions; Emilia helps facilitate the mechanism of the tragedy of *Othello*, Nerissa the comedy of *Merchant*. Both have hungry ears for the troubles and plots of their mistresses, the female leads.

Jessica* in *Merchant* and Bianca in *Othello* are more or less the girls from the other side of the tracks, true in their love for their respective beaus. Where I could, I consolidated or eliminated characters. Pocket becomes Lancelot Gobbo, Shylock's servant. The vengeful Montressor, from *The Cask of Amontillado*, becomes Brabantio, and Pocket also becomes Poe's boastful harlequin, Fortunato, both bearing nicknames given them by the doge. I might have trimmed Antonio's entourage

---

*Interesting bit of trivia I found: the first time the name "Jessica" appears in print, anywhere, in any language, is in *The Merchant of Venice*, although it may be derived from the Hebrew name Iscah.

a bit, but I felt it only fair to leave a substantial number of "red shirts" in the cast to entertain Viv's appetites.

The Chorus is a presence in a few of the plays, most notably *Henry the Fifth* and *Romeo and Juliet,* where they both get some of the better lines in two very poetic plays with some of my favorite speeches. In other plays (*Pericles* comes to mind—one of Shakespeare's lesser-known plays), he uses named characters as onstage narrators. But there is no Chorus in either *Othello* or *The Merchant of Venice.* I love the poet's voice on the stage, walking around, describing the action, appearing invisible to all the other characters, so I thought it might be amusing to shine the spotlight on him. *Othello* is more or less narrated by Iago, who spends an enormous amount of time in soliloquy, telling the audience what evil shit he is plotting, so it only occurs to me now, with the story finished, that I should have had him accuse the Chorus of sleeping with Emilia.

ATTITUDES

Let me make it clear here that when I'm talking about "attitudes" what I'm talking about are racism and anti-Semitism. Based on criticism I've read of *The Merchant of Venice,* and the criticism of the criticism, it seems that somewhere in the latter end of the twentieth century, academics declared *The Merchant of Venice* to not be an anti-Semitic play, but a play with anti-Semitic characters. "You have to see it in the context of the time it was written," we are told. Shylock, next to Hamlet, is probably the most analyzed of Shakespeare's characters. He is eloquent, although he speaks in a different cadence and manner from everyone else in the play, and he is both greedy and clichéd in the way he is written, but is also a product of much oppression and prejudice, and he makes an eloquent case for his thirst for vengeance.

The play is set as contemporary to the time in which it was written (we know this because in the play, one of the Antonio's ships is coming from Mexico, so it is necessarily after 1492), a time shortly after the beginning of the Inquisition (also 1492), when Ferdinand and Isabella expelled the Jews from Spain, and many Catholic countries followed suit. Venice, however, as a state, was resistant to the Inquisition, and while Jews were persecuted there, it was to a much lesser extent than in other Catholic countries, another instance of Venice resisting the authority of the church, as was the case in their adventures in the Crusades. Jews from Spain, France, and other parts of Italy fled to Venice. This may be why Shylock speaks strangely and is considered by Portia's citation of the law to be an "alien." The play doesn't say he comes from another place. Perhaps Shakespeare knew about this refugee status, perhaps not.

I suppose it should be noted, as well, that in Shakespeare's England, anti-Semitism was a crowd-pleaser in the theater, beginning with Christopher Marlowe's play *The Jew of Malta* (1590), which is outrightly Jew hating, with his main character Barabbas more or less the blueprint for the clichéd craven money-grubber and scoundrel. (Which endures in English literature even into Dickens. Fagin, in *Oliver Twist*, is referred to repeatedly as "the Jew.") A few years after *The Jew of Malta* appeared on the stage in 1594, Rodrigo Lopez, the queen's doctor and a Jew, had been tried and beheaded by Queen Elizabeth for plotting to assassinate her. Elizabeth was a very popular monarch (almost by necessity, because she was pretty indiscriminate about cutting off the heads of people who didn't like her), and so the public was happy to get their anti-Semitism on again with *The Merchant of Venice* (1596–1598). Compared with Barabbas, Shylock is, as they say, a *mensch*. (Shakespeare was less of a trendsetter than a trend follower. His *King Lear* followed a play called *King Leir* written four years prior by another playwright. It's his genius for language, not his plotting, that has made his work immortal.)

So yes, in context, Shakespeare's play is certainly less anti-Semitic than Marlowe's, but Antonio is the protagonist of *Merchant*, the hero, if you will. He's anti-Semitic through the play, and Shakespeare implies he is such because Shylock is practicing "usury," or charging interest on money he loans. Talented directors and actors have portrayed Shylock as the sympathetic lead, though, in recent times, without altering a word of the text, and it's really a credit to the craft of acting and directing that it can be done. Al Pacino's Shylock in the 2006 film version of *Merchant* is a good example of a sympathetic Shylock, and filmed in Venice, it's a pretty film to look at.

That said, *The Serpent of Venice* is set in medieval times, three hundred years before Shakespeare's play, and conditions were quite different. Jews in Venice were required to wear a yellow hat, and there were stricter controls on what they were able to do with property. Across Europe, Jews were persecuted; the reference to the burning of the Jews at York is true. All Jews were expelled from England in 1290, and from France in 1306. The plagues of the time were often blamed on Jews, as well as the failure of crops, and they were accused of poisoning wells, no doubt an early application of statistical medicine linking cholera to water, with Jews as the scapegoat. In short, it was tough being a Jew in the Middle Ages, so Shylock in my setting would have to be tough, resilient, and resourceful, or at least have an advocate who was.

I also found it interesting to insert a Jew into the context of a holy war between Christians and Muslims, basically over who would occupy Jerusalem. By seniority, of course, the Jews get Jerusalem, but Shylock never inserts himself into that dialogue. He's just trying to get by, and be faithful. The contrast of vengeance and mercy in the trial of *The Merchant of Venice* is obviously Shakespeare doing a compare and contrast between the Old Testament God and the New Testament Christ, but he's completely ducking the religious question of his time, which was between the Catholics and the Protestants. (Elizabeth was adamantly Protestant, while her successor, her cousin James I, was Catholic, and Shakespeare had to write to please both of them, as Elizabeth died at the midpoint of his career.)

So, was Shakespeare an anti-Semite? I don't think so. I think he was writing for his audience, just as I write for my readers. (Interesting, I think, that Shylock is referred to as "the Jew" twenty-eight times in the play, and by his name only three.) And neither do I think he was racist, but race is definitely an issue in *Othello*.

The person who mentions Othello's color most often is Othello himself, referring to himself as "black" a number of times, and professing often how rough his manners and speech are in very poetic prose. Brabantio is completely out of his mind about Othello's race, and Iago and Rodrigo whip him into a frenzy at the beginning of the play by talking about the "black ram tupping his white ewe" and using other racist ways of saying that a black guy is bonking his daughter. After the play leaves Venice, however, and proceeds to Cyprus, the racism settles down and Iago just hates Othello because he hates everyone. It was very difficult to not put the word *sociopath* in Pocket's mouth when referring to Iago, but I had to settle for *lunatic*. For Iago, Othello's race pales in comparison to so many other reasons to hate and undermine the Moor.

Yes, there are racist elements to *Othello*, but Othello is the hero of the play, of high and pure morals, courageous, and an extraordinary commander. (Even Iago concedes this in the play, and Iago does not give a lot of credit to anyone.) In *Merchant*, however, Portia has the racist lines. When the Prince of Morocco is coming to have a try at the caskets, she says he has the "complexion of a devil," and when we first meet the prince he apologizes for his color, and asks her to overlook it. When he goes away, she sighs with relief, and says that she hopes that all of his color should meet the same losing circumstance. While Portia has some brilliant speeches later in the play, specifically "The quality of mercy" discourse during the trial, she is a brat in that and other "casket" scenes, so I portrayed her thus through most of my story.

More interesting for me than race, when the story is set in the context of the Crusades, is that a Moor would have been from North Africa, a predominantly Muslim culture, and now he is in command of a force that may lead a major attack on the Muslims. Othello, we are told by Iago, is not a Muslim, but a Christian, but, you know, he might be a secret Muslim. I mean, he's so African looking, and he has that funny name . . .

Yeah, I went there.

Anyway, I don't think that Shakespeare was a racist, and his sonnets 127–151 are about the famous mistress he refers to as his "dark-lady" who is, by description, of African descent.

The point of this, I suppose, is that I didn't intend *The Serpent of Venice* to be a story about discrimination, although discrimination is manifest among the characters. For me, it's a story about hypocrisy and greed, courage and grief, anger and revenge. But most important, I wanted it to be a story that shows how cool it would be to have your own dragon, which I have wanted since I was five.*

Christopher Moore
San Francisco, California
January 2013

---

*No, I didn't and don't want to have sex with a dragon, I just thought that would be funny.

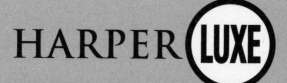

HARPER LUXE

THE NEW LUXURY IN READING

We hope you enjoyed reading
our new, comfortable print size and found it
an experience you would like to repeat.

Well – you're in luck!

HarperLuxe offers the finest in fiction and
nonfiction books in this same larger print size and
paperback format. Light and easy to read, HarperLuxe
paperbacks are for book lovers who want to see
what they are reading without the strain.

For a full listing of titles and
new releases to come, please visit our website:

www.HarperLuxe.com